08-BVV-277

"London's writing bubbles with high emotion as she describes sexual enthusiasm, personal grief and familial warmth. Her blend of playful humor and sincerity imbues her heroines with incredible appeal, and readers will delight as their unconventional tactics create rambling paths to happiness."
—*Publishers Weekly* on *The Devil Takes a Bride*

"This tale of scandal and passion is perfect for readers who like to see bad girls win, but still love the feeling of a society romance, and London nicely sets up future books starring Honor's sisters."
—*Publishers Weekly* on *The Trouble with Honor*

"A delectably sexy hero, an unconventionally savvy heroine, and a completely improper business proposal add up to another winner for ever-versatile London."
—*Booklist* on *The Trouble with Honor*

"This series starter brims with delightful humor and charm."
—*RT Book Reviews* on *The Trouble with Honor*

"Julia London writes vibrant, emotional stories and sexy, richly-drawn characters."
—*New York Times* bestselling author
Madeline Hunter

**Also available from Julia London
and HQN Books**

*The Trouble with Honor*

# JULIA LONDON

# THE DEVIL TAKES A BRIDE

HQN™

Recycling programs
for this product may
not exist in your area.

ISBN-13: 978-0-373-77890-4

The Devil Takes a Bride

**Printed in U.S.A.**

HQN™

To Nitty, who has made my life immeasurably easier

# *PROLOGUE*

*Autumn of 1810*

AT THE END of the hunting season, before the winter set in, the Earl of Clarendon hosted a soiree at his London home for the families of Quality that had come to town. He included, in his coveted invitations, his closest friends, all of whom had august titles and impeccable social connections.

The Earl of Beckington and his wife; his son, Lord Sommerfield, Augustine Devereaux; and his two eldest stepdaughters—Miss Honor Cabot and Miss Grace Cabot—were invited to attend. That the two youngest Beckington stepdaughters, Miss Prudence Cabot and Miss Mercy Cabot, were not included in the invitation caused quite a ruckus at the Beckington London townhome, which resulted in many tears being shed. The youngest, Mercy Cabot, vowed that she would vacate that house while the others attended the soiree. She would steal aboard a merchant ship that would carry her as far from London as one might possibly sail.

Miss Prudence Cabot, who was three years older than Mercy and who had just passed her sixteenth birthday, said she would *not* steal aboard a merchant ship.

But if she was so worthless as to not merit an invitation, she intended to walk about Covent Garden unattended and sell her body and soul to the first person who offered a guinea.

*"What?"* cried twenty-year-old Grace when Prudence cavalierly announced her intentions. "Prudence, darling, have you lost your mind? You would sell yourself for a *guinea?"*

"Yes," said Prudence petulantly, and lifted her chin, her gaze daring anyone to challenge her.

"Should you not at least aspire to a *crown,* dearest? What will a guinea say of your family? You must agree that a guinea is insufficient for your body *and* your soul."

"Mamma!" Prudence cried. "Why do you allow her to tease me?" And then, unsatisfied with Lady Beckington's indifferent response, she'd flounced off, apparently encountering several doors in her haste to flee, judging by the number of them that were slammed.

The Cabot girls were as close as sisters could be, and even Prudence's hurt feelings could not keep her from the excitement of watching her older sisters dress for the evening. Honor and Grace were highly regarded among the most fashionably dressed—that was because their stepfather was a generous man and indulged their tastes in fine fabrics and skilled modistes.

On the evening of the soiree, in preparation, gowns were donned and discarded as too plain, too old or too confining. In the end, Honor, the oldest at twenty-one, selected a pale blue gown that complemented her black hair and blue eyes. Grace chose dark gold with silver filigree that caught the light and seemed to sparkle when she moved. Honor said it was the perfect gown to set off Grace's gold hair and her hazel eyes.

When they descended to the foyer, their stepbrother, Augustine, who was to accompany them as the earl and his wife had declined the invitation, given the earl's battle with consumption, peered at them. Then he rose up on his toes and said dramatically, "You surely do not intend to go out like that?"

"Like what?" Honor asked.

Augustine puffed out his cheeks as he was wont to do when he was flustered. "Like *that*," he said, studiously avoiding looking at their chests.

"Do you mean our hair?" Honor teased him.

"No."

"Is it my rouge? Does it not appeal to you?"

"*No,* I do not mean your *rouge.*"

"It must be your pearls," Grace said with a wink for her sister.

Augustine turned quite red. "You know very well what I mean! I think your gown is too revealing! There, I've said it."

"It's the fashion in Paris," Grace explained as she accepted her cloak from the footman.

"One cannot help but wonder if there is any fashion left in Paris, as it all seems to be upstairs in this house. I wonder how you *know* the fashion of Paris seeing as how Britain is at war with France."

"Men are at war, Augustine. Women are not," Grace said, and kissed him lightly on the cheek. "Don't you *want* us to be fashionable?"

"Well, yes, I—"

"Good, then it is settled," Honor said cheerfully, and linked her arm through her stepbrother's. "Shall we?"

As was often the case, Augustine was overwhelmed by his stepsisters. With a good yank on his waistcoat to bring it down over a belly that had gone a little soft, he muttered that he did not care for their revealing clothing but allowed them to lead him out all the same.

THE CLARENDONS' GRAND SALON was so crowded that there was hardly enough room to maneuver, and yet, all eyes turned toward the Cabot sisters.

"As is ever the case," said Grace's friend, Miss Tamryn Collins, "all gentlemen are held in thrall by the Cabot sisters."

"Silly!" Grace said. "I'd wager the only gentlemen held in any sort of thrall are those who have been pressed by their families to make an offer to a debutante who will bring with her a generous dowry."

"You underestimate the appeal of a pleasing décolletage, I think," Tamryn said dryly.

Grace laughed, but Tamryn was right. Honor and Grace, separated by only a year, had been out for more than a year. By all rights, they ought to have received and accepted an offer of marriage, for wasn't that the point of coming out? But Honor and Grace were beautiful young women and had quickly discovered they enjoyed the chase far too much to give it up for marriage just yet—not chasing, mind you, but being chased.

And they were very well chased.

It was no secret that the alluring Cabot sisters were

as good a match as any young gentlemen might hope to make—pleasing to the eye and in spirit, and backed by the wealth of the Earl of Beckington.

"Oh, no," Honor said, and took hold of Grace's arm. "Grace, you must intercept him."

"Who?" Tamryn asked, standing beside Grace as she peered into the crowd.

"Mr. Jett!" Honor whispered loudly. "He's coming across the room, straight for us."

"For *you,* you mean," Grace said, and slipped her hand into Tamryn's. "We must flee, Tamryn, lest we be locked in boring conversation for the rest of the evening. Have a lovely evening, Honor."

*"Grace!"* Honor exclaimed, but Grace and Tamryn had already escaped on a wave of giggling, leaving Honor alone to graciously rebuff Mr. Jett's most ardent attention.

With Tamryn gone off to have a word with a friend, Grace wended her way through the ballroom.

Grace danced, too, one set after the other, never lacking partners. But when the odious Mr. Redmond cast an oily smile in her direction and began to move toward her, she was relieved that Lord Amherst should suddenly step before her and bow grandly.

"Come quickly," he said, holding out his hand. "I mean to rescue you from Redmond."

"My hero!" Grace said laughingly, and slipped her hand into his, following his lead onto the dance floor.

Grace liked Lord Amherst. As did every other debutante. He was handsome and always had a warm laugh for her. He never failed to charm, and in fact, that was his reputation; he charmed every woman he met with his outrageous flirting and suggestive innuendo. That's why Grace liked him so—she rather enjoyed flirting and suggestive innuendo.

He bowed as the dance began and said, "I've been trying to reach you all night, fighting my way through this bloody crowd for you."

"What? There were no other dance partners for you?"

"Miss Cabot, you tease me mercilessly. You know there's not another woman in this room that can compare to you."

"Not even one other?" she asked as they rose up on their toes and then down, twirling around and facing each other once more.

"Absolutely not," he said, and winked.

"My lord, you are the king of compliments."

"Can you blame me? A woman as beautiful and spirited as you deserves nothing less than to be continually flattered. My heart has been quite lost to you."

Grace giggled at his silliness. "Confess—you've said that to every other girl in attendance tonight."

"Miss Cabot, you wound me. I have *not* said that to every other girl in attendance tonight. Only the beautiful ones."

Grace laughed. They turned to the right, then to face each other again as they made their way up the line.

"Lord," Amherst suddenly muttered. He was looking at a point over Grace's shoulder. When Grace glanced back, she happened to notice Amherst's brother, Lord Merryton. She was surprised to see *him* here. There were never two brothers more unalike. Amherst was always about, but Merryton rarely came to town. Amherst was quite diverting, and his brother brooding. That's what he seemed to be doing now, standing with his back to the wall, his hands behind him. He had dark, curling hair, his expression grim.

Grace turned back to Amherst. "Your brother doesn't seem to be enjoying the evening."

*"No,"* he drawled. "He does not enjoy society as I do."

"Doesn't enjoy society?" Grace laughed. "I pray you, what else is there but society when it rains for days on end as it has?"

"Yes, well, he disapproves of gaiety in general. Balls in particular. He has no use for them."

Grace was incredulous at this news. To have no use for balls was so far beyond her comprehension that she felt compelled to glance over her shoulder at the strange Earl of Merryton once more.

Amherst laughed. "You won't find any answers there, Miss Cabot. He is rather adept at not allowing his true feelings to be known. Decorum in all things, you know."

Grace smiled at her partner. "The same can't be said of *you,* my lord."

"Certainly not. I should like the world to know my very fond feelings of the most beautiful of the Cabot girls. In fact, I think I shall announce it. The moment we reach the top of the line, prepare yourself for a declaration of great esteem."

Grace laughed at his teasing. She forgot about Merryton after that dance. After all, there were so many gentlemen, so much dancing, so many opportunities to *flirt*.

She forgot about him altogether until roughly eighteen months later, when her fortunes had shifted, and she was bitterly reminded just how disagreeable Lord Merryton was.

# CHAPTER ONE

*Spring of 1812*

THE FRANKLIN SISTERS of Bath, England—one a widow, the other a spinster—presided over a small tea shop on the square near the baths and the abbey. It was their pleasure to serve tea and fresh-baked pastries to the denizens and visitors to their fair town. They knew most everyone by name. They lived above their shop and were open every day, without fail.

The sisters reasoned that, being as close to the abbey as they were, they might offer up their daily prayers in a more official manner than in their rooms, and every evening, at precisely six o'clock, they closed their shop. Those who resided near the abbey knew that they were so exact and so regular that even the abbey's grounds-keeper had noticed and had quite literally set the abbey clocks by them.

Once their daily prayers were offered, the sisters returned to their shop, lit a pair of candles and shared tea or soup and nattered on about their day. On certain special occasions, such as those evenings when a chorale was sung in the abbey, Reverend Cumberhill accompanied them back to the shop, and a bit of brandy was poured into the tea.

Grace Cabot was depending on the sisters' routine. A routine she was confident went undetected by most of the fashionable people in Bath, as the fashionable people in Bath were not in the habit of attending evening prayer. She knew this because she was one of that set that spring, and she was in the habit of attending one soiree after the next along with the rest of them.

Had it not been for a chance call to her old friend Diana Mortimer, who lived near the abbey, Grace wouldn't have known about the sisters' routine. But she had made that call, and Diana had remarked upon it.

Diana Mortimer was also the one to tell her about the famed Russian soprano's upcoming performance at the abbey. "The Prince of Wales has favored her," Diana said. "And you know very well that if the prince has favored her, there won't be an empty seat."

That was the moment Grace hit upon the perfect plan to lure Lord Amherst into her trap.

She risked everything to set her plan in motion on the night the Russian soprano sang. It all hinged on the Franklin sisters arriving at the precise and *most* inopportune moment.

Grace did not think she was the sort to be annoyingly proud of her accomplishments, but this meeting with Lord Amherst, on this night, had taken exceptional cunning to arrange. She'd come to Bath a month ago after hearing his lordship had come for the waters, for the sole purpose of convincing him that she was quite sincere in her esteem of him, without appearing too wanton. But Grace had made her social debut at the age of eighteen, and in the three years hence, she'd learned her lessons in the finest salons of London and knew a thing or two about how to entice a gentleman, especially one like Amherst.

And yet, Amherst had surprised her. In spite of his reputation for being a randy and rambunctious rake, in spite of declaring his esteem for her more than once, he'd not been persuaded that a private meeting with Grace was the thing to do.

Grace had not anticipated his reluctance when she'd devised her plan. On every occasion they'd met in London, Amherst had been attentive—one might even say eager—to please and charm her. He was forthright about his esteem for her, and Grace had been certain his affection would lend itself to a clandestine meeting. Indeed, when Grace had arrived in Bath, and made the necessary rounds to the necessary parlors, Lord Amherst had not been the least reluctant to whisper in her ear during the Wickers' soiree. Nor had he been reluctant to walk with her in the park near the Royal Crescent or keep his hands from her as they strolled.

But he'd absolutely refused to meet her in private when she'd first suggested it.

She had wondered if he had suspected her and her motives, but quickly dismissed that notion—she'd been too clever in her deceit. Having three sisters and a stepbrother had taught her how to connive. Then perhaps she'd not been conniving enough, and in the privacy of the room she'd taken in the home of her mother's dear friend Cousin Beatrice she'd thought hard about what she must do.

One night, it came to her—no one could resist a secret. Not even Amherst. She'd told him that she had something very important to tell him, something that *no one* else could hear. And Grace had been right—Amherst couldn't resist and had agreed to meet her.

One might assume that Grace wanted to seduce Amherst for her own pleasure, but nothing could be further from the truth. This scheme had become necessary because her stepfather, the Earl of Beckington, had recently died. Grace, her mother, Lady Beckington, and her sisters Honor, Prudence and Mercy had been completely dependent on the earl. *Completely.* Now, her stepbrother, Augustine, was the new earl, and every day that passed with her mother under Augustine's roof was a day that her mother's terrible secret could be discovered: Lady Beckington was going mad.

That secret would ruin the Cabot sisters, for if it were known among the ton that Lady Beckington was mad, and her four unmarried daughters now had modest dowries instead of generous ones, no one would have them. No one. There wasn't a gentleman in London who would chance introducing madness into his family's lineage, especially without the incentive of grand wealth. More important, Grace had two younger sisters who were not yet out. They would have no opportunity to make a good match.

She and Honor had worried over it for weeks now, and while Grace didn't like that it had come to this, that she should find herself in a position of having to conspire to something so morally reprehensible, she could see no other viable or expeditious solution. She must marry Amherst before her secrets were discovered.

Everything was set. The little tea shop across the square from the abbey was closed at six o'clock. There was quite a crowd gathered at the abbey this evening to hear the Russian soprano. Grace knew the Franklin sisters would return after the chorale with Reverend Cumberhill. She'd even stood across from the tea shop, watching when the Franklin sisters departed for the abbey at six o'clock, then testing the door herself. It was open. It was always open—the abbey was only steps from the shop.

Tonight, Grace's life would change forevermore. She would suffer a great scandal, would no doubt be made a pariah among polite society. She was prepared for it—at least her younger sisters would have what they needed.

At the chorale, she caught Amherst's twinkling eye. Just as they'd planned, she stood and walked briskly from the abbey's sanctuary before the chorale was ended. She knew that Amherst would be right behind her, unsuspecting that the Franklin sisters and the reverend would be right behind *him*.

A light rain had begun to fall, and that worried Grace. A few moments too early, a few moments too late, and everything would be ruined. She pulled the hood of her cape over her head and hurried across the abbey courtyard to the tea shop. She had a moment of breathlessness at the realization she was actually stooping to such wretched manipulations—up until this moment, it had been nothing but a scheme—but that was followed by an exhalation of desperation. She had never in her life been so desperate as this.

At the door of the tea shop, she pushed her hood back

to look around her before she opened the door. There was no one about—everyone was in the abbey, hearing the last stanzas of the chorale.

Grace reached for the handle and pushed. She knew a moment of panic when the door would not open—but she put her shoulder to it and it opened with a creak so loud she expected the entire town of Bath to spill out of their doors and accuse her of thievery. Grace slipped inside, leaving the door slightly ajar so that Amherst would know it was open, and paused, listening for any sounds that would indicate she'd been seen.

She couldn't hear a thing over the pounding of her heart.

The room was very dark; the embers at the hearth were so low she could hardly see her hand before her. Another bolt of panic hit her—she hadn't thought of the dark. How would Amherst find her? She was too fearful to speak. She'd stand near the door; she'd reach out and touch him when he entered.

Grace began to feel about for the furnishings. She'd been in this tiny tearoom many times, and knew there were two small tables just at the door, a desk to her right. With her hands sweeping slowly in front of her, she brushed against the back of the chair at the desk.

All right, then, she had her bearings. She knew where she was standing, where the door was.

Grace removed her cloak and dropped it somewhere nearby, then nervously smoothed her hair. Her hands were shaking; she clasped them tightly together, waiting. A clock was ticking somewhere, and every second that ticked by, her heart beat harder.

She heard the footfall of Amherst as he strode across the abbey courtyard. He was walking quickly, purposefully, and suddenly Grace's breath deserted her entirely. She gulped for air, straining to hear. She heard Amherst pause just outside the door and swallowed down a small cry of tension. It sounded as if he was moving about, and Grace imagined Amherst was having second thoughts. He moved away from the door, and she gasped softly.

But he came back almost at once.

A silence followed, and Grace could not quell the shaking in her. Why did he not open the door? When he did, pushing the door so that it swung open, a rush of cool damp air swept across Grace's face. Her breath was so shallow she felt faint; her hands were so tightly clasped that she was vaguely aware of her fingernails digging into her skin.

Amherst stepped cautiously over the threshold. He looked taller than he normally seemed, which Grace attributed to the bit of light outside that framed him in the doorway. He turned his head to one side, as if he were listening for her.

Her nerves would strangle her. "Here," she said.

His head snapped around to the sound she'd made, and in a moment of sheer panic, Grace launched her body at him. She expected him to say something, but he froze, as if she had startled him. She threw her arms around his neck; he caught her by the waist with a soft grunt, and stumbled backward to keep them from falling. Somehow, Grace found his mouth in the dark. It was much softer than she would have thought. It was lush, wet and warm, and—

And he was suddenly devouring her lips. Hungrily. Grace hadn't expected such a powerful kiss. She couldn't say what exactly she'd expected, but it wasn't *this*. Her blood felt hot in her veins, sluicing through her. She was a pot boiling over, and she liked it. His tongue swept into her mouth, and she was rocked by the prurient sensation of it. She felt strangely free and anonymous in the dark, not like herself at all. Not a debutante with at least *some* sense of propriety. His kiss was stunningly arousing, and Grace pressed against him without regard for herself or her reputation, feeling the hard length of him—

He suddenly picked her up by the waist, and Grace cried out with surprise against his mouth. He knocked into the chair at the desk, and she heard it crash to the planked floor. He sat her on the desk, and something there dug into her back, but Grace didn't care—his tongue was stroking her mouth and driving her wild. He nipped at her lips with his teeth, drew them into his mouth, and Grace realized now exactly how Amherst had derived the reputation for being something of a rake, for his kiss was the most exciting thing that had ever happened to her.

She was sliding down a very sensual path. She felt too damp, too hot in her clothes, pushed to the edge of reason by every stroke of his tongue in her mouth, every bite of her lips.

He suddenly moved, and his mouth was on her décolletage, his fingers digging into the fabric of her gown. Grace thought she should stop him before this game went too far, but his hand had found her leg, was under her gown! And his fingers were tracing a burning path up her leg.

*Stop him, stop him now!* She wanted to be discovered in a fierce embrace, *not* in the full throes of lovemaking. Where were the Franklin sisters, for God's sake? Grace couldn't find her voice—rather, she didn't *want* to find her voice. She much preferred to close her eyes and feel the extraordinary sensations. She dropped her head back and allowed herself to experience every moment of this carnal onslaught. His fingers dug into the meaty part of her thigh, and she gasped with the tantalizing sensation of a man's hand between her legs. She sank her fingers into his hair as his lips closed around the hard tip of her breast through her gown. She could not believe she had accomplished it! She would be happy with him, if this is what she might look forward to.

He freed her breast with a yank to the fabric of her gown. He took it in his mouth, suckling it, and the sensation was so shocking, so arousing, that it pooled in her groin.

Amherst growled against her breast, a guttural, animal sound of desire, and Grace's body reverberated with it. When his hand moved deeper between her thighs, Grace brazenly lifted her leg. His fingers slipped into the folds of her sex. She gasped for breath, lifting off the desk. She hardly knew herself!

"I wasn't sure you'd come," she whispered into his ear.

His hesitation was so slight she wasn't sure it was real. But he said nothing as he moved to her other breast and pressed an erection against her that both alarmed and incited her. She'd never felt a man's desire, had never seen it. It felt mysterious and hard against her leg, and the lusty image of how it would fit inside her filled her head as a strong current of desire skated down her spine, overwhelming her senses, tingling in every patch of her skin.

Everything began to fall away. Grace forgot her deceit, or even where she was. She forgot everything but the way he was making her feel, the way her body was responding, wanting more, *craving* more. So when a lantern of light suddenly filled the room, she was startled and cried out.

Amherst whirled about, spreading his cloak to cover Grace while she desperately sought to cover herself.

"My lord!" Reverend Cumberhill cried, his voice full of censure and alarm. "God in heaven, what have you *done?*"

Grace frantically tried to remember her part in this theater. "Please," she said. *Please what?* She looked down and realized that Amherst had actually torn the bodice of her gown. She held the fabric together with her hand, and cast frantically about for her cloak.

"My lord, this *cannot* stand!" the reverend cried. "You have taken cruel advantage of this girl!"

"Young lady, are you *harmed?*" one of the sisters demanded, and suddenly light was shining on Grace. She heard the Franklin sisters' twin cries of shock at her appearance. Grace spotted her cloak and dipped down for it.

"Miss Cabot!" one of them cried. "Come, darling, let

me help you," she said, and Grace felt her hands on her shoulders, felt her pulling the cloak around her neck.

"By God, Merryton, I never thought you capable of rape! I will call the authorities!"

Rape! *Merryton?*

Grace's heart stopped beating. And then it started again with a painful jerk. No, no no no *no—Merryton?* How could she have made such a horrible, wretched mistake? It was impossible, and Grace whirled about to face the man who had driven her to wild desire—

Her heart plummeted to her toes.

She felt ill, could feel the blood rushing from her limbs, and thought she might collapse. She had *not* coaxed the affable and randy Lord Amherst into a compromising situation as she had planned. She had thrown herself at his brother, Lord Merryton, the most disagreeable man in England.

She had to fix this. "He did not harm me!" she cried, panicking now. There was sacrifice and the real desire to save her sisters, but then there was sheer terror, and *this* was sheer terror. She could not allow this to happen. It could not! Where in heaven was Amherst?

"Miss, do not speak," the reverend warned her. "I will not allow him to intimidate you!"

Merryton's cold green eyes bored through Grace. His face was dark, his expression stormy, and an unpleasantly cold shiver raced through her.

"I take full responsibility," he said curtly.

"As well you ought!" the reverend said sharply, and stalked forward, holding up his lantern to see Grace.

Grace quickly put a hand to her bodice and only then realized a long tangled hank of hair hung over her shoulder.

"Dear God," the reverend said, his voice hushed, his expression truly horrified. He shifted that look of horror to Merryton. "This will *not* be borne! You have *ruined* this young woman, ruined her irrevocably, and for that, you will pay the price! Ladies, please, do see her to safety at once," he said brusquely. "Take her from this place and send Mr. Botham to me as quickly as you can," he added, referring to the local magistrate.

One of the ladies pulled the hood of her cloak over Grace's head.

"There has been no crime," she tried again. "It was my doing—"

"Quiet!" the reverend bellowed. The sisters shushed her as they flanked her, forcefully ushering her to the door.

Grace stumbled along, her breath short and thin. What a horrible, *horrible* mistake! She'd done something quite wretched. Worse than wretched! She felt as if she might vomit, and doubled over so that she wouldn't. She wondered wildly if Amherst would have felt as helpless as she was feeling in that moment if he'd come, if her plan had worked.

"Oh, dear. Take heart, Miss Cabot. The reverend will see to it that man faces justice for what he's done."

"He committed no crime!" Grace cried helplessly. "It was *I* who brought this on him! *I* lured him."

"Dearest, it is only natural that you would want to take the blame for your indiscretion, but you mustn't," one of the ladies said. "He has used you ill!"

That made no sense to Grace, but they were pulling her out the door and into the abbey courtyard, where dozens were now emerging from the abbey. Several heads swiveled in Grace's direction—it wasn't often that one saw two women dragging a third between them—and voices began to rise around them.

"Hurry along, Agnes!" one of the sisters hissed, and Grace was stumbling between them to keep up.

She would never recall how, exactly, she was returned to Cousin Beatrice's house on Royal Crescent. She could only vaguely recall being there at all when the gentlemen came to speak with her, to ascertain what had happened in that dark tea shop. Grace tried desperately to explain to them that it was her doing, but when pressed to give a reason as to *why* she would do something so heinous, she could not tell them the truth.

The gentlemen assumed that as she could not adequately explain her reasoning for doing something so horrific because she was lying. She was lying, they carefully explained to her, because she feared Merryton.

Grace *did* fear Merryton. She'd never heard a kind word said about him. He was known to be aloof and distant and disdainful.

But he did not deserve what she'd done to him.

## CHAPTER TWO

*ONE TWO THREE four five six seven eight.*

There were precisely eight steps from the breakfast room to the study, and eight panels of wallpapering in the room. Jeffrey knew this because he counted them every day on those occasions he resided at his townhome in Bath, sometimes several times a day. And yet he couldn't be entirely certain of the number of steps in the early-morning hours after his spectacular downfall. He kept walking back and forth between the breakfast room and study, counting the steps.

He had to do it; he had to count until he was completely certain, for it was the only thing that could annihilate the image of him thrusting his body into that young woman's sex.

The vision—unwanted, uninvited, mistakenly placed in his brain—was new to him. Generally, the vulgar and salacious thoughts that tended to plague him every day were of two women pleasuring each other with their tongues and fingers. He couldn't say why that was, only that he had begun to experience that particular image around his seventeenth year. He'd begun to act on it in his twenty-first year, carefully seeking out the sort of bedmates who were willing to perform for him and with him. But in society, Jeffrey had learned to keep the dark images deep in the corners of his mind, hidden away. Always proper, always a model of propriety, just as his father had taught him to be. When Jeffrey made a concerted effort to banish the images, he was generally successful. They seemed only to emerge when he was very tired or felt the pressure of his title.

His title, the Earl of Merryton, as well as two lesser titles, was the heavy mantle he wore. He was the head of a large family with impressive holdings. He was Jeffrey Donovan, the man everyone assumed to be above scandal and immoral behavior, just like his father before him.

But the truth was that Jeffrey was not above it all. He'd merely found a way to restrain himself.

Until last night.

And now, a new, monstrous image was residing quite firmly in his thoughts and he could not subdue it. Bloody hell, he didn't even know her name! Cabot, Mrs. Franklin had said. Jeffrey knew no Cabots. He knew nothing about her, except that she had tasted like honey, had felt like silk.

*One two three four five six seven eight.*

Eight. Eight. Eight.

This thing, this demonic obsession with eight, had invaded Jeffrey so many years ago that he could no longer remember how. But in his sixteenth year, when his father had died and he'd become the earl, responsible for carrying on the family's name and its impeccable credentials, responsible for being the one above all reproach, the eight had begun to loom in his heart and mind. Like the salacious images, Jeffrey was at a loss to understood how or why it had happened. He thought himself mad, really, particularly as the eight was imperative to him but also torture at the same time.

The necessity for eight in his everyday life had manifested itself when Jeffrey had lain with a woman the first time. How old was he then, eighteen? He'd been seduced—willingly—by an older woman. She had shown him what his body wanted with her hands and her mouth, things he hadn't realized, had not imagined. Those things seemed incongruent with the lord he was supposed to be, and he had not been able to douse his shame except by counting.

But then, the images, vile and lustful, had come at him, worse than he'd ever imagined. And the eight demon had grabbed him by the throat, choking the life out of him, forcing him to walk on the sharp edge of a blade—think bad thoughts, banish them only with eight. Now, at thirty years of age, Jeffrey knew that to fall off his private blade was to fall into the chaos of his thoughts, to obsess about women's bodies and sexual plunder and the number eight.

He had learned to control it, to keep it quite under wraps. He rarely made mistakes.

*Rarely.*

And yet, he'd made a colossal one last night.

He had his brother to blame, damn him. John Donovan, the Viscount Amherst, was the bane of Jeffrey's existence. It seemed John strove to make every mistake he could. He'd been unapologetically involved in one scandal after another. From the time he'd reached his majority, he'd racked up gambling debts that he could not repay, leaving Jeffrey to deal with them from the family's coffers. He would not settle on a woman and make an offer, and instead preferred to dally with every debutante who happened to drift in his path, creating scandal in London and among some of the finest families in the Quality.

John was the reason Jeffrey was presently in Bath. He'd heard John was here, and he'd come to speak to him. Because he'd also heard things from his sister, Sylvia. Sylvia was at her home near the border of Scotland with two small children. Jeffrey hadn't seen her in some time as her children were too young to travel, but she kept in touch through correspondence. In her last letter, she'd reported hearing that John had run up some gambling debts and owed more than one gentleman in London, including a prominent viscount.

The news had angered Jeffrey. More than once, he'd begged John to consider an occupation, anything to keep him from trouble and ruin. He would very much like to see John accept a naval commission. He was more than happy to arrange it for his brother. He just had to make John see the benefit in it, to get his brother to agree that he ought to leave England and all her vices until he could put his life to rights. To settle on a woman who would give him heirs and for God's sake, beget those heirs.

And then, last evening, when Jeffrey had given into the insistence of his friend, Dr. Linford, to accompany him and his wife to hear the Russian soprano, he had seen the young woman with the golden hair leave the concert at the abbey. He'd watched as John had followed only moments later, and his blood had heated with his rage. There was his brother, following after a woman for the whole world to see and titter about.

Jeffrey had walked out into the abbey courtyard and looked around for his brother. He was nowhere to be seen, and Jeffrey had turned to go back into the abbey when he noticed a movement, a slip of color, against the darkened window of the tearoom.

That was when he noticed the door was slightly ajar.

Jeffrey had counted eighty steps to the door. The tea shop was dark, and he could hear no sounds within. But in looking around the courtyard, he believed there was no other place his brother could be. He'd fully expected to find his brother rutting in some girl there, and Jeffrey's mind had filled with the awful images. He could see her legs spread wide apart, could see his brother sliding in and out of her. He'd tapped his thigh eight times in an effort to banish those images, but it had been hopeless. By the time he walked into that room and felt her mouth on his, he'd been lost.

What he'd done to that young woman!

Jeffrey closed his eyes in an attempt to banish the sight from his mind—her torn bodice, her golden hair mussed and falling, her hazel eyes wide with shock— but it was useless. He had done that. He'd unleashed his demon on the young woman. She'd tasted so sweet, and her skin so fragrant, he'd not been able to stop himself. He'd been too rough, had done untold harm to her.

With a groan, he pressed both fists to his temples, squeezing hard. He knew himself to be many things, but he had never believed himself capable of harming a woman, under any circumstance. When he had immoral thoughts, he kept his distance from society, retreating to Blackwood Hall, his country estate.

Now, he didn't know where to go to escape his tortuous thoughts.

"My lord."

Jeffrey started at the sound of his butler, Tobias. "Yes?"

"Mr. Botham, the Reverend Cumberhill, Mr. Davis and Dr. Linford are calling."

Jeffrey drew a breath. Perhaps they would be his salvation. Perhaps they would see him directly to some jail. "Send them in," he said, and stood in the middle of his study, silently tapping eight times against his thigh. And again. And again.

Reverend Cumberhill could scarcely look him in the eye when he entered, and Jeffrey could hardly blame him. Mr. Botham, the magistrate, seemed only perplexed. Mr. Davis, the town's mayor, eyed him curiously, as if he were examining a scar on Jeffrey's face.

Dr. Linford, however, looked at him with a bit of sympathy in his eyes. He was the one person on this earth in whom Jeffrey had confided his dangerous thoughts.

"Gentlemen," he said, and gestured toward seating in his office. "Tobias, tea, please."

"I think that is not necessary, my lord," Mr. Botham began. "I shall not draw this unfortunate matter out any more than is necessary. We have called on Miss Cabot and have questioned her thoroughly. She will not turn against you, and insists that this was her doing."

Jeffrey wondered if that was her attempt to protect John? Or was she foolishly honest?

"However, she has agreed, as has her cousin's husband, Mr. Frederick Brumley, that because of the heinous nature of what has occurred, the only options available are to accuse you of rape…"

Jeffrey's gut seized. He was a powerful earl, but even he could not escape such an accusation.

"Or," Mr. Botham said, glancing down at the carpet, "to marry you to avoid what would be a very damaging scandal for you both."

Jeffrey swallowed. He counted the buttons on Mr. Botham's waistcoat. There were only six. *Six*.

"We counseled her that to marry a brute is to consign oneself to enduring a brute for a lifetime," Reverend Cumberhill said curtly.

Jeffrey didn't speak. He was suddenly plagued with the image of her body, her legs open to him and his cock pumping into her.

"We have counseled her," Mr. Botham agreed, casting a look at the reverend, "but she insists she will take that risk rather than sully your name, or the name of her family."

Jeffrey didn't want to marry her, for Chrissakes! He wanted nothing to do with her! And yet, he had no other option. "Who…who is her family?"

He saw the exchange of looks between the men, the disgust that he didn't even know who he'd sullied. "She is the stepsister of the Earl of Beckington."

*God in heaven*. Jeffrey tried to recall Beckington, and could not. It scarcely mattered. The man was an earl. If Jeffrey didn't take his sister to wife, the man would surely see him hanged for rape; Jeffrey would do no less in his shoes. He lifted his chin. "I am an earl," he said tightly. "I have a duty to my family and my title to oversee our fortune and produce a legitimate heir." He glanced at Dr. Linford. "Have you examined her?"

"For harm, yes," he said. "She does not appear to be harmed."

That wasn't what Jeffrey meant. "I mean, is she a virgin?" he asked bluntly.

The reverend made a sound of despair or disgust, and Davis looked appalled.

"We are speaking of Miss Grace Cabot," Mr. Davis said. "She is the stepdaughter of the late Earl of Beckington, who only recently passed, and the stepsister of the new earl. She comes from a fine family, my lord."

Jeffrey began to clench and unclench his fist, eight times. "That is all well and good, but you are surely aware that a proper pedigree does not weight a woman's hem."

Dr. Linford and Mr. Botham both glanced at the floor; the reverend covered his face in his hands. They were appalled by him, yes, but Jeffrey noticed that none of them contradicted him.

"She has assured me she is…intact," Linford said tightly.

Mr. Davis cleared his throat. "May we assume, then, that a marriage will take place?"

Jeffrey hesitated. He thought of Mary Gastineau, the daughter of Lord Wicking, his second cousin. Mary was the second daughter of the second Lord Wicking, and she was the second woman he had seriously courted.

He had courted Miss Gastineau for two years, grooming her to his way of life and his need for perfection. While Mary Gastineau did not excite him in any way, Jeffrey thought she would be the wife that he needed. He did not imagine her naked body, did not think of his body sliding into hers. The woman did not make mistakes, and seemed perfectly suited to walking the edge of the knife with him.

And still, he had put off making an offer as long as he reasonably could. For symmetry, he'd told himself. *From fear,* his conscience barked at him. Nevertheless, Jeffrey had been prepared to make the offer this Season.

"My lord," Mr. Botham said, his low voice drawing Jeffrey out of his rumination, "if you do not agree, we will accuse you of the crime of rape. We will not ignore what you have done to that poor young, innocent woman."

*Innocent.* Inexperienced, perhaps, but she was not innocent. Jeffrey lifted his gaze, and four pairs of eyes steadily met his. Their minds were made up then— they would see him prosecuted if he did not solve the very real problem he had created for them. "Yes, I will marry her."

No one spoke at first; the three men looked at the reverend, who was the most aggrieved by what had happened. He stood, rising to his full height, which was still considerably shorter than Jeffrey's. His expression was sour, as if he were displeased with the decision. But Reverend Cumberhill was a shrewd man. He knew that to go against the powerful Earl of Merryton would not work in his favor. He clenched his jaw, peered at Jeffrey. "You will make this marriage straightaway?"

"Not only will I do it straightaway, I shall remove myself and this woman to Blackwood Hall at once."

"Then we are agreed," the reverend said crisply.

COUSIN BEATRICE'S LACE cap had been askew since the night the Franklin sisters had brought a disheveled Grace to her. Like everyone else, Beatrice assumed that Grace had suffered a great trauma to her person. She'd cried as she'd helped Grace undress. "Your mother will never forgive me!" she'd wailed.

Her mother, were she in her right mind, would never forgive Grace for what she'd done. Grace would never forgive herself. Yes, she'd suffered a great trauma, all right, but not to her person. The trauma was in the awful truth that she'd trapped the wrong man into scandal. Moreover, now that the trapping had been done, Grace was appalled by how deplorable an act it truly was. Would it have been any different had it been Amherst? Would he not have looked at her with the same loathing she'd seen in Merryton's eyes? How did she ever come to believe this horrible, wretched plan would work?

Honor had been right when Grace had shared her scheme with her before traveling to Bath—it was a ridiculous, impossible plan. Why was it that this would be the *one* time that Honor was right? Could she not have been right that it was perfectly fine for two young women to race their horses on Rotten Row? Could she not have been right that the coral silk Grace had coveted was the best color for her? No, she had to be right about this.

Cousin Beatrice was pacing in front of Grace again, wringing her hands. Grace had never seen Beatrice wring her hands, but then again, she supposed Beatrice had never had to wait for the Earl of Merryton and the authorities of Bath to come for her. They were to arrive at eight o'clock, only minutes from now. The deed had been done, the agreement made and now, Grace would marry him.

What else could she do? She was irrevocably ruined. She felt nothing but angry disappointment at herself and dread for what was to come. She had *not* miraculously saved her family as she'd grandly imagined. Ah yes, the self-sacrificing heroine, saving her dear sisters from ruin! In fact, nothing at all had changed! The only new bit was that Grace would now suffer the shame of her ridiculous scandal *not* in the company of the affable Lord Amherst as she had planned, but with disagreeable, cold Lord Merryton.

"Your dear mother will be so *very* disappointed," Beatrice said. "In you, in me— Grace, it is not to be borne! Why did you refuse to send a messenger to her at once? Why did you not ask for the help and support of your stepbrother at such a time as this?"

Grace could not possibly make Beatrice understand. "A messenger would never reach her in time, and as I explained, I could not possibly taint the wedding of my stepbrother. He's waited so long! And my stepfather, gone only a month! Can you imagine, adding that scandal to what the family has already endured? Think of my young sisters, not yet out. No, cousin, there is no other course but to take responsibility for my indiscretion, just as Mr. Brumley has said."

"Oh, Mr. Brumley!" Beatrice wailed, referring to her husband. "He doesn't understand these things, Grace. Those men have pushed you into an agreement knowing very well you have no counsel!"

Of course, Beatrice would believe that, since Grace had not been truthful about why she'd done what she had. But Beatrice had not seen her friend Lady Beckington in quite some time, as she had been wintering in Bath and had not been to town this Season. Beatrice had no way of knowing that her old friend had gone almost completely mad, scarcely recognizing her own daughters on some days.

Keeping such news from Beatrice was something Grace could add to the growing list of reprehensible things she had done. But until Grace or her sister Honor were married, until they had secured a place for their two younger sisters and their mad mother to go, Grace would not breathe a word of it.

Time was of the essence, too, when Grace had undertaken the awful task of trapping a husband. Her stepbrother, Augustine Devereaux, the new Earl of Beckington, was set to marry Monica Hargrove within the month. Monica was Honor's nemesis, and she, along with her mother, was aware of Lady Beckington's deteriorating mind. They had already begun to speak of a manor in Wales for the Cabot girls.

Wales. *Wales!* It was as far from proper society as Monica could send them all. As far from opportunity

as Grace's sisters Prudence and Mercy could possibly
be. It was intolerable, and as Honor had failed to save
them all from that fate with her equally ridiculous plan
of having a gentleman seduce Monica away from Augustine, Grace had felt as if the responsibility fell to her.

Which is why Grace had come to Bath—to lure
the charming Lord Amherst to her. His reputation as
a scoundrel was legion, yes, but he was also kind, and
quite a lot of fun, and Grace had reasoned that if it had
to be done, why not Lord Amherst? She could imagine that after the initial shock and scandal, they might
be happy.

*Dimwitted child,* she thought as Beatrice paced and
carried on. She and Honor had long bemoaned the fact
that as young ladies without significant resources of
their own with which to solve their growing problems,
they had no other options but to use their passable looks
and cunning to change the course of their lives. Their
cunning, however, was sorely lacking. Their plans were
so...*ludicrous.*

She could see that now. She could see just how naive
and doltish she'd been.

The question that burned, that kept her up these past
two nights since the awful mistake had occurred, was
why hadn't Amherst come? How had *Merryton,* of all
people, arrived in his stead?

Every time Grace thought of it, she shuddered. The
moments with Merryton in that darkened room had
been the most exciting thing she'd ever experienced. He
had stoked something fiery in her, something that felt
as if it meant to consume her. But the moment Grace

had realized those passions had been stirred by *him,* she'd been repulsed and intimidated.

Just thinking of it now, she shuddered again. Titillation. Revulsion. It was enough to make her head spin.

"Oh, dear, you are afraid," Cousin Beatrice said, and hurried to Grace to rub her hands on Grace's bare arms. "I would that I could repair this situation for you, darling, but I cannot. There is nothing I can do, you must surely see that."

"I see it quite clearly, cousin. No one can help me now."

"Please, let us send for Beckington!"

They'd had this argument several times in the past few days. "I *can't!*" Grace exclaimed. "Can you not see? There is nothing that can be done for this predicament. I can't recover from it, cousin—never! No one will have me after this. No doubt word has already spread, and I am already ruined. And I haven't even begun to contemplate the consequence to him. I *will* marry him today. There is nothing more to be said."

At least she assumed a wedding would take place today, that all the necessary arrangements had been made. After her spectacular fall from grace, Grace scarcely knew of or cared about the negotiations for her marriage to Merryton. Mr. Brumley conducted them on her behalf with a scowl and air of disapproval about him.

Grace understood it had been mutually agreed that Beatrice would gift ten thousand pounds to Grace as her dowry—which was the figure Grace recalled her mother had once set aside for her—with the full expectation that the new Earl of Beckington would be quite happy to reimburse the money to avoid a wider scandal.

Grace's task was to send a letter to her stepbrother requesting the dowry. That was the easier letter to write. Grace imagined that Augustine would be happy to see her wed—not in this way, of course, but to have it done—and would take the dowry from the money Grace's mother had brought into the marriage.

The letter to Honor was much harder to pen. Grace spent the better part of an afternoon crafting it, imagining her sister's horror when she read what had happened, as well as the sum that her family must now pay. Perhaps the hardest thing to write was that Honor was right. Honor had warned Grace that the plan would never succeed, but Grace had been so stubbornly sure that it would, that her plan was vastly superior to Honor's. She'd been so certain that Amherst's flirtations and playfulness with her person was indicative of a particular esteem for her, and that he would, when it was all said and done, be willing to accept it.

Even worse, far worse, Grace had thought herself rather clever with her daring subterfuge.

*Fool. Wretched, naive, silly fool!*

Well, then, she'd set her own course for calamity, hadn't she? And now, she was entirely alone, cast out onto a rough sea without so much as an oar. What she wouldn't give to hear Honor's unsolicited advice now! To hear Prudence play the pianoforte, or Mercy's gruesome tales of mummies. What she wouldn't give to sit at her mother's feet, lay her head on her lap and feel her mother's sure hand stroke her hair, as she had done when they were girls.

The day of reckoning had come. Grace would be married to a humorless man. Lord, but he couldn't be more ill-suited for Grace if he woke up every morning with that express desire.

Grace had heard nothing from Merryton in the days since the disaster, not a single kind or unkind word. Not that she expected it, for what would it be? *My dear Miss Cabot, thank you kindly for utterly ruining my life.*

No, she didn't expect anything, really, and had tried to push aside her conflicting and terrifying thoughts by methodically packing her belongings into her trunk. She'd folded her stockings into neat little squares, her gowns into bigger squares. Today, she had dressed for her wedding, hardly caring that she broke with tradition by putting away her mourning garb. Wasn't black too macabre, in spite of how somber she found this day? Didn't the silver gown seem too sprightly for such an unbearable event? She'd chosen the pale blue gown Mercy had once declared went very well with Grace's hazel eyes and the brass tones in her hair. Subdued, and yet, it would not appear as if she'd crawled out a dark tomb to wed.

Grace added a chemisette with a collar so that no skin was revealed to her future husband. She knew it was absurd to feign modesty now, but it seemed the thing to do. She pulled her hair into an austere knot at the nape of her neck, and the only jewelry she wore was a strand of pearls about her neck. It had been a gift from her mother on the occasion of her sixteenth birthday, and it made her feel close to her mother now.

A light rap on her door signaled the time had come.

"Oh, dear. I suppose it's time," Beatrice said fretfully.

At least there was one bright spot to Grace's day— she would soon be out from under Beatrice's tearful gaze. If there was one thing she could not abide, it was the female penchant for the tearful gnashing of teeth. So much time and effort spent in crying! Grace wouldn't cry. She'd created this mess and, heaven above, she'd suffer the consequences with her head held high. And if she couldn't manage that, she'd certainly cry in private.

She opened the door to the Brumley butler. "I'm to bring your trunk, miss," he said.

Grace pointed to it; she couldn't find the will to even speak. As the butler and a footman took her trunk down, Grace wrapped a cloak around her and picked up her bonnet. She turned to Beatrice and smiled. "Thank you, cousin—for everything."

Beatrice's eyes filled with tears. "How lovely you look, dearest. I wish your mother was here to see it."

Grace smiled ruefully. "I don't."

*"Tsk,"* Beatrice said. "Not even this day could make you any less lovely. You are your mother's daughter, a true beauty. That man is quite fortunate if you ask me."

Grace almost laughed. He was so fortunate his life had been ruined.

Beatrice hugged Grace to her. "Mr. Brumley and I will be there to serve as witness, of course."

Grace gave her a wan smile. She didn't care who

saw her now. All she could think about was marrying him, then being spirited away to Blackwood Hall, which sounded as bleak as her life stretching all the years before her. She toyed with a fantasy that when the scandal had died down, she would run away—from him, from society, surviving by her wits in the wild—

"Oh! I almost forgot! A letter has come for you this very morning!" Beatrice said.

"A letter?" Grace said, brightening.

Beatrice took the letter from her pocket and held it out. Grace instantly recognized Honor's handwriting. "It's from Honor!" she exclaimed. "How could she have received my letter so soon? I sent it only yesterday."

"This one came late last night," Beatrice said. "It passed yours in the post."

Grace's excitement instantly flagged. There would be no proposed escape for her, no promise of help knocking at her door at any moment. She tucked the letter into her reticule.

"Chin up, darling," Beatrice said as she wrapped her arm around Grace's shoulders and began to walk with her. "I hear that Blackwood Hall is a grand estate with a dozen guest rooms. After things settle, you might find it to your liking."

Grace would never find it to her liking, she was certain of that.

In the foyer, Grace fit her bonnet on her head, low over her eyes so that she'd not have to see any happy people walking about, and followed the footman to the small carriage.

"Mr. Brumley and I will be along behind you, darling!" Cousin Beatrice called from the walk when Grace had settled herself inside, and waved her handkerchief at Grace as the carriage pulled away, as if she were going on holiday.

In the carriage, Grace retrieved Honor's letter and broke the seal.

Dearest Grace,

I pray this letter finds you well. You must forgive me, dearest, for I have been remiss in my duty to write you faithfully as I promised. We've been quite well occupied in London. Mamma is no better, but seems to retreat into her private world a bit more each week. It's rather difficult to keep her calm at times. Hannah was given a tincture by a woman in Covent Garden, of which I did not approve. It does seem to help when Mamma is particularly agitated, and yet I don't care for it, as the ingredients are not known to us.

Prudence and Mercy are very well. They were made very happy with an invitation to dine at Lady Chatham's. She has invited all the girls not yet out. I suspect she wants a preview of next Season's debutantes so that she might begin to meddle before anyone else is allowed the privilege.

I do have a bit of joyous news and I hope you will not be cross with me. Easton and I have married! I regret that I could not get word to you in time, for I would have liked nothing more than to have my dearest sister stand up with me. How-

ever, owing to a bit of bothersome scandal, time
was of the essence.

Grace gasped. "You *didn't!*" she cried. "When?"

We were married a fortnight ago at Augustine's
insistence. We are residing at Easton's house on
Audley Street, but I must honestly inform you
that my poor dear husband is near to penniless as
he has lost his ship, and he is determined that we
will relocate to more modest housing. I do have
his word that there will be room for the Cabot
girls wherever we might land. When you return
from Bath, you must join us! I cannot bear to be
apart from you, and you have surely determined
by now that yours is a fool's errand. Come home,
Grace, please do come. We all miss you so and
we need you desperately. I know you won't care
for this news, but truly, I love Easton with all my
heart and I couldn't possibly be happier than if
he were king.

There was more to the letter, mostly having to do
with how deliriously happy Honor was with Mr. Easton,
and how Grace might hear some talk of what happened
in a gaming hell in Southwark, but that Honor would
prefer to explain it in person, as it was far too complicated to write.

Grace hardly cared what Honor had done, or that she
was penniless and happy about it. Had Grace known a
fortnight ago that scandal had touched the Cabots and

there was no hope of saving them from it, she never would have put her own foolish plan into motion.

To think Honor might have *spared* her this fate. *"Oh!"* Grace cried, and kicked the bench across from her.

That did not help at all. And it seemed she had injured her toe.

## CHAPTER THREE

THE CARRIAGE BEGAN to slow, and Grace leaned forward, looking out the small window. They'd come to a plain building, but up the road, she could see a small chapel next to a field where sheep grazed. When the carriage came to a halt, the Brumley footman opened the door and held up his hand to assist Grace.

She stepped out and looked around. "What place is this?" she asked, peering up at the building.

"Office of the magistrate, miss," he said, and shut the carriage door.

The door of the building swung open, and a portly gentleman stepped outside. "This way, if you please," he said, gesturing to Grace.

Grace slipped Honor's letter into her reticule, picked up her skirts and walked up the uneven path to the door. The gentleman showed her into a small dark office and gestured to a wooden bench against the wall. "If you would, miss. Someone will be along to collect you when the time has come."

"What is—"

He'd already shut the door.

Grace looked around the room and sat reluctantly. A few minutes later, she was startled to her feet when the door swung open.

Merryton stepped through the door. He seemed surprised to see her; he was still wearing his cloak—as was she—and boots muddied from his ride. She wondered where he had come from.

His green eyes scraped down her body and up again. A shiver ran through Grace; she thought of that darkened tea shop, the feel of his body hard against hers, his lips soft but demanding. She looked down, uncertain what to do in this situation, and afraid he would somehow read the memory in her face.

Why did he not *speak?*

She couldn't bear the silence and lifted her gaze.

The man whom she had dishonored was staring at her, his gaze dark and devouring. She didn't understand it completely, but she felt the intensity of it, and her hand fluttered self-consciously to her neck.

He clasped his hands behind his back. But he did not speak.

"My name is Grace," she said, her voice sounding too loud in this room. "Grace Cabot." The moment the words came out of her mouth, she realized how absurd she must sound. As if he'd not gone to the trouble to find out who, precisely, he was marrying. But whatever Merryton thought, she would not be allowed to know. His expression did not change.

Grace's heart began to pound in her chest. She suddenly imagined him taking her in hand, taking her on the small, cluttered desk. Isn't that what his gaze meant? "I, ah, I realize we've not been properly introduced." She nervously cleared her throat. "I wish I knew how to…to adequately express my deepest apology," she said with an uncertain gesture.

One of his dark brows arched slightly above the other, which she assumed meant he found her effort to apologize lacking.

"I can't begin to apologize enough, my lord," she quickly amended, trying to convey the depth of her regret. "But I am truly and deeply sorry for what I have done."

Still, he did not speak. He had piercing, all-seeing eyes, and she wondered if he could sense how uncomfortable, how uncertain, she was. She didn't want him to see it—she knew instinctively that to show this man any weakness would be like dangling meat before a lion. So she tried to smile a little. "So…here we are." She nervously shifted up onto her toes and down again. "What shall I call you?"

He almost looked surprised by the question. "My lord," he said, as if that were perfectly obvious. "Excuse me." He turned around, his cloak swirling behind him, and walked out of the small room, closing the door firmly behind him.

Leaving Grace alone in that small dark office, staring at the place he'd just stood.

She snatched in a deep breath she hadn't even realized she needed until that moment, and sank heavily onto the wooden bench. "My *lord?*" she repeated to the closed door. "That's what I'm to call you? *My lord?*" Would he loathe her always? Would he ever speak?

Her mind raced alongside her heart for the next several minutes. Or hours—who knew? It seemed an interminably long wait, and she did not move from that bench. Her limbs ached, her head ached more. She wished someone had opened the blinds and given the room a bit more light, but it was as bleak and as dark as her mood. She did not feel at liberty to open them herself.

Occasionally, Grace would smooth out Honor's letter from its crumpled state and read it again, but her sister's words filled her with an overwhelming desire to stab a pen into the hard wood of the desk before her, or kick it with both feet until it broke in two. How different this day would have been had she known! How different her *life* would have been had Honor written her sooner!

Grace almost sobbed out loud with relief when the door swung open, and Merryton stepped inside. He stood just at the door, one fist clenched at his side, lightly tapping against the jamb. *One two three four five six seven eight.* He dropped his hand. "It is time, Miss Cabot," he said simply.

"Well. Here it is, then," she said, resigned. In the time it took her to stand, the life Grace had known flashed before her. A privileged childhood, three sisters whom she loved more than anything else. An elegant, sophisticated mother. A life at the brilliant center of London's highest society.

Merryton, she noticed, tapped the jamb again, eight times.

Grace shoved Honor's letter into her reticule. She tried to avoid his fierce green eyes. His jaw was clenched, his expression cold. The feeling was mutual, she supposed, and swallowed down the lump of trepidation that was choking her.

Merryton glanced at a small mantel clock. "Come now." He spoke as if she were a servant.

"I'm coming as quickly as I can force myself."

"It would behoove you to force yourself a bit faster."

She could scarcely look at him as she moved past him, taking care not to brush his clothing with hers as she did. She stepped out and winced when she heard the door shut resoundingly behind her. She clasped her hands tightly before her and walked beside him, aware of his physical presence so much bigger and powerful than she.

Another shiver raced through her, and honestly, Grace could not say if it was a shiver of fear, of revulsion or, if she were perfectly honest with herself, of titillation. As heartsick as she was about this wedding, that night in the tea shop was still very much on her mind.

How in heaven had she managed to create such a prodigiously complicated shambles of her life in such a short amount of time? She would write Honor straightaway, as soon as the vows were said, and beg her to come. If she were allowed to post letters, that was. Grace wasn't entirely certain what to expect any longer.

Merryton paused before another door in the back of the small offices. He rapped on the door, and as they waited for it to open, he tapped the jamb with his fist.

Grace glanced heavenward and sent up a silent prayer for courage.

The door opened, and a man of the cloth stood behind it. He was the same height as Grace, and his disdainful gaze slid down to her toes and up again. "This way, my lord," he said to Merryton, and gestured behind Grace to the front door of the offices.

Merryton swept his hand before him, indicating Grace should precede him. She followed the clergyman out of the offices and up the road to the little chapel. She could hear Merryton walking behind her, but she could not see him. She glanced over her shoulder at him. His gaze was locked on her.

Why did he not speak? At the very least he might tell her he was so angry he did not intend to ever speak to her. Surely she deserved at least that explanation.

Grace slowed her step so that he had to walk beside her. She glanced at him from the corner of her eye, debating what she might say to somehow improve this wretched situation. "Perhaps," she said carefully, "this…arrangement…won't be as bad as one might fear." She looked at him hopefully.

Something dark flashed in his eyes.

"I mean only that, sometimes, it is best to look for hope than to find fault." Oh, that sounded ridiculous.

He must have thought so, too, because he said nothing. Grace was beginning to think his silence might be the worst of it all—that he would never utter a word.

Cousin Beatrice and her disagreeable husband were waiting inside the chapel for them, and Beatrice looked again as if she might burst into tears at any moment. Grace sincerely hoped she would not.

There was no one for Merryton, she noticed. Not even Amherst.

Her heart was pounding as they moved up the aisle

to the altar. She'd never felt so alone—they may as well have been leading her to the gallows and her execution.

The clergyman spoke in near-whispers to Merryton, almost as if Grace was not even present. He announced he would begin. He drew a breath and fixed his gaze on Grace. "We are gathered here today in the sight of *God,*" he said, as if Grace wasn't aware that God was watching. As if she needed to be reminded. As if she wasn't acutely aware of how dreadfully she must have disappointed her maker.

She surreptitiously pressed her damp palms against the skirt of her gown. She felt a little light-headed as the weight of what was happening began to sink in, and fixed her gaze on the stained glass over the vicar's head, of Jesus on the cross. Her thoughts jumbled and raced ahead to her duties as this man's wife. She was aware when Merryton shifted beside her, felt the heat in his much-larger hand when he took hers—literally picking it up from her side to hold it when Grace failed to hear the vicar's instruction. The vicar began to read the assumptions of a married couple, including fidelity and honor. She noticed that Merryton's eyes seemed to narrow the more the vicar spoke.

"My lord," the vicar said, his voice soft and even kind, "will you take this woman…" He began to rattle off the requirements of him. To hold her from this day forward. To honor and cherish, for better or worse—

Now there was a laugh. There was no accidental honoring and cherishing at this altar. The notion that he should have to vow such a thing was so absurd that

Grace could feel a slightly hysterical, completely irrepressible smile begin to curve her lips.

As the vicar continued to speak, Merryton looked at her curiously at first, then crossly. He undoubtedly did not find any of this amusing, and in spite of her attempt to hide her hysterical smile, neither did Grace. But the more the vicar spoke, the more absurd it all seemed, and Grace's laughter was rising in her like a storm tide, threatening to explode on the gentleman standing before her. She bit her lip, but she couldn't keep that damnable smile from her lips.

"I will," Merryton said curtly.

Grace hadn't even realized the question had ended.

"Miss Cabot," the vicar said, "will you take Jeffrey Thomas Creighton Donovan to be your lawfully wedded husband, to have and to hold from this day forward, for better, for worse, for richer, for poorer, in sickness and in health, to love, to cherish, to honor and obey until death do you part?" he asked quickly, his gaze on the book he held.

Oh, dear. Until death parted them seemed an *awfully* long time. Grace thought of her fantasy of escaping, of running away. She would do that long before death ever thought to part them, and that, therefore, begged the question—

Merryton squeezed her hand. Her hesitation had earned her twin stern looks from the vicar and from Merryton. "Oh, yes," she said quickly, and looked at the vicar. "I will." Her voice was surprisingly strong for all the roiling in her belly. She shifted her gaze to Merryton. His expression was either a devouring one, or it was a very heated one, and she was mystified as to what, exactly, his gaze meant.

She looked away, finding the stained glass once more, praying for wisdom, forbearance, hope.

The vicar reminded them both that they had said these vows in the presence of God, and then intoned, "I pronounce you man and wife."

The moment he said it, Merryton dropped her hand.

"If you would, my lord, sign the parish register," the vicar said, his hand on Merryton's elbow, showing him the way to the register.

Grace didn't move from her spot at the altar, feeling quite at sea.

The vicar paused and looked back. "Mrs. Donovan!" he said, as if she were a lagging child, and held out the pen to her.

Well, then, that sealed it. If she was addressed as Mrs. Donovan, she must be married. Grace signed the marriage book, her hand shaking beneath the firm strokes of his signature. *Merryton,* he'd written. Cousin Beatrice signed as witness, wiping tears from her face as she did. Her husband signed next, and when he laid down the pen, he looked at Merryton and said, "My sympathies, my lord."

Grace gasped with disbelief and gaped at Brumley, but she was so inconsequential to him that he never even glanced in her direction.

Merryton did, however. He turned that dark, cold gaze to her and said simply, "Come." He turned on his heel, walking from the chapel, his cloak billowing behind him. He had not even removed his cloak.

A sob came from somewhere behind her, and in the next moment, Beatrice's hands were grasping at Grace, turning her about, pulling her into her chest. "You poor dear," she whispered. "Please let me write to your mother! She will be a source of great comfort to you now."

Grace had to physically push away from Beatrice to draw a breath. "I've already sent a letter," she lied.

"Oh, right, of course you have," Beatrice said, and clasped Grace's face between her hands. "Be brave, darling. It will not do to cry and carry on when you yourself have brought this on yourself."

Grace blinked. She gave a small, rueful laugh. "No, of course not," she agreed.

"Lady Merryton," Merryton called sternly from the entrance.

It was a moment before Grace understood that he was speaking to her. She peeled Beatrice's hands from her face and stepped away. She could still hear Beatrice's whimpering as she walked down the aisle toward the sunlight streaming through the open door. Bright, cheerful sun, as if this was the happiest of days.

Grace stepped out into the sunlight and lifted the hood of her cloak over her head.

At the bottom of the hill, Merryton stood beside a black coach pulled by a team of four. It was deceiving in its lack of ornamentation; Grace knew it was one of the new, expensive landau coaches. The only nod given to the rank of the man who owned it was red plumes that billowed up from either side of the driver's seat. Four coachmen in livery stood at attention, and she could see her trunk strapped to the boot.

With a curt nod of his head, Merryton commanded the coach door to be opened and the step brought down. He looked at Grace.

She took a breath and did not release it until she reached the coach. And even when she did, hardly any breath left her, all of it absorbed by her trepidation.

Merryton held out his hand, palm up, to help her into the coach. She hesitated before laying her hand in his. He didn't look at her as he handed her up. When she was seated he stepped back. "Godspeed, madam."

"Wait—pardon?" she said, confused, and lurched forward, bracing herself in the open door of the coach. "Aren't you coming?"

"I will ride."

"But I—" *But she what?* What could she possibly say? She wanted him to ride with her? No, no, she didn't want that. Hours of cold silence was far worse than being alone on her wedding day—

Before Grace could work out what she meant, he'd shut the door. She surged toward the window, pushing aside the curtain. She had to crane her neck to see him, but she watched him stride to a horse that a boy held and easily swing up. He looked like a king on that horse, taut and muscular, his shoulders squared, his countenance stern. He turned to speak to the coachman, and then spurred his horse, galloping away from the chapel as if the devil chased him.

A moment later, the coach lurched forward, tossing Grace back into the leather squabs. She blinked up at the silk-covered ceiling. That was that, then. She was married to him, until death parted them, and he despised her. She abruptly bit down on her lower lip to keep tears from falling. She agreed with Cousin Beatrice—it would not do to cry when one had brought the situation on herself.

She would *not* cry, bloody hell, she would *not*.

# CHAPTER FOUR

IT WASN'T LONG before the scattering of cottages grew farther apart, and soon, there was nothing but forests rolling by, broken by the occasional pasture dotted with sheep or cows or, as Grace saw in one pasture, dozens of pigs grazing around their little hovels. Occasionally, she would spot the chimneys of a grand estate over the tops of trees, but that was the only sign of people on this road.

She was hungry; she wondered if it was acceptable to ask the coachman to stop in a village, to allow her to rest, to eat something, to freshen herself before she arrived at Blackwood Hall.

She reread Honor's letter to take her mind off her discomfort, but found nothing but more anxiety in the happy loops and swirls of her sister's handwriting. Grace put the letter away, folded her arms and leaned her head back against the squabs, squeezing her eyes shut against the images of the life about to unfold before her. The constant rocking of the coach made her limbs and eyelids feel heavy; Grace was aware she was sinking into exhaustion, but she didn't recall sliding down onto the bench. That was where she was when the coach hit a bump, and her head struck the side of the coach, waking her. "Ouch," she said, wincing and putting a hand to her head.

She pushed herself up and swept aside the curtains. The day had turned gloomy, and they were rolling past some barren cliffs. But the road turned, and the forest began again, rising up dark against the hills. The coach slowed and turned north, into the thick of the forest. The trees were so dense that they blocked what little light existed. The forest was truly black wood.

The coach began to slow. They passed through a massive stone gate, its height so tall that from Grace's vantage point through the small window she could not see the top of it. Once inside the gate, the trees had been thinned, and gray light dappled the pristine lawn.

Grace gasped softly when the house came into view—it was quite large, at least as large as Longmeadow, the Beckington seat where she'd spent her youth. But where Longmeadow was light and cheerful, Blackwood Hall was dark and foreboding. The stone was gray, the windows black eyes. The chimneys were covered in soot, and there was no color that Grace could see, other than the green ivy that covered one corner of the house.

The house looked just like its master—bleak, dark and foreboding, the only color in his face the stark green of his eyes.

The house staff was scurrying out the door, lining up in order of rank as the coach rolled in. There were fifteen in all, the butler and the housekeeper at the head of the line. They came to a halt, and the door swung open. The bench was set before the opening. A coachman held up his hand to assist her down.

Grace swallowed down a small lump of fear, and stepped out.

The staff were looking straight ahead, but more than one pair of eyes slid in her direction. She let her hood fall back and glanced around for Merryton. He came striding across the drive, his crop tapping against his leg. Eight times. A pause. Eight times again.

"Mr. Cox, Mrs. Garland, may I present Lady Merryton," he said matter-of-factly. He announced it so casually, in fact, that one would reasonably assume he must have sent word ahead of his marriage. But it was clear that when the two principle servants both froze, and the ripple ran through the rest of the servants gathered, that none of them knew.

"My lady," Mrs. Garland said, the first to recover as she dipped into a quick curtsy. She looked to Mr. Cox for guidance, but the tall, thin butler had yet to regain his composure. Not that Merryton cared, apparently, because he looked at Grace, clenched his jaw and strode inside, the crop still tapping against his leg. Eight times.

"Ah…" Grace glanced over her shoulder; the coachmen were unlashing her trunk. She turned back to the group of servants. "How do you do," she said, forcing a smile, nodding at them. "This…this must come as something of a surprise."

There was a murmur of agreement, more shuffling about.

"Yes, well…it was meant to…be a surprise," she said

hesitantly, reaching for anything to ease her arrival as a Fallen Woman.

"You are very welcome, my lady," Cox said, having recovered from his initial shock. He jostled two chambermaids out of the way and walked briskly forward, bowing before Grace, then gesturing for her to precede him into the house. "If I may, I shall show you about the hall. Mrs. Garland, please do see that the lady's chambers are made ready? Make way," he said, and the servants instantly split into two lines, stepping back to allow Grace to pass.

Grace smiled again, lifted her chin as if she were entering Lady Chatham's sitting room, nodding and murmuring a greeting to the servants as she passed by them and walked into the foyer of Blackwood Hall.

She had expected grandeur, and while the house was certainly grand—the marble floors, the winding formal staircase, the Grecian columns—there was not the usual assembly of paintings and armor that, in Grace's experience, generally graced the entrance to a grand home. This foyer was stark, as if the owner had only recently taken possession.

Mr. Cox walked her down long hallways, showing her small salons and larger, more formal salons, the breakfast room, more than one dining room and one formal one that would seat sixty. There was a ballroom and so many guest rooms that Grace lost count. The house was magnificently constructed, but somber in its decor. There were no paintings on the walls, no familiar signs of family history, no evidence of ancestry for all to see. There were only identical vases of identical hothouse flowers—roses—cut at identical height.

In the main salon, Grace paused before the massive hearth and glanced up at the mirror that hung above it. "I have noticed there are no paintings," she said to Cox.

"No, madam. His lordship prefers that the frames be made uniform, and if they cannot, he prefers they not hang."

"Pardon?" Grace said, glancing over her shoulder at the butler.

Even though Cox's hair was thinning, he was unexpectedly young for the position he held. He said again, "His lordship prefers uniformity," he said.

What on earth did that mean, he preferred uniformity? She glanced up to the mirror, the only thing in the room to adorn the walls. Moreover, there were four chairs set before the hearth, two facing two, all of them at equal distance from the other.

How odd.

"Shall I show you your lady's suite of rooms?"

"Please," Grace said.

She was happy to see that her suite of rooms faced south and west, which promised sunlight to chase away the gloom of this house. The rooms themselves were tastefully appointed, painted a pale creamy pink, with white shutters at the windows and embroidered draperies. The wood floor had been covered with a thick rug. It was very inviting. Except that, again, there was nothing on the walls to brighten the room.

"Is there anything you might require?" Mr. Cox asked.

"Yes," she said, and pressed her hands to her belly. "I am quite hungry, Mr. Cox. Might I have something to eat?"

Mr. Cox looked strangely uncomfortable at her request. "I beg your pardon, madam, but supper is served at precisely eight o'clock."

Grace looked at the mantle clock. It was a quarter to five o'clock. "Do you mean to say that I may not have anything to eat until eight o'clock?"

Cox swallowed; his cheeks colored slightly. "His lordship prefers food be served at those hours. Breakfast is likewise served at eight o'clock, and luncheon at twelve o'clock, tea at four o'clock."

Grace stared at the butler, thinking she would see the hint of a smile, discover that he possessed a jovial streak. But Cox merely stood, awaiting her direction.

"No exception might be made today?" she asked.

"If his lordship agrees, of course." But he made no move, which led Grace to believe that she would have to be the one to inquire. If that was the case, she preferred to feel the pangs of hunger.

"Might I have a bath?" she asked. "Or…are there requirements for the time they might be drawn?"

"No, madam. I will have one drawn right away." Mr. Cox gave her a curt nod and strode briskly from the room.

When he'd gone, Grace let her reticule fall to the floor. She wasn't sure what she was going to do next— her belly was growling and she was exhausted from the strain of this day. A bath would help that, and then she would count every minute to supper and the moment

she'd be allowed to eat something. After that, well…
whatever came after that, she couldn't contemplate
without feeling a bit ill.

But also a wee bit intrigued.

After all, not every moment in the tea shop had been
dreadful.

JEFFREY'S PRIVATE CHAMBER was situated in the front hall
of the first floor, overlooking the entrance to Blackwood Hall. It was twenty-four steps long and sixteen
steps wide.

The master suite, which Mr. Cox frequently brought
up in the hopes that Jeffrey would one day occupy it,
was at the southern corner of the first floor. It had two
walls of windows, with three windows each, overlooking the more picturesque bits of his estate. It was also
thirty-one steps long and twenty-three steps wide.

Mr. Cox believed that Jeffrey preferred not to sleep
where his father had passed away, and Jeffrey was content for him to assume so. But in truth, he preferred it
here, in the quiet comfort of eight. It settled him, made
him feel at ease.

Until today. This room was uncomfortably close to
the new Lady Merryton's suite of rooms.

He had taken refuge in his rooms when they'd arrived from Bath, pouring himself a generous portion of
whiskey and removing his boots. He'd sat down onto the
upholstered chair before his hearth, had leaned his head
back and closed his eyes, his mind racing around the
improbable fact that he was now married to a woman
he did not know.

As he sat there in his quiet, he heard the servants in the hall. "Have a care, Willie, mind you not make a noise," one footman said harshly to the other. "I told you, one bucket, each hand. If Mrs. Garland notices you've sloshed water on the carpets, she'll have you sent to the stables."

Jeffrey slowly opened his eyes. He realized that they were hauling buckets of water so that Lady Merryton could bathe.

He downed the rest of his whiskey, clenched his jaw and closed his eyes again. He tried his best not to imagine her naked body sliding into steaming water, her breasts floating on the surface. But the more he tried to banish the images, the faster they came at him. He saw water swirling around her sex, caressing her as he ached to do. He saw her lifting a slender, tapered leg from the water and running her hands over it, then her breasts, then leaning her head against the back of the bath and sliding her hands lower to where he wanted to put his hands—

Jeffrey suddenly came up with a start. He walked to the windows and flung one open, leaning into the casing, taking deep breaths of air. He had to control himself and his ugly thoughts. He had to learn to exist in this house with that woman—that treacherous, *beautiful* woman.

He whirled around from the window, grabbed up his boot. He silently counted to eight, then shoved his foot in. Again on the other leg. And then he strode out of his rooms, bound for the study, his fist tapping in a futile effort to ease his racing thoughts.

There he remained, burying his thoughts in an avalanche of work. He reviewed invoices, examined the ledgers, wrote his own correspondence. At ten of seven, Cox entered the study. "Will you dress for supper, my lord?"

"No," Jeffrey said without looking up from his work. His response no doubt caused Cox a bit of consternation, for Jeffrey was nothing if not habitual. "Quite a lot to be done," he said vaguely, and looked at the papers before him. "Please inform her ladyship of when and where we might dine."

"Yes, my lord."

Jeffrey stared blindly at the page before him as Cox went out, counting the butler's footsteps. *Six.* Only six. Everything around him was off-kilter, out of balance, and Jeffrey didn't know how to get it back. He couldn't avoid the feminine presence in his house. He could already feel it seeping in through the walls, surrounding him like a vapor. He had spent so much of his adult life carefully constructing the boundaries around him that he'd not thought of what he might do if those boundaries were breached.

He certainly didn't know what to do now, and continued working, filling his head with figures and the problems of managing a large estate until the supper hour. As much as he would have liked to have dined alone in his rooms, his sense of order and habit was much stronger. He strode down the hallway—sixteen steps in all—to the family dining room. He walked in, and the woman, his *wife,* was standing at the buffet.

His entrance clearly startled her; she jerked around, knocking into the buffet and causing the stack of plates to rattle. She quickly put her hands around the plates to still them and smiled apprehensively.

Her hands, he noticed, were slender and elegant. Long, tapered fingers. He looked down, pushing an image of those fingers sliding into body orifices.

"Good evening, my lord," she said with as much cheer as one could muster, given the day. Her voice sounded melodic.

"Good evening, Lady Merryton."

"Ah…Grace," she said, as if perhaps he hadn't re-membered it, as if he hadn't signed a marriage book and a special license with her name clearly spelled out for all eternity: Grace Elizabeth Diana Cabot. Twenty-four letters in all.

"You will forgive me if I do not feel the familiarity necessary to address you by your given name as yet." He thought he was being helpful. He couldn't very well explain to her that certain things had to happen before he could call her by her given name—even he wasn't sure what—but he couldn't speak to her as if they were known to each other. As if he had courted her, had asked her permission to address her more intimately.

Clearly, his helpful explanation had not had the de-sired effect; he could see her delicate swallow course her neck. She pressed her lips together and nodded po-litely.

She apparently had given up any pretense of mourn-ing her stepfather, as she was wearing a shimmering gold gown with intricate embroidery of crystals on the skirt. They caught the light and made it look as if she were sparkling. The gown hugged her body tightly, and her breasts, heaven help him, were two creamy mounds that looked as if they would burst from her décolletage at any moment. Her golden hair was swept up in a simple roll at her nape. Jewels that matched the glitter of those around her throat dangled at her earlobes.

She was, in a word, *lovely.*

Jeffrey gestured to a seat at the table; a footman instantly moved to hold the chair for her.

She sat elegantly, her hands in her lap, her gaze on the setting before her. Jeffrey admired her long neck, the tiny wisps of hair that were not caught in the roll of her hair. She took a deep breath, her chest lifting with it, then smoothly falling again as she silently released it.

Jeffrey sat heavily in his seat at the head of the table, prepared for what he assumed would be a difficult evening. He tried not to look at this stranger, this beauty, his wife. To look at her was to imagine the claiming of her, the possession of her body. It was within his right, but Jeffrey could not bear it. He feared what he would do, that he would lose control, that he could, God forbid, *hurt* her. It was one thing to seek the company of women who shared his appetites, or could be persuaded to like them with a generous purse. It was something else entirely when the object of his desire was a virginal debutante.

He couldn't help himself; he tapped his forefinger

against the table eight times as nonchalantly as he possibly could.

"Shall we serve, my lord?" Cox said behind him.

*Yes, please serve, let this day be done!* "Please," he said, and leaned back, his fists on his thighs, his jaw clenched.

The place settings had been laid perfectly—the water goblet four inches above the center of the plate, the wine goblet four inches to the right of that. The china plate, purchased from a rather desperate aristocratic Frenchman, boasted a fleur-de-lis in the center of the plate. The top of the fleur-de-lis pointed to the center of the water goblet. Jeffrey did not look at the plate's border; it was a terrible hodgepodge of scrolling evergreen boughs and tiny fleur-de-lis that made no sense to him and disturbed him.

"You have a lovely home."

The dulcet tone of her voice slipped through Jeffrey; he risked a look at her. The first thing he'd truly noticed about her—the first time he'd seen her in light, in that wretched office before they were wed—was her eyes. They were hazel, more green than brown, and they reminded him of the colors of late summer. Her lashes were darkly golden but long, her brows feathery arches over her eyes. He'd been struck by her beauty, something that he'd failed to notice the night in the tea shop.

What he noticed tonight was that her fingers were tapping lightly on the stem of the wine goblet. She had pulled the goblet out of its place, closer to her, and that it was out of place gave him a feeling of uneasiness. "Thank you," he said. He looked away.

"Have you always resided here?"

Bloody hell, conversation could not be avoided. He turned back to her, his gaze sweeping over her. She was wearing a choker of amber stones about her neck, and he could imagine himself removing that necklace, his hands sliding over her shoulders, the jewels sliding into her cleavage, followed by his fingers.

That image was inexplicably and unavoidably followed by one of him at her breast, his mouth surrounding the tip of it, his tongue flicking across the hardened peak.

She was speaking, he realized. Jeffrey pressed the heel of his shoe into the carpet to settle himself. "Pardon?"

"I was inquiring if your family has been long at Blackwood Hall."

"Generations," he responded tersely. "This has been the Merryton seat since the title was bestowed on us. I am the fifth earl." Her lips were full, plush and an amazing shade of coral.

"Do you live alone here?"

He shifted in his seat. "Mostly."

She looked as if she wanted to ask more, but thankfully, the serving of the meal ended any talk for the time being. When Cox had filled their plates with lamb and potatoes, and had filled their wineglasses, Jeffrey sent him and the footman out with a single gesture.

He picked up his fork and began to eat. He was aware that his wife picked uneasily at her food as if she had no appetite, but drank her wine with more enthusiasm. When he finished, he settled back in his seat and placed his napkin on the table beside his plate. He noticed she'd only taken a few bites. "Do you not find the food to your liking?"

"What? No, it's perfectly fine."

Then why did she not eat it? He shifted his gaze to the buffet. Eight drawers, four by four.

"If I may," she said, "I should like to…offer an apology for what happened."

She *had* apologized to him. He didn't know what she thought he might do with another apology.

"The tea shop," she said, apparently thinking it necessary to explain what she meant. As if something else had happened between them, as if she'd made some other catastrophic gash across his life.

He did not care to think of that night, of his complete loss of control. "It is unnecessary."

"But I—"

"Madam, as I said, unnecessary," he said, and shifted uncomfortably again. "You were there to meet Amherst. You mistook me for him. We have both made a mistake of enormous consequence that has linked us, inextricably, for eternity. What is done is done. Have you finished your meal?"

Her brows knit in frown. "Yes."

"Then…if you will excuse me." He stood.

His wife looked surprised. She moved to stand, too, and the gentleman in Jeffrey, bred into him at an early age, quickly moved to pull her chair away. She straightened, only inches from him. Her eyes blinked up at him, the candlelight making them seem to sparkle. Jeffrey felt a swirl of emotion and heat rising up in him. He had an unbearable urge to take her in hand, to kiss the plump, moist lips, to put his hand and his mouth on her chest, to bend her over this table and lift her skirts, bare her bottom to him, move his hand between her legs—

He stepped back, curtly bowed his head. "I will not come to you tonight, Lady Merryton." He clasped his hands at his back so that she would not see the way his hand curled into a fist, trying to control his desire. "I will allow you the time to be comfortable at Black-wood Hall."

Her eyes widened. An appealing blush rose in her cheeks as she glanced around them, as if searching for something. An exit, perhaps.

"You may inquire with Mr. Cox about the services of a lady's maid."

That brought her gaze quickly back to him, but this time, instead of bewilderment, her gaze was cross. She folded her arms across her body and tilted her head to one side, and Jeffrey could not help but admire her neck. "I am curious—are you this aloof and command-ing with everyone you know, or have you adopted this demeanor entirely for my benefit? For if you mean to punish me, you need not bother. I am punishing myself every moment of every day."

Her bit of cheek surprised him. He wasn't punishing her. He was more at fault than she.

"I understand you are angry. I would be, were I in your shoes. I have apologized—"

"There is no need to apologize again," he said brusquely.

Her eyes narrowed slightly. "Good, because I didn't intend to apologize *again.* After all, there are only so many ways one might beg for forgiveness, and I believe I've exhausted them all. But I rather think that here we are, my lord, and we may as well determine how we are to endure it."

Jeffrey was caught completely off guard. He lived a solitary life—most people deferred to him. They certainly did not challenge him. "I beg your pardon, madam, if I've not been suitably garrulous for you. I find idle chatter tedious and I am not very good at it."

"Why yes, you have demonstrated that very well, my lord. But I don't think of it as idle chatter. I was attempting to know you."

That declaration made him feel uncomfortably exposed. He wondered what she would think if she knew she'd trapped herself into a marriage with a madman. "Frankly, I don't care to be known," he said truthfully. "Good night."

He turned away from her and walked to the door. But as he reached it, he heard her say something quite low. He paused at the door and looked back. "Pardon?"

"I said, good night, my lord," she said with mock cheer. She looked lovely standing there, her color high, her eyes blazing with ire. The images began to come to him—images of those eyes blazing with passion—

He turned away and walked into the corridor. He turned left. He walked sixteen steps to the turn into the main corridor, then thirty-two steps to the foyer, which required him to shorten his stride. In the foyer, he began the count again, going up the steps.

It was the only thing that would banish the image of his wife caressing her naked body while he watched.

## CHAPTER FIVE

GRACE LOCKED THE door of her room. She stood there, her arms akimbo, studying it. She debated pulling a chair before it to make doubly sure he couldn't enter. She would no more allow that wretched man to touch her than she would eat her shoe.

Actually, under the right circumstances, she might be persuaded to eat her shoe.

She studied the door, imagined him breaking it down, demanding entry. He said he would not come to her...but when he said it, he was looking at her so intently, his gaze so ravenous, that Grace didn't believe him. She thought it a trick.

No, no, she was being ridiculous. He said he would not come to her. And if that man said something, it was painfully true. *"I find idle chatter tedious,"* she mimicked him under her breath. *"Frankly, I do not wish to be known."*

Grace rolled her eyes. What a miserable figure! And *she,* a woman who was accustomed to fawning men and high society, was married to him. "Oh!" she said to the ceiling, and gripped her hands in frustration.

Yes, the lock was sufficient. And honestly, were he to come through the door now, she might brain him with the fire poker. Grace was never one to contemplate violence, but she had already contemplated it several times today, so exasperated was she with her situation. "Come through *my* door, sir, and see what awaits," she muttered.

She backed away from the door, expecting to see the handle turn at any moment, and bumped up against the bed. She sat, her hands on either side of her knees, her breath a little uneven. *What was the matter with him?* He was a man with a broad reputation for being aloof, for being more concerned about his place in society and propriety than his own family. But his flaws seemed more to her than that. There was something very different about him than anyone she'd ever known, the signs of a private struggle, as if he was making a concerted effort to isolate himself from everyone around him. Not only would he scarcely utter a word to her, it seemed to take quite a lot for him to look her in the eye.

And yet, when he did look her in the eye, his gaze was so intent, so hungry, that she couldn't suppress the small shock of fear that sliced through her even now.

"Now you're imagining things," she muttered wearily. He might be a strangely aloof man, but he was an earl, a gentleman. He had said he would not come to her tonight and he would keep his word. Grace sighed with the exhaustion of prolonged agitation and stood up. She'd forced a marriage with the man and she could not avoid the marriage bed, no matter how much she might like to. Part of her was repulsed by it, by *him,* by his cold manner. But another part of her felt a bit of heat sluice through her every time she thought of their fateful encounter.

*You were there to meet Amherst. You mistook me for him.*

How did he know what she'd done? And if he knew, why did he kiss her so thoroughly that night?

Grace mulled that over as she reached behind her to unbutton her gown but was startled almost out of her wits by a knock at the door. She gasped and hopped to her feet, running to the hearth to grab the fire poker. "Who's there!"

"Hattie Crump, mu'um. I've been sent by Mrs. Garland to attend you."

Grace's relief swept out of her, making her feel suddenly limp. She drew a breath to find her composure, put aside the fire poker and walked to the door. She opened it to a small woman with dark red hair pinned tightly at her nape. She was wearing a severe dark blue gown with a prim white collar that Grace had seen on the other female servants today. She had an unfortunate pair of dark hollows beneath her eyes, as if she'd not slept in years.

Hattie Crump curtsied. "Mrs. Garland said I should help you until you've hired a lady's maid."

Grace's initial instinct was to send her away, but she was so grateful for company of any sort that was not that awful man, she pulled the woman in. "Thank you."

"How may I help?"

"Ah…" Grace glanced around the room. "My trunk. If you would put away my things?"

"Aye," Hattie said, and started briskly for the dressing room.

Grace followed her. She stood in the doorway nervously fidgeting with the cuff of her sleeve as Hattie began to remove her gowns and underthings from the trunk, opening the doors to the armoire and neatly stacking them inside.

"Have you been long at Blackwood Hall?" Grace asked.

"Aye, mu'um, more or less all my life. As my mother before me."

Hattie looked at least as old as Merryton. "Then I suppose you've known his lordship quite a long time," Grace said, watching the woman's face for any sign of revulsion.

"Oh, aye. He's only a wee bit younger than I am. He was a lovely lad. Always had a kind word for the servants."

Grace thought she must mean Amherst and said, "I was referring to Lord Merryton."

Hattie looked up, surprised. "Aye, Lord Merryton."

Grace blanched—Merryton, kind? There was suddenly so much she wanted to know, to arm herself against the devil. "It's a beautiful house," she said, avoiding Hattie's steady gaze. "Quite far from town, however. I suppose his lordship is often away?"

"No, mu'um. Lord Amherst is rarely about, but Merryton, he remains here most of the year. Except when he travels to Bath. The family takes the waters there."

Just as she'd feared, she'd be stuck in this wilderness, away from her mother and sisters, with perhaps an occasional trip to Bath. Grace pushed away from the door frame and walked to a window. She tried to see out, but the night was an inky black. "There must be quite a number of tenants," she said with a sigh of tedium.

"I suppose, mu'um. The church pews are filled on Sunday, that's all I know."

In the mirror's reflection, Grace could see Hattie holding up her black gown and eyeing it as if she were confused by it. Grace thought perhaps she might acquaint herself with this woman before she explained she'd married while in mourning. Put her best foot forward first, as it were. "Is there a village nearby?" she asked.

"Aye, Ashton Down. It's a two-mile walk through the woods."

Grace couldn't imagine taking as much as a step into these dark woods. "Perhaps I shall walk there on the morrow," she said, surprising herself. Apparently, she could imagine it if it meant escaping this bleak house and its bleaker master.

Hattie finished putting the clothing away, closed the doors of the armoire and turned around. "Mrs. Garland says to inquire if you will need me in the morning, mu'um," she said.

"No, thank you. I shall be quite all right on my own." Grace smiled.

"Very well. Mr. Cox, he's to bring you a lady's maid. His lordship said you must have one."

"Why can't it be you?" she asked Hattie.

The poor woman looked so shocked that Grace almost laughed. "Me!" Hattie said, glancing around the room. "I'm no lady's maid, mu'um. I do the cleaning."

"It's not a science, Hattie. It's really quite simple. Help button me up and pin up my hair. That sort of thing."

"I…I don't know, mu'um," Hattie said. Her neck was turning red with her fluster.

"I shall speak to Mr. Cox," Grace said confidently. She would not allow Hattie's fluster to dissuade her. She liked the small woman. And she certainly didn't want a girl from the village who would be as fearful of Blackwood Hall as Grace. She needed someone who understood this house and its master.

Grace put her arm around the woman's bony shoulders and squeezed. "It will be quite all right, you'll see. I'm very good at persuading gentlemen to my viewpoint." She smiled, and thought the better of pointing out that the predicament in which she found herself just now was all the result of having persuaded a gentleman to meet her in the dark.

When Hattie had gone, Grace locked the door again, changed into her nightclothes, and when she'd finished her toilette, she climbed into the four-poster bed. But she couldn't sleep; every creak, every moan, was Merryton coming to claim his conjugal rights. She closed her eyes, tried not to imagine him looming over her, his expression cold, his eyes shuttered. She tried not to imagine the number of lonely days and nights stretching before her in this house, with no society, no one to talk to, no one to advise her.

*What a shambles you've made, Grace Elizabeth.*

*Thank you, but I am acutely aware,* she silently responded to herself.

SHE AWOKE THE next morning feeling as if she hadn't slept at all. She relinquished the last bit of pretense at mourning garb—it seemed ridiculous, given all that had happened. And it wasn't as if anyone in society would see her here. There were far better things to gossip about now, weren't there?

She dressed in a brown gown with a high neck and long sleeves, a somber color for her somber mood. She looked at the clock—it seemed that her eye found it every quarter hour. It was too early for breakfast, too early to walk. Grace decided to use the time to write Honor. She went into the sitting room that adjoined her bedroom and looked around. There was a pair of chairs before the hearth, the seats covered in the same chintz as the settee. Up against one long window was the writing desk Grace had seen yesterday. She opened the drawers, found vellum and ink and sat down.

My dearest Mrs. Easton, I assume this letter finds you well enough. You have succeeded in shocking me, as I am certain I have shocked you. I should like to think you've found your happiness in your foolishness, for I have found nothing but misery in mine. His lordship is aloof and somber, and he does not enjoy the slightest bit of conversation.

I have arrived at Blackwood Hall, and find it quite grim. There is no society, no one whom I may take in my confidence. The maid tells me the earl rarely leaves this place and I fear I shall never look upon the faces of my mother or my sisters again. I have never felt quite so alone or so foolish. You must advise me, Honor. Tell me how to bear it.

Before she knew it, Grace had filled two pages, front and back. She folded them together, sealed and addressed them and put it in her pocket to give to Mr. Cox. She glanced at the clock, saw that it was time for breakfast and, with trepidation, began her way downstairs.

Cox was in the corridor of the main floor and bowed when he saw her. "Shall I direct you to the breakfast room?"

"If you would," Grace said. She followed him in a new direction, past more blank walls, more empty consoles. He opened the door of a room, and stepped aside to allow her entrance.

The room was small, the drapes pulled back to reveal a bright day. At a small round table in the center of the room, she saw one place setting, a vase with a pair of roses and a pot of tea. There was no evidence of Merryton, no evidence that anyone else would be dining here, save her.

She looked at Mr. Cox. "Where is his lordship?"

"He did not take breakfast this morning. Tea?"

"I will pour it, thank you," Grace said, mildly annoyed that Merryton didn't at least bother to greet her.

"The bellpull is just here," Cox said, gesturing to the pull beside the door. He went out.

Grace looked at the sideboard, laden with enough food to feed four people, much less one. She walked to the window and looked out. The breakfast room overlooked a vast garden. The hedges had been planted into four series of scrolls, and at the center of each were rosebushes in full bloom. At the center of the garden was a large fountain. Beyond the garden, she could see a small lake, the path to it mowed and lined with more roses.

She helped herself to some toast and a spoonful of eggs, but in spite of scarcely having eaten in the past twenty-four hours, even that bit of food felt more than she could possibly choke down.

That exasperated Grace, too. She had always possessed a healthy appetite. She would *not* exist like this—she refused.

A thought came to her on a sudden wave of determination. She would not wander about from room to room, casting about for anything to occupy her. Merryton could despise her as he wished, but she would not stand to be cast out of her own life by what had happened. What was it her mother had once said? *One is happy when one learns how to face up to life.* Of course, her mother had been talking about a tiff between Grace and Prudence, the reason long forgotten. But her point was that each person made his or her own happiness.

Well, then, Grace would make her own happiness, because she refused to live any other way. No more moping about. No more living in dread.

When Cox returned to clear her dishes away— her toast and eggs still on the plate, her tea only half drunk—Grace stood up. "Mr. Cox, I should like to have Hattie as my lady's maid, if you please."

Cox's eyes widened slightly; he put two hands under her plate, as if he feared he might drop it having just heard that news. "But Hattie is a chambermaid, madam. You would prefer a proper lady's maid, I should think."

"I cannot imagine there is a *proper* lady's maid in Ashton Down. Hattie is sensible, she knows Blackwood Hall and I prefer her."

She saw the apple of Mr. Cox's throat bob as he swallowed down the news. "I shall speak to his lordship straightaway."

"Oh. Is he here?" she asked, looking at the door.

"No, madam. He has gone out for the day."

Merryton had gone out and left her here? Alone? One day after she had wed him? Grace couldn't imagine why that would surprise her, but it did seem rather rude. "Very well," she said, lifting her chin. "Then I suppose I shall spend this day acquainting myself with Blackwood Hall. Is that acceptable to you, Mr. Cox?"

"To me?" he asked, startled. "Yes, of course, my lady, whatever you wish."

"That is what I wish," she said. "And, if you would, see that this letter is posted?" she asked, and withdrew from her pocket the letter she had written to Honor and held it out to him.

"Will there be anything else, madam?" Cox asked.

Yes. She would like to rewind the past fortnight and do it all again. But as that was beyond Cox's abilities, she said no, gave him a bright smile and walked out the door.

She moved down the main corridor to the foyer, paused there and looked around her. Her eye fell to the crystal vases filled with red roses. The vases were set atop half-moon consoles. There were four of them, two by two, each set in perfect mirror image across the foyer by the other one, all of them sporting identical vases. Each vase had exactly eight red roses.

Grace absently fingered one of the roses in the vase. It was drooping a little, and she guessed it had been cut and left without water too long. She pulled the vase from the wall, removed the drooping rose and held it up to her nose. She pushed the vase back and walked on, carrying the rose, determined to have a look about the place.

JEFFREY NOTICED INSTANTLY that one of the crystal vases in the foyer was not in its place when he returned to Blackwood late that afternoon. And it had been carelessly pushed against the wall. He bit down remarking as much to Cox, who was busy receiving Jeffrey's cloak, gloves and hat, as well as his riding crop. He was reluctant to speak, certain that every word he uttered revealed his sickness in some way. He struggled to keep the evidence from everyone, although he thought that he had no doubt failed miserably to hide it completely from Mr. Cox or Mrs. Garland.

"If I may, my lord," Cox said, his arms laden with Jeffrey's things.

Jeffrey took his gaze from the offending vase and fixed it on his butler.

"Lady Merryton has requested that Hattie Crump serve as her lady's maid."

Hattie, the tiny woman with the dark red hair, was quite plain, her face reminiscent, to Jeffrey at least, of a goose. He did not wish to be so uncharitable, but when it came to women, it behooved his sanity to take careful note of their looks. Hattie had been in service at Blackwood Hall since she was a girl and he'd known her all his life. She was the one he allowed to tend his study and his private rooms. Hattie was quite efficient at what she did, and moreover, so plain that she did not provoke disturbing images to crowd his brain.

"I explained that she is not a lady's maid to her ladyship, but she said that she preferred Hattie to anyone we might find in the village."

An image of Lady Merryton lounging naked in her bath while Hattie brushed her golden hair flit like a butterfly through Jeffrey's mind. "I shall think on it," he said, and turned to go. He paused at the console with the offending vase, and straightened it. "We are missing a rose, Cox," he said with his back to the butler, and walked on. He knew that Cox would be scrambling to right that terrible wrong, beginning with a tongue lashing for the poor servant who had miscounted.

He dressed for supper, as was his habit, combing his hair eight times, untying and tying his neck cloth eight times. When he'd finished, he studied himself in the mirror above his basin, looking for any sign of madness, of the obsession that gripped him. But he looked as he always did—filled with ennui. Expressionless. He'd spent a considerable amount of time over the years affecting the look so that he'd not reveal his terrible inner thoughts.

Even now, composed as he might appear, he couldn't bear to think of laying eyes on his wife again, of seeing the swanlike neck, the golden hair, the sea-stained eyes. He was a man, for God's sake. He was strong, he was virile—he wanted his wife and he would not allow this illness to hold him hostage.

He strode from his room, determined.

She was in the dining room before him, just as she had been last evening. Tonight, she was dressed quite plainly in a brown day dress with a high neck. It did not hide her beauty; if anything, it accentuated it. Now, there was nothing to distract from the eyes, or the creaminess of her skin, or the coral lips.

She was holding a glass of wine as she curtsied, then sipped from it as she eyed him curiously over the rim. She did not appear as anxious as she had yesterday evening. Tonight, she appeared restless.

Jeffrey clasped his hands tightly at his back. "Good evening, Lady Merryton."

"Good evening. By the by, my name is Grace," she said.

"I am aware." His gaze slid to her glass. "You enjoy wine." He meant nothing by it; it was merely an observation, something to say to prove to himself that he could indeed converse. But he saw an almost imperceptible lift of her chin, as if she thought he disapproved, when in fact, he did not approve or disapprove.

"I do," she said. "Sometimes, I like it far better than

other times." She drank deliberately, her gaze steady on his.

"My lord, supper is served," Cox announced, and placed a glass of wine at Jeffrey's place.

Jeffrey glanced to the footman. Ewan was a young man, a handsome man, Jeffrey believed, not that he was a particularly good judge of it.

Ewan instantly moved to seat Lady Merryton, holding out his gloved hand to help her into her chair. Jeffrey watched her slip her hand into Ewan's, and he suddenly thought of Ewan's hand on her bare skin, on her breast. That image plagued him as took his seat and as Cox filled their plates. Jeffrey was relieved when Cox had finished, and nodded to Ewan, and the two of them quietly quit the room. He picked up his fork.

So did his wife.

He ate a bit of the beefsteak, aware of the oppressive silence in that room. "I understand you have asked that Hattie serve as your lady's maid," he said.

She looked up, her gaze wary. "I did. I rather like her and I think she would suit me."

"Be that as it may, I cannot allow it."

"Pardon?" She put down her fork. "Why ever not?"

Jeffrey had intended to suggest that as he did not care about the expense, perhaps she might write someone in her family and ask for a referral. He did not expect to argue, and honestly, he didn't know how to argue. What was he to say? The truth? *Because she will be replaced with a comely lass, and I will think of nothing but her body, of bending her over the basin and sliding into her over and over again....* He swallowed and glanced at his plate. "She is a chambermaid," he said. "She is not a lady's maid." It seemed an obvious explanation to him.

His wife was not satisfied with that, clearly. She twisted in her seat so that she was facing him. "Why is it that men seem to believe a lady's maid requires a mysterious skill? That's not the least bit true, you know—Hattie is perfectly capable of helping me dress and undress. I am confident she is acquainted with a corset and is adept at folding undergarments."

Jeffrey picked up his glass of wine and drank generously.

"I don't want another lady's maid. I like Hattie."

He could see the spark of ire in his wife's eyes, but he couldn't help her in this. He wanted—he *needed*—Hattie for himself.

When he did not speak, she made a sound of exasperation. "It seems a trifling thing to me."

"I beg your pardon, but are you accustomed to argument?"

His wife blinked. And then she unexpectedly grinned. Her smile illuminated her face and shone in her eyes and Jeffrey was surprisingly moved by it.

"You cannot possibly imagine *how* accustomed I am to argument, my lord," she said gaily. "I have three sisters and a stepbrother. We argue about most things."

"I see," he said.

Now she responded with a gay little laugh that shimmered down Jeffrey's spine. "Oh, I'm rather certain you don't see at all." She picked up her fork. "I think you would be quite shocked by the arguments I have witnessed at the supper table. Once, my youngest sister Mercy—she's thirteen years—appeared in the dining room wearing my sister Pru's new gown, only just delivered from the modiste. Prudence was quite upset, and my sister Honor tried to reprimand Mercy for her thievery. But Mercy cleverly turned the tables on Honor with the mention of having seen her in Hyde Park in the company of Lord Rowley." She grinned. "You're not acquainted with my sisters, so it is perhaps a bit difficult to understand the terrible crimes that were committed that evening, but I assure you, they were *terrible* crimes. Nonetheless—yes, my lord, I am accustomed to argument."

She seemed pleased with herself for mysterious reasons that completely bypassed Jeffrey. He wasn't even sure what she was talking about now and struggled to find his place in this argument, this discussion, whatever the bloody hell it was that was happening at this table.

"In spite of your apparent joy in arguing, you may not have Hattie as your lady's maid," he said. "Choose any other lass in the land, but not her."

Her joviality left her then. "Ah," she said, nodding. "I *see*."

"*See?* Judging by the tone of your voice, you think you have stumbled on to something. There is nothing to discover other than I am ultimately the one who will assign the servants their posts."

"Of *course*," she said, far too agreeably. She turned her attention to her plate. "But I *do* understand how men such as yourself will seek…*comfort*." She gave him a very coy sidelong look.

That took Jeffrey aback—was she suggesting he kept Hattie as his lover? If he'd not been so surprised, he might have laughed. "You could not be more wrong."

"Oh, I suppose not," she said with such mock gravity that it was clear she didn't think herself wrong at all. She forked a generous bite of beefsteak, and popped it into her mouth.

This woman, his wife, was not like any woman in Jeffrey's acquaintance. Mary Gastineau would have been far better suited to him—she hardly spoke at all. But this one? Jeffrey couldn't even say what she was, precisely.

She saved the rest of her remarks for the food, proclaiming the beefsteak the best she'd ever eaten. She ate with gusto, her appetite clearly having returned to her. Jeffrey finished his meal and began to count the minutes until he might reasonably take his leave of her.

When she had finished her plate, she leaned back and put her hand on her belly. "I feel quite full."

It was a wonder she hadn't popped. Jeffrey put aside his linen napkin. "If you have finished your meal, I shall give you leave."

His wife slowly brought her attention away from the table and to him. "Then I shall take it." She stood abruptly, catching the chair with her hand before it toppled over.

Jeffrey quickly found his feet.

She walked to where he stood, tilted her head back and looked up at him. She stood so close he could see the storm in her eyes, could smell the sweet scent of her perfume. It was at once unbearable; his pulse began to pound as his mind filled with the thought of burying his face in her hair, his body in her wet warmth. He envisioned the arch of her back as she found her release, the curve of her neck as she dropped her head back in ecstasy. He clenched his fist, tapped eight times against his leg.

"You've done exceedingly well in conveying your disdain, and really, I can scarcely blame you," she said, sounding almost cheerful about it. But then her brows dipped into a V. "However, for better or worse, we are inextricably bound to each other, and my *name* is *Grace*."

Surprised again, Jeffrey arched a brow as he took her in, from the pert tilt of her nose, to the high cheekbones and slender chin. How innocent she was, how unaware of his ugly thoughts, of how he saw her, with her legs spread wide, her pink lips glistening, beckoning. The yearning for it was thrumming in him now, pushing him past reasonable thought.

"Good night," she said pertly, and stepped around him, headed for the door.

"You're right," he said, and took some pleasure in having unbalanced her, judging by the hitch in her step and the way she twirled back to him. "We are inextricably bound for all of eternity. And, as such, I see no point in putting off the inevitable."

The color bled from her face. "By that do you mean conversation?" she asked hopefully.

"No." He walked closer, peered down at her mouth. "I will come to you tonight as your husband, as is my right...*Grace*." He struggled to say her name. He had not been able to say it, to be so familiar, and the sound of it from his throat sounded harsh, untried. He spoke so roughly that he sounded as if he was taunting her.

She looked truly horrified. Her lips parted, and he was certain that his expression betrayed the terrible thoughts that were slamming through his head in that moment. If she meant to speak, she thought the better of it, for she merely nodded and went out.

Jeffrey waited until he could no longer hear her footfall, clenching and unclenching his hand, over and over again, his eyes closed as torrid images filled his head. He had to keep his wits about him, had to *breathe*. He would devote his attention to his duty and his privilege, and nothing else. *Nothing else.*

# CHAPTER SIX

JEFFREY WAITED A suitable amount of time so that she might prepare herself, pacing, tossing back a pair of whiskies.

His fear was unfounded, he knew that, and yet he couldn't relieve himself of its grip. He was no stranger to lying with women—fortunately for him, there were women in this world who at least appeared to relish a man's firm hand or peculiar thirsts. But none of them ladies, none of them innocents, none of them proper debutantes.

Jeffrey removed his coat and neck cloth, his waist-coat. He pulled his shirt from his trousers. The fear of harming her, of his lust blinding him to his actions, made him miserable. But it had to be done. He could not take a wife and not put a child in her. It was expected, it was his duty, it was necessary. He stalked down the hall to her rooms and rapped twice on her door, resisted the urge to rap six more times, and abruptly opened the door.

She was standing at the foot of her bed. She'd taken her hair down, and it hung to her waist in gold silken waves. She was wearing a silk dressing gown, and Jeffrey was instantly seized with the vision of what she must look like underneath—long, slender limbs, a dark thatch of hair between her legs, voluptuous breasts.

He noticed that her chest was rising and falling with each breath, her nerves apparently having the best of her.

Jeffrey shut the door and turned the key. He didn't speak at first, certain that his voice would give away the desire that already raged through him. How could he help it? His gaze wandered over her form, a woman's shape, the core of his ravenous desire. She was a beautiful woman, quite extraordinarily beautiful, and *this* woman's shape, *this* woman's body, belonged to him and him alone.

He would have this over with sooner rather than later—to dally was to lose his control. "Remove your gown," he said.

"Pardon?"

He gestured to her dressing gown. "Remove it."

She did not remove it; she folded her arms tightly across her body.

*A lamb to slaughter,* that's what she was. Jeffrey fixed his gaze on hers, reached for one end of the tie that held her dressing gown together and pulled it.

Her eyes fluttered shut for a moment, as if she dreaded this above all else, and yet all Jeffrey could think of was how her lashes would flutter shut in the throes of ecstasy—

*No.* No matter how they had come to be here, she was an innocent, and he was a beast. He abruptly took her by the elbow and turned her around, so that her back was to him. He slid his arm around her waist and dipped his head, touched his lips to her neck. Her skin was soft and fragrant; his desire slipped into his veins and began to snake through him, a translucent thread of heat. His wife stiffened; Jeffrey tightened his hold, and moved his mouth down, to the point where her neck curved into her shoulder. He lightly bit the taut skin, felt the thread of heat in him spread and grow, rooting in his groin and making him thick and hard.

The sensations were torturous; he turned her around again, his mouth finding hers. They were soft, moist, and he was reminded of the night in the tea shop, the way she'd felt in his arms, of how he'd fallen so quickly, unable to find any traction as he'd slipped and slid into the pit of his lust. His desire threatened to swallow him whole—she was so lithe, so soft. Jeffrey cupped the side of her face, and teased her lips open with his tongue. The stiffness in her began to ease.

He deepened his kiss, his body wanting more, wanting it all, and his mind pushing back. But when his wife began to kiss him back, Jeffrey felt his tenuous hold on restraint begin to disintegrate. His desire rushed to the surface; he wanted to rip her gown from her body, put her on her back on the bed, spread her legs and drive into her with a roar. He groped for her breast, squeezing it, the buoyancy of it fanning the flames in him. He slid his hand down her side, to her hip, and pressed her into his cock. She shifted away from him, but he pulled her back into him, made her feel his arousal, feel what she had unleashed that night in the tea shop.

She began to squirm.

*Was he hurting her?* He had to make quick work

of it, have it over and done before it ruined them both. He pushed her dressing gown from her bare shoulders, but she clutched at it, desperately trying to hold it to her naked body.

The dressing gown would not stop him. With one hand around her waist, he lifted her off her feet and put her on the bed. He crawled over her and stared down into her eyes.

She was frightened of him, perhaps even repulsed, but her revulsion could never match what he felt for himself. He put his knee between her legs and pushed them open, then unbuttoned his trousers. His wife gasped and turned her head, her hair falling over her eyes and shielding her sight.

"Be easy," he said. He had no idea how to calm a virgin. He only knew how to incite women to lust. He nudged her legs farther apart. She clutched her gown tightly to her, her breath coming in short gasps now, as if her lungs had filled. With his cock in hand, he pressed lightly against her sex. The folds of her flesh were thick and warm, and he inwardly convulsed with want.

But her legs were tensed and shaking around him. "Be easy," he said again. "I don't want to hurt you." How did he instruct an innocent? He could feel his muscles tensing, his body straining to keep from shoving into her. He slid the tip of his cock to her sheath, tried to establish some distance and slowly pushed.

She gasped; her body tightened around him.

Every muscle in him tensed, constricting, holding his lust in check. He pushed again, moving her leg, trying to ease inside of her. But with no help from her, it was almost impossible to do. He moved again and felt her maidenhead.

She had told Dr. Linford the truth, then.

Jeffrey gripped the counterpane on either side of her. He clenched his hips and pushed past the barrier.

His wife gasped softly. He clenched his jaw and slid deeper, withdrawing to the tip, sliding slowly again so as not to hurt her or frighten her. It was excruciating work, the anxiety of harming her and the pace of his movements depriving him of any pleasure. But as he neared his release, he began to move faster, wanting it done.

When his release at long last did come, he quickly withdrew. He was acutely aware that she'd found no pleasure in it. He knew of no bridge between his beastly desires to giving her maidenly pleasure. He was disgusted with himself for not knowing how to ease her into the carnal world. Perhaps, in time, after she had given him an heir, she would discreetly find a kind man who might please her.

He stood, and watched her roll onto her side, pulling her dressing gown tightly around her, covering herself. Her hair still obscured her sight of him.

Jeffrey buttoned his trousers. "Do you require any… anything?" he asked uncertainly.

"Please go."

He reviled himself in that moment. He had done what he feared and he'd hurt her.

*Eight panes of glass in the window. Eight steps across the dressing room. Sixteen stalls in the carriage house, forty-eight hours since he'd married.*

Jeffrey walked to the door and unlocked it, then stepped out, shutting the door behind him. He closed his eyes, pressed his fists against his temples.

*Sixty-four miles to London, eighty tiles in his bath, eight horses in the stable.*

SINCE HER HORRIBLE misstep in Bath, Grace cried for the first time. *Really* cried, with big hot tears and a leaky nose. She buried her face in her pillow lest anyone hear her, for she could think of no greater humiliation than to be found sobbing on the night she had been made a wife.

She was appalled by what had happened in this bed. *Appalled.*

But *not* hurt.

She pounded her pillow several times with great frustration.

The experience had been nothing as Ellen Pendleton had whispered to Grace and Honor one evening at a supper party. Ellen had insisted there was an awful pain and tenderness associated with the wedding night. Grace had felt a prick, and the discomfort of a foreign object inside of her, but she would not call it painful.

It was, however, the most wretched thing she'd ever endured. Was this what she was to look forward to for the rest of her life? Was this what she had heard women titter about all her life? She'd found nothing to titter about!

Just waiting for her husband to come to her room had been exhausting in and of itself. He'd been tender with her in the beginning, and she'd thought perhaps it might be as pleasurable as before. She'd been hopeful when his first kiss had felt...exotic. But then suddenly, something had changed, and he was aloof, detached. And when he'd entered her, he could hardly look her in the eye.

Grace miserably supposed she deserved that lack of attachment seeing as how she had forced this marriage. Be that as it may, she couldn't do *that* again. She couldn't bear to feel him so thick and hard inside her, or his hands and mouth on her skin, no matter how arousing it might feel. Those actions were lustful. Lust was what men did with ladies of the night. Not their wives. Not that she had any particular knowledge of it, but she firmly believed at least a bit of affection was to be expected.

But once again, what else could she expect? She had brought this on herself.

She slept fitfully, and the next morning, as she stared at the shadows beneath her eyes, she decided it would not do. She was married to an indifferent man, yes, but she would *not* become the strained and downtrodden woman she was beginning to resemble. She wasn't quite sure how to keep it from happening, but Grace would be damned if she was going to curl up every night and cry herself to sleep.

She dressed and went downstairs to a breakfast place setting for one. Nights with a cold stranger, lonely days with nothing to occupy her? No, she would not accept it. Theirs was not a love match, clearly. But she was still his wife, and she would assume the privileges of that role. She suddenly pushed her plate away.

The footman looked uncertain what to do.

"Please take it," Grace said, and stood. She walked out of the breakfast room, determined to find something, anything, to occupy her.

In the foyer, she paused as she had yesterday, looking at the crystal vases that were in their precise places. She found the perfect symmetry of their arrangements vaguely annoying. Before her mother had gone mad, she would bring in big blooms from the hothouse and stuff them into vases without regard for arrangement, creating what looked like a fountain of flowers. Grace much preferred that than this perfection.

She walked on, pausing to look in the various rooms as she had the day before, and seeing nothing new, nothing to divert her, moving on to the next.

At the end of the hall, she noticed that the door to Merryton's study was open. Mr. Cox had pointed out the closed door to her yesterday and told her that Merryton did not like to be disturbed while he was working.

She assumed he was not there as the door was open, and quickened her step, wanting to peek inside. But when she reached the open door and looked in, she must have gasped with surprise—Merryton was seated at his desk, his head bent over a document. When he heard her, he started and came instantly to his feet. He gripped an ink pen in his hand. Tightly. Grace had obviously and accidentally intruded, and he did nothing to put her at ease.

For that reason alone, she was not leaving.

She stepped across the threshold. That's when she noticed something curious. Merryton appeared to be flustered. A man as uncaring as he would not be flustered, would he? *She* ought to be flustered, especially after last night, but she was quite beyond that—she felt nothing but indistinct irritation racing through her veins.

"Madam?"

"My lord," she said, finding herself again. She looked around her at the austere decor and bare walls. "This is your study?"

The grip of his pen tightened, she noticed. He glanced around, too. "Obviously so."

Everything was pristine, everything set perfectly, the chairs at the hearth at identical angles. His desk, Grace noticed, was placed in the center of the window. To her right was a small writing table and, on its surface, four ink pens lying neatly in a row. She absently picked one up, needing something to do with her hands.

Merryton's gaze went immediately to the pen. He put his down.

She looked at him, then at the pen she held. His gaze was fixed on it; she put the pen down. What had she done?

"If there is something you wish—"

"As it happens, there is something I most desperately wish. I wish to know what I might do."

He blinked. *"Do?"*

"Yes, do!" she said, taking a few more steps into his study. "I need something to occupy my time. If I don't have it, I will wander about like a madwoman."

He stepped out from behind his desk, walking around to the front. "Madam, do as you like. You are mistress here." He was moving toward her and the door. He meant to show her out.

"I feel as if I am mistress of nothing but long and empty hours. There must be *something*—"

"You may inquire of Mr. Cox," he said abruptly, and gestured to the door. He stood at the writing desk, and as he waited for her to take her leave, he put his hand on the pen and moved it slightly, so that it was perfectly aligned with the others. Then he clasped his hands behind his back. "Now, if you will excuse me, there are matters that require my attention."

Yes, but s*he* required his attention.

He looked at the open door, then at her. He wanted her to leave.

Grace wasn't leaving, not like this. She folded her arms and stared up at him. "Is this how it shall be?"

"I beg your pardon?"

"This marriage," she said. "So formal and…distant. Is there nothing we might enjoy together? No society we might enjoy?"

He looked astonished by her straightforward question. "My family is my society. Beyond that, I don't find society either particularly comfortable or redeeming in any way."

"If you are never *in* society, how do you know? I happen to find society redeeming in many ways."

His gaze darkened. He leaned closer, so that she could see how deep the green of his eyes seemed to go. "Have you not altered the course of my life enough?" he asked low. "Did you somehow believe that after the manner in which this marriage has come about, we would somehow live as a happy couple, forever united, hosting parties to satisfy you? I suggest that you might turn your attentions to charitable works if you would like to mitigate the damage you have done, and not seek *society*."

Grace felt the nick of pain those words were intended to inflict. She felt herself shrink with guilt, and that made her angry.

"Please do see Mr. Cox," he said curtly. "If you will excuse me."

He seemed so tense, so ill at ease. But Grace was angry. She reached for the pen and, with the flick of her finger, moved it out of alignment again.

He stiffened. "That was a childish thing to do."

"And so is assuming that things should go only your way." She whirled away from him. "Good day, Lord Merryton," she tossed over her shoulder.

"Madam."

*"Grace!"* she said, and went out.

## CHAPTER SEVEN

GRACE MARCHED ABOUT in a bit of a snit, but found nothing to do. The household was run far too efficiently; nothing—*nothing*—was left undone. So Grace spent another tedious day peering out windows and trying to read the dry books from the library. There was not a fictional title among them.

In the afternoon, Mr. Cox presented two girls from the village whom he'd deemed suitable to be her lady's maid. The girls both were cheerful and eager to please. Grace was happy to speak to someone other than Mr. Cox and inquired after their families, and of the various activities one might find in Ashton Down. She prolonged the conversation as long as she could, until one of them began to squirm as if she needed to heed the call of nature.

When the girls were sent back to the village, Mr. Cox came into the green salon and bowed. "May I inquire, madam, if you found either of the girls to your liking?"

Grace absently drummed her fingers against the arm of her chair, debating. "They are fine girls, Mr. Cox. But I prefer Hattie."

Cox, the poor man, was entirely discombobulated by that. "Yes, well, I… Shall I speak to his lordship?"

"Please," she said with a sunny smile.

Grace took her time dressing for supper. It hardly mattered what she wore, as she would see no one but him. She chose one of her favorite gowns, the pale green silk with the tiny embroidered pink birds. She put up her hair as best she could, fastening it with pearl-tipped pins, and wore a long pearl necklace.

She arrived in the dining room before him, and nodded to the footman to pour wine for her because, yes, husband, she did indeed enjoy wine.

Merryton arrived a few moments later, and as cross as Grace was with him, she couldn't help but note that he looked resplendent in his formal tails and snowy white collar. He was a handsome man in spite of his piercing green eyes. He was trim, his shoulders broad. She tried to imagine his smile, tried to picture how his eyes might shine with it, but it was impossible. He looked distant and stoic and she was fairly convinced he never smiled.

His gaze flicked over Grace, from the top of her head to the tips of her slippers.

"Good evening," she said with only the slightest dip of an irreverent curtsy, still holding her wineglass.

"Good evening." He looked at Cox and nodded, indicating the supper was to be served.

The footman stepped forward and held out Grace's chair. With a sigh, she took her place. She set her wineglass on the table; Mr. Cox quickly swept behind her and moved it to match the glasses at Merryton's setting. That small, innocuous movement rankled Grace. She considered it tiresome that every blessed thing in the house had to be in its proper place. She instantly reached for the wineglass to move it and, in her haste to claim a bit of imperfect space, spilled a splotch of the red wine onto the white tablecloth.

Merryton's gaze riveted on her. Grace smiled prettily. "I beg your pardon, I've spilled."

He looked away as Mr. Cox hurried to blot it up with his serving towel. When he had finished, Grace smiled at him and held out her glass for more. She could almost feel the waves of disapproval coming from her husband, but when she glanced over her shoulder at him, silently challenging him to speak, he would not.

She spent another interminable supper watching him eat without enthusiasm, his finger tapping absently against the table. Tap tap tap tap—pause. Tap tap tap tap—pause.

When the first course had been cleared from the table, Merryton said, "Cox informs me you did not find the village girls he'd brought around to your liking."

Well, then, the ogre spoke, after all. "No, I didn't. I prefer Hattie. I rather like her."

Merryton's unflinching gaze locked on hers. "As I said, you may have anyone you like. But you may not have Hattie."

"Then I can't have anyone I like, can I?"

His expression did not change, but he slowly leaned forward, bracing his arm against the table. "You tend toward obstinacy. I cannot make myself more clear— Hattie will not become your lady's maid. Choose anyone else you like or choose no one at all. It makes no difference to me."

Grace despised him. She didn't care any longer that she was the cause of this marriage—she despised him. She shrugged insouciantly. "*You* tend toward the inflexible."

He drew a slow breath. "By God, you are impudent."

Grace laughed. "Thank you."

"It is in no way a compliment."

"Yes, I know," she said, still smiling with delight. "By the by, today you suggested I mitigate the damage I have caused you by performing charitable acts. But I don't see how I might do that if I am never to be beyond the walls of Blackwood Hall."

He had one hand on the table, watching her, his gaze sharp, like a hawk. "You may inquire of the vicar, Lady Merryton. He will be more than happy to assist you in atoning for your sins."

Oh! He was maddening, truly maddening! She picked up her fork, but she could scarcely eat now, as angry as she was. Therefore, the meal was finished as it had been every night since they had arrived at Blackwood Hall—Merryton impatiently waiting for her to finish so that he might take his leave.

This evening, when he so eagerly left the dining room, Grace took a candelabrum in hand and wandered aimlessly about. Her strolling took her past his study. She paused before the closed door. With a glance up the hall to assure herself that no one followed, she opened it. It was dark within, of course, and the room cold. Grace stepped inside, saw the four pens on the writing desk, still neatly and perfectly aligned. She ran her hand over them, sending them in various directions, and smiled to herself as she stepped out of his study and shut the door.

She carried on to the music room. She'd found it earlier today tucked at the back of the house near the garden doors.

It was a cozy room, with a pair of music stands and a pianoforte and harp.

Grace sat at the pianoforte, idly picking out notes to play. Prudence was the most musically inclined of the family. When she played, Grace, Mercy and Honor would dance, practicing their reels and their minuets. Naturally, Grace had been instructed in music as all wellborn girls were, but she didn't have the same ear for it as Prudence. She put her hands on the keys and played a chord and smiled at the cheery sound. At least this was one diversion available to her. Perhaps she would practice her music on lonely afternoons and hone her skill.

She remembered one piece, *Autumnal Melody,* and began to play. Her rendition was fraught with discordant sounds that she quickly sought to correct. It was a bit jarring to her own ears, but if there was anyone in this house who took issue with her admittedly awful playing, they did not come forward.

When she had tired of attempting to regain her musical dexterity, she retired to her rooms. Someone had built a cheerful fire and had turned down her bed. She grimaced at the bed and walked past to her dressing room and donned her nightclothes. She braided her hair, performed her toilette and then climbed onto the bed.

She propped herself against the pillows to begin her wait for her husband.

He did not come.

Was there a rule for how long one waited? Did husband and wife generally discuss these things, arriving on a time and place agreeable to them both? Or did every wife sit in her bed, waiting?

Grace waited long enough that she fell asleep. She was awakened by the creaking sound of the door and sat up with a start. Her candle had burned down; only two inches of beeswax remained.

She could see Merryton looming in the doorway, one hand on the door handle, the other on the frame, as if he were uncertain he would enter. He was dressed the same as last night, in his trousers and his shirttails. When he saw her stir, he stepped inside, then shut the door behind him.

As he neared the bed, she could see the low light glimmering in his eyes, making Grace think of the demons Mercy liked to talk about at every turn. He stood over her bed, looking down at her, and something about the light in his eyes changed. It stunned Grace—she thought she saw a glint of tenderness. And then he casually touched her face with the back of his hand.

It surprised Grace so that she treated it suspiciously, recoiling from it. It was so incongruent that she couldn't understand what he was doing or what she was to do in return. He caressed her cheek, and with his gaze on hers, he slowly and deliberately leaned over her, bracing himself on his hands on either side of her. His gaze slipped to her lips and he lowered his head to kiss her.

His kiss was gentle and his lips like velvet, and it swirled through Grace—a delicious and deceptive heat growing warmer as it moved. His lips were moist, his tongue a whisper against her lips. He shifted, cupped her chin with his big hand and kissed the corner of her mouth.

A thousand tiny ripples of delight rushed through her, tingling on her skin. Grace's eyes fluttered shut; she tilted her head slightly so that he might kiss her neck. He moved to her chest, leaving a warm, wet trail of butterfly kisses across her skin. The pleasure he stoked in her made her feel weightless. His hands and mouth were incredibly provocative as they moved on the body, drawing a spark from deep within her and flaring in the surface of her skin. He moved to her breast, mouthing the hardened peak through her nightgown. She gasped softly and lifted to his mouth without conscious thought. He teased her with his tongue as he slid his hand down to her abdomen, down her leg. His hand, warm on her bare skin, slid up her thigh and in between her legs.

The sensation of his fingers on her intimate flesh sent a white-hot flame through her. Grace could feel the dampness of her body, desire thrumming and rising up in her.

Merryton released a long breath. His touch grew more urgent, and he returned to her breast, pulling at her nightgown until she felt a button fly off. With a groan, he took her bare breast in his mouth, nipping and sucking her. She raked her fingers through his hair, holding him to her as she lost herself in the utterly gratifying sensation of his mouth and hands. It was an exquisite, a perfect stir of feelings. *This* is what she had experienced that night in the tea shop.

He freed his cock and moved between her legs. He grabbed her by the waist and pulled her down, so that she was on her back, then shifted between her legs and rubbed his erection against her.

Grace pressed against him. She lifted one knee, ready for him, eager for him—

Merryton suddenly thrust his arm beneath her back and lifted her up, roughly turning her over. He drew her up by the abdomen and, without a word, pushed her knees apart, and entered her from behind, almost as if he did not want her to see him. He began to move in her, keeping his arm around her waist, pulling her into his body as he thrust into her, one hand on the bed to brace himself. He made quick work of it, pumping into her, his strokes faster and faster.

It was all terribly confusing. Grace's body was responding to his touch, but her mind was not. She tried again to turn, to sit up, but he put her back down.

He made a guttural sound as he spilled his seed hot and hard into her. He bent over her back, kissed the nape of her neck and then withdrew himself from her person.

Grace was stunned. She fell onto her side and pulled her nightgown down. She lay with her back to him. He didn't speak, but he stroked her hair. She closed her eyes, silently willing him to leave her.

"Are you all right?" he asked, his voice rough.

"Fine," she said.

"Did I… Are you hurt?"

She was hurt, but not in the way he meant. *"No,"* she said firmly.

She felt him stand, could hear him dressing. He stood

a moment, waiting, she supposed, for her to turn and face him. When she did not, he stroked her hair and said quietly, "Good night, Grace."

*Grace*! He would use her name now?

Grace didn't cry this time. She rolled onto her back when he'd gone, her arms splayed wide, and stared up at the embroidered canopy above her head.

She thought of murder. Mercy was particularly fond of gruesome tales, and she imagined how her youngest sister might create this man's demise. Grace liked the image of him tumbling from his horse and bouncing down a ravine. Or perhaps a tragic fall from the grand staircase, wheeling head over toe to the marble tiles below.

Better yet, the unexpected kick of a goat right between his bloody eyes.

But then Grace thought of her mother. Before the carriage accident that had begun her mother's descent into madness—before her mother had begun to unravel the embroidery of her sleeve and call Grace by the name of her deceased sister, or believe she was living in a past year—she'd been an elegant, beautiful woman.

Joan Cabot was a mainstay in London society, a clever, witty woman considered to be one of the true beauties among the ton. Scarcely a year after Grace's father, a bishop, had died, her mother had received an offer of marriage from the older Earl of Beckington.

Once, Grace had asked her mother how she'd managed to love Beckington after loving Grace's father. Grace was only ten years old, and then, Beckington had seemed rather ancient to her. But her mother had laughed gaily and had folded Grace into an embrace. "Oh, my darling! There is so much of the world you've yet to learn!"

"But you do love him, don't you?" Grace had asked. She could think of nothing worse than being married to a man one did not love. She couldn't imagine wanting another husband after Pappa.

"Oh, I do. But that took time, darling. And I had to convince him that he loved me first," she'd said, and had laughed gaily while Hannah, her longtime lady's maid, had giggled, too.

Grace had been shocked—she'd assumed anyone who met her mother would love her. "He didn't love you straightaway?" she'd asked incredulously.

Her mother had smiled and touched her fingers to Grace's face. "No, darling, he scarcely knew me. But I persuaded him to desire me above all others. Do you want to know how?"

Grace had nodded.

"By making myself desirable in a manner that he himself wanted to be desired."

"You make it sound very simple, my lady," Hannah had said.

It hadn't sounded simple to Grace at all; it had sounded nonsensical. She recalled how her mother had laughed at her expression. "One day, you'll understand."

Grace wasn't sure she understood it even now, but the thought occurred to her that perhaps she was going about this all wrong. Perhaps the key to turning this awful marriage into one that both of them could endure would be to become what Merryton wanted Grace to desire in him.

"That's not the least bit convoluted," she muttered sarcastically to herself. She could hear Honor now, wailing about how Grace was her own person, and should command to be treated as such. And while Grace would find merit in what Honor would say were she here, she also understood that as she had caused this, it was her lot to repair it, however she could.

For the thousandth time in the past year or so, she wished for her mother to come back to her. She wished desperately she could ask her now what to do with this strange man. But the mother she'd known all her life had slipped away, and in her place, a woman whose madness had pushed all that she knew from her mind.

Grace would have to go this alone.

## CHAPTER EIGHT

HOT RED SHAME filled Jeffrey.

He had rutted in his wife like a pig, the carnal sensation taking over all rational thought. He feared he'd been too rough. Jeffrey closed his eyes and tapped his fist against his leg.

But he could not banish the images of her, lying there with her eyes closed, the lustful, earthy sounds of pleasure escaping her. Her scent was still in his nose, still torturing him, an intoxicating mix of perfume and the scent of an aroused woman, and it had been all he could do to keep from unleashing his base desires on her.

She was beautiful, and she was a hellish temptation to the beast in him. Today, he would leave Blackwood Hall. He would put some distance between them, find his balance once more. He would ride into Ashton Down and hopefully displace the inflaming images that littered his brain.

He left quite early, riding hard, pushing his horse to a gallop. The more he exerted himself, the better he was able to contain himself. He pushed until he could breathe normally. Until the shame had been pounded out of him.

He trotted into town, reining up at the Three Georges, Ashton Down's public inn.

"My lord Merryton!" Dawson, the innkeeper, called out to Jeffrey when he entered. "You are welcome, sir!"

"Thank you," Jeffrey said. "An ale, please." He walked to a table before the window and sat down. Before him, on the wall near the entrance, Dawson had tacked seven plates to the wall.

Jeffrey turned his chair so that he could not see the plates and gazed out the window.

"Good day, milord," a woman said.

Jeffrey glanced up to see Nell, a serving woman who had, on more than one occasion, spread her legs for him and allowed him to use a crop on her bare bottom.

"I've no' seen ye in a time, milord," she said. "Ye are welcome upstairs as always."

He nodded. She'd always fascinated him with her ample hips and breasts, but today, she held no interest for him. His mind was fixated on a beautiful young woman with pale skin and eyes that reminded him of summer.

*My name is Grace.*

It was a peculiar thing, his inability to say her name aloud, but her name carried so much weight. If he said it, if the name fell off his tongue with any sort of familiarity, he feared he would slowly incorporate her into his depravity. Her name would be intertwined with his debauched thoughts, and there would be no hope for her.

A jostle at his table brought his head up.

"I thought it might be you, my lord." Mr. Paulson, a member of the landed gentry, was standing before him, his hat in hand. He was dressed fashionably in gray trousers and a blue superfine coat. "I understand felicitations are in order," he said, bowing grandly.

"Thank you," Jeffrey said, and gestured to the chair beside him.

Paulson flipped his tails and sat, balancing his hat on his knee. "I've just come from London," he said. "I had not heard of your nuptials until just yesterday. Many happy returns."

Jeffrey smiled.

"May I ask, where is the lovely Lady Merryton? Have you brought her to the village?"

"She is resting, presently."

"It is quite a lot of bother, a wedding, isn't it?"

Jeffrey didn't know what that was supposed to imply exactly, but gave Paulson a curt nod of his head. He thought of his wife now and tried, with difficulty, to put away the images of her bathing the bruises from her body. He *must* have inflicted bruises. The memory of last night's encounter had swelled in him, and now he believed it had been much rougher than it had seemed at the time. He'd gripped her too tight, had been too rough, too lecherous, he was certain.

"If I may, you are a fortunate man indeed, my lord," Paulson continued. "The Cabot girls are renowned for their looks."

Jeffrey was unaware of that and looked at Paulson curiously.

"They say the younger ones, who are not yet out, are even more beautiful than the eldest two," Paulson said.

"A pity that I am already married." He laughed politely, but he was eyeing Jeffrey shrewdly.

Jeffrey said nothing.

"I will admit to some surprise when I heard the news of your nuptials, given your aversion to scandal," Paulson added, far too casually.

Jeffrey knew the day would come when someone would mention the circumstances of his marriage, but he was not prepared to hear it this morning.

"That was rather a stink with the oldest sister, was it not? What with the gambling and the public declaration for Easton?"

Jeffrey knew of George Easton, the notorious bastard son of the Duke of Gloucester. He was not aware that his wife's sister had married Easton as the result of a scandal. And now he had married under a similar cloud. God help him, but his life had twisted out of control, slipping through his fingers so quickly, so easily. He'd maintained such tight control, never erring, and in one evening, he'd managed to lose it all. The consequences of that one indiscretion were astounding.

Paulson thought that Jeffrey's look somehow constituted an agreement with him. "I know that you are averse to even the suggestion of scandal," Paulson said low, as if they shared a confidence. "But I think you are far enough removed from it."

Jeffrey merely looked at him.

"There now, we must have you and Lady Merryton to dine!" he said jovially, redirecting the conversation. "My Lucy will be quite keen to make her acquaintance."

"Likewise," Jeffrey drawled, and stood. "Speaking

of my wife, you will excuse me, will you, Paulson?"
Jeffrey put a few coins on the table, nodded at Paulson
and went out, studiously avoiding the seven plates as
he did. But it was useless—he could feel the discomfort of seven in his chest.

As he'd found no relief in Ashton Down, he walked
down the street for his horse. But he happened to pass
a dress shop, and a pair of kid gloves in the window
caught his eye.

Jeffrey paused and looked at the gloves. They were
kid leather. His wife would like gloves, wouldn't she?
Didn't all women desire such frills? He stepped into
the shop, his head brushing against the little bell that
tingled, announcing a visitor.

A woman stepped out from a back room. Her jaw
dropped with surprise when she saw him. "Oh! Welcome, *welcome,* my lord!"

He nodded and walked deeper into her shop. He was
surrounded by frilly, pretty things.

The proprietress dipped into a proper curtsy, sinking down so low that he had a clear view into her cleavage. Jeffrey's pulse ticked up, and he clasped his hands
tightly at his back. "You've a pair of gloves in the window," he said.

She looked toward the window. "Yes. They are
Swiss made, kid leather. Quite exquisite." She hurried
to fetch them and returned to him, holding them across
her palms.

The fingers of the gloves looked small to Jeffrey.
"They will fit a grown woman?"

She smiled. "Yes, of course, my lord. Someone with delicate hands."

He withdrew his purse. "I'll have them."

She beamed with delight and whirled around to her counter. She dipped down below and rose up with a plain white box, which she opened and lined with a bit of linen. "May I offer you anything else, my lord?" she asked smilingly as she wrapped the gloves in the linen.

He glanced at her and her shining eyes. She was a good, decent woman, and as it often happened with his demented mind, he thought of her sinking to her knees and taking him in her mouth. But then, something shifted, and it wasn't this woman who looked up at him. It was his wife. It was Grace.

"My lord?"

"Yes," he said, and looked down. "Perhaps you may be of some help. I am in need of a chambermaid. Preferably an older woman." He handed her the coins for the gloves.

"A chambermaid," she said, and her fingers fluttered around her bodice. Jeffrey thought of his wife's breasts. They were firm and sweet, the nipple dark against her pale skin, taut beneath his tongue.

"I think I know someone who might fit that description. Julia Barnhill."

Jeffrey glanced up at her.

"She was the old rector's caretaker. But now that he has gone, and the new rector has come, she hasn't a proper situation."

"Where might I find her?"

"At the rectory, my lord."

"Thank you." Jeffrey fit his hat on his head. "Have the gloves delivered to Mr. Cox at Blackwood Hall," he said, and went out.

It was a short walk to the rectory. He stepped through the gates and stalked past a pair of hens that waddled toward him. A dog barked at him from the corner of the courtyard, but Jeffrey didn't bother to look at him.

When he rapped on the door, it was opened by a woman who was rather too large for her gown. The bodice was far too tight, and the hem too short. Her boots were scuffed and her hair was tied in an unforgiving bun. She had a bulbous nose, and two small eyes set too far apart. Better still, she was at least twenty years older than he.

She would do nicely.

The woman wiped her hands on her apron. "Sir?"

"Merryton," he said, bowing his head. "I am from Blackwood Hall."

Her small dark eyes widened. "Oh. Milord," she said, and dipped into an awkward curtsy. "The rector's not here, milord. He's gone to read the last rites to old Mr. Davidson."

Jeffrey nodded and looked behind her, into the front room of the rectory. It was tidy. "Do you keep this house?"

"What?" She looked behind her. "Aye, milord, I keep it," she said, looking at him as if she expected some criticism.

"I understand you are without situation since the rector has died," he said flatly. "I am in need of a maid to clean my personal rooms."

She stared at him.

"I am very exact in my requirements for cleanliness and order. I expect my private apartments to be cleaned every day and things to be kept in their place. I prefer a minimum of fuss. Are you capable of that?"

"I... Me?" she asked disbelievingly.

"Yes. You. The pay is generous."

She sized him up, her small eyes shrewdly taking him in. "If I might inquire, why me?"

The answer to that was so complicated that Jeffrey couldn't begin to sort through a response. He merely shrugged. "Why not you?"

She eyed him suspiciously. "Did you say how much the pay, milord?"

Jeffrey hadn't the slightest idea how much a chambermaid was paid on his staff. "Fifteen pounds per annum in addition to food and lodging."

It must have been a good sum; the woman's little eyes nearly bulged out of their sockets. "When shall I report?"

"As soon as you free yourself of your obligations here. Thank you, Miss Barnhill." He touched his hat and went out of the rectory's courtyard, pleased that he would at least be able to offer his wife the services of plain Hattie. That seemed small consolation for what he'd done to her, but at least it was something.

Jeffrey felt much more in control of his thoughts when he returned to Blackwood Hall. He walked into the foyer and handed his hat to Cox, which was the moment he heard the sounds coming from the music room. It was not pleasant music that was being played on the pianoforte, but fits and starts, with many wrong chords struck and then attempted again. Jeffrey looked at his butler, who wore a pained expression.

"Her ladyship has expressed a renewed interest in learning the pianoforte," Cox said. "She informs us that she's not had a music tutor in many years."

That was quite obvious. Jeffrey nodded and started for his rooms, but as he walked through the foyer, he stopped. He looked at the consoles. The identical crystal vases of roses had been replaced with a chaotic arrangement of hothouse flowers. Nor were the vases in their places. Jeffrey's pulse began to ratchet. He looked questioningly at Cox.

"Lady Merryton has made the arrangements today, my lord," he said apologetically.

Jeffrey bit his tongue. He walked on, jogging up the stairs, twenty-four steps in all, swallowing down his discomfort.

But no matter how hard he tried, he could not stop thinking of the storm that seemed to be brewing in his foyer.

His discomfort was so great that he went down to supper early, so that he might see for himself that nothing had actually happened in the foyer. It was absurd, he knew it was absurd to believe that somehow those bloody flowers had damaged his foyer, but the fear of it was quite compelling.

He found the chaotic arrangement of flowers just as they'd been when he'd come in. But there was nothing else amiss.

Jeffrey was waiting for his wife in the dining room

when she arrived, dressed in a silver gown, her hair bound in a chignon at her nape. She was clearly surprised to see him standing there; he could see it in the flicker of her eyes. She paused at the threshold and curtsied.

"Madam," he said.

*"Mmm,"* she said, and walked in, looking to Cox.

Cox was ready with her glass of wine, offering it to her on a silver tray. "Thank you." She smiled at Cox.

Jeffrey felt that smile swim like a pretty little goldfish through him.

He waited until they had been seated for the meal before he could begin the conversation that was burning in his brain. "How did you find your day, Lady Merryton?"

She looked up with surprise. "Tedious."

He arched a brow. "I noticed that you arranged the flowers in the foyer."

"I did," she said, watching him closely. "The hothouse is teeming with them. I thought something different might be nice."

*Different.* Chaotic. Impulsive, disruptive, *wrong.* He took a bite of his fish. "I prefer roses."

He did not expect silence from her on that—he did not expect silence from her at all—and when he looked up, he found her gaze locked on him. "*I* prefer a variety."

The poor lamb had no idea how quickly she would be defeated in this. Order was the air that Jeffrey breathed. "By the by, I have given your request for Hattie more thought. She will begin as your lady's maid on the morrow."

Suddenly, everything in the room seemed to change. She gasped and smiled with such delight that he felt the warmth of her happiness wash over him. "I may have Hattie?"

He nodded.

"*Thank* you." She laughed a little and leaned back in her chair, smiling as if she'd just won a prize.

Jeffrey's gaze flicked over her shapely body. "Another matter has been brought to my attention," he said.

"It is my music, isn't it? It is fairly obvious that it makes Cox uncomfortable, and yes, I will admit I am quite unpracticed. But I am confident I might regain my competency."

"I think there is a great hope among the staff that you will," he said. "But I was referring to the matter concerning your older sister."

That certainly garnered her attention. "Honor? Why, has something happened?"

"I understand she has married George Easton."

His wife swallowed. She folded her hands in her lap like a chastised schoolgirl. So it was true, then.

"I was not made aware of the scandal," he said.

"No, I rather imagine you were not."

He leaned back in his chair. "Madam, I shall be perfectly clear. I will not tolerate scandal of any sort to besmirch this family's name. What has happened between us is scandal enough, is it not? I pray you tell me now if there are any other skeletons in your closet, for I don't think you will care for the consequences if I learn of more at a later date."

She looked at her plate.

"My father spent a good part of his life building our name into one that is synonymous with respect and decorum." Bloody hell, it was as if he was speaking to John. How many times had he said these things? "It is my duty as his son and as the current earl to ensure that our name remains free of scandal and gossip. Do you understand?"

She looked up, and peered straight into his eyes. "Yes, I understand. My family has an excellent reputation, as well, my lord. You need not concern yourself."

He couldn't imagine how fine her family's reputation now with *two* daughters married under scandalous circumstances. "For your sake, I hope that you are right."

"I think you mean for yours," she said. "If you bring more scandal to our families, I won't blame you."

Jeffrey stilled. It was such an odd thing for her to say, and the sentiment behind it was so foreign to him as to make him uncomfortable. He'd been judged for his actions all his life. Everything he did was scrutinized, first by his father, now by him and, he supposed, society. He looked at her again, but his gaze fell to her décolletage.

Jeffrey looked down, ate more of his food.

This was how it had all begun. The pressure to be good, to be perfect, even as a young man had made him crave that which wasn't good or perfect. He was craving it now. Just the mention of scandal and he was thinking of his wife's fragrant skin, of his fingers in her wet flesh. Image after image filled his brain, and with those images, a rising fear of harming her. He wanted to put his fist through a wall, to break a window.

But he didn't do that. He lifted his gaze to his wife's and said, "Shall we retire?"

She looked startled by the suggestion. "Now?"

"It's late." He stood up, offered his hand.

She looked at his hand, then braced both of hers against the table and slowly rose to her feet. She seemed repulsed. Disgusted. He couldn't blame her. He was a disgusting man, no one knew it better than he, and yet, he was powerless against it.

As he led her from the dining room, and they made the long walk upstairs with her hand on his arm, her head down, he counted to himself. She must suspect by now that he was depraved. She surely understood that he had no choice but to subject her to it, as they were both bound to produce an heir.

He told himself he was a necessary evil.

In her room, he shut the door behind them, then turned her about. He undid the clasp of her necklace and put it aside. He turned his attention to the buttons of her gown, his fingers moving deftly down the loops. He noticed she was trembling as he pushed the gown from her shoulders and slid his hands with the gown down her arms, to her fingers.

She was afraid of him. What else could those trembles mean?

He wished for all the world that he was a normal man with normal appetites. He wished he could explain to her that, in his mind, it was reasonable to imagine her pleasuring herself, to imagine her bound by the hands and wanting him to have his way with her.

The gown pooled at her feet; she stepped out of it.

Jeffrey traced a line from the top of her neck down her spine, to the top of her hip. He pulled the string of her corset and began to unlace it, one loop at a time, letting it drop to the floor when he had loosened it.

She tried to turn around to face him, but he held her there, with her back to him. He drew a steadying breath and pushed her chemise from her shoulders, watching the silk ripple down her body, sliding over her hips and landing on top of her clothing.

She turned her head slightly and glanced at him from the corner of her eye.

Jeffrey withdrew the pins from her hair and let the golden tresses fall over his arm and down her back. He lifted one thick strand and put it to his face, closing his eyes as he brushed it across his lips. He pushed it over her shoulder and kissed her nape, and moved down her bare back, trailing a line of kisses along her spine, caressing her skin with his hands, to her hips. He lightly bit one hip, then the other, and kneaded the plump flesh with his hands.

His wife was shivering. She grabbed the bedpost to steady herself. Jeffrey was hard, his cock throbbing with want. He imagined her on the floor before the hearth, her fingers on her breasts, his mouth on her sex. He squeezed his eyes against such images, unable to bear the desire that flooded his veins, the strength it required to keep from putting her there. He rose again, his hand sliding up, to her neck, then slowly, but firmly, bending her over the bed.

"No," she said, and tried to stand.

But Jeffrey stepped between her legs and palmed her

sex, sliding his finger over the sensitive core and into her body. She was slick; she gasped as his finger slid inside her, and he felt her entire body shiver. *"Yes,"* he whispered. What a monster he was, a bloody monster.

He slid his cock into her, pressing gently at first, clenching his jaw as her body opened to him, admitted him and drew him in. He sank deep into her wet depths, and the feeling of it was the most pleasurable torment. He wanted to pump into her, to feel her body tighten around his and draw his release. He moved carefully, one hand on her hip to keep her down as he moved in and out of her. But his mind began to fill with images of what he was doing to her, of what he would like to do to her, and he felt himself losing control. He closed his eyes, but his need was too powerful—a deluge of want.

He could hear her gasps, her moans, and it alarmed him. If it had been any other woman, he would have believed she was finding pleasure in his body. But this was his wife, an innocent young woman who had played with fire in a tea shop and been burned. He guessed she was whimpering with dismay. He moved faster, harder, now desperately seeking his release.

It was explosive. He grabbed the bedpost, gripping it tightly as he sought his breath. When he had found his bearings, he realized he still had her bent over the bed. Jeffrey quickly withdrew and picked up her chemise, pressing it against her.

She wordlessly took the chemise and pulled it over her head. She said nothing as she pulled her hair free from the garment. He worried that he'd been too hard, too animalistic.

His fear was confirmed when she turned around. Her eyes were blazing with fury. It startled him; he didn't know what to say, how to ask her forgiveness. He tapped his finger to his thumb. "Are you hurt?" he forced himself to ask.

*"Hurt?"* she repeated, as if that were entirely too obvious. "I am not *hurt*— Just go. Please."

"Grace—"

"Will you please leave me now?" she asked, her voice low and cool.

He hesitated before walking to the door, where he paused there and glanced back. "Good night, Grace."

She did not respond. He walked out of her room. It was thirty-two steps to his rooms. *He was wrong, all wrong.* Eight steps to a sideboard. *He was demented.* Four fingers of whiskey. He tossed it down his throat and closed his eyes against myriad immoral images. Another four fingers of whiskey, drunk like water, until the liquor began to drown the acid in his belly and he could breathe again.

## CHAPTER NINE

GRACE AWOKE THE next morning full of physical and emotional frustration, her thoughts still reeling from what had happened last night. She despised how Merryton made her face away, as if she were too hideous to gaze upon. Did he find her ugly? Did he find her revolting in some way?

It was even worse than that. Grace had felt herself sliding down a path of pleasure, her body desperately wanting its landing. She had liked the way his body and his hands and mouth had made her feel.

But then he'd withdrawn from her, and she'd felt unfinished and homely and used.

Hattie came at half past eight to help her dress, holding a box tied with a white ribbon. "His lordship bid me give this to you," she said.

"For me?" Grace asked incredulously. She took the box and pulled one end of the ribbon, laying the box open. She moved the linen wrap and looked down at the gloves. Fine gloves, by the look of it, made of supple leather. Grace lifted the gloves, looking for a note and finding none. "There's no message?"

"No, mu'um," Hattie said as she leaned over to have a look at the gloves. "Just said I was to give them to you."

Of course there was no note. That would require some effort at civility. Grace tossed the gloves into the box and turned her head. She didn't want the bloody things.

"Shall I...shall I put them away?" Hattie asked uncertainly.

"Yes, please," Grace said coolly. "In a drawer somewhere I will not see them." She turned away from the offending gloves and walked out of her room.

Unsurprisingly, she found the breakfast room empty, save Cox, who stood by ready to serve. At least her appetite had returned with a vengeance, and Grace ate. When she had finished, she said, "Don't wait luncheon for me, Cox," she said. "I intend to take a very long walk." Perhaps all the way to London. Or at least Bath. Well, she couldn't be certain how far she'd go, but she was determined to remove herself from this gloomy house.

The day was a fine spring day, crystal in its clarity, the sun glinting off the dew on the rosebushes and the water in the fountains. The hedgerows were trimmed and the rosebushes groomed to perfection. All of them red roses. Only red. It was as if he had aversion to any other sort of flower or color.

There was an iron gate at the manicured gardens and, beyond that, a mowed path down to the lake's edge. Ash trees towered above Grace as she set down the path, her stride long, her mood improving with every step away from Blackwood Hall.

She lifted her face to the sun, felt its warmth on her skin and closed her eyes. A sound—a cough, a clearing of a throat—caught her ear; she turned toward the woods.

What was that, a gate?

Yes, she could just make it out, a gate behind the tangle of vines. That was a fence, too, she realized, and, if she were not mistaken, a thatched roof behind the trees.

She walked over to the gate and pushed aside some of the vines, peering in. There was a lovely garden behind that gate, a true English garden. Roses and columbine, hydrangeas, peonies and delphinium. A cat was stretched lazily across a tree stump, sunning itself, its eyes on Grace.

Who lived here? The cottage looked charming from what little she could see. She stepped back and looked around. There was another stump beside what she now could see was a stone wall around the garden. Grace picked her way through the undergrowth and climbed up on the tree stump and peered over the wall. She could see all of the cottage then.

The front of the cottage faced the lake. There were flower boxes in the windows spilling over with touch-me-not flowers. A pair of hens were pecking the ground in the corner of the garden, and a curl of smoke drifted up from the single chimney. The cottage was quite charming, and Grace was delighted to have found it—at last, something that put a smile on her face.

A woman suddenly appeared on the path around the side of the cottage carrying a basket of flowers. With a gasp of alarm, Grace dipped down, mortified that she should be caught spying. She crouched there, listening.

"You may as well come in, but you best come around the front. That gate's been woven shut by the vines."

Grace held her breath.

"Yes, you, dear, on the other side of the wall." The woman's gray head suddenly appeared above Grace at the wall. "Oh, dear, I should clear out the undergrowth, shouldn't I? Quite untidy. Come around, and I'll make you some tea."

Grace slowly rose, her cheeks stained with her embarrassment. "I beg your pardon," she said apologetically. "I was passing by, and I... Well, I suppose you've guessed. I climbed on this stump to peer at your house. And I am happy that I did. It's so very charming."

The woman smiled. "Thank you."

"But I couldn't possibly impose," Grace said, and hopped down from the stump. "I apologize."

"Impose!" the woman cried. "But I'd be delighted! Do come in, Lady Merryton."

Grace gasped. "How do you know my name?"

The woman tittered at that. "I daresay everyone here knows who you are, milady. I'm Molly Madigan. Come around to the front." Her head disappeared from view.

With one glance behind her to Blackwood Hall, Grace was persuaded. She hurried around to the front of the cottage.

Molly Madigan was waiting at the front gate, holding it open.

"Thank you," Grace said, and stepped through. Molly was a head shorter than Grace and was wearing a stained apron around her middle, a handwoven shawl about her shoulders and a wide-brimmed gardening hat.

She picked up her basket of flowers and walked to the door of her cottage. "Fine day for a walkabout," she said cheerfully, and shooed the cat away when it tried to wind around her legs.

Grace stepped up to the door and peered inside as the cat brushed against her on its way inside, its tail high.

She could see a wooden settee and two cushioned rocking chairs. A single oil lamp was on a table near one chair and, beneath the table, a sewing basket that looked to be overflowing.

"You needn't be timid here. Come in!" Molly called to her.

Grace looked in the direction of her voice. Molly Madigan was in an adjoining room holding a tray with two cups.

"I'll just fetch the kettle. The water will still be hot." She put the tray on a small table at the window and disappeared into the back of the cottage.

Grace hastily removed her bonnet. She sat gingerly in one of the chairs at the table and folded her hands in her lap. On the wall opposite the window were three framed sketches of two smiling boys, obviously siblings, and a young girl between them. All of the children looked to be about ten years old in the drawings.

Molly Madigan returned a moment later with a kettle. "Here we are," she said, and poured the water, then set the kettle aside and let the tea steep.

She had a lovely countenance, Grace thought. "Thank you, Mrs. Madigan."

"Not a missus, no. And you should call me Molly.

Everyone does." She offered Grace a cube of sugar. "How do you find Blackwood Hall?"

"It is…grand," Grace said carefully.

Molly laughed. "It's grand indeed. It always seemed a bit lonely all the way here on the edge of Somerset. And inside that grand house, dear me! One can ramble about for days!"

"Yes." Grace had done precisely that, rambling about for three days. She hid her feelings about that behind a sip of tea. The cat jumped up on the table and sat before her, his yellow eyes staring into hers. Grace absently stroked him.

Molly's gaze, she noticed, was firmly fixed on her.

"Are those your children?" Grace asked, nodding at the sketches.

Molly looked at the sketches on the wall. "In a manner of speaking, I suppose you might say they were. I was their governess. That's his lordship when he was but a boy," she said, pointing to the one on the right. "And his sister, Lady Sylvia."

"Lord Merryton?" Grace asked with astonishment. The picture was of a happy boy, not a dark and humorless man.

Molly laughed. "My artistic skills are somewhat lacking."

"You drew them? But…he's smiling." Grace could see the resemblance now, especially in his eyes.

"Ah, yes," Molly said. "He does indeed find it difficult to smile, doesn't he?"

Grace looked curiously at Molly. "You've known him for a very long time, then."

"Since he was a lad of six years," she said. "He's a good man," she added, as if she had guessed at Grace's unspoken question. "He's given me this cottage, for he knows how much I enjoy gardening. Do you garden?"

"No. I've always lived in town. And there have always been gardeners about." She smiled a little.

"I can teach you," Molly brightly suggested. "You will find there is nothing quite as satisfying as putting one's hands in dirt and bringing something to life."

Of all the things Grace had imagined for herself, puttering about a garden was not one of them. She had imagined herself a grand doyenne of proper society, the one who would host the teas and balls that mattered to the social lives of countless debutantes. In London, she and Honor had scarcely spent an evening at home; they were always out in society. They'd had many suitors and they'd both put off proper courting so as not to gain any marriage offers. They had enjoyed their privilege and their freedom. She supposed they had truly believed that they could do whatever they liked.

That life seemed forever removed from her now, and she was struck again by how foolish she had been.

Grace glanced at the window and tried to picture the years stretching before her, filled with nothing more diverting than gardening. Growing roses, of course. Red roses. Merryton would not tolerate any other bloom, would he? She wondered if there was any particular talent that was required for proper gardening—she'd yet to find her particular talent. The only thing she seemed particularly adept at was attracting dance partners.

Molly suddenly leaned forward, her blue eyes smiling. "Is something the matter, madam?"

"Pardon?"

"You look…well, I wouldn't presume, but you look a bit sad."

"I do?" Grace said.

"Perhaps a bit fatigued."

Grace almost laughed at that. "I am *very* fatigued," she said with a slight shake of her head. "I have discovered marriage to be a rather confounding business."

"Oh, my dear," Molly said sympathetically. "The beginning of *any* marriage is difficult for everyone."

Grace resisted a roll of her eyes at that. Miss Madigan had no idea. "Some more than others, I should think."

"Take heart, my dear. It will get easier with time." Molly put her hand on Grace's arm and gave her a reassuring squeeze.

The touch of her hand was the first kindness Grace had received since that fateful night, and she mentally collapsed with gratitude for it. She didn't even realize she was sinking until her head touched Molly Madigan's table. "It's *awful*," she said weakly.

"Oh, my dear!" Molly said again, her voice full of alarm. She scooted around in her chair, and soothingly stroked Grace's head. "Surely it's not as bad as that."

"It's worse!" Grace insisted. "He doesn't care for me in the least. He thinks I'm *ugly*—"

"No, that is impossible! How could he? You are beautiful!"

"No, I'm not. He won't *look* at me—"

"Because he is shy," Molly said, stroking her hair now. "He is very reticent."

"Shy!" Grace scoffed.

"Dreadfully so," Molly said soothingly. "When he was a boy, he could scarcely look his father in the eye. His father was a big imposing man with a bellowing voice, and he insisted on perfection. The poor lad never knew precisely what to say, and his father would shout at him to speak up, which only made him more anxious, to the point he was stumbling over his words."

That did not sound like the man she'd married, and Grace lifted her head and looked skeptically at Molly. "Merryton?"

"Yes, Merryton," she said, nodding firmly. "He has a kind heart, but he is not at ease with people. Were I you, I would tell him how you feel. He shall do everything in his power to put it to rights."

But Grace shook her head. "I couldn't," she said. What would she tell him? That she found the conjugal relations unbearable?

"You must try, dear. I assure you, he will do whatever he might to make things better for you. But you cannot expect him to guess at what you need, can you?"

"You don't understand," Grace said morosely. "I have tried. I have told him I should like some society, something to occupy me, and he said I might do whatever I wish."

"There, you see?" Molly said brightly.

"But how can I have any sort of society without proper introduction? I've no acquaintances here and he has left me to myself."

"Then perhaps you might arrange to have the introductions you'd like," she said cheerfully. "Tell him you'd like to invite the local gentry. Cox will arrange it all for you—Blackwood Hall has been the site of many gatherings, particularly when Lady Sylvia is here. She lives too far north now, unfortunately, and doesn't come as often as his lordship would like."

"Why not?" Grace asked curiously.

"Oh, well, she has two very small children and it's too far for them to travel yet. But when she is here, the hall is quite lively. Now when you've finished your tea, you might return to the hall and speak to Mr. Cox. I am sure you will find your path, Lady Merryton. And when you do find your path, you must call again and tell me how it has gone for you."

Grace smiled. She was feeling immeasurably better. "Will Merryton mind that I have called on you?"

"Not in the least! He frequently comes to tea himself. Oh, dear, you seem astonished. But his lordship rather likes the simplicity of this cottage. Why, I wouldn't be the least surprised if he were to appear now." She laughed outright. "Can you imagine his delight to find you here?"

"No, I cannot imagine his delight," Grace said dryly.

"You will," Molly said confidently with a friendly nudge of her arm. "When you come to know him as I know him, you will understand him."

Grace doubted that, and yet, something Molly said resonated with her. She wondered if there was a way to reach that shy boy, buried in that aloof man.

She left Molly to work in her garden and continued

with her walk, following the path around by the lake, and on toward the woods. There were a few outbuildings near the woods, and Grace wandered over to see what they were. She was delighted to discover the kennels. There were about eight spaniels, all of them in the middle of a fenced-in area, tails wagging around three men who were talking.

One of them, holding a rifle, noticed Grace and came forward to greet her. "Milady," he said, swiping his hat off his head. "Is something amiss?"

"Not at all. I'm having a walkabout." She smiled.

"Mr. Drake, the gamekeeper here, at your service."

"How do you do. What fine dogs!" she said, leaning around him to see the dogs. She noticed a puppy still in a kennel. It had its paws planted on the slats and was yapping to be let out. "Are you hunting today?"

"No, mu'um. We're training the wee ones," he said.

With a whistle, one of the men sent the dogs bounding for the gate that led to the fields beyond.

Grace laughed at their exuberance. Her mother had always had one or two dogs about, and she was fond of them. The puppy, she noticed, was frantically trying to dig out of his kennel and go with the other dogs. "It would seem you forgot a little fellow."

Drake looked over his shoulder at the puppy. "No, mu'um. He's not to go."

"Why not?"

Drake shook his head and adjusted the gun on his shoulder. "The pup is too fearful of the guns. Afraid he won't be much of a hunter."

Grace looked at the puppy, who was now stretched up the gate of the kennel, crying. "Then what will he be?"

"Be? Beg you pardon, mu'um, but the dog's no use to Blackwood Hall." He looked at her with such trepidation that Grace instantly understood what he was telling her. They meant to kill the puppy, dispose of him. Her heart leaped and she looked at the spaniel with his one red ear and a big splotch of red on his side. "May I see him?"

"You want to *see* him?"

"Yes. I want to see him," she said emphatically.

Mr. Drake seemed uncertain, and looked back at the kennel. But Grace had already started in that direction with the new thought that perhaps she might find her way here at Blackwood Hall, after all—gardening with the affable Molly Madigan and taking care of a puppy afraid of guns. When the puppy's tail started to wag as she approached, the day suddenly seemed a little bright to Grace.

"Good afternoon, little lad," she said, dipping down by the kennel gate and sticking her fingers through the slats for the puppy to lick. "We're lucky to have found one another, aren't we?"

# CHAPTER TEN

THE BLACK TENTACLES of remorse had slipped into Jeffrey once again, latching on to his veins and wrapping around his heart, squeezing painfully. The previous night's events had been very much on his mind all day, as was the murderous look Grace had given him when he'd left.

And still, obscene thoughts of his wife crept into his head.

He couldn't blame her for her disgust with him. He'd bent her over the bed like a whore. He'd tried to keep his distance, he'd wanted desperately to be gentle, but as usual, his demons had overtaken his desires.

Jeffrey released another tortured breath—his body ached with regret and disgust.

How desperately he wanted not to be the animal that lived inside him. He wanted to be the man his father had raised him to be, the man everyone expected him to be. He did not want his wife to fear him. Yes, he wanted his conjugal rights—he needed them, every man needed them—but he did not mean to *harm* her. He was a man, a strong man, and yet, he was not strong enough to fight the unnatural urges in him. He wanted children, and yet he did not want them to carry the burden he'd known all his life.

This marriage had muddied every part of his life. Before that night in Bath, he'd been quite content in his carefully ordered days. Now, his mind was filled with salacious images and he was desperately counting, looking for the comfort of eight.

He was losing the control he'd worked so hard to construct.

He heard a commotion outside and glanced at the clock on the mantel. It was a quarter to three o'clock. It was too late for lunch, too early for tea. Jeffrey checked that the arrangement of things on his desk—the inkwell, the blotter, the paperweight and Merryton seal— were spaced equally apart. Everything was in balance, which somehow allowed him to leave his study before the appointed time.

It was madness.

He walked out of his study and down the hall toward the sound of the commotion, which grew louder as he neared, culminating with a crash of glass. He heard Cox's alarmed voice, and when he entered the foyer, he saw why. A spaniel puppy was prancing about with a pair of mangled roses in its jaws. Apparently, it had knocked into the console and sent the vase crashing to the floor. Cox looked as if he would faint.

But his wife was laughing. "I am very sorry, Mr. Cox. He's scarcely even whelped!" As if to prove it, the young dog hiked his leg against the console.

"No!" Grace cried, and shooed him off before he made his mark.

Jeffrey swallowed down his rapidly increasing pulse.

"My lord, I beg your pardon!"

Jeffrey had not seen Mr. Drake at the door until that moment. "Drake, did you give this dog to Lady Merryton?"

*"No!"* his wife said cheerfully. "In spite of Mr. Drake's best efforts to save me, I absconded with him." She scooped the pup up in her arms and the dog licked her face. "I refused to allow Mr. Drake to drag him off to the hangman. I was quite determined. Wasn't I?" she cooed to the dog.

The pup squirmed free of her arms and leaped, sliding over the tile before gaining traction, and then bounding over to where Jeffrey was standing, his tail wagging furiously as he sniffed at his shoes.

"The hangman?" Jeffrey repeated as the dog caught his trouser hem and began to tug. The chaos in that foyer—the broken glass, which a footman was hastily sweeping up, and the asymmetry of the flowers, the dog running about—it felt as if the walls were closing in. He clasped his hands at his back and tried to shake the dog off.

"The whelp won't take to the gun," Drake said apologetically. "Scared of his own shadow, this one."

"I will not listen to another word, Mr. Drake," his wife said firmly. "I have taken the dog under my wing and I mean to keep him there." She suddenly shrugged out of her Spencer jacket and marched forward, dipping down to tie the arm of her coat with the puppy's collar. She stood up, holding the other arm of the jacket in her hand, having fashioned it into a sort of lead. She forced a smile at Jeffrey. "It's sinful to toss aside one of God's creatures because he's not perfect, isn't it? I'm not perfect, either."

"Madam—"

"You said I might do what I like, to find something to occupy me," she said. "Well, I have found something to occupy me. Now, then, if you gentlemen will excuse us, the dog and I are going to have a look about his new home." She smiled warmly at the men gathered in that foyer, a lovely smile brimming with happiness and youthful beauty. She laughed with joy when the pup began to growl and attack her hem, and God help him if Jeffrey would be the one to douse that smile.

Not that his wife had any intention of allowing him, apparently, for she marched off to the staircase leading the pup with her jacket.

Jeffrey glanced back at Mr. Drake. "It's all right," he said. "Have a proper lead sent up to the house."

"Aye, milord." Mr. Drake quickly ducked outside.

That left a stricken Cox standing in the middle of the foyer, staring at Jeffrey.

"I will allow it for a time," Jeffrey quickly assured him. "Until she has settled here."

"Yes, milord," Mr. Cox said, and started a bit when the sound of barking reached them.

Jeffrey turned and headed for the sanctuary of his study, trying not to think of a dog running, unfettered, through his house.

But that afternoon, he heard her wretched playing of the pianoforte, accompanied by the yapping of the puppy. He could hear his wife's laughter drifting down the hall to him. He closed his eyes. *Eight*.

Jeffrey was expecting the dog to be bounding about the room when he came down to dine that evening, but thankfully, the dog was nowhere to be seen. His wife was there, however, standing at the window, beaming with delight and, he thought, triumph.

There was no sign of the dog, but there were flowers on the table, the sideboard and, most disturbing, in a bud vase in the center of his plate setting. His senses were assaulted with the riot of color and variety.

"I hope you don't mind," she said apologetically. "The hothouse is full of these beautiful spring flowers, and I thought it would be an awful thing to ignore them. I didn't put them in the foyer," she added quickly, assuming, incorrectly, that the foyer was his objection. "I know you like your roses there." She looked around the room. "Aren't they *beautiful?* I've never seen so many beautiful flowers in one place."

Good God, *she* was beautiful. Her creamy skin and her hair seemed to glow in the low candlelight. He thought of taking her now, of putting her on his lap, teaching her how to ride him—

"Do you agree?" she asked.

He thought it was bedlam. He couldn't think in the mayhem of different blooms and colors and felt a bit of perspiration under his collar.

"I adore spring," she said. "It is the start of so much new. The Season, of course. Country house gatherings." She looked at him as if she were waiting for agreement.

"Where is the dog?"

"Oh! Mr. Drake recommended a portable kennel be brought up for him. We've put him in the kitchens, near the hearth. He's had a bowl of milk and a bone Cook gave him and he's quite content."

At least something in this house was content. Jeffrey felt as if his heart would leap out of his chest with so many thoughts mixing wildly around so many flowers. He was relieved when Cox entered from the serving door to serve.

But his wife, the cause of the chaos in this room, looked at him, and at Cox. "Will we not have a bit of wine first to aid in our digestion?"

The only thing that would aid in Jeffrey's digestion was to escape this room as quickly as possible. But he gestured to the wineglasses, then caught Cox's eye and nodded at the bud vase on his place setting.

Cox moved immediately, sweeping it off his plate.

His wife watched Cox, her mouth falling open in surprise as he picked up the vase at the center of the table and carried it out of the room, as well. That left a vase on the sideboard, another on a serving table near the window.

"Where did he go?" she demanded as the service door swung shut behind Cox. "Why did he take the flowers?"

"Please sit," Jeffrey said, and Ewan moved to pull out her chair.

She looked at Jeffrey in bewilderment as she reluctantly took her seat. "I don't understand your aversion to flowers!"

"I have no aversion to flowers. Look around you, there are many in this room yet."

She did not seem appeased.

Jeffrey noticed the pearls threaded through her hair. He tried not to think of last night, but the image was suddenly in his brain. He swallowed hard against it.

Cox reappeared, carrying a soup tureen. As he ladled soup into bowls, his wife suddenly straightened and took a long breath before saying, "By the by, I have taken your advice, my lord."

"My advice?"

"The dog and I took a long walk this afternoon, down to the vicar's house. I thought to call and inquire where I might begin my charitable works. So that I may *atone*," she said, emphasizing the word he had used.

Jeffrey had nearly forgotten the remark.

"But as it happens, the vicar is away just now. His mother is ailing and his return is indefinite."

Ah, yes. Jeffrey had forgotten that, too, in the chaos of the past week.

"But I've thought of an alternative. I thought perhaps you might introduce me to some of your tenants."

She had caught him off guard and she knew very well she had. He could see it in the slight curl of one corner of her mouth. "Mr. Cox informs me that you intend to call on a few of them on the morrow," she said smoothly. "It's perfect, is it not?"

She cast another lovely smile at him that made his blood heat. *Bloody hell.* "These are not social calls," he said curtly. "I've the business of the estate to see after, and I intend to ride—"

"Splendid!" she quickly interjected "I am an excellent rider. I won't be a bother. I want only to meet your tenants so I can begin my charity. In *earnest*."

Jeffrey kept his expression flat, but he gripped the arm of his chair. "What of your dog?" he asked dryly.

"He should come, too!"

"No."

"All right. I'll find someone to tend him. What time shall I be ready to ride?" She smiled triumphantly again.

He was cornered, and she knew it. To deny her would spark some sort of war where flowers of all shapes and sizes would bloom and his house would be overrun by disobedient puppies. "Nine o'clock," he said. "Don't be tardy. I will not wait."

She laughed as if he'd said it to be amusing. "Somehow, I had guessed as much, my lord. Oh, and I should like to change the music room about a bit. I hope you don't mind. And I would like a music tutor. My play needs some tidying up, really. I wish I'd been more attentive when I was a girl, but there were so many distractions." She shrugged. "No time like the present, is there?"

She continued to chatter through the meal, waxing about music and dogs, the latter being much on her mind, as well as the need to settle on a name for the pup. Jeffrey scarcely heard her—he gazed upon the shape of her mouth. On the swell of her bosom, the flesh spilling out of her bodice.

His wife lingered over the last course, purposely prolonging it, he suspected, as she knew he waited. But when she at last put her fork down, he put his linen aside. "If you will excuse me."

"By all means," she said, and smiled in a way that made his blood race.

Jeffrey went straight to his study, locked the door, then yanked furiously at his neck cloth in search of air. He had not felt this disconcerted since that night in Bath. There were dogs, and music rooms and chatter. So much chatter! And he, unable to think of anything but rutting on her, of his mouth on her sex, his cock sliding between her breasts—

Jeffrey counted, divided, multiplied, added and counted again to quiet his thoughts, to bring him back to familiar ground and to sanity. It had been so long since he'd been this troubled by his affliction that he found himself dwelling on what the bloody hell it was, and why in God's name it involved the number eight.

He suspected that whatever was his illness, his father had suffered from it, too—the earl was determined to have precise order in his life and demanded the same from his children. They were to move through life lock-step, and when they did not, they all felt his wrath. His father had been especially demanding of Jeffrey, his firstborn and his heir. Jeffrey could clearly recall several incidents of where the punishment for the perceived infraction was severe. Once, when he was eight years old, Jeffrey had failed to properly greet a gentleman caller. His father had made him stand in the center of the foyer so long that Jeffrey had watched the sun sink from the sky. His knees had buckled, he'd felt sick with despair and hunger, but his father would not release him from his punishment until Jeffrey had reached some standard only his father could see.

John and Sylvia had suffered their father's harsh punishments, too, but not like Jeffrey. He'd tried to shield his younger siblings where he could, taking the blame for things he'd had no part of, just so they would not be subjected to their father's twisted sense of punishment.

But in spite of his strict upbringing and his father's peculiarities, it wasn't until Jeffrey's father died that Jeffrey began to notice signs of his own moral corruption, of the depravity that had knit itself into his bones. There was nothing—*nothing*—Jeffrey could do to banish it. Eight was his only relief. Somewhere, somehow, eight had become his tether.

Fortunately, he was not generally as mad as he'd been this past fortnight. He had learned to live with his affliction, and if he followed his prescribed path each day, if he lived simply, he lived contentedly. Not happily, but at least contentedly.

Jeffrey didn't know how long he'd been in his study, but when he emerged, Cox had already made his rounds, dousing the wall sconces.

He walked in the dark, his steps measured, his breathing shallow. He had no intention of entering his wife's rooms, convinced that he had to stay away from her if he was to have any hope of banishing the images. As he undressed, however, his body was turning damp from the exertion of pushing down the images. He was bedeviled, consumed with the lurid, immoral thoughts. He did not want to go to her, *he did not*—but there was nothing to keep him from it. There was no law, no tug of virtue, that could or should keep a man from his wife.

Jeffrey donned his dressing gown and was in the hall before he could think. He rapped once on her door, then opened it.

She was seated at a writing table, her pen moving furiously across a sheet of vellum. She dropped the pen when he stepped through the door and hastily came to her feet. Jeffrey saw something flicker across her face at the sight of him—fear? Yes, fear, it was obviously fear, because she took a step back as he moved deeper into her room.

That pained him terribly. But it was too late for them both—he had slid too far into his debauched thoughts, could find relief only in her body.

He walked across the room to where she stood, grabbed her by the waist and crushed her to him and thrust his tongue hungrily in her mouth. He was ashamed, so ashamed, and he ignored the little cry in her throat. He guided her hand to feel his lust for her, opening the gap of his dressing gown and closing her fingers around it.

She did not recoil or shriek as he expected. But she tortured him with her innocence. Her hand began to move on him, her fingers sliding up, her thumb brushing across the tip. The sensation was unbearable; he suddenly picked her up with one arm about her waist, and in one swift stride he had put her on her back on her bed. She was still fully clothed—there was no time for her to disrobe. Jeffrey groped for her hem, pushed her gown up, then slipped his hand under her back and took hold of her, intending to turn her around so that she would not have to look at him as the plunged into her depths.

"No!" she cried, and grabbed his shoulders, her fingers digging into his flesh.

"It is my right—"

"Jeffrey!" she cried, startling him with the use of his Christian name. "Do you find me so ugly?"

That rendered him speechless. She was *beautiful*.

"Do I revolt you?" she cried, pushing against him. "No!"

"But you make me turn. Why won't you look at me?"

He didn't know what to say, how to explain the mad thoughts in his head.

She suddenly cupped his face with her hands, her eyes shimmering up at him. "*Look* at me. Count to eight if you must, but look at my face."

His breath froze in his chest—she couldn't have stunned him more. How could she know, how could she have deduced his affliction?

"Say my name, I beg of you. *Look* at me. I am your wife."

His blood was raging now, rushing through him, carrying him away.

"Please don't turn me away as if I was some loathsome task to you." She lifted up, kissed him lightly on the lips. It was a timid kiss, but it was as powerful as any he'd felt in his life. "My name is Grace."

"*Grace,*" he whispered, and wrapped his arms around her and kissed her.

She couldn't know how hard he struggled to restrain himself, how her tender kisses didn't leash his lust, but inflamed it. She couldn't understand that if he said her name, if he allowed that whisper into his heart, he could not let it go, he could *never* let go, and he would obsess over her, no matter how much she might come to hate him.

But once again, it was too late for him. "Grace," he said again, and eased her onto her back, then proceeded to remove her shoes, one at a time. "Grace," he said again, and reached under the hem of her gown. *"Grace,"* he muttered as he lifted the hem of her gown and pushed it up, to her waist. She was exposed to him now, just like in the images in his mind. Dark and glistening, beckoning him. He leaned over her, kissed her mouth, then kissed the hollow of her throat, and down, to her chest, her bare thigh. He said her name, kissed her flesh.

Her scent incited him. He sank before her, his entire body engorged with desire. He pushed her legs apart and touched his tongue to her, sliding in one long stroke. Grace jerked at the touch and gasped loudly. He would not stop, and grabbed her hips, holding them firmly in his hand, lapping his tongue across her folds, dipping into the darkest recesses.

Grace bent one knee. She clutched at his hands, curling around his as he continued the onslaught. He sucked her into his mouth, teasing her with his lips and his teeth, making her writhe. He dipped his tongue into her again, swirling up, then sucking her into his mouth.

Grace, his wife, cried out. She arched as her body released into pleasure, pressing against him, seeking more.

Jeffrey stood up. He lifted her legs, put them around his waist and then guided his cock into her. He stroked her at first, but the depravity in him was too powerful, and he began to thrust, his pace unrelenting.

He looked at her beautiful face, never moved his eyes from it. He unleashed the fury of lust on her, reaching for a powerful climax. When he thought he could bear it no more, she closed her eyes and groaned again, arching her back, tightening around his body and pulling an explosive response from him.

*"Grace,"* he said roughly, and collapsed over her, completely spent.

# CHAPTER ELEVEN

FOR THE FIRST time in a very long time, Grace woke up feeling refreshed and happy. She smiled as she stretched her arms high over her head, and then suddenly remembered why she felt so well—a shudder of pleasurable memory shot through her, fluttering in her chest, as she recalled Merryton's mouth on her. Grace had felt almost delirious last night, having been fully initiated into her marriage—she'd never felt such pleasure, had never imagined the possibility of it.

She wanted more. She wanted to know all the things her husband could do to make her feel that way again

A noise in the dressing room brought her arms down. She paused, listening, then grinned with delight. "Come here, you wee beast," she called, and the next moment, Dog came trotting out of her dressing room dragging her shoe with him.

"No, you mustn't!" Hattie cried, running in behind him. But the dog thought Hattie intended to play and growled with delight as she tried to tug the shoe free. "Milady, he'll ruin it!"

"I don't care!" Grace said gaily, and leaned over the edge of the bed, whistling to him. Thankfully, the puppy was easily distracted and came running to Grace, attacking the hank of her hair that hung to the floor while Hattie swept up the shoe.

"He ought to be in his kennel, milady," Hattie said. "Cook said he was making such a wretched racket that I was to bring him up."

"I'm very glad she did," Grace said. She picked up the dog and brought him up on the bed and pressed her cheek against his fur. "I'll need my riding habit today, please," she said cheerfully.

An hour later, Grace ran down the grand staircase, the braid of her hair swinging above her hip. Her hat dangled by its ribbons from her hand, and her very bad dog—according to Hattie, anyway, as Dog had managed to shred one of Grace's chemisettes when Hattie had turned her back for a moment—trailed behind her on the lead Mr. Drake had sent up.

Grace expected to find Merryton waiting for her. She expected the barrier between them to have been breached, and that today would begin the true course of their marriage. But then again, Grace had always suffered from an overabundance of hope and lofty expectations.

She smiled at Cox, who tried to pretend as if he didn't notice Dog was chewing at his shoe. "Where might I find my husband?"

"He is presently in his private study and asks that he not be disturbed."

"Oh," Grace said, slightly taken aback. Perhaps he meant disturbed by others. Yes, surely, that was it— after last night, he would not mind if she were to poke her head into his study, would he?

She turned about and walked into the corridor. "Madam?" she heard Cox say, but she kept walking, pretending she hadn't heard him, pausing briefly to chide Dog for digging at the carpet.

At Jeffrey's closed study door, she stood debating a moment. But Dog was eager to begin his day and yapped.

"Well, thank you for that," she muttered and knocked on the door.

*"Come,"* was his muffled reply.

Grace opened the door and peeked around it, forgetting that Dog was with her. The pup dashed in and ran straight for Jeffrey, who was standing at the window with his back to the door.

"Dog! Come here!" Grace cried, but the puppy had a mind of his own and darted off to have a smell about the hearth. Grace looked sheepishly at her husband. His dark curling hair was brushed over his collar. He was wearing buckskins and a black superfine coat worn taut across his broad shoulders. He held one hand at the small of his back, and the other at his side. He was tapping his forefinger to his thumb, always in a pattern of eight.

"Good morning!" she said.

For a sliver of a moment, Grace thought she saw something spark in those hard green eyes, but they quickly shuttered into inscrutability. "Good morning."

"We are ready," she announced.

His gaze flicked over her. "I see. The wind is a bit high," he said. "Perhaps you should not expose yourself to the elements."

"Oh, that's quite all right. My mother always said I had an indefatigable constitution." She laughed.

His jaw bulged slightly with his clench. "Then I'll have the carriage brought around—"

"Carriage! I thought we were to ride."

"It is several miles across terrain that is not suited to gentle riding."

She didn't understand his demeanor at all, but she instinctively understood that backing down was quite the wrong thing to do. She glanced at Dog, who was gnawing on the corner of the rug. "As luck would have it, neither am I suited to gentle riding."

His gaze flicked over her again. "Very well," he said. "I'll have the mounts brought around."

She tilted her head to one side, trying to find any crack in his expression. Impossible. He was as practiced as she was in maintaining a serene countenance. "I'll be waiting," she said cheerily. She bent down to scoop up her dog and noticed a small puddle. "Oh, dear," she said, wincing a little. "He's not yet learned that he shouldn't do so."

Merryton looked down. His expression turned dark.

"I'll tell Cox," she said, and quickly went out with the naughty dog, who was trying to apologize for his blunder by licking her face. "That won't do, Dog," she whispered to him. "I can't seem to make you understand that you are a guest here, and not a welcome one."

As she walked along, some of Grace's confidence began to flag. She tried to understand Merryton as she walked outside and headed for Molly's cottage. Did Merryton not feel the same sense of euphoria as she?

Or the intimate attachment that could only come in a marital bed? Why was he so distant to her now?

It was not to be borne. After last night, she'd truly believed that they *would* find happy ground on which they could endure their forced marriage, and she was not giving up.

Molly was more than happy to keep an eye on Dog, but her cat was not excited by the prospect. He swiped the puppy's nose and sent the poor thing dashing around the corner of the cottage, yelping.

"Oh, dear," Molly said.

"I'll be back soon!" Grace said, making a hasty departure, fully prepared to offer up a cornucopia of apologies later. At present, she had a husband to tame. The dog would have to come later.

Merryton was on the drive, his weight on one hip, his crop in hand when she returned. Beside him, a boy held two saddled stallions. Grace recognized the black horse with white socks as the mount Merryton had ridden from Bath. The taller horse had been outfitted with a sidesaddle.

Merryton looked at her, then at the boy. "Certainly you have a more suitable mount for the lady?"

"That one will do," Grace said before he could find another excuse for her not to accompany him.

"Seems rather a big mount for a woman."

"For most women. But I am not like most women. I happen to be an excellent rider."

Merryton almost smiled at that. "I've heard many women say they are and find it is rarely true."

"Then you might be rarely surprised," she said pertly,

grateful for the riding lessons her stepfather had insisted she and her sisters take when they were young. *"You'll earn a man's respect by sitting a saddle well and keeping it beneath you,"* he'd said.

Merryton looked dubious, but he gave the boy a curt nod. The boy handed him the reins of the black, and then led the white horse to Grace. A groom appeared with a mounting block.

The horse was still too tall, even with the mounting block. Grace had to put both hands on the saddle and hop into it while the boy steadied the horse. When she had situated herself as best she could on the sidesaddle, the groom handed her the reins and a crop. "He's got a bit of a temper, mu'um. He won't like to be held back."

"Is that so?" Grace said pleasantly. The stallion flexed his shoulders and shimmied his torso, testing her.

Grace leaned over, caressed the horse's neck and murmured, "Don't misjudge me—I've as firm a hand as he."

The horse bucked his head in response.

"Shall we?" Merryton asked, looking almost amused. As if he'd wagered on this ride and was already counting his winnings. Bloody rooster.

Grace adjusted her riding hat. "Please," she said, and gave her horse a tap of the crop, sending him into a trot without waiting for Merryton.

Merryton was quick to catch up, however, and took the lead, slowing down the pace considerably. Grace's horse followed behind, but the groom was right—she had to keep a firm hold of him. He was chafing, wanting to run. Of course he did—it was a brisk spring day, perfect for people and horses alike. Grace was chafing, wanting to run, too.

When the road widened, Grace moved in beside Merryton. "The park is lovely," she said, looking around them. "The estate must be very large."

"Yes," he said, his eyes on the road ahead of them.

So taciturn! "I suppose you have quite a lot of sheep and cows that wander about."

"Quite a lot," he agreed.

He could be as taciturn as he liked, but Grace would not be put off. She was clearly new to the intimate secrets between a husband and wife, but she was *not* new to gentlemen. He had just made himself a puzzle she intended to solve.

He continued at a slow pace, his gaze straight ahead, one hand on the reins, the other one on his thigh. Grace's horse grew increasingly restless. "Perhaps we might improve the pace?"

"In what way?"

She smiled. "I mean faster," she said. "My mount and I are restless."

When Merryton made no move to quicken the pace, Grace nudged her horse to a canter. Her mount eagerly complied, lurching forward ahead of the other horse, proudly snorting and tossing his head about. Grace led him to lope around Merryton in big, wide circles while her husband watched her impassively.

"Has this horse a name?" she called out to him.

"Snow," he said.

"Snow! How very original!"

"I should think a woman who has named a canine *Dog* might be more appreciative."

She giggled. "Touché! The right name hasn't come to me, but it will." She reined the horse into a trot alongside him once more. "You are no doubt wondering after my skill in riding."

"I wasn't."

"I have been taught to ride by the finest instructors in London," she said. "My sisters and I are often seen racing on Rotten Row in Hyde Park. *Racing!* Isn't it scandalous? Lady Chatham—do you know Lady Chatham? For she knows everyone in England, I think. She says it will not do to have young ladies racing like thugs through Rotten Row. I will confess, that is precisely why we do it." She laughed again.

Merryton looked at her with slight astonishment.

Grace spurred her horse to trot another circle around him. "I only mention it so that you are aware I am from London. I thought that might interest you...where I have lived."

"I know from where you hail," he said, his gaze on the road again.

"But do you know that I also spent quite a lot of my youth at Longmeadow? That is the Earl of Beckington's seat. Rather far from here, I think, perhaps as much as two days' ride."

He said nothing.

"My father was a bishop. He died when I was eight years old. My mother married the earl, and he very kindly took in four daughters and treated them as his own. His son, the new Earl of Beckington—well, he's

Augustine to us—he'll marry as soon as he has completed his mourning. He is affianced to Miss Monica Hargrove. I would think you've not met her." Grace did not say aloud that, until recently, Monica did not travel in such august circles as Merryton.

He looked away, out over the fields they were passing.

Bloody recalcitrant man, Grace thought. "Oh, but I miss my family terribly. Do you miss yours? I've never been away from home for as long as this. It's a terrible thing to be without one's siblings, isn't it? You must know very well what I mean, as your siblings are not here, either."

She glanced at Merryton and was surprised to see him looking at her. She made a sound of exasperation. "For heaven's sake, why will you not *speak?*"

A slow, half smile appeared on his face. "I was not aware there had been an opportunity."

Grace was so shocked by that smile—only half of one at that—that it was a wonder she didn't topple right off her horse. "I don't see the need for us *both* to be so tight-lipped."

"Apparently not," he agreed, his smile widening slightly.

"If you prefer, I will cease to speak. Shall we ride, then? Are you holding your horse under such close rein because you fear I will not keep up? If so, you needn't fret—I should very much like to run."

"Then by all means," he said. *"Run."*

Grace frowned at him. The many gentlemen in London who had sought her company were eager to please her in any way they could. This one seemed determined to do anything *but* please her, and damn his eyes if he wasn't succeeding brilliantly. "Do you know what I think? I think Snow is a ridiculous name for such fine horseflesh." And with that, she slapped the crop against Snow's flank.

Snow responded instantly and began to run, his stride lengthening as she nudged him into the center of the road. Grace bent over his neck. She could feel her braid of hair bouncing against her back, the hem of her riding habit flapping about her ankles. She didn't even particularly care where the horse ran—at present, she was content with the knowledge that Merryton and Blackwood Hall were fading far behind her. She wondered briefly how long it would take her to ride all the way to London. Had she known the direction, she may very well have tried.

But at the next turn in the road, she encountered a crofter cottage. There were three people in the field beside it, two men with hoes and a woman with a basket. *Thank God! Civilization!*

All three of them stopped their work when Grace pulled up on the reins of her horse, bringing him to an abrupt halt. She hopped too eagerly off her saddle and landed on all fours. One of the gentlemen lurched forward as if he meant to catch her, but Grace bounced up and smiled, waving her hand in greeting. "Good morning!"

The other man doffed his cap and took a cautious step forward. "Milady?" he said. "Are you lost, then?"

"Lost?" She glanced around them. It looked like the

rest of the estate—dark and uninhabited. "No, I don't think so. You're tenants of Blackwood Hall, are you?"

"Aye," the older gentleman said. "And you are…?"

"Oh! Me, yes…I am Lady Merryton."

Not one of the tenants moved. Not one of them spoke. They all stared at her as if they didn't speak the king's English. Before any of them could even peep, the sound of an approaching rider caused them all to turn and look up the road.

Merryton trotted casually into their midst. He looked at Grace standing there, then dismounted fluidly from his horse and walked to where they all stood. "Good morning, Mr. Murphy." He nodded to the other two.

The woman was quick to dip a curtsy. "Milord," she said.

Merryton smiled thinly and nodded as he tapped his crop against his leg. Grace wondered if the habit was so ingrained that it was always eight times without a thought.

"Good, you are preparing to sow," he remarked.

"Aye, milord. Should have it all planted by week's end," Mr. Murphy said.

The younger man and woman were still staring at Grace. What must they think? As Merryton made no move to introduce her, she touched his hand in an attempt to remind him. He flinched slightly and looked at her. "Forgive me," he said at once. "Allow me to introduce Mr. Murphy, and his son and daughter-in-law, Mr. and Mrs. Murphy." To his tenants he said, "My wife, Lady Merryton."

Grace beamed at them. "A pleasure. I hope to see

you about Blackwood Hall. You do come to the hall on occasion, don't you?"

The three Murphys all exchanged a look. "Yes," Mr. Murphy said. "Forgive us—our felicitations."

"With many happy returns," the woman said, recovering. "We…" She glanced at the two men. "We weren't aware you'd taken a wife, my lord."

"Yes." Merryton said no more than that, and clasped his hands tightly at his back. *Very* tightly.

"Only recently," Grace added, and reached for his hand. He resisted her, but she dug her fingernails into the bit of exposed wrist she could feel and tugged it free. She held his hand tightly in her own. "In Bath," she added. "We intended to have a grand wedding, but we were so in love we married straightaway."

That earned her a sharp squeeze of her hand, but Grace squeezed right back. "We'll host a gathering to celebrate properly, very soon. You'll all be invited."

Now Merryton squeezed her hand hard enough to make her wince slightly.

"Oh!" Mrs. Murphy said, smiling now. "That would be lovely!"

"We will leave you now to carry on," Merryton said, and looked down at Grace. "Must get my bride home."

Grace smiled up at him. She could see the warning in his green eyes and flatly ignored it. "What a pleasure it has been to make your acquaintance," she said to the Murphys again.

"Good day," Merryton said, and with his hand now firmly in the small of her back, he ushered her to her horse. When he cupped his hands to help her up, Grace offered her foot with a bit of a kick. He vaulted her up with a bit more enthusiasm than was necessary.

As they rode away, Grace waved at the Murphys. The three of them had moved to the middle of the road, watching them curiously. When they had ridden a distance, Grace said, "Could you not say a *bit* more to them? They were so clearly curious of your sudden marriage!"

"So much in love?" he repeated with incredulity to the sky.

"Would you rather I have told them the truth?"

"Of course not! Has it ever occurred to you that there is some virtue in prudence? It is none of their concern."

"*Prudence!* What do you know of prudence? You scarcely even spoke to them! Those are the people who till your land—you might at least show them the courtesy of introducing your unexpected wife!"

"When exactly would I have gathered around my tenants and shared the happy news?" he shot back, and gripped his reins tightly, shifting in his saddle. "Do not think to instruct me on etiquette."

"I happen to be an *expert* on manners and etiquette, particularly in difficult situations," she said. "I will have you know that I am a frequent visitor to the grandest salons in London. I am never without invitation, because I understand the social graces and how these things are done."

"How grand for you. But *this,* as you may have noticed, is not London."

"It hardly matters!"

"Of course it does," he said curtly, looking away from her.

"Of course it does *not*. People are people, Merryton! It hardly matters if they are standing in a ballroom or in a field—we all like to think that the person addressing us respects us enough to tell us that they have married!"

As usual, he said nothing, but she could see the way his fist curled on his thigh.

She suddenly remembered what Molly Madigan had told her about him and drew a breath to calm herself. "I realize your bashfulness makes it difficult—"

"My *what?*" he roared, jerking his gaze to her.

"Your bashfulness!"

"You think *bashfulness* plagues me?" He gave a bark of astonished laughter and shook his head.

"If you are not bashful, then there is another name for what you are, my lord, but I am too much of a lady to say it," she said pertly.

"You mistake bashfulness for impatient tolerance," he said gruffly.

Grace was not a violent person, but if she could have managed launching herself at his neck, she would have done so. Instead, she spurred her horse forward, galloping away from him once more.

This time, however, Merryton allowed his horse to join in the running. She could hear him gaining on her, and it angered her. She spurred Snow on. But Merryton's horse matched Snow, and they rounded the corner galloping at a breakneck speed—so fast, in fact, that Grace had trouble keeping her seat. She tried to slow Snow, but the horse was racing Merryton's and was not inclined to pull up. It wasn't until Merryton raced alongside and caught Snow's bridle, giving it a hard yank, that Snow slowed.

They were in the middle of nowhere, but Grace was seething. She slid off the horse—landing on two feet this time—and marched forward into an untended field.

"Where are you going?" Merryton called after her.

*"Home!"*

"You forgot your bloody dog!"

She gasped and whirled around. Merryton had come off his horse and had settled his weight onto one hip. He was holding his crop at his side. "You are so heartless!" she shouted at him.

He scoffed. "Not heartless. Practical."

"You are! You are heartless to me, you are heartless to them," she said, gesturing in the direction of the Murphys. "What is the matter with you?"

"Nothing," he said. But he tapped his crop against his leg in his customary pattern. He glanced uneasily around them, at the towering trees, the open field. And then he sighed. He took off his hat and shoved his fingers through his hair. "I am not heartless," he said, speaking as if he was carefully considering each word. "But I find it exceedingly difficult to converse without a distinct purpose. It causes me to become impatient."

He needed a purpose to converse with someone? "So you *are* bashful."

"No, it's...it's a bit more complicated than that."

"How so?" she asked curiously.

"It doesn't matter," he said, and fit his hat back on his head. "I don't mean to be cruel. Or cross. But perhaps you should understand that I cannot indulge in a lot of nattering."

"Nattering!" Grace protested. "I'm not an old woman in my dotage. I am trying to *understand*—"

"There is nothing more for you to understand," he said crisply, effectively cutting off any prolonged discussion of it.

"Well. You clearly would like me to believe that. But I don't," she said, and started the march back to her horse, weary of him. But as she moved to pass him, he caught her arm.

"I know you are trying," he said hesitantly. "But I don't...I'm not like the gentlemen you have known, Grace. And I would therefore advise you not to tell the tenants ours is a love match because I can't add to that fantasy. Or to bring in untrained dogs—"

"Or what?" she challenged him, jerking her arm free of his grip at the mention of Dog. "You will be unkind? You will refuse to accept this marriage? At least Dog shows me some affection." She snorted disdainfully and started to move past him again. Jeffrey reached for her arm a bit more firmly this time, and when he did, Grace tried to swerve out of his reach. He caught her all the same, and her feet were tangled with his, and she swayed off balance, tumbling to the ground.

Jeffrey tumbled with her.

She pushed him away and rolled onto her back and splayed her arms wide. "Go on, then. Strike me, beat me, whatever it is you want to do to me for having put you in this situation. For heaven's sake, do what you must!"

Merryton groaned. "For God's sake, why do you think I want to beat you?" He stood up, then leaned over and picked Grace up and set her on her feet.

"You obviously want to do something to me," she muttered as she shook out her skirts and tried to pick the grass from her braid. "I can see it simmering in you like an overcooked stew."

"For the love of heaven," he muttered.

"Will you deny it?" she asked, unthinkingly pushing him away from her.

Jeffrey pressed his lips together, then slowly lifted his crop and touched it to her chin.

Grace swayed backward. "Is that it? You want to beat me with your crop?"

He moved the tip of the crop from her chin, sliding it down her throat, to her chest, then lightly flicking the end of it against her nipple. "*Beating* you is the last thing I want to do." He slid the crop down farther, tracing a line down her abdomen and stopping at the apex of her legs.

His behavior confused her. Grace could feel the wave of desire coming from him, could see the heated look in his eye, and found it strangely titillating. "If it is the last thing you want to do to me…then what is the first?"

His jaw clenched, but there was a flash, a glimmer of raw emotion in his eyes. A surprising flash of bold desire mixed with a bit of vulnerability.

She suddenly grabbed the crop and yanked it away from him. She touched him with the tip as he had done her, sliding it down his chest, to the top of his trousers. "What do you want, Jeffrey Donovan?" she demanded.

Grace didn't mean in that moment, precisely, although she would like to know what he meant to do with the crop. Hers was a bigger question, and her husband seemed to understand that as she slid the crop down, to the bulge in his trousers. He didn't move, but kept his gaze locked on her, his expression raging with desire and anger and something else that Grace didn't understand. "What I want is to return you to Blackwood Hall, straightaway," he said. He grabbed the crop and took it from her. His expression had changed; it had shuttered again and he had hidden away that glimpse of raw emotion. He turned and began to walk back to the horses.

Grace slowly followed, considering him and these last strange moments. She had noticed it before, she realized, that hint of vulnerability in an otherwise iron-clad facade of utter detachment.

She was still studying him when she reached the horses. He was standing next to hers, ready to help her up. She looked up at him, trying to find that moment in his eyes again. But he was, she was learning, a careful man, closely guarded and a master at protecting the gates. For some reason that made her feel sorrow for him. What must have happened to him to be so guarded? To refuse to let even the slightest ray of affection inside? How lonely that must be, she thought, and couldn't help herself—she touched his face.

Merryton flinched and turned his head slightly, but Grace was not deterred. If anything, that flinch emboldened her. She rose up on her toes and kissed him lightly on the lips. She expected him to recoil, but he didn't.

She lingered there, her lips lightly touching his, a chaste and simple kiss. And then she melted back to her feet.

His gaze poured into hers, reaching down, filling her up for one long moment, and Grace had the sense that he was trying to understand *her* for a change. He wordlessly put his hands on her waist and lifted her up. His hand grazed her thigh when she was seated. He stepped back, his gaze fixed on her, quietly assessing.

Then he turned and walked back to his horse.

They rode in silence back to Blackwood Hall, Merryton slightly ahead, which Grace believed was his way of avoiding any "nattering." At the gates of the hall, he slowed so that she might catch up. "I have business in the village. I trust you will see yourself safely to the house."

"I thought perhaps—"

He had already spurred his horse.

"I thought we might take luncheon together, you impossibly ill-mannered husband," she said to herself.

She rode down to the house, handed her reins to the young man who hurried out to greet her and hopped down. She strode away, her crop in hand, and walked through the immaculate garden, through the iron gates at the end of the garden into the park, bound for Molly Madigan's cottage.

As she walked in through the wooden gate, the cat jumped onto the windowsill, and swished its tail several times as it fixed its eyes on Grace. The cat almost appeared to be scowling.

She rapped on the door. A few moments later, the

door opened and Dog came bounding out with what looked like the tongue from a leather boot.

"Oh, no," Grace said, and squatted down to receive his exuberant greeting and wrench the leather free.

"Lady Merryton!" Molly said with delight, appearing behind the dog. "Come in, come in!"

"Please, you must call me Grace," she said as she stepped across the threshold. "I hope Dog hasn't been too much of a bother?" she asked, and handed the chewed leather to Molly.

Molly looked at it and winced. "Um...*well,*" she said, and gamely tried to smile. Grace could see why—the rest of the boot was lying in various spots around her parlor.

"Oh, dear," Grace said, and sighed with frustration. She needed something to be right today.

"Is everything all right?" Molly asked as she shut the door and shooed the puppy away from her foot. He growled at it and pounced on her toe.

"What a little bother you are!" Grace said, and scooped him up. "Yes, everything is fine. I'll just take this bit of bother away." She turned to the door. And then she abruptly turned back to Molly. "No, everything is *not* fine."

"Oh, dear. Come now, and sit. I shall give you some tea."

"What of my bother?" she asked, gesturing to the dog.

"Put him down, please. He can't destroy much else, can he?"

Grace winced and allowed Molly to usher her into

one of the chairs before the hearth. The dog trotted to the hearth and lay down, too, sighing long and loud, as if he'd had a hard day chewing boots.

"He's not what you say, Molly," Grace said abruptly.

"Oh, no. He's really a good dog—"

"No, I mean Merryton. I can't seem to make any gains with him. I think he must truly despise me."

"Oh, that can't be true," Molly said soothingly, and hurried into the adjoining room to fetch the tea service.

"But it is. He's ashamed of me. He could scarcely bring himself to introduce me to his tenants. I had to do it."

"Oh, my," Molly said, and put the tea service on the table between them and began to pour.

Grace told Molly about the Murphys, and how he had neglected to even acknowledge her. "He resents me terribly," she said with a groan.

"I don't believe it!" Molly insisted. "He was all set to marry Mary Gastineau, but he married *you,* my dear. How could he be ashamed of you?"

"Pardon?" Grace had not considered that he'd held esteem for someone else. That he'd been set to *marry* someone else. She'd just assumed— Good God, she'd done a lot of assuming, hadn't she? "Mary Gastineau?" she repeated distantly.

"I thought you knew."

"No," Grace said, shaking her head, and gave Molly a sheepish look. "I don't know if you are aware, but our union came about after an…indiscretion. There was not time for familiarity."

"Ah." Molly did not seem surprised or scandalized,

which left Grace to assume that word of the scandal had already traveled. That did not help her mood in the slightest—if anything, it made her feel worse. How long before word reached the nice people she'd met today?

"Well, no matter. I am certain he will grow to love you."

Grace snorted. "I can't imagine it. He barely even speaks to me."

"Perhaps you might show him a kindness," Molly suggested, and lifted her gaze to meet Grace's. "He must be trying very hard to accept the marriage and to be the husband you deserve. But perhaps it is not as easy for him as it is for you."

"Why must it be so difficult?" Grace asked. "It's not a new and baffling thing, marriage. Men and women have been joined in matrimony since the dawn of time."

"Well, yes, but some marriages are not always pleasant, are they? His lordship's upbringing was difficult," Molly said, her pleasant smile contradicting those words. "His parents were unhappy with each other. He's not had the privilege of witnessing a happy marriage."

"I had no idea," Grace said.

"I don't suppose that is something he should like to be known."

No, she supposed not. Grace had heard talk of unpleasant marriages. Rumor had it that Sir Brendon treated his meek wife to regular beatings, but even that was gossip—Grace had never seen any evidence of it. She wondered what it was Merryton had tried to convey when he'd touched her with his riding crop.

"But I am fully confident that you'll discover how

to improve things with his lordship," Molly said cheerfully. "Now then, I've made some fresh scones and clotted cream. I should be honored to serve you." She stood up, and when she did, the dog bounded to his feet. As Molly started for the other room, the dog bounded ahead of her, almost tripping her.

Grace sighed and wearily propped her chin on her fist. Perhaps a scone would help her think. "I am a bit hungry," she muttered to no one in particular. But not for food, exactly. She was hungry to understand, to open the locked door to her husband's heart. To discover what it was that kept him at such a great distance not only from her, but what seemed like the world.

## CHAPTER TWELVE

At PRECISELY EIGHT minutes to eight o'clock, Jeffrey went downstairs to supper. All day, he'd felt the strange current of agitation running just under his skin. It was as if he was waiting for something to happen, for someone or something to come, to leave, to rise, to fall. He despised the uncertainty.

He arrived at the dining room, fully expecting to find a sullen wife, a wineglass in her hand and an angry spark in her eye, given her obvious displeasure with him this morning. He could not have been more wrong.

She was dressed in a sunny yellow gown, a curious color given her stepfather's recent passing. She had put up her hair with glittering pins and wore diamonds at her throat. She did not hold a wineglass, and in fact, he didn't see glasses on the table. She did, however, hold the lead in her hand. The puppy was sitting patiently beside her, his tongue hanging long.

There was only one real spot of chaos in the room, and that was in the vase of hothouse flowers, neatly tucked away at the sideboard, directly across from her seat so that she might see them as she dined.

It was remarkable that Jeffrey noticed these things at all, because Grace smiled as he entered, and what

# FREE Merchandise is 'in the Cards' for you!

Dear Reader,

## *We're giving away FREE MERCHANDISE!*

Seriously, we'd like to reward you for reading this novel by giving you **FREE MERCHANDISE** worth over $20. And no purchase is necessary!

You see the Jack of Hearts sticker above? Paste that sticker in the box on the Free Merchandise Voucher inside. Return the Voucher promptly...and we'll send you valuable Free Merchandise!

Thanks again for reading one of our novels—and enjoy your Free Merchandise with our compliments!

*Pam Powers*

Pam Powers

P.S. Look inside to see what Free Merchandise is **"in the cards"** for you!

**W**e'd like to send you two free books like the one you are enjoying now. Your two books have a combined price of over $10, but they are yours to keep absolutely FREE! We'll even send you 2 wonderful surprise gifts. You can't lose!

**REMEMBER:** Your Free Merchandise, consisting of **2 Free Books** and **2 Free Gifts**, is worth over $20.00! No purchase is necessary, so please send for your Free Merchandise today.

# FREE MERCHANDISE VOUCHER

2 FREE
BOOKS
and
2 FREE
GIFTS

Please send my Free Merchandise, consisting of
**2 Free Books** and **2 Free Mystery Gifts**.
I understand that I am under no obligation to buy
anything, as explained on the back of this card.

### 246/349 HDL GEHD

*Please Print*

|  |
|---|

FIRST NAME

|  |
|---|

LAST NAME

|  |
|---|

ADDRESS

|  |  |
|---|---|

APT.#          CITY

|  |  |
|---|---|

STATE/PROV.     ZIP/POSTAL CODE

### *NO PURCHASE NECESSARY!*

HH-714-FM13

a bloody brilliant smile it was, one that seemed to brighten the entire room. "Good evening, my lord," she said cheerfully, and curtsied deeply.

Before he could respond, the dog suddenly leaped up and bounded toward him with such force that the lead was yanked from Grace's hand. The dog rushed to Jeffrey and planted his paws on his trouser leg, his tail wagging as he peered up at Jeffrey.

"Bother!" she cried, and quickly stooped to grab up the lead. "Oh, I *do* beg your pardon! He's not to do that. *No,* Bother, no!"

"Bother?" Jeffrey echoed, and pushed the dog down, giving him a scratch behind the ears.

"I've named him," she said proudly. "He's been such a bother to everyone that it seemed a perfect name. I hope you don't mind, but Cook requested of Cox that he not be in the kitchens while they are preparing the evening meal. It would seem some food has gone missing."

"Has it," he said, looking at the dog.

"Not to worry! I've sent for Mr. Drake."

He looked up. "You've given up?"

"What? No, certainly not!" she exclaimed. "I never give up! But I have asked Mr. Drake if he might teach him not to take things from Cook's table."

The pup jerked on the lead again and wandered under the table, his tail high, his nose on the floor. Grace sighed dramatically, then smiled and clasped her hands demurely before her. "Would you care for wine before supper? Cox has decanted it for us." She walked to the sideboard. She poured a glass and held it up to him as the dog began to sniff around the drapes.

For some reason, that made the prickling beneath Jeffrey's skin worse. Her smile was the kindling to the fire growing in him. He took the glass, his fingers brushing against hers. He did not drink, but gripped the glass tightly.

"Oh!" she said as she poured a glass of wine for herself, as if just recalling something. "I hope you won't mind terribly, but I requested Cook prepare one of my favorite dishes this evening."

Jeffrey sincerely hoped her favorite dish was not something he couldn't possibly ingest. "Fish stew," she said. "I am quite fond of it. How do you find it?"

"I have no opinion."

"Astounding," she said, one brow arching in graceful dubiousness. "I can't imagine there is another man in all of Britain who has *no opinion* of fish stew."

There was something strange at work here. The room felt different. Lighter. Disordered. "Where is Cox?" he asked.

"Gone to find Mr. Drake, I suspect. I will confess that Cox has not taken to Bother." She glanced at the dog, who had managed to pull up a corner of the rug and was chewing it. "May I tell you something? I rather like it when Cox is not here. It's difficult to speak candidly with servants hovering about, don't you agree?" she asked, and looked at him coyly from the corner of her eye.

"Do you need to speak candidly?"

She smiled. "Not at the moment."

She made no sense. Why seek privacy for a candid conversation if one had nothing candid to impart?

A knock at the door caused Bother to bark uncontrollably. Grace picked up his lead and quickly pulled the door open. "Ah, there you are, Miller," she said to one of the footmen. "Has Drake come?"

"Yes, mu'um."

She handed the lead to Miller, then bent down to pet the dog. "Go along, Bother. Go and learn how to be a good dog from Mr. Drake." She watched as Davis led the dog away, even leaning partially out into the hall. When she was apparently satisfied, she shut the door and turned back to Jeffrey. "Shall we sit?"

As there was no servant, Jeffrey put her in her chair. She daintily slipped into it, arranging her skirts just so. Standing above her as he was, Jeffrey could see her breasts nestled in the bodice of her gown. He put his hand on her shoulder before he knew what he was doing and brushed his fingers across her collarbone. Her skin left a searing heat in his fingers, made worse when she glanced up at him and smiled.

Jeffrey took his seat.

A moment later, the service door swung open and Cox entered with a silver tray. Behind him was Ewan, who carried the bread. Jeffrey observed the young footman as he served, watched him lean over his wife and put bread on her plate. He was certain he saw the footman's gaze move to her bodice.

He closed his eyes against the hideous image of the young footman at his wife's breast.

Cox ladled fish stew into their bowls, and with a curt bow and flourish of his hand, he sent Ewan out and followed him. Jeffrey made a note to have Ewan removed from service in the dining room, to some other, more obscure part of the house. Chimneys, he thought idly. He picked up his spoon.

So did Grace.

Jeffrey dipped his spoon into the stew and tasted it. He was right; he had no opinion of it, good or bad.

"Well?" Grace said eagerly.

Jeffrey looked at his bowl.

"It's all right to say you don't agree with my assessment of fish stew, you know. I won't bite," Grace said.

A sudden and lurid image of her mouth on him, her teeth nibbling his skin, suddenly flashed through his mind and rushed to his chest in a dark heat. He looked up, startled.

"I meant it in jest," she said, looking at him curiously. "Of course I'd not *bite* you." She smiled.

No, but he would. "It is…good."

She laughed. "If that is good, I shudder to imagine your expression if you found it not to your liking."

The same, Jeffrey thought.

"Well, I like it very much," she said, and took several bites. "By the by, I wanted to thank you for allowing me to ride with you today. I was very happy to feel the sun on my face, and it was a pleasure to meet your tenants."

Funny, but she had not seemed very pleased earlier today.

"I believe there must be more society here than I originally believed," she continued, clearly determined to converse. "And many more of your tenants who haven't the slightest notion you've married."

He shrugged.

She put down her spoon. "Perhaps we might invite a few of your friends to dine and perhaps announce it."

He balked at the very idea. Of course, Blackwood Hall had seen quite a lot of balls and supper parties, but as long as he'd been earl, they'd all been overseen by his sister, Sylvia. But now that Sylvia was at her home in the north with babies, she couldn't make the trip to Blackwood Hall as often she once had. Frankly, it seemed none of his family—his siblings, his cousins and aunts—came round as they once had. He assumed it was because Blackwood Hall was quite far from them. He didn't like to think that it was because of him.

Jeffrey was a wretched host, he knew, and he couldn't possibly do anything like Sylvia had done—he feared he would lose his mind completely in the uneven numbers, the dizzying array of colors, in the perfumes of women. He feared he would say something entirely offensive under the duress of hosting. "I think it not necessary," he said flatly. "Word has spread without any formal announcement."

Her smiled seemed to dim a bit. "Not a large affair, but something small," she said, as if he hadn't spoken. "Your closest friends."

His friends? What friends? "I don't care to host a… soiree," he said.

A moment of silence passed. But only one dizzyingly short one. "Haven't you any friends?" she asked.

That was impossible, given his depravity. He put down his spoon and looked at her. "As I said, it is not necessary."

"Perhaps it is not necessary for *you,* but it is for me.

I will wither away without some sort of society, something to occupy me. And really, this is something you need not worry with the details—with Cox's help, I will take care of everything. I've a lot of practice." As she ate her stew, she began to speak of all the soirees that had been held at Beckington's house in London. This one with a small string quartet, that one in the garden, this one again, with a marzipan made to resemble a bowl of fruit. She was very pleased with her hosting, and was careful to stress how meticulous she was with the details, so much so that even her mother had not had cause to fret that something was undone.

How could he possibly explain to her that details were precisely the thing he *had* to worry about?

She mistook his silence for disagreement. "Please," she said. "I should very much like to have a friend or two."

Her eyes were pleading with him, tugging at his conscience. Of course, she should have some friends. He couldn't allow his depravity to keep her from it. Perhaps that was the thing—if she had friends, if she had places to go, to be, she would be removed from his sight. God help him if her friends proved to be as alluring as she. He tried to push down the images of women in his house with their perfumes and silken hair and flawless skin. Women who would entice him. His fist curled in his lap and he tapped against his knee. "Then you should have them," he said.

Her face instantly lit with pleasure that illuminated some place deep inside him.

"Make your friends, invite them to dine if you'd like. But don't expect me to join you."

He turned his attention to the stew.

"But that's the point," she said. "I thought if we had some friends in common, we might...well, we might become friends, too."

She would never understand that his mind was not his own. That because of the carnal images that possessed his mind, he must keep his distance from her or risk destroying their fragile union. Friends? Routine may seem unfeeling to her, but it was entirely necessary to him. He put aside his spoon. "Grace—"

He was interrupted by a knock at the door. It was Miller again, and this time, he was carrying a silver tray. He bowed. "A letter has come for her ladyship," he said.

Grace sat up and eagerly took the letter from his tray. "Honor!" she said breathlessly, and looked at Jeffrey. "Will you excuse me?" But she was already standing, hurrying from the dining room, leaving the scent of her perfume behind to torment Jeffrey.

When she'd gone, he looked down the empty table, at his empty bowl of stew. Apparently, he liked fish stew more than he knew. Cox entered and began to clear the dishes.

"Cox...Ewan should find another post in this house," Jeffrey said.

Cox stopped what he was doing. "My lord? Has he done something to displease you?"

"No," Jeffrey said. "But I prefer someone older in the dining room. Billings—he'll do."

"Billings," Cox repeated, his voice full of disbelief.

"If you will forgive me, my lord, but old Billings can scarcely lift a tray."

Jeffrey felt the flush of remorse, but he could not abide a young and handsome footman near his wife. Not because he doubted the loyalty of his servant or, even at this early stage of his marriage, the loyalty of his wife. But because he couldn't trust himself. "He'll do," he said. "And…give Ewan an extra pound or two this annum."

Cox looked at the dishes he held. "Yes, my lord," he said, and went out through the service door, leaving Jeffrey alone.

Until several days ago, this had been the pattern of his evenings. He dined alone. He ruminated alone. He allowed his fantasies to roam about his head, all alone. He looked around at the stark dining room and was reminded of another meal in this house, many years ago. He'd been a boy, perhaps ten years of age. He couldn't any longer recall if his family had gathered for breakfast or luncheon, but the sun had been streaming through the windows, and he could remember thinking that bright sunlight seemed so wrong for such a menacing day.

Sylvia and John had been at the table, as well as his parents. His mother had received a letter, not unlike Grace had tonight. Jeffrey never knew who'd sent it. Not that it mattered—the letter had sent his father into a rage. He'd banged the table so hard with his fist that glasses tumbled and platters rattled. He bellowed that Jeffrey's mother had dishonored him, and took the letter before she had the opportunity to read it.

His mother had gotten up from the table and run, and

his father, his face red with anger, had instructed his three children to remain at the table until he had said they might stand. He went after his wife, and the three of them could hear his father's vile shouts, his mother's screams. Doors had slammed and furniture had toppled, all of it audible to the children in this room. The physical struggle between their parents and the disgusting victory of their father over their mother had been heard by nearly everyone at Blackwood Hall.

The children, Jeffrey remembered, had been too frightened to leave their chairs, too afraid of what their father would do to them. Even the footmen had stood against the wall, too afraid to leave their posts, all of them listening to the same wretched event.

Jeffrey remembered feeling responsible for it. That made no sense to him now, but he could remember the feeling of helplessness, and the belief that he should *do* something. But what he'd done was remain seated, his head down while his father brutalized his mother, tapping his fists against his knees to keep from crying before his siblings. Sylvia was weeping, and John so young he wanted to be down from his chair to play. Jeffrey forbade him, and kept tapping. Eight times. Pause. Eight times, again.

*Why eight?*

He wondered now, twenty years later, how much time had actually passed before his father had returned wild-eyed, his clothing askew, his lip bleeding. He had stalked into the dining room, had looked each child in the eye. "Never," he said, his voice quavering with anger. "*Never* dishonor me, for the consequences will be dear. Ask your whore of a mother if you don't believe me." And then he'd ordered them all from the room and had resumed his meal, as if brutalizing his wife had given him an appetite.

Jeffrey swallowed down the horrid memory, which, in retrospect, was only one of many.

It was little wonder that he preferred to dine alone.

Unfortunately, that was now impossible.

# CHAPTER THIRTEEN

What mad thing have you done? Oh, Grace, dearest Grace, how could you do such an extraordinarily foolish thing? How could you have made such a terrible, terrible mistake? The moment I received your letter I wanted to come to you straightaway, but Easton says we haven't the funds for it, and besides, there is the matter of our mother to consider. She can't possibly travel now—I fear we would lose her, and even if we managed to hold her close, there is her unfortunate tendency to engage others in nonsensical speech. Augustine tells me he and Monica have decided to marry in private before the summer and that we must make accommodations for Mamma. What am I to do? I must obviously remain in London for her and our sisters until all is settled. I can't possibly come to you now.

Oh, dearest, I don't know how you will bear it! Your situation sounds truly wretched. My only advice is to make yourself as willing a wife as you are able. You really must try, and above all, keep a pleasant countenance! Easton says that a man is made pliable to his wife's wants if he is kept well occupied in the marital bed. My face burns at the mere mention of it, but I don't know what else to advise you. I'll come as soon as I am able. Take heart, darling, and be strong. Remember Mamma always said a woman makes her own place in this world, and now you must make yours. Our love and sympathy, and do be patient until I can come to you! Fondly, Mrs. George P. Easton

*WELL OCCUPIED* IN THE marital bed? Grace rolled her eyes—Honor's advice was not always helpful. How exactly did Honor think Grace was to do that with a man who had his way and then left? A man who was as cold to her outside of these rooms as a hard winter? The marital bed, as Honor put it, seemed to be the only thing he wanted from her. He clearly didn't care to know her otherwise.

If her sister only knew how Grace longed to know more of the marital bed, to experience more, to be swept away on that cloud of pleasure. But something was missing from Grace's introduction to intimacy, although she couldn't say exactly what. She only knew if he continued to be aloof and distant with her, she didn't care to experience more at his hand—no matter how pleasurable it felt in the moment.

Because even when she enjoyed the sensations, she felt as if she were scarcely more than a vessel to him.

A rap at the door startled her. Before she could stand, her husband walked into her room. He had that darkly lustful look about him that made her heart skip and her blood race. It almost felt as if her clothes fell away every place his gaze touched. He shut the door at his back, then reached for his neck cloth and unknotted it. "You have not yet prepared for bed."

"No."

He glanced around her rooms, as if he thought Bother would hop out of Grace's dressing room to surprise him.

"How do you find your new maid, my lord?" Grace asked as she slyly moved around to the end of her bed, putting some distance between them.

"What?" he asked, his attention on her once more.

"Your maid."

He seemed perplexed by the question. His gaze slid down her body, lingering on her breasts and her abdomen. She noticed that he held one hand clenched at his side. Always clenched or tapping. He reached for her, taking her hand in his and drawing her into him.

"Hattie has done very well for me, if that was what you had wondered," she said.

"I hadn't."

"Why did you give her to me?"

"Why?" He said it as if the answer was obvious as he moved toward her. "Because you wanted her."

Grace opened her mouth to speak but he shook his head. "Any more conversation on the topic is unnecessary."

"Unnec—" she started, but he cut her off with a kiss. Grace wanted to resist, but his fingers splayed across her chin and his lips were so soft. His hand slid down her back to her hip, and Grace felt herself softening....

Until she heard the word *unnecessary* in her head. She suddenly brought up a hand between them and pushed on his chest. That was it, the thing that seemed so wrong—she was only a body to him. Everything else was unnecessary. *"No,"* she said sternly.

Merryton's brows dipped into a dark V above his green eyes. *"No?"*

"I want to talk—"

He sighed impatiently heavenward.

"It is not an unreasonable request," she said, trying to keep control of her temper.

"Talk, then," he said, and gestured impatiently, as if she was to present a list of sentences.

She wasn't going to be put on the spot like that. "Would you like to play a game?" The idea just came to her, but there seemed no better option at the moment than to force him to sit and actually speak to her.

"No."

"Cards," she insisted. "You do know how—"

"I know *how,* Grace. I don't understand the purpose."

"If you know *how,*" she said, mimicking the stern tone of his voice, "then I have a challenge for you. Do you accept it?"

"How can I possibly accept it? I don't even know what it is."

"And therein lies the fun!" she said with false brightness. "Do you accept?"

He sighed, clearly debating. But if he were like every other man Grace had ever been even slightly acquainted with, she knew he would not refuse a challenge of any sort.

For once, her instincts proved right, for he said tersely, "Very well."

She beamed, delighted to have won a tiny battle. "Shall we play Vingt-et-un?" she asked. "The first player to reach the value of twenty-one with his or her cards wins the hand."

"I am familiar," he said. "Have you a purse, or do you expect I will not only indulge you in this game but pay your debts, as well?"

"I pay my own debts," she said smartly. "I'm not as clever with cards as Honor." She suddenly thought perhaps it was best not to mention Honor and her antics in the early stages of their marriage and laughed. "Honor has always been rather unique in society. Well, that's neither here nor there," she said with a dismissive flick of her wrist. "I had in mind gambling with something far more diverting than coin."

"And what would that be?"

"You needn't look so suspicious," she said. "For every hand I win, you must answer a question. *Truthfully,*" she hastily added.

"What sort of questions?" he asked suspiciously.

"Questions about you."

"That again, is it?" he said. "And for every hand I win?"

"I'll answer whatever you like," she said.

He withered her with a look. She hadn't thought far enough into this impetuous plan to know what she would do if he didn't want to indulge her. But she knew if she didn't present something quickly, he would deny her. So she seized on the one thing she knew he desired. "For every hand *you* win…you may point to an article of clothing that I must remove."

Her suggestion had the desired effect; one dark brow rose slowly above the other. "That certainly makes your proposition more interesting." His voice was smooth and deep, and Grace could imagine any number of women would swoon at the sound of it.

"Are you up to the challenge?" she asked, taking another step back. "Will you answer truthfully?"

"Do you suppose I would answer any other way? Have I not been truthful with you?"

"I wouldn't know," Grace said with a shrug. "You want to remain a stranger to me."

"Yes, well…" His gaze was suddenly piercing. "This will be diverting. You're not opposed to diversion, are you?"

He looked entirely opposed to a diversion and even a little tense at the suggestion. Lord—she'd not asked to look at the household books, she'd not asked for money, she'd not done anything but ask that she might know more about him. She impulsively reached out and touched his arm; he flinched.

Grace was not offended by it. She was, surprisingly, sorry for him. "It's only a game, my lord. I promise not to delve too deep."

He clenched his jaw, tapped his finger against his leg. "Very well," he said at last.

## CHAPTER FOURTEEN

IT WAS ANOTHER small victory and Grace was a little astonished that she'd won again. She moved before Merryton could change his mind, a hop and a step around him, to her writing table. She gave it a tug, dragging it from the window to the hearth.

"What are you— Allow me," he said brusquely, and stepped in, lifting the table up and swinging it around. Grace hurried ahead of him and pushed the chaise from in front of the hearth. Merryton put the table down in that spot.

"There we are!" Grace said, and hurried to fetch the chair. She handed it to Merryton, and then picked up the bench from her vanity, placing it on the other side of the table.

Merryton looked at her, then at the table, and with a sigh, he swept his hand in the direction of it, indicating she was to sit.

Grace took the bench, leaving him the chair. He walked around to the other side of the table, flipped his tails and sat. The ends of his neck cloth dangled down his chest and his hair curled around his ears. He had the dark shadow of a beard and, as always, the piercing green eyes. He braced one hand against his knee, his other arm on the table. "Well, then? Have you any playing cards?"

"Yes!" She'd found them rummaging about the writing desk. Unfortunately, they were on his side of the table. Grace stood up and leaned across the table, aware that his gaze was now on her bodice and, more specifically, affixed to her cleavage. As she leaned forward, drawing closer to him, he did not move, so that when she finally reached down to open the drawer, he was only a very few inches from her breasts.

Grace could feel his breath on her skin, could feel her blood warming under his scrutiny. She quickly reached down and pulled the drawer open, grabbed the cards and sank back onto her bench. "Not yet," she said silkily. "Would you care to deal?"

"After you."

With her back rigid and straight, Grace shuffled and dealt the cards.

They played the first round in silence, with Grace winning easily. Merryton's gaze came up when she turned over the winning card.

"I win. My first question—"

"First?"

*"First,"* she said firmly. "You didn't think I'd be satisfied with one, did you?"

He smiled faintly at that. "Quite the opposite. Go on, then. Ask."

"I should like to know if you are still angry with me for the circumstances of our marriage."

He hesitated. "No."

Grace clucked her tongue. "You promised to be truthful."

"You doubt me?" he asked incredulously.

"Oh *dear*," she said with mock concern. "You think me naive."

His lips twitched, and for a brief moment, Grace thought he might actually smile. "I hardly think you naive. That is the furthest from what I think you." He arched a brow, as if daring her to challenge him.

"Then you may as well admit it. I ruined your life, quite plainly, and your anger is evident."

He suddenly leaned forward, his eyes locked on hers. "Any anger that is *evident* is not aimed at you, but at myself."

Grace blinked. "It's not *your* fault. Why should you be angry with yourself?"

"That is two questions."

"But related to the first, so really only one," she countered. "Why should you be cross with yourself? It was all my doing."

His gaze was so steady, so unyielding, that it was a bit unnerving to her. "Quite simply because I do not generally allow myself to lose control."

"Yes, well, that is clear. But *I* kissed *you*. In the *dark*. Ardently, I might add," she said, blushing. "But it was all my doing."

He frowned slightly and gestured for the cards. She handed them to him. "Not all," he softly admitted. "There were two people in that room."

Grace glanced down as he dealt, trying to sort through her own feelings about that night. She felt guilty. In fact, the guilt she felt was worse than before, especially now that she understood he blamed himself.

The next game went quickly; Merryton won easily. He tossed his cards onto the table and leaned back in the chair, his fist pressed against the edge of the table. "Your hair," he said quietly. "Take it down."

The command, spoken with such authority, yet so softly, sent a shiver of anticipation down Grace's spine. She slowly lifted her arms, pulled one pin free and a thick tress of her hair tumbled down, falling over her shoulder.

He motioned for her to continue. She removed two more pins, helping her hair to fall, untangling it from the binds until it was completely down.

Merryton swallowed; the grip of his hand tightened. He silently pushed the deck of cards across the table.

Grace was so flustered by his visceral reaction that she lost the next hand, too.

"Stockings," he said roughly.

Heat rushed to her face as Grace leaned over, dipping her hand under her gown.

"No," he said, and with his foot pushed the table aside. He nodded at her gown. "Lift the hem so that I may see you."

Grace was reluctant to be so bold. But at the same time, the power her flesh and bone seemed to hold over him excited her. She kept her gaze on her husband and slowly lifted her hem up over her knees. She removed one shoe, then the other, and rolled down her stocking.

She could see how quickly desire sparked in his eyes, and heard the sharp intake of his breath. She lifted the other leg and rolled down the stocking. She tossed it at him.

He caught it deftly in one hand, touched it to his nose, and Grace's blood rushed.

*"Deal,"* she commanded.

But Merryton suddenly leaned forward and covered her hand with his, curling his fingers around hers, and a hot jolt of awareness shocked through her. "I've lost interest in the cards. Ask what you want, but ask it quickly. My patience is waning."

He was watching her like a cat. Grace took him at his word, dispensing with polite conversation. "Are you in love with Mary Gastineau?"

His eyes widened with surprise, and miracle of all miracles, he *smiled* at her. The effect was astounding; the man was stunningly handsome when he smiled—it transformed his face, gave him tiny little fans at the corners of his eyes and dimples in his cheeks. He didn't look distant, he looked...*warm*. Approachable. Human. Grace's heart skipped; she couldn't find her breath.

"I wonder where you might have heard of her," he said curiously, tilting his head to one side.

"I've made a few acquaintances."

"Quite industrious of you. You surprise me."

"Do you love her?" she asked, and a small part of her desperately wanted the answer to be no.

"She was as proper a match as I might have hoped for. I esteemed her. But I cannot say that I loved her."

That answer, which should have satisfied her, only served to perplex Grace more. She didn't know what he meant by "as proper a match as he might have hoped for." An earl with his wealth could have anyone he might want. "Does she know that you've married?"

His gaze settled on her mouth. "Yes."

Grace could feel the heat of her shame creeping up her neck. "I beg your pardon. That must have been difficult for you."

"It was," he agreed. "I called on the morning we were wed and explained my situation. I had given her certain expectations."

Now guilt would swallow her whole. Had Mary Gastineau been attached to Merryton? Had she destroyed that woman's happiness, too? Grace had not considered the possibility that she'd ruined even more lives, and the idea distressed her. How shameful she'd been, toying with the lives of others.

"What more do you want to know?" he asked, and turned her hand over, brought it to his mouth and kissed the center of her palm, drawing a small line with the tip of his tongue.

"Do you have a mistress?"

"That's personal."

"But fair."

He smiled again. "I swore a vow of fidelity to you, did I not? I am a man of my word."

What did that *mean*? She didn't know if she could trust anything he was telling her, really, but, oh, how she wanted to trust him now. She wanted to believe that there was some hope, no matter how small, that they might find their way to a happy future. She wanted him to be faithful to her. She knew it was common for men like him to keep mistresses, but she wanted to *be* the mistress. She wanted to be the only one.

"No more questions—"

"Wait," she said, and pulled her hand free to remove her necklace, putting it on the table between them. "I am still dressed. A question for an article of clothing."

"You are determined," he said, amused.

In response, she removed her bracelet and earrings and added them to the necklace.

Merryton chuckled softly, and settled back in his seat, clearly enjoying her slow disrobing. "The gown, then."

Grace put her hands on the table and pushed herself to stand. She felt conspicuous as she reached behind her to unbutton the gown.

"Come here," he said, gesturing to her. At Grace's skeptical look, he added, "You can't reach all the buttons."

That was true. She walked around to his side of the table; he was sitting with his legs casually sprawled, and Grace had to step in between them to present her back. Merryton made quick work of the buttons, and with his hands, he slowly pushed it from her shoulders, his fingers following the trail of the gown down her arms. As the gown slid down her body, he put his arm around her abdomen and pulled her onto his lap. He pushed her hair aside and kissed her nape.

More liquid fire slipped down her spine. Grace closed her eyes, wanting to feel more of it, but she remembered her goal, and pushed his hand away from her middle. She stood up and moved out of his reach.

"Why are there no paintings, no portraits, on the walls in this house? No adornment at all?"

He clasped his hands together, and Grace had the feeling that it was to keep himself from tapping. She had no reason to suspect it, but she would have wagered a fortune on it.

"I prefer a certain symmetry," he said, his voice having lost the lightness. "But as no two frames are alike, it is impossible to achieve. I prefer bare walls to misaligned portraits and paintings."

Misaligned paintings! She had expected him to say he'd given the paintings to his sister, or he'd sold them to pay some debt. But the frames lacked perfect symmetry? It was illogical, too exacting. It was a quest for perfection so perverse that it was completely imperfect.

Oddly enough, Grace couldn't help but think of her mother. How could she ever survive in a house like this? Her entire world was misaligned and imperfect, with no hope of ever being aligned, or made proper. She felt a swell of sorrow, but in that moment, she wasn't certain who she mourned. Her mother? Or her husband?

"The stays," he said, referring to the corset she wore. His gaze was on her breasts now.

Grace didn't move straightaway, still stunned by his response to the paintings. He didn't like her hesitation, for he suddenly surged to his feet. He put his arms around her, his fingers pulling the ties of her stays free, then pushing it off her shoulders.

The stays fell away. Grace stood before him wearing only a thin chemise now. She could see the hunger in his gaze, could see his body responding to hers, and the power she felt was intoxicating.

His eyes were dark and unreadable. "Do you fear that I will harm you?"

There it was again, the fear of harming her, which also seemed illogical to Grace. If he was fearful of it, he would be mindful not to hurt her. Wasn't that how everyone behaved? Managed their behavior so as not to harm or offend? "I don't fear that you will harm me, Jeffrey," she said, and noticed the flutter of his lashes when she said his name. "I fear that you will abandon me."

She wasn't certain he'd even heard her, for his eyes had gone dark, and he reached for her—

Grace backed several steps away. "I have one more question—"

"No more," he said sternly, reaching for her again.

"Answer one more and I will remove the chemise."

He paused. He reached for a tress of her hair, rubbing it between his finger and thumb as he considered it. "One more," he said silkily. "But then the game is done."

It wasn't a game to Grace. "Why do you do so many things to the count of eight?"

He looked as if she'd struck him, had punched him in the soft belly. He dropped her hair. Grace was struck with the thought that she had somehow trampled on something important to him, although she couldn't possibly guess what that was. "I've seen you," she said, suddenly feeling the need to explain, and mimicked the tapping he often did with her finger and thumb. Eight times, pause. Eight times, pause.

"What of it?" he snapped. "It is an anxious habit."

An anxious habit would not garner a response like this—if it were only an anxious habit, he would dismiss it, make light of it. Grace saw something in his eyes that she had yet to see in him—fear. *Fear!* But what could he possibly have to fear? What had the number eight to do with it? No, no, it wasn't fear, she suddenly realized as he shoved his hand through his hair, his eyes wildly searching her face. It was *shame.* The man was utterly ashamed.

Something about that twirled uncomfortably about her heart. Merryton was a noble man, a proud man who, by all accounts, demanded perfection. And yet there was something terribly imperfect about him. There was pain in him, so different than anything Grace had ever seen in another person. He looked embattled, bewildered, and he looked, she thought with shock, very much like her mother had looked before she'd gone completely mad. As if she were bewildered by the betrayal of her mind.

Was *that* what Merryton was feeling? What was wrong with him, what was he hiding?

He watched her apprehensively, as if he expected her reaction to be bad.

In truth, Grace had to fight the urge to physically recoil from him. She had enough madness in her life and the idea of being married to a madman frightened her. And yet, for the life of her, she couldn't fathom how a *number* could be the source of madness. Surely she was making too much of it. And yet she could plainly see that no matter how uneasy she was feeling, he seemed

to be feeling worse. Her heartfelt instinct was that to
show him any negative emotion at this moment would
be the very wrong thing to do. If anything, he needed
her compassion just now.

Grace felt as if she were slipping and sliding along
a very slender beam here, uncertain of what she was
doing, moving by raw instinct alone. She made a decision in that single moment; she pushed the straps of her
chemise from her shoulders and down her body. She
stepped out of it, tossed it aside and stood before him,
completely bare.

Merryton breathed in so deeply his nostrils flared
with it. His gaze moved down her body and up again,
and at his side, his fingers did the strange bit of tapping.

When he lifted his gaze to hers, he opened his
mouth to speak. It seemed difficult for him, but he said
roughly, "You are beautiful, Grace. My God, but you
are beautiful."

The compliment, so rawly offered, took her breath
away. How this man baffled her! There was so obviously a need in him—not for her, or her body, precisely,
but strangely, she thought she understood he needed
not to be judged. That was a need born from pain, and
Grace could not bear to see it in a man's eyes.

She moved without thinking, putting her arms
around his neck. He stiffened, but she pulled his head
down to hers and kissed him. It was meant to be a soothing kiss, and her fingers skirted lightly over his jaw,
feeling the stubble of a day's beard.

She felt his body fill with his breath, felt the tension
in him ease a little. His arms went around her, squeezing

her to him. She could feel his cock harden and lengthen against her, and longing took hold of her thoughts. She pulled his neck cloth free, then opened his collar.

He pressed his forehead to hers, his eyes closed, his breath coming in deep draws.

Grace unbuttoned his waistcoat and pushed it open. She pulled his shirt free of his trousers and slipped her hand under his shirt. His muscled stomach rippled beneath her fingers, as if he couldn't bear to be touched. She ran her hands up his chest, over his nipples, and kissed his chest through the open neck of his shirt.

Merryton pushed her back until she bumped up against the bed. He suddenly shifted her around and sat on the bed, pulling her onto his lap, guiding her to straddle him. He pushed both hands into her hair as he kissed her. His mouth was warm and wet, as tormenting as it was pleasurable. Heat pulsed in her, pooling between her legs. Grace desired him more than anything.

His response to her was powerful and demanding, as it always was, but tonight it felt different than it had before. In his caresses, in the way he looked at her, *really* looked at her, it felt to Grace as if he was feeling something beyond the physical pleasure.

That jolted Grace, rattled every bone and nerve in her. Her body responded from some primal place, and she pressed against him after he hastily discarded his shirt, fitting into his embrace as if she had been there all along. His tongue swirled around hers, and his hands caressed her sides, her torso, her breasts. Grace could forget everything that had happened in the past few weeks. She saw, she felt, only Merryton. She was emboldened by his desire for her and her need began to clash with his, then entwining with it and demanding as much from him as he demanded from her.

He eagerly explored her mouth while his hands moved on her body, sliding down one curve, up another, and in between her legs. He stood up, still holding her at his waist and, with one hand, discarded his trousers. When he sat again, he nestled his erection in the wet valley of her sex.

Pleasure and prurience engulfed her, and Grace dropped her head, her hair forming a curtain between them. Merryton pushed her hair back, sought her breast with his mouth. White-hot shivers slammed through her, and when Merryton pressed the hard tip of his erection against her, her breathing turned ragged.

He pushed her hair from her face, lifted her by her hips and guided her onto his cock, sliding deep inside her. Grace gasped at the sensation; she clutched at his shoulders, moving delicately, uncertainly. He kissed her with uncharacteristic tenderness as he helped her to glide on him, showing her the rhythm. When Grace took over, his hands went to her breasts, kneading them, his eyes on hers.

She began to move with more urgency, seeking release; Merryton slipped his hand in between them and began to stroke her. His touch was electrifying—she encircled his neck with arms, watching his face as they moved as one, until she could bear it no longer. She closed her eyes, felt the pleasurable release swirling around in her groin, rising up and up, until at last she splintered as the pleasure swept over her.

In a moment, he had her on her back and was driving into her, racing toward his own climax. He touched her lips with his and pushed into her, faster and harder until she felt his body shudder, heard him growl with the relief of his release as he spilled into her.

Grace wrapped her arms around him. She kissed the side of his head, and smiled up to the canopy, luxuriating in the warm glow of their bodies.

He lifted his head, kissed her cheek tenderly, and her forehead, then gathered her in his arms and rolled onto his side.

Grace had never felt quite so content. Her heart was still beating wildly, and against his chest. His skin was damp, his arms strong in their hold of her. She felt a lightness, as if everything around them shimmered, cocooning them in her bed.

Several moments passed before Merryton put his palm to her cheek and kissed her, softly, languidly. And then he rolled onto his back, still trying to catch his breath.

After a moment, he pushed himself up. "I shall leave you—"

"No," Grace said, and caught his arm. "Please stay."

"You should rest."

"Jeffrey, stay." She smiled at him and caressed his arm.

He stroked her cheek, then slowly eased back, lying beside her.

Grace smiled and kissed his shoulder and draped her arm across his abdomen as she nestled in beside him. She felt as if some chasm had been crossed tonight. She felt hopeful for the first time since coming to Black-wood Hall. She believed in that moment that she could grow to care for Merryton very much.

But when she awoke an hour or so later and found herself alone in her bed, the warm glow turned cold. She pushed herself up, looking around. Merryton and his clothes were gone.

Grace fell onto her back, her arms splayed wide, and glared at the canopy above her, angry and perhaps even a bit hurt by it. There *had* to be a way to reach Jeffrey Donovan, but blast it all if Grace knew what it could possibly be.

JEFFREY HADN'T HURT her. He'd done no harm to her, as evidenced by her request that he remain with her. It was all there, in his mind's eye, the whole astounding experience. He'd lost himself, had let himself be free, and now, he could rest knowing that his worst fear had not come true.

But he couldn't rest. He couldn't sleep. He thought of the card game she'd convinced him to play, of the questions she'd asked. He'd been able to answer them all until she'd asked him about eight.

Jeffrey closed his eyes and banged his fist against his forehead in a futile attempt to knock loose the demon. There was nothing that could relieve him of the ter-rible desires that so freely and mercilessly inhabited his thoughts other than to count in multiples of eight.

But as his depraved thoughts began to root into his brain, the path of eight steps in his room was not enough. Jeffrey made his way in the dark down the stairs and to the main corridor.

That corridor was a last resort, one he reserved for those rare occasions when the lack of control in his life was raging. He'd not been here in months, perhaps even as much as two years. It was for emergencies only, as the fear of being seen by the servants generally outweighed any other consideration.

Tonight, he would risk it.

The main corridor was precisely eight feet wide and, from one end to the other, thirty-two steps, even forty if he altered his gait. He chose thirty-two. Thirty-two steps to the end, turn, thirty-two steps back. Repeat.

He hadn't hurt her, he thought as he counted his steps. He had feared the worst, and the worst had not come to pass. The images he was experiencing now—of her naked body on his, of his cock ramming into her— were nothing more than that, nothing more than images.

On his third round of counting, Jeffrey could admit to himself that the experience had been very agreeable moments afterward, when he had been persuaded to lay there with her head on his shoulder, her body nestled against his. But he couldn't stay with her, not indefinitely, not in her bed, not with his many secrets and the rituals he could not forego. He'd felt a bit remorseful for slipping away as she lay sleeping, but he reasoned that he would feel far worse if she knew the truth about him.

As it was, she now knew too much about him. He was intrigued by her, aroused by her. He was angered by her, inconvenienced by her. He'd always been a man who took pride in the fact that he could always find an answer, could always bring order to any situation. Could always control himself. But with Grace, there was no order. There was no control. It was a messy, muddy hole of emotions and secrets and chaos. For the first time in a very long time, the chaos inside him was growing.

He would hurt her. If he hadn't already, he would.

As the minutes clocked by, Jeffrey was increasingly unable to calm his racing thoughts He was astounded, flummoxed and even a bit frightened. How could she possibly know about *eight?*

Dr. Linford was the only one to whom Jeffrey had ever confessed his unnatural need. He'd told him in hopes there was some medicine or tincture that would cure him, or at least some plausible explanation for why his world was divided into eights. Dr. Linford had not only been shocked by it, he hadn't the slightest notion of what could be done.

Jeffrey suspected Cox had guessed at his affliction with the number eight, but he was far too good a butler to mention it. The man quietly and very efficiently incorporated Jeffrey's foibles into his daily routines.

But to have this woman, a stranger, really, guess at his obsession? To have seen how he relied on eight, how everything in his life came back to it? If she had seen the full extent of his depravity, who else had seen it?

He could not have the world know of his affliction. He'd be made the laughingstock of England.

Worse, even if she did recognize his need for eight and somehow managed to overlook it for the sake of this marriage, she would never overlook his sexual perversion. She would never consent to being bound or to feeling the crop against her skin. She would never understand his desire for more than one woman.

*I didn't hurt her.*

She will cry off this marriage and flee to London.

Could he stop her? Would he? Wasn't he morally bound to let her go if she desired, given that the perversion in this union was within him? She would have every right to flee him, every right to be disgusted by him.

He walked the corridor for hours that wretched night, but the weight of his shame became unbearable. He had to get away, to be somewhere safe where he might think.

To Cox's great surprise, Jeffrey left the next morning at precisely eight o'clock. He asked Cox to tell his wife that business had called him away to Bath. He did not mention when he would return because he honestly didn't know.

Jeffrey rode to Bath and his town house there, surprising Tobias, his butler and caretaker. Tucked away there, with its eight steps from study to dining room, and eight panels of wallpapering in his salon, Jeffrey felt at ease for the first time since entering Grace's rooms the night before.

He was finally able to sleep—so well, in fact, he awoke just before noon the following day. When he arose, Jeffrey sent his footman to inquire if Dr. Linford might receive him.

Dr. Linford returned word that he would be delighted to receive his lordship in his home.

"My lord," Dr. Linford said when Jeffrey arrived, coming across his salon, his hand extended, and bowing over it. Mrs. Linford, a dark-haired beauty, was seated on a settee. A young maid who was at work tidying the study stole a look at Jeffrey.

"My lord, you are welcome," Mrs. Linford said.

Jeffrey nodded. He was struck by the realization that for the first time in recent memory, he could look at the lovely Mrs. Linford and the maid without the image of their hands and mouths on each other appearing in his head. It seemed that his corrupt mind had focused entirely on his wife.

"Perhaps we might speak in my office?" Dr. Linford said, and gestured to the door.

Jeffrey gave Linford's wife a curt nod and followed Linford out of the room, down the narrow hall and into a small office. He declined the seat Linford offered him, preferring to remain standing, as he was now questioning the wisdom of having come at all.

"How may I be of service, my lord?" Linford asked.

Jeffrey folded his arm so that his hand was behind his back and tapped eight times. "I have...struggled with...peculiar thoughts," he said.

"Ah," Dr. Linford said. "You've had another spell of the eight again?"

A spell, as if it was something brought on by the ingestion of too much wine or some such thing. "Yes."

Dr. Linford eyed him thoughtfully. "Has it to do with your recent nuptials, do you suppose?"

Now he was to name a reason for his degenerate thoughts? That it had been made much worse, *far* worse, by his marriage to a complete stranger? Yes, of course it had! "Perhaps."

"As it happens, I've done a bit of reading on your unusual situation," Linford said. "Not yours, precisely, but unnatural thoughts in general. My recommendation is that we attempt to purge the poisons that obviously lead to these thoughts with a bloodletting, and follow that with a course of laudanum to establish calm."

Jeffrey instantly recoiled at the mention of bloodletting.

"Just here," Linford said, pointing to his own neck. "To balance the humors and hopefully promote productive thought."

"No," Jeffrey said instantly. He recalled with some horror the bloodletting that had been done to his father as he laid on his deathbed.

"My lord, I cannot stress enough that it is entirely necessary. If you want to be free of it—"

"Yes, all right," Jeffrey said impatiently. If that's what it would take, he was willing to try it.

They arranged for the treatment to begin the next morning.

The bloodletting itself hardly registered to Jeffrey. Other than the nick where Linford cut him, he didn't feel anything leaving his body. He felt nothing but a little weak from it.

Dr. Linford left Jeffrey with two vials of laudanum and strict instructions on how he was to take the medicine. Jeffrey ate a bit of luncheon—he really had no appetite—then locked the door of his study, pulled a chair around to face the fire and sprawled onto the seat. He took the dosage Dr. Linford had prescribed and settled back, waiting for the medicine to take hold and calm his thoughts.

An hour or so later, he watched the flames in the hearth—huge, chimney-creeping flames—curve and curl into eights before his very eyes, then disappear, evaporating into smoke. Jeffrey counted sixteen of them. In that altered state, he believed he had been freed, that the eights were disappearing, one at a time. He was quite encouraged by it, even ecstatic. So much so that he took more of the laudanum, wanting to hasten it along.

But then shadows began to creep out of the chimney and march on the walls, on the ceiling, closing in on him, surrounding him. He thrashed at the shadows, but he seemed to have lost the ability to move his body efficiently.

There was no hope for him.

## CHAPTER FIFTEEN

GRACE LEARNED OF Jeffrey's abrupt departure from Hattie.

"Quite a ruckus this morning, mu'um," Hattie said as she puttered around Grace's rooms. "Julia Barnhill, she'd not do as Mrs. Garland asked, said she was brought on to clean the earl's rooms, not the parlors. But Mrs. Garland said that as his lordship's away, there's no cleaning for her to do, and she could surely help with household chores. She took the matter to Mr. Cox, and suddenly, Miss Barnhill is charity and grace, ready to serve." She puffed out her cheeks and shook her head. "Mrs. Garland, she doesn't care for that Miss Barnhill."

"His lordship has gone away?" Grace said, startled by the news.

Hattie colored. "Aye, mu'um, to Bath. So says Mr. Cox."

Grace went immediately to inquire of Cox, who confirmed Jeffrey had left early that morning. "When will he return?"

"His return is indefinite, madam."

Indefinite? Just like that, he'd up and left her without a bloody word? It made Grace quite angry. So angry that she wanted to kick something. Or scream. But as neither of those was practical, she came up with the idea to *change* something. She would not allow him to ruin the gains she'd made this week. She would take this opportunity to enhance the music room.

She asked Ewan to come to the attic storage with her and rummaged through stacks of paintings and furniture. In addition to finding some paintings for the music room, she was thrilled to find chairs for the dining room. They were upholstered in rich red velvet—not the plain brown wood of the chairs that she'd sat upon every night thus far. When she inquired why they were in storage, Ewan pointed to a dark stain on the master chair. "Someone spilled a bit of wine."

That was it—the chairs had been banished for a bit of wine. She wondered what else he had banished for being less than perfect. The thought of her mother popped into her head, and Grace's anger swelled alongside a vague sense of sorrow. How had perfection become so necessary to Merryton? How had he allowed it to rule him in an imperfect world? And how in heaven could she ever bridge the gap between his perfect order and her family? "It can be cleaned," she pointed out.

"Aye, mu'um. But his lordship said to take them away."

"Please have them cleaned and brought up to the dining room," she said confidently.

Cox was a bit disagreeable about it, insisting, when he found her in the music room, that his lordship did not care to have the red chairs. Or the yellow flowers she'd put in the vases. The more he mentioned what his lordship did not care for, the more Grace was determined to have them.

"Does he not?" Grace asked sweetly. "Then perhaps he shall return to his wife and tell her so himself." She smiled.

"Very well, madam," Cox said. The poor man appeared resigned to change at Blackwood Hall. "But the paintings," he said, referring to the two the carpenter was hanging. "He's been quite adamant that they not be hung. He does not care for them."

"He does not care for them to be misaligned," Grace corrected him. "And I haven't asked you to bring *all* the paintings from storage. Just these two." With that, she sat down and began to play the pianoforte, confident that would send Cox from the room.

She was right—he left straightaway.

Grace continued to pound away while Bother fought a feather that had appeared from heaven knew where.

Grace scarcely noticed what she was doing; her mind was swirling around Jeffrey's strange disappearance. He confounded her so completely! He was as ill-mannered as she'd first believed.

On the second day of his absence, Grace complained of it to Molly Madigan as she'd helped her take cuttings from the garden. "On my word, I don't understand him," she'd said as she angrily snipped a stem. "Could he not imagine I'd want to know that he'd gone? To ask him where he might be, what I was to do in his absence, how long he'd be away?"

"Yes, of course he should have imagined it, but I suppose he is not yet accustomed to having a wife to consider," Molly had said, as if it were all very simple. "For many years he has done as he pleased."

"Yes, well *that* is painfully obvious," Grace had grumbled.

"It may be difficult for you to see yet, but he is a considerate man."

Grace snorted.

Molly smiled and handed Grace a basket of yellow roses. "*All* men need to be prodded into good manners from time to time."

"But how? I can hardly *scold* him."

"Children often learn when the consequences of bad behavior are plainly evident."

"He's not a *child*," Grace scoffed.

"Oh, no…but I suppose all men are a bit childish, are they not? Were I you…"

"Yes?" Grace asked quickly, her gaze riveting on Molly, hopeful for any piece of advice.

Molly clucked her tongue and pretended to rummage about in her basket. "I've said too much. I would never advise you about such matters that concern your husband."

"No, of course not," Grace said, inching closer to her. "But if you were *me,* you would…?"

"Well," Molly said, "I suppose I'd go and find him."

Grace stared at her. The thought had not occurred to her.

Molly colored slightly. "As I said, I would *never* presume—"

"But you're absolutely right, Molly!" Grace said, filled with renewed determination. "How else will he know it will not do to leave without a word?" She laughed with delight. "Oh, but I can scarcely wait to see his face when I arrive in Bath."

Molly smiled uncertainly.

Once again, Cox was reluctant when she asked to have a coach brought around with a team of four and a driver.

"A coach, madam?"

"Yes, Cox. I am to Bath."

One of his eyes twitched. He cleared his throat, took a breath. "Allow me to inquire of the carriage house if one is available and if we have drivers."

Grace had anticipated his reluctance. "If there are no drivers, I will drive myself. I'm perfectly at ease driving a coach, did you know? I've driven them all over Longmeadow and Hyde Park." That wasn't precisely true—what Grace had driven were pony carts, and while Grace wasn't at all certain she could drive a team of four, she was not going to be put off.

Poor Mr. Cox looked very conflicted. She guessed he wished perhaps as much as she that Merryton would not disappear. Or perhaps he wished that she and her dog were the ones to disappear. She smiled sympathetically at him and said, "I'll just fetch my things."

As she began to walk away, Cox said, "Madam, if I may— I would be remiss if I allowed you to leave unattended. I can assure you his lordship would not approve."

"I agree *completely*," she said, and put a comforting hand on his arm. "Which is why I've asked Hattie to gather her things. Now, don't look so astounded, Cox.

I think Hattie is the sort who could be very useful if we found ourselves in a scrape. And we're only going as far as Bath." She patted his arm and walked on before he could think of any other reason to dissuade her.

HATTIE LOOKED AS unhappy as Cox when Grace met them on the drive with Bother in tow. She also looked a bit frightened.

"Come along, Hattie," Grace said. "In London, ladies may come and go as they please." That wasn't true, either, but certainly Grace and Honor had done so to the delight of many gentlemen about town.

Hattie looked up at Mr. Cox for affirmation of that fact.

"Mr. Cox does not hail from London and is not acquainted with the customs there," Grace said, linking her arm in Hattie's and turning her away from Cox's reproachful eye. "But I am. Now really, we must be away. It's not a short drive to Bath."

Hattie climbed into the coach. Grace followed her, waved cheerfully to Cox and knocked on the ceiling to signal the driver.

Grace was forced to do quite a lot of what her husband would call *nattering* on the way to Bath. After Hattie confessed she'd never been beyond Ashton Down, Grace understood her trepidation. She tried to put the maid at ease, but Hattie was anxious. So Grace talked. She talked until Hattie's chin dropped to her chest and she began to snore softly.

She leaned across the squabs to pet Bother, who sat with his paws on the window sash for most of the drive.

He seemed content to watch the passing countryside for rabbits or birds, occasionally lifting his snout in the air as if he'd detected something important.

Grace was uncertain what to expect in Bath—other than a tongue-lashing. She was fully prepared for that. But the thought had occurred to her that perhaps he was with a mistress. In spite of his claim to be a man who honored his vows, nothing else made sense. And his sudden disappearance had to make *sense*. He sought perfection in all things. Well, she sought reason.

Hattie woke just as they entered Bath, and she gasped at the sight of the much larger town, joining Bother to peer out the window.

The coach rolled slowly through the narrow streets, garnering the attention of pedestrians, many of whom stopped to watch it roll by. The coach eventually rolled to a halt in front of a first-rate town house on a picturesque square. Grace caught an anxious breath and grabbed Bother's lead. She landed on the sidewalk when the coachman opened the door, looked up at the door and squared her shoulders.

They were met at the door by the Bath butler, or rather, Grace was, as Hattie stood on the sidewalk. "Good afternoon," Grace said. "I am Lady Merryton."

The butler looked stunned. "Yes, *yes,* madam. Of course!" He bowed.

"Have you a name?"

"Tobias, my lady. I am the butler here. At your service." He bowed again as Bother sniffed around his shoes before lifting his leg against the boot scrape.

Tobias didn't seem to notice. At first Grace thought

that perhaps he was more accommodating than Cox, but then she realized that the gentleman seemed rather anxious. Grace smiled and tried to see past him. "Well, then, Tobias, will you leave me standing here, or allow me in to see my husband?"

Tobias blinked.

"He is here, is he not?"

"Ah…" The butler glanced over his shoulder, and Grace's heart sank. No wonder Tobias was acting so strangely. Jeffrey was here, with his mistress. Or worse. She didn't know what worse might be, but clearly, something was terribly amiss, and she felt ridiculous for having come all this way only to be humiliated.

"He is, madam, but he is…indisposed."

"Yes, I can guess that he is," she said. She turned around, gestured for Hattie. When Hattie was close enough, she put her hand on her arm and pulled her forward, almost thrusting her at Tobias. "Please show Hattie to our rooms and have our things brought in." She moved forward, forcing Tobias to move aside, and walked into the foyer.

"Yes, madam. If you will follow me," he said, gesturing to a drawing room on the right.

Grace pulled back. "No, thank you, Tobias. I should like to see my husband now."

She noted the slightest dip in Tobias's shoulders. "Yes," he said gloomily. He gestured for a footman to come forward, and instructed him to show Hattie up. "This way," he said softly, and led Grace and Bother to a door at the end of the hall. He rapped lightly on the door. "My lord!" He leaned forward, listening.

There was no answer.

Tobias rapped louder. "My lord!" he called again.

What was this happening here? Grace pushed past the butler and tried the door, but found it locked. "Have you a key?"

Tobias removed the keys from his pocket and turned the lock.

Grace pushed the door open. Bother darted past her and into the room. "Bother!" Grace called. She stepped inside, saw Jeffrey lying on the floor, and her heart seized with fear that he was dead. But then he groaned and moved.

Lord, was he *drunk?* She looked at Tobias for explanation, but Tobias had regained his composure and his expression was unreadable. "Thank you," she said. "I'll ring for you if I need you." She gestured for him to go. Tobias went reluctantly, his gaze on Jeffrey. Grace closed the door firmly when he'd gone out, and turned to look at Jeffrey on the floor.

Bother had his nose to the ground, his tail high as he examined the room. It looked as if there had been a fight in this room. Chairs were overturned and a candle had fallen and burned a hole in the carpet. One of the drapes hung haphazardly, and Grace had the odd image of Jeffrey swinging from it. Some piece of china—a figurine, she supposed—had been shattered at the hearth.

She moved slowly toward her husband, looking for an empty bottle of whiskey. And then she saw it—there, near his elbow, a brown vial. She knew precisely what sort of vial it was—the Lord knew they had given her mother enough laudanum to calm her over the past few months. Grace dipped down and picked it up. There was still liquid sloshing about inside. She tossed it into the embers.

Was he addicted to the laudanum, then? Was that the reason for his odd behavior? Was that the invisible wall he'd erected around himself? Grace had heard of it happening. She stepped over him, and spotted a bottle of whiskey lying on its side. She panicked, wondering if she had married a man who could not free himself of demons. And yet, that didn't seem like Jeffrey. She glanced down at him, lying on the floor. His brow was creased, as if he were in pain. His chin was covered with the stubble of his beard. How long had he been like this? The room was dank and smoky, leading her to believe it had been more than a few hours.

Bother had reached Jeffrey and was sniffing the leg of his trousers, then his face. He licked his cheek.

Jeffrey's eyes fluttered open. He scowled at the dog, then looked up at Grace with dull eyes. Where were the vibrant green eyes that always seemed to look straight into her? Grace didn't know what had happened to this man, but her heart went out to him. There was something bruisingly vulnerable in him, something quite sad. She crouched next to him and brushed a curl from his forehead. "Poor thing," she murmured.

He grimaced, gently pushed the dog away and then sat up. "Why are you here?" he asked, his voice rough.

"Here?" She looked around. "Do you mean *here,* in this room? Or do you mean here, in Bath? I think the answer is the same—I am here because my husband left without a word to me. What are *you* doing here, my lord?"

He closed his eyes a moment, as if he were pushing down his pain. "You shouldn't have come."

"Really? It looks to me as if you are fortunate that I have come. What has happened, Jeffrey?"

He shook his head. Bother nudged his hand, crawling onto his leg. Jeffrey didn't stop him.

"I don't understand you." Grace sighed, sliding onto her knees beside him. "For all I knew, you had abandoned me. I couldn't imagine why you would not have the courtesy to at least inform me you were leaving."

"Would it have made a difference to your displeasure?" he asked, and rubbed his temples.

Grace tilted her head to one side. "No," she said as she studied him. "It would have made for a different sort of displeasure entirely." She noticed a bandage on his neck and reached out to touch it. "Oh, dear, what happened?" He instantly recoiled and pulled her hand down from his neck.

"Something is wrong," she said again. "If you tell me, I will help you. I *want* to help you."

For some reason, that made him smile. He looked at her. He took her hand and lifted it to his lips, kissed her knuckles. And even though Grace was wearing gloves, she could feel that kiss seeping into her skin, leaving a sizzling little trail as it moved into her veins and flowed through her. He said, "You would not understand it."

"But I might." She squeezed his hand. "Whatever is the matter, you can't hide it forever, can you?"

"Don't press me, Grace," he said low, and came unsteadily to his feet. "You mean well, but you have no idea what you're doing."

"I know very well what *I'm* doing," she said, rising up beside him. "I'm trying rather desperately to be a wife to you. I am trying to find my way in this marriage, but it's very difficult because you keep insisting I don't understand, and then I find you like this."

"This is private—"

"I won't accept that, Jeffrey, I won't." She looked around at the broken room. "It's…it's *madness*—"

"Yes. It is," he said, his gaze casting about the room, too. "Bloody *madness*."

He started to move away from her, but Grace caught his arm, gripping it tightly. "I won't leave it, you know. I will follow you to the ends of the earth if that's what it takes to discover what secret you are hiding."

Jeffrey gave a bitter laugh to the ceiling and yanked his arm free of her. He pushed his hands through his hair, then found his waist and stared at her, swaying a bit unsteadily on his feet. "Very well, madam, you have demanded it. You have pushed me to the truth. Have you any idea what I want right now, this very minute?"

"A bath?" she said, arching a brow.

"I want you to kiss me. What you cannot possibly understand is how completely and *utterly* I desire you."

That proclamation was so unexpected that Grace was made speechless by it.

"I *desire* you," he said, and clenched his fist as he stepped closer to her. "God help me, how I do. But I don't desire you merely as a man desires a woman.

It is much more than that—it is far more *challenging* than that."

Quite honestly, Grace didn't know if she should be flattered or insulted. "That makes no sense."

He snorted derisively. "Nothing about me makes sense, you may as well know."

Good God, he *was* mad. "I don't understand!" she exclaimed, casting her arms wide. "Why should a man not desire his wife? What is the *matter* with you?" Grace cried.

"You see? I've only told you that I desire you completely and it daunts you."

"I am not daunted!" She suddenly threw herself at him with such force that he stumbled a bit with surprise. She put her arms around his neck, pressed her body against his and kissed him. Truly *kissed* him. She sank into him, her back curving as she melted against his body. She angled her head and opened her mouth, slipped her tongue into his.

Jeffrey's response was hard and immediate; he drew her tighter into his body, whirled them around and flattened her against the wall. His hand found her hip and roughly kneaded it, pulling her into him. He cupped one of her breasts, his fingers sinking into her flesh through her clothing.

His lusty response incited Grace—she was only beginning to understand the breadth of the power she could wield with just her body—and she pressed against him, moving her pelvis against his sudden erection. But at the same time, the pleasurable assault of his hands and his mouth on her made her weak; she splayed her arms against the wall and closed her eyes as his mouth moved on her skin. How had she become this woman? Not a fortnight ago, she could scarcely look at him. Now, she craved his touch, his attention—

He suddenly lifted his head and dropped his hands. He was breathing hard, and his eyes looked as if they were on fire. He dragged the back of his hand across his mouth. "For God's sake," he said through deep breaths, "don't challenge me, Grace. You don't understand what sort of beast you unleash—"

"Beast! Because you desire me? Because you want me to kiss you?"

"You are too young, too innocent, to understand," he said, and suddenly braced his hand against the wall at her head, dipping down and leaning into her, his eyes level with hers. "Heed me—I am a man for whom control is *difficult*," he said, the words sounding hard to say. "God, how do I make you understand? I lose control—look around you! I *lose control!* And this?" he said angrily, gesturing between the two of them, "this will never end with a kiss. I will only want more and more. I will want until you are spent, physically and emotionally. You have no idea what I am," he said roughly. "God hope you never find out."

He turned, and started to walk across the room. Grace whirled about and slammed her fist against the wall. Bother began to bark, and Grace instantly grabbed her hand and winced at the pain. The puppy began to paw at her skirts.

"What in God's name are you doing?" Jeffrey exclaimed, reaching for her hand.

Grace had never struck a wall in her life. Not when her sisters vexed her, not in all the fear and uncertainty her mother had aroused in her. But then again, she had never been so frustrated as this. "My patience is spent," she said angrily as he moved her fingers, one by one. "I have somehow managed to put myself in a marriage with the most impenetrable, intractable man in all of England! When I think of all the years before me in which I will be forced to live with whatever it is that ails you, without benefit of even understanding what it is, I can scarcely abide it!" She jerked her hand away from him and stretched her fingers long, then curled them.

"You're right," Jeffrey said, his voice gone soft, and shrugged. "Are you certain you want the truth? Can you bear it?"

Her heart skipped with apprehension, and for a slender moment, she wasn't certain she could bear it. But her burning desire to understand him quickly buried that uncertainty. "More than anything."

"Then you must prepare yourself, Lady Merryton, for your husband suffers from madness."

"Don't say that unless it's true."

He smiled ruefully. "It's true. I will tell you things that may repulse you, and I won't blame you if they do. But it doesn't change the truth."

"First you are a beast, and now you are mad? You're not *mad*—"

"I am ruled by the number eight."

Grace didn't think she heard him correctly. "Pardon?"

He smiled sadly, ran his hand over his hair again.

"Don't expect any of what I will tell you to make sense. I've been trying to make sense of it most of my life." He turned away from her and walked to the window, bracing himself with one arm against the frame. "I am *ruled* by the number eight."

"But…how can a number rule you?" she asked.

"It all seems quite simple to me, really. I am plagued with images," he said, gesturing to his head. "Immoral, vile images. Of…women," he admitted. "Of women pleasuring themselves…and pleasuring one another." He did not look at her, and Grace was thankful he didn't. She was certain the blood had rushed out of her face.

"It began as a young man, these images, these thoughts of vile acts with women, or in watching women. I began to imagine what I might do to a woman, and the images became more fantastic. Those thoughts, those visions, fire my blood." He glanced at her over his shoulder, his gaze flicking over her. "And when I look at you, my improbable wife, I see the most beautiful of women, and I can't stop the fear that I…that I will hurt you in the grip of my lust." He swallowed, and looked down.

"The only thing that can calm me, the only thing that can push the images away is the number eight. Counting, dividing, multiplying." With a heavy sigh, he shook his head. "It is madness."

Grace had truly believed he couldn't shock her, but he had. As if her mother's madness wasn't difficult enough, this was quite uncomfortable to hear. She sank down the wall, sliding to her haunches on the floor.

"I have been this way most of my life, although it

seems to have worsened with age and…and with solitude. It is beyond my ability to control these obsessive thoughts and these compulsions to count. I can't even explain to you why I have them. I only know that the less chaos in my life, the more symmetry—simple, clean lines, uniform color—the easier it is for me."

Suddenly so much of what Grace knew of him made sense. The lack of paintings, the single type of rose. Now she could almost see his struggle to maintain order at Blackwood Hall, to keep the secrets of his mind. She could see by the ravages of his face as he unburdened himself to her that it had taken a hard toll on him.

She also realized that he would never be able to accept her mother into his life. That realization wrapped around her heart and squeezed painfully.

"I have been fighting against the need for absolute perfection since I was a boy," he said. "I've always known it was unreasonable, but of late, it has become intolerable. My days are spent worrying that I might harm you, that I might coax you into an act of depravity that no young woman should ever have to endure."

She was to endure depravity? Grace looped her arm around Bother's neck, holding him close. Jeffrey sighed wearily, as if telling the truth had sapped him. She could see the desperation in his eyes for her to understand him, but at the same time, he seemed almost resigned that she would not. "I suppose it is little wonder to you now why I remain at Blackwood. Out of sight, undiscoverable, where I might control the urges. I come to Bath to take the waters on the very thin hope that will help. I go to London when I must, but I am truly comfortable only at Blackwood Hall."

"Is there no help for it?" she asked softly.

He smiled lopsidedly. "That's why I came to Bath. After our night together, I felt…uncontrollable. Linford performed a blood-letting to rid me of the poisons," he said, gesturing to his neck. "He gave me laudanum to calm my thoughts. It would seem that neither has done as he—or I—hoped."

It was all too much—Grace couldn't make sense of her thoughts. She pitied Jeffrey. She wanted to help him somehow, for he seemed so desperate and alone, and her heart truly went out to him. But at the same time, she possessed a fierce desire to protect herself, her family, her life. She didn't know what to make of what he'd told her, of the warning of depravity foisted upon her, of what that truly meant, precisely. And she couldn't help but wonder about any children born of this union. Would they, too, think vile thoughts? The very idea sent a shudder down her spine.

"You are revolted," he said quietly. "I can see it."

She wasn't revolted; she was disturbed. Deeply disturbed. Grace tried very hard to smile reassuringly but failed miserably. "I'm confused." She pushed up again, picked up Bother's lead. What did this mean for them now?

She needed to think. She needed a bit of time to absorb this and *think*.

She didn't even realize she was walking to the door until he said, "Where are you going?"

She looked at the door, then at him.

He winced as if he'd been struck by an inward pain. "If you want…" He swallowed. "If you want to leave, I will not stand in your way."

Did he mean the room? Or his life?

He grimaced again, and his fist closed tightly. "I will understand." He tapped it against his leg, eight times, and she wondered if it was so ingrained in him now that he didn't even realize he was doing it.

"I don't…I don't know what I mean to do," she said honestly. "I only know that it's been a long drive from Blackwood." It was hard to look at him, to see the need for acceptance in his eyes, particularly when she didn't know what she was capable of giving him. "I need to think, Jeffrey. It's quite a lot to take in."

"Of course." He averted his gaze.

"Come, Bother," she said softly, and went out of that wrecked room, her thoughts rushing ahead of her feet.

## CHAPTER SIXTEEN

GRACE HAD UNNERVED HIM. Jeffrey had been on a precipice after the blood-letting, and her unexpected appearance had pushed him off balance. It was a fact that he did not bear up well under surprises.

And yet, in spite of the failures of Dr. Linford's remedies, he felt a great relief in having unburdened himself to her. He hadn't realized how much he'd needed to say aloud what plagued him. It was the first time in his life he'd admitted his secret to anyone, and after a bath, and a bit of food in his belly, Jeffrey felt lighter than he had since his first encounter with Grace Cabot. He'd felt in control of his thoughts, of his habits. Perhaps all he'd needed was a bit of time alone, to absorb this sea change in his life. Perhaps he could navigate this marriage, after all.

No more secrets.

But God help him, Grace was never the same one day to the next. She'd been contrite and subdued in the beginning. Then angry. Then cheerful and spirited and quite awful on the pianoforte, and kind to useless dogs.

And now she was missing.

She'd gone out with the dog shortly after finding him as she had. "To walk," Tobias informed him.

She had not come back.

When she did not appear for the evening meal, Jeffrey could only assume the worst. Had she fled him, then? Had he horrified her so completely that she'd stolen away while he was in his bath? Jeffrey's feeling of lightness began to turn heavy. Now he wondered how he might endure the lack of predictability from her, if she returned to him. He thought of Mary Gastineau and how that marriage might have gone. Mary was timid and far more restrained than Grace. Bloody hell, entire squads of debutantes were far more restrained than Grace. He could safely assume that Mary would not have impetuously followed him to Bath.

He smiled a little at that, and imagined his golden-haired wife in the coach with Hattie and her dog, chattering as if it were a tea party.

But the waiting was impossible. He finally rang for Tobias. "Has she come yet?" he asked when Tobias appeared in the parlor.

"No, my lord," Tobias said. "Her maid informs me that she has dined at the home of Mr. and Mrs. Brumley."

The Brumleys, of course. They would wonder why he hadn't accompanied her, wouldn't they? God help him, what would she tell them? Were they gathered around her even now, their faces twisted with horror as she whispered the ugly truth about him? No, no… Grace wouldn't do that. He truly believed she did not want to hurt him, no matter what she might be feeling about him now.

Still, he felt uneasy, and debated going to fetch her,

to at least make an appearance. What would John do in a situation such as this? Jeffrey had always envied his brother's easy way with others, his ease as he moved through society. John was gregarious and very sociable, quick to please their guests.

Jeffrey could never seem to think of trite things to say. And given the sickness of his mind, conversation, even smiling, was quite difficult for him. He knew that people perceived him to be aloof and haughty, but it wasn't true. The truth was that he was frozen, locked into the madness that had consumed his life. In his life, society was the most dangerous ground he walked. In the presence of strangers and acquaintances, Jeffrey had to concentrate entirely on his affliction so that he'd not show any sign of it. He was painfully aware that madness, more than any other disability, could ruin this family and this prestigious name. More than scandal, more than frailty, more than lack of fortune, more than a failure to pay one's debts—nothing turned people away like the hint of madness. Society had a tendency to lock the maddest away in dungeons, leaving them to rot. Certainly no one in his lofty circles would allow a daughter to wed a madman, or the brother of a madman, for what if that taint was carried in the blood? Then even Sylvia's two young children, one of them a newborn, would be suspect.

Passing on his madness to a child was the worst thing Jeffrey could possibly imagine. The carnal pleasure he sought from Grace was made even more disturbing when he considered that, in every act, he risked creating a child that would be just like him.

And yet, he couldn't stop himself.

He had to go and get her. He dressed, nervously tying and untying a neck cloth before he was satisfied with it. He walked down to the foyer, and as he took his hat and crop from Tobias, the door opened and Grace walked in, the dog scampering ahead of her. Her cheeks were flushed, and she smiled a little uncertainly. "Bother and I had a bit of a walk. Rather, he dragged me around behind him."

"If I may, Lady Merryton, I'll take him around to the stables," Tobias said.

"Thank you." She handed the lead to Tobias. She dipped down, cooed to the dog and scratched him behind the ears before he was led away.

When Tobias and the dog had gone, Grace and Jeffrey were alone in the foyer. She eyed him nervously.

"Did you enjoy your evening?" he asked.

"Well," she said on a sigh, "Cousin Beatrice insisted I describe each room of Blackwood Hall in great detail. In *great* detail. Down to the number of candles and such."

Jeffrey arched a brow. "That is a lot of rooms and candles."

"Indeed it is. But I was effusive in my praise," she said with a funny little nod of her head. "I might have embellished a bit. I proclaimed it the grandest of houses and a favorite of the king's."

"The *king*," Jeffrey said, smiling.

"You are not acquainted with Beatrice. She likes things to be quite grand. You may trust that she adored the notion and was sitting so close to the edge of her seat that I feared she would topple over and smother poor Bother. And then I explained to Beatrice it was so grand that you'd given yourself a bit of an ague with the running of it. She sends her best wishes for your speedy recovery."

Jeffrey smiled with relief and gratitude that she hadn't divulged his true ailment. "Perhaps we might have a port," he suggested, and gestured to the parlor.

"Might we have tea?" she asked, her hand going lightly to her abdomen. "I've drunk enough wine this evening."

"I'll see to it," he said, and gestured for her to wait in the drawing room. When he returned, having asked for tea, Grace was still standing. She had removed her cloak and was wearing a gossamer green silk gown with a train that had been beaded with tiny crystals. Ah, but she was a beautiful woman, as beautiful as she was when lying naked in her bed, her skin cast gold from the light of the hearth. He admired her honey-colored hair, the plump pink lips, and could feel the vile thoughts crowding in at the edges of his brain. He glanced down, tapped his fingers together eight times.

When he looked up, she was watching him. "I wasn't certain you would return," he said.

"Quite honestly, neither was I." She brushed the back of her hand against her cheek, and looked absently at the window. "I spent the better part of the evening trying to understand what you have told me, and I can't seem to."

Jeffrey's heart sank a little. Of course she couldn't understand his madness. And Grace was too clever, too rational, to make sense of something so baffling.

"But as I thought about it, I realized that I had forced you into this untenable position, and then forced you to reveal your...dilemma. I won't abandon you with it now. I don't know what to think of it really...but I think you should know that I'm not afraid."

It was the kindest thing she might have said to him. He took as step forward. "Grace—"

"May I ask you," she said before he could say anything, before he could touch her, "is there anyone else who knows?"

He gripped his hand in a fist, and swallowed down his natural tendency to say nothing. "Linford knows perhaps a bit of it. My brother and sister suspect—John most of all. But no one knows the extent of it."

"I wonder, shall I ever be presented to your family, or am I a secret, as well?"

"You're not a secret," he said. "They will come in summer to escape the foul air in London. Much as I presume you might have moved to...Longmeadow, is it?"

She smiled. "You remembered."

"I remember everything you have said." He meant that quite earnestly.

"What will they think of me?"

"Pardon?"

"Your family," she clarified. "What will they think of me?" She was fidgeting with the tail of the ribbon that cinched the gown beneath her bodice. It was one of the rare shows of angst he'd actually seen from her.

They would think he'd lost his mind, certainly, for if there was one person in the family who could be depended upon to stay quite out of scandal, it was him.

But they would find Grace lovely, he had no doubt. "I believe they will say that fortune has smiled on me," he answered honestly.

Her eyes widened with surprise and she smiled with pleasure. "*Thank* you. I expect they'll think me quite shameful. Or worse. Now I must know if you intend to meet *my* family?"

Jeffrey didn't realize he was tapping his fingers until Grace shifted closer and took his hand. She looked up at him, her eyes curious but kind as she linked her fingers with his to keep him from tapping.

Tobias entered with the tea service, and Grace's fingers fluttered away from his. She moved to the mantel and lit another candle as Tobias arranged the tea and biscuits.

"Thank you, that will be all," Jeffrey said, and waited until his butler had gone out.

"I rather like this room," Grace said, glancing around as Jeffrey poured tea for her, her gaze steady on his face. "It reminds me of a room at Longmeadow, a small parlor where my mother liked us to dine, informally. She said that allowed her to mind our table manners more closely." She smiled at the memory, then looked at him again. "What of *your* mother? You've said nothing about her."

Jeffrey didn't remember much about his mother. She had spent most of his youth in her bed, suffering from this illness or that. He believed that the truth was that she'd been too idle, and had grown accustomed to the art of lying about. Which came naturally when one drank brandy as she did.

"My mother did not concern herself with children," he said matter-of-factly. He looked down at his plate, suddenly plagued with a hard memory. His father had been angry with him for something that Jeffrey couldn't even recall any longer and had locked him in a cupboard. Jeffrey remembered calling out to his mother. *Mamma!* He would count to eight and call again. And again. His mother never came. No one came. It had been hours before his father returned to free him.

"I don't recall her very well at all," he said, more to himself than to Grace, and gestured for her to sit, handing her a cup of tea.

"Oh, dear…I'm sorry."

He shrugged indifferently as he sat beside her on the settee.

"I *am* sorry," she said. "I can't imagine it. My mother, she…" She suddenly looked away, to the hearth. "She has been the kindest, most loving of mothers." She said nothing for several moments and seemed lost in her own thoughts, her finger going around and around the rim of her teacup. "Do *you* wish for children?"

A bitter taste filled his throat. He wished for whiskey and abruptly stood, walking to the sideboard. "I am obliged to produce an heir," he said as he poured whiskey into a tot.

"Do you want children merely because you are obliged?"

"That is a difficult question to answer," he said truthfully, and tossed the whiskey down his throat, and poured another. "I am clearly obliged. It is the only thing that is truly expected of me, barring any natural impediments." He turned back to her. "But I don't *wish* for children, Grace. How could I wish for them, knowing what afflictions I might pass to them?"

"Well, I should like to be surrounded by my children, to raise a large and happy family, with much love and laughter. I would not like to spend my days with no one to care for."

She looked at him expectantly, and Jeffrey thought it quite clear that she wanted him to agree, to want the same thing. If he'd been anyone other than a man who had to count to eight to endure life, or could not erase from his mind the images of her with her legs spread open to him, he might have offered her that reassurance. He resumed his seat next to her. "Do you want them yet, given what I've told you?"

She steadily held his gaze, her eyes seeking something in him. "It gives me pause, I won't deny it," she admitted. "But I have faith, and yes, I want them." She nibbled a biscuit. "Will you describe the images?"

The request caught him off guard. He was doing his best to be open with her, but there were some parts of him he could scarcely look at, much less reveal. He could not look in the seas of her eyes and say aloud the voracious and vile thoughts he'd had about her.

Grace suddenly put aside her teacup and leaned forward, framing his face with her hands. "I don't fear them, Jeffrey. I don't fear anything about you."

Jeffrey closed his eyes and swallowed hard.

*"Jeffrey,"* she whispered, her voice a soft whisper, floating in past the torrid thoughts, the overwhelming urge to count. "Help me understand."

"They are how I desire you," he heard himself say. "The incomprehensible and debauched manner in which I *desire* you." He opened his eyes, grabbed her hand and kissed her palm. "The images," he said, gesturing at his head, "are shocking."

"Images of what?"

"Grace, I beg of you, don't push me. I have been as honest with you as I know to be."

She shook her head. "I don't understand how a man's desire for his wife can be *debauched*."

"Because you are too innocent to understand what depravity exists in this world."

She drifted back away from him, her gaze steady on his, studying him. "I may be innocent, but I'm not naive, Jeffrey. I've heard tales—"

"You've heard nothing like this," he said quickly, and stood up, walking to the sideboard again. "I desire you in ways that could harm you."

"But you haven't harmed me in the least. The obsession with it is not real."

"By the sheer nature of the acts I imagine, I harm you."

She frowned a little, as if trying to make sense of that. She stood up, taking a tentative step toward him. "Tell me how you would harm me. I have a right to know."

His blood was churning with regret, with desire, with a torrent of emotions that had been bottled up and tucked away all his life. They were building to a boil, and he could feel the danger of them boiling over. He drew a breath, clenched his hands tightly. "I imagine you bound and gagged," he said flatly. "You cannot either move or speak."

Grace paused. "Am I clothed?"

"In the beginning. But then I remove them, laying you bare to me." He swallowed, hard, his mind filling with that image.

Grace's chest rose. "Go on," she said.

"Your…your arms are tied over your head," he said, gesturing to her hands. "Your legs are spread apart."

Grace bit her bottom lip. "And then?"

"And then," he said, moving closer to her, "I reach inside you with my fingers," he said, holding up two together, and mimicked sliding inside of her, "to ascertain if you are enjoying your bondage."

"Am I?" she asked, tilting her head back to look up at him.

"Yes." He tilted his head next to hers and whispered, "And then I reach for my riding crop." He heard the soft intake of her breath. "I use it for something other than its express purpose."

Grace slightly turned her head toward him. "To hurt me?"

His lips grazed her temple. "No. To see your undiluted pleasure. But I fear, in my zeal, I will harm you."

She stood for a moment, then moved away from him. He thought he'd gone too far—she was moving to the door. But she went to the table and picked up the riding crop he'd laid next to his hat. She turned around with it in her hand. "Show me," she said.

"Grace, no—"

"Jeffrey Donovan, I should rather my husband desire me so much that he fears it will harm me than not desire me at all." She tossed the crop at him, forcing him to catch it. She reached behind with both hands and began to unbutton her gown. Her bodice came loose, and she pushed the gown from her shoulders, stepping out of it. She was not wearing a corset, only a chemise underneath.

"*Show* me," she said again.

He could not have been more aroused if she'd put her mouth on his cock and twirled her tongue around the tip. He gripped the crop tightly, then flicked it lightly against the tip of her breast.

Grace lowered her head, pushed her chemise down. It drifted to the floor, too, and now she stood before him, starkly naked, her skin cast glowing in the light of the hearth, the thatch of hair between her legs as golden as the hair on her head.

Jeffrey was lost now, falling into the pit of his desires. He traced a line across her chest to the other breast, and flicked the end of the crop against the tip. Both peaks were rigid now. Grace gave him a sultry smile. He shifted to her right, tested the crop against her bottom. Grace hopped a little when he did, and turned eyes blazing with heat to him.

"How do you find it, Lady Merryton?" he muttered, and slapped the crop against her again.

"Interesting," she said. She drew another deep breath as he moved the crop in between her hips, sliding in between her legs. He stepped up behind her, put his hand on her waist and leaned down, nibbling her shoulder.

Grace twisted around in his arms. She reached for

his neck cloth, quickly undoing the knot and drawing it free. She held up the neck cloth. "Bind me."

"No," he said, but Grace pressed the neck cloth into his hand, then stepped back and pulled the pins free from her hair. Gold hanks of hair fell down around her shoulders. She lifted her hands, her wrists pressed together. "Bind me, Jeffrey."

Jeffrey looked at her delicate hands, uncertain if he should leave or allow this young woman, this innocent, to convince him that there was no depravity in him. He didn't know if he had the strength to deny himself; his cock was already straining against his trousers.

It was no use. He was going to take her here. He was going to toy with her, then plunge into her. "Touch yourself," he commanded.

"Pardon?"

He flicked the crop against her breast again, only a bit harder this time. "You want to know what my desire is? Then *touch* yourself."

She hesitantly lifted her hands to her breasts.

It was hardly anything at all, but Jeffrey found it strangely erotic. Grace slowly spread her fingers across her breast, squeezing her stiffened nipples between them, and Jeffrey could almost feel her fingers on his nipples.

He yanked his collar free of his neck and tossed it aside. He pushed away from the door and started walking toward her. "Slide your hand down, between your legs."

Grace did as he instructed, her hand moving slowly over the soft plane of her abdomen, slipping in between her legs. She lifted her head slightly, as if the sensation of it had pricked her.

Jeffrey reached her, ran his hands down her sides. He let his gaze slide down her body, taking in the dark aureoles of her breasts, the hardened nipples, the goose skin of her arms. He took one of her hands, then the other, and bound them with his neck cloth. Her eyes sparked as a seductive smile curved on her lips. Jeffrey brushed her hair back from her face. "You amaze me," he murmured.

He turned her about, then guided her to bend over the settee, her bottom exposed to him, and slapped the crop against it.

Grace made a sound—of distress? Of pleasure? He panicked a moment, but then Grace turned her head and looked at him. "You see?" she said silkily. "You've not harmed me."

He lifted his gaze to her, and myriad images, all of them starkly prurient, rushed through his brain. He slapped her again with the crop, then tossed it aside. He could scarcely draw his breath now. A flame had ignited in his groin. He bent over her. "Spread your legs." He slipped his hand between them, his fingers into her slit.

He felt vibrant, animated, and pushed her bound hands up, high over her head. She was stretched over the arm of the settee and across it now, a feast for him. *"Yes,"* he breathed, his mind racing, his body moving ahead of his thoughts. "Now close your eyes."

Grace did as he bid her. "You are forbidden to open them," he said. He grabbed her chin in his hand and leaned down so that he was only a moment from her lips. "Are you afraid?"

"No."

He dipped his finger in a pot of honey that had come with the tea service and first painted her lips with it, then spread a line of it down her back, to her hips. He rubbed it against the pink patches of skin where he'd spanked her with the crop. He watched her dip the tip of her tongue to taste it, then scrape her teeth over her bottom lip, the honey into her mouth.

It was wildly erotic, and she seemed quite at ease with his play. He didn't hold his desire—there was nothing left for him but to have his way with her. That notion seemed decadent to him, but at the same time, it felt incredibly freeing. Exhilarating. He could feel her body quivering with anticipation beneath his. He could feel his own heart pounding with it, as well.

A bit of honey ran down her hip; Jeffrey sucked it from her skin. He applied honey to more of her, licking it and sucking it from her skin. When he bit her, Grace moaned and lifted to him, and the tremor of lust rattled all the way to Jeffrey's feet.

He continued the honeyed assault on her skin, working his way down between her legs, lapping honey from her slick sex as she gasped and squirmed against him. "Untie me," she said breathlessly.

He thought he'd gone too far and felt the apologies and self-loathing, begin to form. He stood up, quickly undid the tie and held his hands up, surrendering. "I beg your pardon. I knew—"

Grace made a clucking sound. She slid off the table

and ran her hand over it, finding the pot of honey. She dipped two fingers into the pot, and with her gaze on him, she reached for his cock, smearing the honey over the tip.

Jeffrey's breath caught in his throat as Grace dipped her fingers into the pot again and smeared it down his chest, his abdomen, following the trail with her mouth, nibbling and licking him as he'd done to her.

The effect was staggering; Jeffrey fell back onto the settee as his chest rose with each sharp, steadying breath. She pushed him, forcing him into a chair, and sank between his legs.

"Grace," he said, but he lost his intended warning when she took him in her mouth. Her tongue swirled around him, and she moved her lips as if tasting him, driving him to madness, until Jeffrey could bear it no more. He suddenly grabbed her, lifting her up, surging with her and putting her on the table. He kissed her almost desperately as he pushed into her. His entry was a shock of raw pleasure; his breath came out in one long and heavy sigh. His hand slipped from her breast to her sex, and he was moving deep and hard into her, pushing her toward release with his body and his fingers.

She came with an animal cry, one arm flailing, knocking something to the floor, shuddering violently with her release and drawing an explosive one from him. Jeffrey fell headlong into pure rapture.

Several moments passed as he clawed his way back to the present. When the fog of ecstasy had cleared, he staggered back into the chair at the table, pulling Grace into his lap.

She kissed his cheek, licked a bit of honey from his mouth and laid her head on his shoulder.

He stroked her hair, overwhelmed and amazed by what had just happened between them. There truly had been nothing to fear…at least not yet. He'd only touched on the edges of his thoughts. The images that would come later would consume him.

It dawned on Jeffrey in that shiny afterglow that perhaps his concern had been misplaced all along. Perhaps he was the one who should fear his thoughts.

# CHAPTER SEVENTEEN

GRACE WORE JEFFREY'S shirt and sat cross-legged on the floor before the hearth. Wearing only his trousers, Jeffrey was stretched long on his side before her. There was a plate of biscuits between them, but the tea had gone cold, and instead, they sipped wine from two small tots.

Grace's hair, a bit sticky in one tress, felt wild to her, hanging loose down her back and front. She felt warm, relaxed and ravenous.

Jeffrey was circumspect, watching her eat the biscuits with her fingers as if she'd been living in the woods. In a strange way, Grace felt as if she'd just emerged from the woods. She felt exuberant, alive, invincible and a bit smart, too, as she believed she had reached this mysterious man. She had climbed a mountain in the past twenty-four hours, and honestly, it had been far more enjoyable than it had sounded.

"Aren't you hungry?" she asked him, and playfully forced a bite of biscuit into his mouth. He smiled, stroked her cheek, his green eyes full of uncharacteristic warmth.

She leaned over the biscuits and kissed him, biting his bottom lip a bit. He caught a rope of her hair in his hand and wrapped it around his knuckles, touching it to his nose. "Does it smell of honey?" she asked him.

"A bit."

"I rather liked it," she said with a coy smile. "It wasn't the least bit vile. Nor was I afraid. Or particularly shy." She laughed at that, having only just realized it herself. "So you may put your mind at ease, Lord Merryton."

"Would that it were that simple," he said. "The problem will come to me later. My thoughts…" He shook his head. "I will begin to see images and believe that what happened was worse than the truth. My mind plays these tricks on me." He sighed, and laced his fingers with hers, his thumb caressing her knuckles. He seemed reticent now, and she sensed he was withdrawing into that place where he kept her at arm's length.

Grace was desperate that he not do that. She leaned across the space between them and looked into his eyes. "Please don't go, Jeffrey," she pleaded.

"I won't leave you," he said. "I shouldn't have done so—"

"I don't mean that." She pushed the plate aside and shifted onto her stomach, propping herself up on her forearms, her face only a few inches from his. "I mean, don't go from here and now. From us. You must see that I don't fear you. You mustn't believe that you might somehow harm me. I'm quite sturdy."

His smiled deepened. "You are very sturdy."

"And you aren't afraid for me or of me."

He tucked a strand of hair behind her ears. "The only time I am afraid of you is when you take the pianoforte."

Grace's eyes widened with surprise, and then she

laughed. "Do my ears deceive me? Does my husband *jest?*"

He lowered his head and kissed her. "Thank you, for allowing me to be candid. But no one must ever know, Grace. If it were even suspected, any children born of our marriage would be suspect. My sister's children would be suspect. My brother's unborn children. You understand."

Grace's eyes fluttered slightly. She thought she should tell him about her mother, just put it in the open as he had done, but somehow in that unguarded moment, having made the gains she had...

"My family can't endure another scandal," he said, tracing his finger across her mouth. "I fear the damage that has already been done. To add madness to it would forever seal it for my niece and nephew, I think."

How did she tell him that madness had already touched his family in marrying her? Would he retreat from her? Would he forgive her? She ought to tell him, she knew she ought to say it, but she feared losing all that she'd gained this night. She decided she needed to think about how to tell him—but before she could, Jeffrey kissed her, and he sank his fingers into her hair, pulling her closer. Before she could even form a coherent thought in her head, he had rolled her onto her back, was at her breast. She stretched her arms above her head, her lips curling into a smile of pure pleasure as his mouth and hands began to move on her once more.

THEY LEFT FOR Blackwood Hall the next morning. This time, Jeffrey rode in the coach with Grace and Hattie and the dog. Grace was buoyant and chatted the entire way, as if she felt obliged to do so. Jeffrey was grateful for it, as he would have seemed rude to Hattie in his inability to participate to carry a conversation, no matter how benign. For her part, Hattie stayed glued to the window with the dog, pressing herself against the wall of the coach, obviously feeling terribly out of place with him.

Grace was clearly determined not to let a moment of silence pass between them. She talked about the weather, and her theories concerning it. She spoke of the last ball she'd been to in London before her stepfather had passed, and cataloged what everyone had worn. Jeffrey noted that she seemed to be inordinately interested in clothing. She remarked that Beckington House routinely hosted suppers of four-and-twenty and then took the time to name the guests that were often in attendance.

By the time they reached Blackwood Hall, she seemed to have exhausted herself with all the chatter. Hattie very nearly sprinted into the house.

"My lord," Cox said, greeting them on the drive as Jeffrey helped Grace from the coach. "So glad that you have arrived. Mr. Ainsley, a solicitor from London, has come down."

"To Blackwood Hall?" Jeffrey asked, trying to recall any correspondence he might have seen warning him of it.

"Yes, my lord. He says it is a matter of some urgency."

Jeffrey looked at Grace. She smiled. "It's such a

beautiful day. I think I should like to ride. Shall I see you at supper, then?"

"Yes," he said, and took her gloved hand and kissed it.

"Where is he?" he asked Cox.

"In the library, my lord."

Jeffrey knew straightaway the matter Mr. Ainsley had come to address was not a pleasant one, given his solemn demeanor when he greeted Jeffrey and the nervous manner in which he handed him a letter. It had been penned by Sir Edmund Read, whom Jeffrey did not know. Sir Edmund wrote that he had retained Ainsley to collect a debt. He claimed that Lord Amherst owed him nine hundred pounds in unpaid gambling debts and that attempts at collection of the debt from Lord Amherst had not been successful.

Jeffrey's pulse had begun to pound at his temples— he had not seen or heard from John since the night in Bath when he'd watched his brother slip out of the abbey during the performance. Jeffrey had sent his own solicitor to find his brother when it became apparent he'd have to marry Grace, but John had disappeared, presumably into the salons of London.

Jeffrey folded the letter eight times into a small square as Mr. Ainsley looked on. "Nine hundred pounds is quite a lot of money," he said. He resisted the urge to crush the letter in his hand as a swell of anger began to push up through his veins.

"It is a large sum indeed, my lord. I've no doubt you understand Sir Edmund's desire to have the debt paid."

"Of course." Jeffrey didn't understand how a man

could give his word and then fail to honor it. He thought of his father, how angry he would have been with John. How he might have accused him of single-handedly destroying the integrity of the Merryton seat. Ah, but now John had Jeffrey in his company.

"You may tell Sir Edmund that I find this matter entirely reprehensible. My father would be quite disappointed in my brother."

"If I may say, my lord, your respect for propriety and decency is well known, which is why Sir Edmund felt comfortable in sending me to you."

Jeffrey flinched inwardly at his own hypocrisy. He wasn't decent. He was indecent. "I'll write a bank draft," Jeffrey said. "Will that suffice?"

"Of course, my lord. No one has reason to doubt the word or deed of the Earl of Merryton." He smiled.

Jeffrey could scarcely speak—the fury of having to clean up his brother's mess once more was sticking like dirt in his throat. He sat at his desk and prepared his draft. He thought of his rudderless brother, flitting from one woman's bed to the next gaming hell with no regard for the debts he amassed and the trouble he stirred.

Jeffrey was reminded, as he dipped the pen in the inkwell eight times, that Sylvia had once told him he was too hard on John, that what John lacked in moral fiber he made up in kindness. Jeffrey was not inclined to agree. He himself suffered privately from moral turpitude, and yet he struggled each day to atone for it. John suffered nothing. He did not atone. He did not care.

He handed the bank draft to Ainsley and thanked him for his candor and his respect for the family's privacy. Something in that made Ainsley look at him strangely. He turned to go, but he paused at the door and looked back at Jeffrey. "If I may, my lord?"

Jeffrey nodded, wishing the man would take his leave.

"I have the sense that you are not aware of your brother's…" He paused, seeming to think the better of what he would say.

"My brother's what?" Jeffrey asked.

Mr. Ainsley took a breath. "I think it is common knowledge around Mayfair that your brother has sired a child."

The news stunned Jeffrey. It should not have been unexpected given John's history, but nevertheless, it caught him completely off guard. He unthinkingly began to tap at his thigh. "A child," he said flatly.

"Forgive me I have overstepped, but you are a man of good character and it seems obvious to me you have been kept in the dark."

Jeffrey had to force himself to speak. He could not trust this man, could never trust a man who would take it upon himself to bring up such a highly personal matter. "Thank you, Mr. Ainsley."

Mr. Ainsley nodded, and his gaze swept over Jeffrey, as if he was assessing him, judging him by some unstated standard.

When he had gone, Jeffrey collapsed into a chair. A *child*. He would kill John. With his bare hands wrapped around his throat, he would kill him.

He had to get to London straightaway.

He reviewed some correspondence that could not

wait, then went in search of Grace. "She is riding around the lake, my lord."

"Alone?" Jeffrey asked as he fit his gloves on his hand.

"Not alone, my lord. The *dogs* have accompanied her," Cox said, clearly disapproving.

"Dogs?" Jeffrey asked curiously.

"It would seem there is yet another one saved from Mr. Drake. This one has a bad leg."

Jeffrey rode down to the lake in search of his wife. He spotted her easily enough; she was racing recklessly around the lake path, the hem of her blue riding habit flying behind her. Bother was racing after the horse, and behind Bother, another dog, lurching along on what looked like only three legs. Normally, the asymmetry of the dog's legs would have been enough to disturb Jeffrey, but he was far too disturbed by Grace's riding. He watched as she reined up hard and wheeled the horse about before trotting back to where Bother had paused to stick his snout into some bushes. That's when she saw Jeffrey, and waved.

"I'm so glad you've come!" she called out to him as he rode around to where she had paused. "Is it not a glorious day?"

"I saw you riding," he said. "You are far too reckless, madam."

She clucked her tongue at him. "You sound like most every man I've ever known. What is the point in riding if you mean to meander along?"

"Perhaps keeping your neck in one piece?" he suggested.

She laughed at him. "You are a man who likes to ride—would you care to race?" she asked, her impertinent smile challenging him.

"That is an imprudent and scandalous thing for you to suggest," he said. "But if you insist—" He suddenly charged past her, bent over the neck of his horse. With a squeal of delight, Grace was quickly after him.

He was an excellent rider, and she couldn't catch him. She at last slowed her mount, and laughed aloud as she tried to catch her breath. Jeffrey turned his horse about and trotted back to her.

"You win!" she breathlessly proclaimed. "And I've lost my bonnet."

"We'll fetch it on the way back. I see you've gained another dog," he said, watching the second one happily hop forward with a mangled leg.

"She was going to be a surprise," Grace said with a wince. "Mr. Drake said she's been made useless after she was caught in a trap."

The dog sat back on her haunches and stared up at Jeffrey, her tail swishing the dirt behind her as her injured paw twisted strangely before her. Jeffrey had to look away—the sight of the paw facing to one side was enough to make discord reverberate through him. "She can scarcely walk."

"Not perfectly, but she can walk," Grace said quickly. "I mean to fix her."

"Some things can't be fixed."

"Perhaps not, but everything deserves at least the attempt."

Jeffrey smiled. "You are determined, aren't you?"

He swung down off his horse and helped Grace off of hers. As she shook out her skirts and tucked strands of hair into her wind-ravaged braid, he led the horses to the edge of the river to drink their fill. The injured dog waded into the water and did a strange sort of swim in a circle. Without her front leg, she was incapable of swimming a straight line. But she seemed undaunted.

When Jeffrey returned to the path, Grace had climbed up on a rock and had drawn her knees into her chest, her arms wrapped around them, her face turned up to the sun. Jeffrey removed his coat and draped it across the grass, stretching out on his back, his feet crossed at the ankles, his arms pillowing his head and his hat covering his face. He couldn't remember the last time he'd done this—when he was a boy, he supposed.

Bother came around, sniffed his neck and ears, then lay down beside him.

"I'll be happy for summer," Grace said with a sigh. "My sisters and I used to swim in the lake at Longmeadow. We were forbidden to do it, but the summers could be so hot." She leaned forward. "We removed our gowns and swam in our chemises," she said low. "And then we'd lie in the grass as you are doing until they dried. But one day, the gamekeeper stumbled upon us." She laughed and straightened up. "He was quite scandalized."

Jeffrey sat up, propping one arm on a knee. "Creating mischief even then, were you?"

"Well, not intentionally," Grace said. "We always wanted to do the right things. It's just that sometimes the right thing is very hard to do." She winked at him.

"That is something the guilty would say," he suggested with a smile of amusement.

"My mother was determined to keep us well occupied so that we'd not be tempted. Prudence was particularly good at music, so she was given music lessons. She is a pleasure to hear, really. Mercy, the youngest, well—she's got a very bright imagination," she said with a roll of her eyes. "But it runs to the macabre. Ghosts and ghouls and the like."

"Ah."

"My mother put her into art lessons, for we discovered she has a very fine eye. And then, of course, there is Honor. She is older than me by one year. Mamma said the first Cabot girl into society makes the strongest impression and she enrolled her in Mrs. Abbot's School for Etiquette. I would never tell her, for my sister is awfully proud of her accomplishments, but Honor is very good at whatever she likes. It was rather maddening to be her younger sister."

"And what is your talent?" Jeffrey asked.

"Mine?" Grace said with a shrug. "I don't quite know. I suppose I'm pleasant enough. I enjoy math and geography and French, but doesn't everyone? I have saved a pair of dogs," she said, looking at Bother.

The dog thumped his tail.

She suddenly hopped off the rock. Bother was instantly on his feet, his tail wagging with happy anticipation. "My mother wanted us to be fine dancers," she said, and stepped over Jeffrey into the middle of the grassy bank. She picked up her skirts and dipped to one side, then the other. "She said that girls who danced well married well, for gentlemen did not care to be saddled to poor dancers."

She went up on her toes and twirled about; Bother leaped around her, thinking she meant to play. The lame dog lay down, her head between her paws, watching.

"I've never heard such a thing," Jeffrey said. "I can assure you that no one has ever advised me to choose a proper dancer."

Grace dipped again. "Then what *did* they advise you, Lord Merryton? To study the size of a debutante's dowry? To closely examine her father's connections?" She held her arms up overhead and twirled.

Jeffrey came up on one elbow to watch her. "They must have," he said. He came to his feet and took her hand, put his other hand behind his back and began to perform the figures of a familiar country dance.

"Then I suppose it's possible that we might have been married the proper way."

Jeffrey smiled. "I rather doubt it," he said, and Grace laughed.

"Oh, but you're a fine dancer!" she said as she moved alongside him, rising up on her toes, and down, back two steps, forward four.

"I'm not. You're attempting to flatter me."

"Perhaps a bit," she said with a winsome smile. "A bit of practice, and you'd be as light on your feet as Lord Grey, who I think must fancy himself something of a *premier danseur noble*," she said, referring to the ballet.

Jeffrey laughed. It was impossible to believe that he, of all people, was dancing on the grassy bank of the lake. He was also aware that he hadn't tapped his finger once since he'd found Grace this afternoon. He felt perfectly at ease, his mind free of the images for the time being. When he ended their dance with a kiss, it was a gentle one. Long and lazy, playful and tender, just like that afternoon.

He hated that he had to go to London. "I've something to tell you," he said as they stood, their arms around each other, swaying to a rhythm only they could hear. "There has been some trouble with John, and I must go to London on the morrow."

Grace's smile faded. "What trouble? Is he all right?"

Her question rudely reminded him that she had come to him by mistake. He had not wondered until now how she felt about his brother. "He's all right."

"What's happened?"

"Nothing to concern you," he said, perhaps a bit more briskly than he intended. He didn't want her to be concerned about John. Not in any way.

"I'll come with you—"

"No," he said. "I must go quickly. I'll ride."

She grabbed his arm tightly. "Don't go, Jeffrey. Not yet."

He didn't know what she meant by *yet,* but he quickly sought to reassure her. "Grace, I'm coming back. But there is a matter that requires my immediate attention."

She looked as if she wanted to say something, but Bother began to bark and she turned to see what had his attention. A reed, moving in the afternoon breeze, was the culprit, but whatever Grace intended to say was lost.

She said nothing more about it that day. It wasn't until the night, after Jeffrey had come to her, after she had suggested he tie her to the bedposts and have his way with her, that she mentioned it again.

She was lying on her stomach, her legs bent at the knees and crossed at the ankles, toying with his discarded collar. Jeffrey was entirely sated, his body heavy from the release of passion. He was making a deliberate and intricate path of kisses down her spine and to her hips, his hand sliding between her legs, dipping into the wet of their lovemaking.

"Must you go?" She lifted her head and closed her eyes, sighing with pleasure as he moved his fingers into her.

"I must," he muttered, far more interested her body than in his trip to London.

"Why can't I come?"

"I shan't be there long. By the time you've gathered what you will need, I will have returned. Why do you have such a strong desire to go on such a quick trip?" he asked. He waited to hear if his brother's name fell from her lips.

Grace glanced over her shoulder at him. "Isn't it apparent? I miss my sisters terribly. I won't need much. But I need my family."

His belly seized a little at the prospect of meeting her sisters. He had found a way to be comfortable in Grace's presence, but he worried what he might be in front of her family. He brushed her hair from her back and kissed her neck, but Grace shifted up, pushing away from the bed. She turned around and sat before him on her knees. Her breasts looked heavy and ripe, and he couldn't resist palming one.

"I *need* to see them," she said. "You could go on the morrow as you planned. I could come the following day, in the coach."

"Grace…a coach will require a day and a half. It's a long journey for a very short visit."

"They are the most important people in my life and I've gone weeks without them. I won't go out into society. I just want to see them. Will it really be so difficult?"

"It's quite a long way—"

"I mean, will it be difficult for *you*," she said, and touched his hand.

It was amazing that she had come to understand his illness so quickly. He looked at her hand, covered it with his. "Yes," he said. "But I understand. You may come for a few days—"

Grace squealed with delight and flung her arms around his neck.

"*Only* a few days," he said, catching her. "I can't… It's difficult to be in London longer than that." He didn't tell her that the chaos of that town would wreak havoc on his counting, particularly coupled with John's problems. He dreaded the prospect of it.

"Yes, yes, only a few days," she said, covering his face with kisses.

Jeffrey twisted her about, onto her back. She sighed as he sank down to her breast, playfully biting her. He could feel her fingers in his hair, twisting a curl around.

"And besides, you would miss me far too much if you left me here."

He squeezed her breast in his hand, kneading the

flesh. The remarkable thing was that he *would* miss her. "Yes," he said, and slid his hand down between her legs again, slipping his fingers inside her. *"Yes,"* he said again. "I would."

## CHAPTER EIGHTEEN

GRACE SAW JEFFREY off the next morning wrapped in his dressing gown with her hair spilling about her. They'd made love well into the morning hours, and she could scarcely keep her eyes open. He cupped the back of her head in his hand and kissed her eight times before finally walking out of her rooms.

She fell back against the pillows with a smile curving on her lips as she burrowed under the covers once more and drifted back to half slumber, her mind playing through the hours now spent in his company.

She was discovering the meaning of conjugal bliss. Jeffrey was teaching her things about her body she had never imagined. And he was teaching her about his body, too. He had taken her into his secret world, always apologetic for it.

But Grace took no offense. She wanted only to experience more of what he could teach her.

A light rap on her door was followed by the opening of it. "Good morning, my lady," Hattie said. "A letter has come for you."

Her eyes flew open; she sat up and reached for the letter Hattie had put on the bed table. She recognized the handwriting as Honor's.

After her greeting and well wishes, Honor wrote:

I'm aching for news of you! I fear you've been locked away in a dark room and forced to dine on something as revolting as eels, which I know you loathe. I should think everyone would loathe eels, but Easton prefers them. Lady Chatham called Wednesday evening for tea. She has not called at all since my marriage to Easton, and I have heard from a kind friend that she's had much to say on the matter all about town. But here she came, her countenance quite cheerful, and I knew at once that she was desperate to speak of you, for of course word has come back to London. Lady Chatham did at last own to her curiosity and confided that Merryton is rigid and fastidious, and thinks of little else than propriety. He has nearly disowned Amherst, and he is said to be a disagreeable and aloof dining companion. Lady Chatham vows that he is so convinced of his own perfection that he looks askance at all else.

"No, that's not true," Grace muttered to herself.

I have thought of little else since her call, and I think that perhaps you should tell him the truth of Mamma. He will no doubt cast you out and end the marriage, and there will surely be a horrible calumny to follow you, but at least you will not be married to that wretched man.

Grace wanted to tell Jeffrey about her mother. She'd been thinking of how precisely to do that, *when* to do that. Why didn't she tell him last night? She'd had the opportunity, but they had been so good together, and she'd felt the affection building between them, and she'd not wanted to ruin it.

Now she worried that he would be angry when he discovered she'd kept this secret from him. She didn't want him to be angry before he left for London. She only knew that he could not be in London without her. It had occurred to Grace that if he saw her mother, and how helpless she was without her daughters, he might perhaps think more kindly of the situation.

Of course you may come to Easton and me. We've not much at present, but we will not force you to eat eels.

"You have it all wrong, Honor," Grace said aloud. She got out of bed and padded over to the writing desk to pen a note, telling Honor she was coming to London with her husband:

You must behave yourself, Honor! Promise that you will! I know how you can be when you have in mind you don't care for someone, but at least allow Merryton the benefit of doubt. I shall call on you as soon as I am situated.

Grace wanted to be confident of what she was doing. As she and Hattie prepared to leave the following morning, she reminded herself that the ugly circumstances of her marriage were slowly peeling away, falling off, discarded. She earnestly believed that she could be happy with Jeffrey, even with his dark ailment. She wasn't so naive to think it would be perfect, or that his predilections or fears of madness would magically disappear, but she had faith that if she was on the path with him, and they understood each other, that in spite of his peculiarities there was nothing but optimism for her future.

Now all she had to do was persuade him to believe it.

THERE WAS A different sort of vitality to London than anywhere else in England, and after an absence of many weeks, Grace felt it more than ever. It reverberated in her blood and her bones, swirled about in her chest. She missed London and the whirl of the Season, the endless procession of balls and soirees and teas. She missed all the lovely gowns and hats and shoes. She missed society and her friends and the bustle of the Mayfair district in the heart of London.

But as the coach crept along a crowded thoroughfare, Grace was astonished to realize she'd also come to appreciate the stark beauty and serene calm of the country.

Blackwood Hall wasn't the same as Longmeadow. At Longmeadow, there were so many families of Quality nearby that society seemed to follow the Beckington household to the country. Grace had spent summers in a whirl of country dances and picnics and horse races. She never rode alone as she'd done at Blackwood, feeling the wind on her face, the freedom of being one in the vastness of the world. She had not visited the kennels and rescued dogs that had not met the gamekeeper's standards. She shuddered to think how many of them she might have saved for being less than perfect had she been aware of anything other than her own need for diversion and attention. She'd been so mired in the whirl of society that she had forgotten to look around her.

Blackwood Hall was its own society and Grace had come to appreciate the beauty in that. Having only herself to rely on these past few weeks had made her recognize the different rhythms in life, of her own feelings. She couldn't suppress a small smile—for the more than two years she'd been out, she had thought of nothing but what she would wear and where she might dine. She'd wanted nothing more than to be admired by gentlemen and befriended by women. What a long way from that debutante she had come in a very short time!

Merryton's town house was among those in a row on Brook Street, not far from Beckington House, and only a short walk across Grovesnor Square to Audley Street, where Grace now resided. The Merryton house was redbrick with two columns marking the entrance. Cox was on hand to greet them, drawing them into the foyer with a black-and-white-tiled floor and a ceiling soaring overhead that made the space seem much larger than it was.

Grace looked around as she removed her gloves and bonnet and noticed the rooms on either side of the foyer were sparsely furnished. That didn't surprise her. What surprised her was that here, there were paintings on the walls. Not many, but enough that the walls were not entirely bare. She guessed that the absence of paintings

in London drew too much attention and invited speculation. Unlike Blackwood Hall, whom few ever saw.

Hattie and Julia, the woman who cleaned Jeffrey's office and personal rooms, stood beside Grace in the foyer
as Cox took their cloaks. Hattie's head tilted back as she
looked at the domed ceiling overhead. "My mother's
youngest brother came to London when he was sixteen
years and was never heard from again," she said in a
near-whisper.

Grace put her arm around Hattie's small shoulders.
"You have my word that you will return to Blackwood
Hall in one piece, Hattie."

"I always thought I'd come to London," Julia said,
and rubbed her hand under her nose as if she had an itch.
"Fancied myself a singer. Thought I'd take up the stage."

Both Hattie and Grace turned their heads to look at
Julia. "You *did?*"

"Oh, aye," Julia said, and rested her hands on her
round belly. "I'm quite a fine singer, mu'um."

"I never fancied I'd be anything but a maid," Hattie said weakly.

"That's what dreams are for, lass," Julia said. "Very
well, Mr. Cox, I should see that his lordship's rooms are
in order," she said, and marched off toward the stairs.

"Is his lordship here?" Grace asked.

"No, madam. He's gone out for the day and bids you
not wait for him. He expects to return quite late. Shall
I show you to your rooms?"

Grace glanced through an open door to one of the
rooms, to a clock on the mantel. She had time to see

Honor before supper. "Yes, thank you. Come, Hattie— we've much to do."

Her rooms—a bedroom, sitting room and dressing room—faced the street. From the corner of her sitting room, Grace could see a bit of Grovesnor Square. Hattie reported that the earl's rooms were just down the hall, a mirror image of what had been reserved for the lady of the house, and his dressing room adjoined hers.

The suite was very pleasingly painted in sky-blue-and-cream trim, with a cascade of papier-mâché ropes serving as the molding. The hearth was faced with marble, the carpets new. It was lovely, and under any other circumstance, Grace would be eager to show her sisters. But she had too many more pressing issues on her mind, not the least of which was how to explain to anyone how she had come to be married to Merryton while mourning her stepfather, without her family to attend her.

If only she'd never gone to Bath. If only, if only.

But then again, if she hadn't done what she had, she would not have married Jeffrey. No matter what happened, no matter what Jeffrey might do when he learned the truth about her mother, Grace would not wish to have missed this experience. She put her hands to her abdomen and drew a deep breath. No, she wouldn't have missed it for the world. She was forever changed by it, and for the better.

But now, there was the issue of how she would explain her sudden marriage to her family and friends. If there was one person who would know precisely what to do, it was Honor Cabot Easton.

Grace left Hattie to put her things away, and set out

for the Easton house across the square. The day had turned gray, and a light rain had begun to fall, washing the ever-present scent of smoke from Mayfair as she walked. The rain began to grow heavier, however, and had turned into a deluge by the time she reached Audley Street. She dashed up the steps of Easton's house, rapping loudly on the door.

The butler there took her things and showed her into a sitting room while he went to announce her to Honor. Grace looked around her while she waited. The home was quite grand, with marble floors, gold-leaf inlays in the molding above and silk-covered walls. It did not look like the house of a man who had lost his fortune as Honor had claimed in her letter. This room was inviting—it looked as if people enjoyed living here. There was no concern for symmetry, no worry for uneven painting frames, no fretting over the proper placement of the accoutrement.

"Grace!"

Grace heard Honor's shriek somewhere above, and then what sounded like a roomful of children running across the floor above her. That sound carried to the stairs, where the clatter of Honor's shoes on the wooden steps must have echoed down the street. She fairly slid to a halt before the door of the parlor before she caught herself against the frame. She stared at Grace. "Good God, it really *is* you!" she cried, and burst into the room, throwing her arms around Grace and squeezing her into a tight embrace.

Much to Grace's horror, tears of relief began to stream from her face. "Honor!" she sobbed. "Oh, Honor."

Honor began to cry, too, and the two of them sank to the floor and to their knees, still clutching each other. But then Honor pushed back, swiped the tears from her face and then those from Grace's face. "No more," she said, smiling in spite of the quaver in her voice. "We are the brave and fearless ladies of London, remember?"

"Oh, how I wish I could forget we ever said we were!" Grace said, and slid onto her bottom, her back against the wall. "I'm so happy to see you," she said morosely, and swiped at her tears.

Honor laughed and came to her feet. "Joy is bleeding from your veins, darling. I'm very happy to see you, too." She grabbed Grace's hand and pulled her up. "Now come and tell me everything. Start with why you're in London, when you arrived and what makes you cry."

"I am crying because I've missed you so, and I've been through so *much*," Grace said. Images from the past few weeks began to fly through her mind.

"You poor dear!" Honor exclaimed. "You're so strong to have married him and have *endured* it—"

Grace grabbed her sister's hand. "God in heaven, how I've missed you, Honor," she said sincerely. "I've missed your ordering me about and telling me what I ought to do from this moment to that."

"I've missed you, too," Honor said. "I missed you worst when Easton refused my offer of marriage—"

*"Refused what?"*

"My offer. He refused me, publicly and dramatically." She waved her hand. "We'll speak of it later. The point is, he has apologized properly for it," she said, pulling Grace to a seat on the settee next to her.

Grace blinked. "What are you saying? I can't *believe*—"

"Of course you will believe it. But enough of that! Here you are, returned to me! I need you with me, Grace." Honor squeezed her hand between hers. "I am terribly happy, more than I ever thought I would be. It's not ideal—we've very little money—but George is very clever and he's not given up on his ship. It won't be long before he turns it all around. There I go again—*enough* of me!" she cried. "What of *you?* I want to know it all. You mustn't omit a single thing. *Merryton?* How could you make such a dreadful mistake?"

How could she indeed? "Because it was dark, and I thought— Oh, I don't know, Honor, it all happened so quickly. I caught a man other than the one I intended, but now, I don't think I made a mistake at all."

"Of *course* it was a mistake."

"No," Grace said with a shake of her head. "I mean that I am glad I mistook him for Amherst."

Honor gasped. She fell back against the settee as if Grace had just admitted treason. And just as quickly, she sat up again, her blue eyes twinkling. "All right. Tell me *everything.*"

"I don't know where to begin," Grace said. "With the night I seduced the wrong man? Or should I begin with how desperate and alone I felt when I arrived at Blackwood Hall? It's dreary, Honor, so very dreary and dark. Or perhaps I should refuse any mention of that at all and tell you how I have come to care for him, but not in the way I ever imagined I would care for a husband. And then again, perhaps none of that matters or will ever matter, for I haven't told him everything."

"What do you mean?" Honor asked.

Grace winced. "I haven't told him about Mamma."

Honor gasped so loudly she startled Grace. "Grace! You *must* tell him! Everyone knows it now! Mamma— we can't hide her any longer. I mean that yes, we *hide* her, for God's sake, for can you imagine what all of Mayfair would say if they saw her wandering about, talking to people who aren't there? But everyone knows that she is *quite* mad."

"They do?" Grace had suspected it, but it pained her to hear it.

Honor suddenly leaned close. "One day, Hannah took her for a turn about the square," she whispered. "She usually says nothing, for she is locked in her own world. But that day, she saw a gentleman and became convinced he'd stolen her reticule. Hannah said it was quite dreadful, her shouting, *Thief!* and what not." She leaned back. "You may rest assured that *everyone* knows it, darling. It is a poorly kept secret. Have you seen her?"

Grace shook her head. "I came to you first."

"And I'm so very glad you did. We'll go around together. But first, you must tell me about Merryton and Blackwood Hall. I am dying to hear it, I'll be honest. I've always thought him so disagreeable."

Grace felt sorrow for her husband, considered by the world to be peculiar and aloof, trapped by his own thoughts. Grace did not tell Honor that, but she told her everything else. She even told her about Molly Madigan, and Bother and the newly named Trois, for only having three legs. She talked of how difficult it was to reach her husband, and how he seemed to resent her so completely in the beginning.

"He sounds wretched and odious," Honor pronounced when Grace had finished telling her everything.

"I thought so, too. But I discovered recently that he's not, Honor. Not really." She told Honor how, by some miracle, he'd begun to be kinder to her, and had actually been affectionate. She admitted there was something quite raw about him. "He reminds me of a wounded animal, as if he's in pain and struggles to hide it. I ache for him, really, for I think it must be terribly exhausting to hide one's pain, don't you?"

"What pain could he possibly have?" Honor scoffed.

"We've all some pain in us, haven't we?" Grace said. "His father was unkind, I gather." She looked down at her hands. "Quite hard on him. And his mother—he scarcely knew her. But I think it is more than that. I see that it is more, and in those moments when we are alone, he lets go of it, and he is…he is everything I ever dreamed of. He is kind and attentive, and he says I am beautiful, and I can see how desperately he desires me."

*"Really?"* Honor said with delight. "And…?" She nudged Grace's knee. "Does he please you in the way a husband ought to please his wife?"

Heat flooded Grace's cheeks. "I don't know if it's the way a husband *ought* to please a wife, but I am quite…happy."

Honor squealed with a laugh, her hand going to her

belly as she fell back against the settee. "The very same happened to me!"

"But then, he turns," Grace said, grabbing Honor's hand and forcing her attention back to more important matters. "It's as if there are shutters on his eyes, green shutters, and they close. And I think, if only I could reach him when the shutters close, I could *help* him."

"Oh, Grace," Honor sighed, and brushed a strand of hair from her face. "Isn't it just like you, to tend to the wounded and the outcast?"

"What do you mean?" Grace asked, surprised by that.

"Don't you know that about you? You have always been able to see something in others that no one else can see. Remember Frederica Morton?" Honor shuddered. "She had an appalling disposition, but you alone remained her friend."

"You were unkind to her."

"Oh, I have no doubt that I was," Honor said, almost cheerfully. "So was most of London. She never had a kind word for anyone."

"She was lonely. She didn't have a single friend."

"Of course she didn't have any friends. If she wanted any, she went about it in a peculiar way, didn't she? But *you* were her friend. I shall never forget the sight of the two of you strolling arm in arm through Hyde Park."

Grace hadn't liked Frederica much, either, but she'd felt such sympathy for her. Frederica never seemed to understand just how unpleasant she was in social situations. "She was tedious. But she truly wanted to be included."

"And remember the baby goat caught in the fencing?"

*"Oh,"* Grace said, wincing at that painful memory.

"You stayed with that poor wretched thing until it died."

"For heaven's sake, Honor, it was mortally wounded! I could hardly leave it to die alone."

*"You* couldn't. But I could, and so could Prudence. It was too heartbreaking to bear! But that's precisely what I mean, Grace. You, of all of us, have always had the ability to see past the surface. You see pain, and you see the good in people. Even in someone as awful as Merryton. I'm not the least bit surprised that you've spotted a bit of good in him. He must be over the moon that he has managed to marry you."

Grace laughed ruefully. "He was hardly over the moon. And while he has warmed to me, he has been very plain that the one thing he will not tolerate is for any dishonor or scandal to touch his name."

"Mmm," Honor said, her gaze narrowing a little. "Seems a little too late for that, doesn't it? Everyone was talking about the sudden marriage of the Earl of Merryton, and now, the disgrace of Amherst."

"Pardon?" Grace said.

"You mean you don't know?" Honor said, surprised. "Isn't that why you've come to London?"

"No—come for what?" Grace asked, her brow furrowing.

Honor cried out with shock. She looked to the door as if she was concerned someone might be listening, and said, "You've not heard! Oh, darling! First, the word went around town that Merryton had married quite un-expectedly, and not under pleasant circumstances, and very soon thereafter a most salacious rumor began to go around—that Amherst had sired a child with the daughter of his tailor."

Grace gasped. *"What?"*

"Yes! Prudence has heard he keeps her in a town house north of Bedford Square."

Grace gaped at her sister.

"Yes, it's shocking," Honor said, nodding her head. "He seems too affable to carry such a deep secret, doesn't he?"

"Are you certain, Honor? It's not merely an ugly rumor?"

"Well, naturally, I can't be *entirely* certain—but I think it is true."

Grace buried her face in her hands, alarmed by her own foolishness, grateful that Amherst had not come. She didn't care that he'd sired an illegitimate child— Lord knew he'd not be the first young lord to have done so. It was the realization that if Amherst *had* come to the tea shop that night, she would have harmed even more people with her folly. A child! And behind that child was a woman who must care for Amherst. Grace had been so naive, and so bloody impressed with her own cunning.

"Oh, no! You mustn't be glum!" Honor said. "I sup-pose given what we know now, if you were determined to snare one of the Donovan men, you ended up with the right one, didn't you? Oh dear, don't fret about it, darling—after what I did in the gaming hell of Southwark, your transgression seems quite mild in comparison." Honor laughed, as if she were proud of that. "I can now scarcely wait to make the acquaintance of Merryton. But first, we must go to Beckington House. Prudence and Mercy miss you horribly, and so does Augustine."

"How are they?" Grace asked as Honor stood.

"Very well," Honor said. "Prudence has been so very helpful in seeing after Mamma. She's taken it upon herself, but you know Prudence, always stepping in to turn things to right. Augustine thought it best that Mamma and the girls stay under his roof until Easton and I can take them. And Mercy…" Honor clucked her tongue. "Mercy is Mercy, sticking her nose in places it ought not to be, and creating wild tales. She keeps Augustine in fits."

Grace smiled fondly. Mercy had always vexed Augustine's tender nature without intending to. "I'm desperate to see them."

"You've not said a word about Mamma," Honor said accusingly. "You do intend to see her, don't you?"

"Yes, of course!" Grace said, gaining her feet, too. "Oh, Honor, I'm a *wretched* daughter! Do you know that I'm afraid to see her, to see how she's worsened? And I don't want to introduce her to Merryton."

"You have no choice," Honor said calmly. "Why have you not *told* him?"

"I don't know," Grace moaned. She felt a little sick inside. It was impossible to convey the war in her head about it, but she did her best to put it into words. "In the beginning, I didn't tell him because he spoke so harshly against scandal and told me explicitly that he would not tolerate any more than what had happened. I feared he would cast me out."

"At least you could have come to us," Honor said. "We're not afraid of scandal, Easton and me."

"That is hardly a superior position to take. Nevertheless, had I known of your marriage, I would never have been in the tea shop," Grace reminded her. "I didn't know until it was too late! I was desperate—I thought we were on the verge of losing all opportunity for Prudence and Mercy. And who could say what Augustine would do with Mamma?"

"I am ashamed that I doubted him, in truth," Honor said. "He has been kind to Mamma. He knows Easton has no money at present. But I'll warn you, darling, he told me very recently that now you've married into privilege, there really is no reason for the Cabots to remain at Beckington. 'Wouldn't they be more comfortable with you or Grace, dearest?'" she said, mimicking Augustine. "So there, you see? You have no choice. You must tell Merryton."

"Of course I must," Grace said. "I should have told him these past few days. But I was so grateful that some barrier had been breached between us, and I didn't want to ruin it. And then, every time I summoned the courage, there was an interruption."

"Mmm," Honor said skeptically, as if she didn't believe that were true. Grace wasn't honestly certain it was true. She only knew that she didn't want to ruin the affection and regard that had sprouted between her and Jeffrey. It was a tender reed, so vulnerable yet.

As always, Honor understood Grace. She reached for her hand. "I understand, darling, I do. I can't even begin to imagine how a man as stiff and unyielding as Merryton will take the truth. But you can't hide her, and we can't desert Prudence and Mercy—they need us more than ever now. You *must* tell him. It won't be easy, but I know you'll do what is right, and you will keep your chin up, and you will carry on as you have. Because you are fearless and daring and you are the best sister I could have ever hoped for."

Grace smiled at Honor and put her arms around her in an embrace. "I hope you will still say so when I am living under your roof, disgraced and wretched and moping about every day."

Honor squeezed her tightly to her. "Oh, dear, I hope so, too."

# CHAPTER NINETEEN

GRACE'S SPIRITS WERE quite low when she left Beckington House sometime later, and trudged through the rain back to the Merryton townhome.

Of course Prudence and Mercy had been thrilled to see Grace, and she them. They had peppered her with questions about Blackwood Hall and Merryton, then had filled her in on all the latest gossip about the Season's newest debutantes.

Augustine was delighted to see Grace, too, hugging her so tightly to him that Grace was robbed of her breath, then suddenly holding her at arm's length to examine her, declaring that she looked very well indeed. "So good that you've come, *so good,*" he'd said. "We must have you and Merryton over at once. Mustn't we, dearest?" he'd said to his fiancée, Monica Hargrove.

"Yes, at once," Monica had said, eyeing Grace shrewdly from across the room, her arms folded. "We are all on tenterhooks to know how you came to marry him so quickly. I wasn't aware that you were even acquainted. Were you?"

"We weren't," Grace had said calmly. "But that's the beauty of Cupid's arrow, isn't it, Monica? It strikes when you are least expecting it, and in some cases, rather deep." She'd smiled sweetly and had promised that as soon as they could arrange it, she would introduce them to her husband.

She sincerely hoped that she would indeed be introducing them to Merryton, and not just another, but larger, scandal.

The time had come for Prudence to lead Grace upstairs, to the two rooms where her mother, Lady Beckington, and her longtime lady's maid, Hannah, resided most days.

Her mother had looked at Grace blankly beneath her unplucked brows. Her sleek dark hair had grayed over the past few months, and was wrapped around in a tight bun at her nape. Grace noticed that both sleeves of her mother's gown had been ravaged by her constant picking at the seams and fabric. It was the fraying of the embroidery of her gowns that had caused Grace and Honor to first notice the change in their mother.

Her mother stood, and her gaze had narrowed as she had studied Grace. At last she'd said, "So good of you to come."

"Mamma," Grace had said, walking across the room to her, her arms outstretched. "It's me, Grace."

"I know you who you are," she'd said tersely, and had darted out of Grace's path to avoid the embrace. "Bets, see her out," she'd muttered.

Bets, Grace recalled, had been her mother's governess.

Her mother took a seat at a gaming table and bent over a backgammon board. She hummed to herself as she moved the pieces about in no particular order or game.

Grace looked at Hannah, who smiled with sympathy. "She's weary, mu'um."

Prudence had linked her arm through Grace's and pulled her aside, "Some days are better than others," she'd confided. "If she hasn't seen you in a while, she forgets. But were you here, she would remember you at times."

"Does she know you?" Grace had asked.

Prudence had shrugged. "Sometimes."

Seeing her mother like that, her faculties even more reduced since she'd last been home, had plunged tiny daggers into Grace. What a harsh world it was when a mother didn't know her own child.

Grace was brooding as she entered the Merryton town house, determined to tell Merryton about her mother, as soon as he returned. Honor was right—it was unconscionable to keep it from him another moment. She stepped inside the foyer and smiled absently at the footman as she handed him her umbrella. When she had removed her cloak, she turned toward the stairs and was startled out of her wits by the sight of Amherst.

He grinned at her and came striding across the foyer from the parlor, his arms outstretched, his hat in his hand. "Sister!" he said, as if nothing improper had happened, as if he hadn't left her waiting at the tea shop for him. He grabbed her up in a tight embrace before Grace could even think what to say and kissed her cheek, then let go and stepped back.

His grin was irrepressible. Curly, tousled light brown locks dipped charmingly over one green eye. He was a handsome man—she'd always thought so, all of London thought so—but Grace was struck by how Jeffrey's quiet and solemn demeanor seemed more masculine to her. Amherst certainly bore a resemblance to Jeffrey, but his jaw was not as strong, his eyes not as vibrant and piercing.

"Are you surprised?" he asked gaily. "You couldn't possibly be as surprised as I was to learn you'd married my brother! But it was a happy surprise."

"Ah…" Grace frantically thought what to say, her gaze sliding to Cox.

"Come, I must hear of it," Amherst said, taking her by the elbow and steering her into the parlor. He shut the door behind them, then turned to look at her. "Marriage agrees with you, Lady Merryton," he said, then abruptly caught her by the waist and twirled her about, as if they were dancing.

"My lord!"

He laughed and let go of her. "You and Merryton," he said with a shake of his head. "What a bit of daring, Miss Cabot—shall I call you Grace? But to set your sights on the Earl of Merryton? I knew the Cabot girls were bold, and yet I had no idea *how* bold. The moment I heard he was in London, I came straightaway to congratulate him and greet my new sister."

A rush of heat swirled up in her. Grace hadn't thought through what she would say to Amherst when she saw him again.

His smile faded. "Oh, dear, I've distressed you. You look troubled, and you mustn't," he said soothingly, and leaned down to whisper, "It will be our secret."

"Our secret? There is no secret!" Grace said crossly. "Of course he knows."

"Of course he knows what?" Amherst asked.

"Honestly, my lord—he knows why I was in the tea shop that night."

Amherst's brows rose with surprise. He suddenly laughed. "Oh, *ho,* that is grand! You don't mean that *he*—"

"Yes, I mean that he came into the shop," she said, folding her arms.

Amherst laughed roundly, as if that was a lark. Grace deserved that—she'd certainly acted as if the entire tryst was a lark. She'd been such a foolish, stupid girl.

"Goodness! I can well imagine his displeasure at that was *great,*" Amherst exclaimed jovially.

"That would be putting it mildly."

"Still…how does it happen that you married him?" he asked, watching her closely. "My brother is not the least bit spontaneous. In fact, he is the least spontaneous person I know. Spontaneity makes him quite cross—"

"My lord!" Grace cried. "Haven't you anything to say for yourself? *You* were to meet me, and you didn't come." It was the question that had once tormented her, but now only a footnote to that fateful night in Bath. She wanted to hear him say it, to admit why he'd abandoned her. "Why didn't you come?"

"Surely you've guessed at things by now," he said.

"I could not have *guessed,*" she said, cross that he would somehow think she would have divined his situation. "How could I possibly have guessed? You gave me every assurance you would come. When our eyes met at the performance at the abbey, you nodded your head."

"Ah, Grace," he said, touching his fingers to hers. "How shall I tell you? I didn't come because I had guessed at your motives."

Grace was stunned—she'd given him no indication, nothing that would cause him to suspect her motives. Had she been so obvious? *"And?"* she demanded, willing him to admit he had fathered a child.

"I see I've offended you. But I'm not a greenhorn, love. I knew very well why you would want to meet under such suspect conditions. You had all but hinted at it in our previous meetings."

"I hadn't—"

He smiled and touched his fingers to her chin. "You had. And as much I esteem you, as much as I care for you…I could not help you in that way."

Grace blanched, humiliated by her foolishness. "But you encouraged me," she pointed out. "For the past two years, you have encouraged me!"

Amherst shrugged casually, as if it were nothing to him to flirt with many women while putting a child in another.

"If you suspected it, then why didn't you refuse to meet me? If you had refused to meet me, it might have at least saved your brother this fate," she said crossly. "He was looking for you in that tea shop, and—" She shook her head. Amherst didn't deserve an explanation.

But one of his brows arched high above the other. "Do I understand you? The great Earl of Merryton made a *mistake?*"

"How can you make light of it?"

"In my wildest imaginings, I never thought Jeffrey would somehow make his way to the tea shop. I was shocked to see him at the concert. He loathes crowds. He loathes tea shops for all I know. And to think he went, and somehow..." He laughed, shocking Grace. "I beg your pardon," he said when he saw her angry expression. "But if only you knew my brother—"

"I know him. I *married* him."

"I mean *really* know him. I am certain he's not allowed you to see his true feelings—he's never allowed anyone to see his true feelings. I am so very sorry, love. I'd not wish him on anyone."

"What—"

"But I can't help you now. It's too late. What is done is done, as they say," he said, as if he'd just finished a meal instead of hearing how his own brother was tricked into marriage.

Good God, Grace had assumed Amherst's affable nature was the sign of a good and decent man. But she was appalled by him.

But then Amherst pushed his fingers through his hair.

It was such a small thing, but she'd never seen him do it before, and it struck her as an anxious sort of gesture. Grace suddenly saw Amherst differently, as a man desperately trying to hide the truth. He was just like his brother in that regard, wasn't he? Both of them determined the truth not be known.

And she was just like them. There was no end to the secrets.

"Come now, Grace," Amherst said, and held out his hand to her. "We are now brother and sister. We might as well be friends."

"You're right."

That seemed to surprise him; he smiled curiously as she slipped her hand into his and gave it an affectionate squeeze.

"You've missed quite a lot this spring," he said. "Shall I tell you the news of London?"

He wouldn't tell her the biggest news of all, Grace was certain of it. And she hardly cared for the rest. But her mind was whirling, her heart aching, and she was glad to let him talk while she tried to gather herself.

He told her what he'd heard about Honor's marriage to George Easton—that her sister had gone to Southwark and had tried to wager an offer of marriage from him in a gaming hell, but he had publicly refused her.

Honor had told Grace a bit of what had happened after she'd left for Bath—Easton had decided he was the worst possible match for her and had refused to see her, so Honor had taken matters into her own hands. Grace knew she'd gone to Southwark and she knew that she had done the offering. But Amherst's version was far more scandalous.

"One never wants for diversion when the Cabot girls are about, does one?" he asked, not unkindly.

He told her how Easton had had a change of heart, apparently, and that the wedding had been done quickly, and all of London was still whispering about the propriety of it, given that Honor was in mourning for her stepfather. "Best hope Jeffrey doesn't hear of it," he said casually.

"Why?" she asked. "Something very similar has happened to him."

Amherst's gaze was quietly assessing. "Because he is a hard man. He has very rigid ideas and expectations."

"He considers things carefully," Grace conceded.

"He considers everything in light of how it may affect *him*. How society will perceive *him*. Don't be shocked— I don't think ill of my brother. I scarcely think he is to blame for these tendencies, really. My father was quite hard on him as the heir, you know. He would not tolerate anything that even hinted of impropriety, and punished us all for it. But he punished Jeffrey most. He was cruel."

"Cruel? Or strict?"

"Cruel." Amherst frowned. "He was quick to resort to beatings to get his point across," he said quietly. "Especially Jeffrey. But wouldn't one reasonably expect that now *he* is earl, he would be kinder? He doesn't use his fists, but his expectations are no less exacting than our father's were. He believes I should have an occupation that he approves, that I should be married to whom *he* approves and carrying on the family name. All in a manner above reproach, naturally." ·

But didn't everyone strive to live in a manner above reproach?

"I suppose he will want the same from you," Amherst said. "He won't tolerate any sort of deviation from what he considers to be proper behavior."

"He's been rather accepting, given the circumstances," she pointed out. Grace didn't care for Amherst's scrutiny of her.

"Grace…" He touched her arm. "May I ask a delicate question? He's not been…vulgar, has he?"

Grace didn't know what to say to that.

"Coarse," John amended.

She could feel the heat flood her cheeks instantly. She was appalled by the impropriety of that question, of the presumption—she began to move, but John caught her arm.

"I would *never* bring up such an indelicate subject to a member of the fairer sex, but you are my sister-in-law, and there have been rumors about his…preferences, so to speak."

Grace could have perished there on the spot. Jeffrey had assured her no one but her knew of the thoughts that plagued him. "I don't know what that means," she said frantically, wanting out of that room and away from Amherst.

"I mean that he has a certain appetite…at least I've heard some talk of it in Ashton Down."

"For what?" she asked, feeling a swell of fear rising up in her.

"For women…but more than one."

John was confusing her. "More than one woman?"

"At the same time," John clarified.

Grace stared at him, unable to fathom *how*.

"He hasn't suggested—"

"No!" Grace exclaimed, and jerked her arm away from him. She was acutely embarrassed, and worse, uncertain. She was only learning of these things, of the sorts of fantasies that plagued her husband, and now she worried that this was what Jeffrey had meant when he'd talked about his depravity. Is that what he desired of her, to share their bed with someone else? God, no—she was an eager student, and she liked what they did. But not that, *never* that.

"I beg your pardon, I didn't mean to alarm you. I shouldn't worry, if I were you, for he has a stronger desire to keep the family name as pristine as snow." This, John said in a tone that indicated he didn't share that view.

Grace didn't understand him. Why was he telling her these things? Why would he mention something so offensive? It felt almost as if he wanted to shock her, wanted to make her despise Merryton.

"I've said enough," he said. "But I thought I should tell you before you heard it from someone else."

That was a lie, and she knew it. He wanted to scandalize her.

"Rumors like that will drift through London."

"Nothing ever drifts through London, my lord. Rumors are blown through like gusts from a storm." She looked at him pointedly, thinking of his secrets.

"I suppose you're right," he said absently.

The sounds of someone in the foyer reached them. She didn't have time to think of what she would say, for the door to the parlor opened and Jeffrey walked in, his gaze running between Grace and Amherst, his expression cool and impenetrable.

IT HAD BEEN a grueling day for Jeffrey, spent searching for his brother. For a man who had trouble absorbing the asymmetry of various establishments and the chaos of all the people and animals moving around London, entering his brother's usual haunts—from gentlemen's clubs to gambling hells—had been the hardest thing he'd done in a very long time.

Jeffrey had kept himself moving forward with the notion that Grace would have arrived by the time he returned to Mayfair. The thought of her, of the things he would like to do to her, of the feel of her, was motivating. But Jeffrey was aware that there was more to it than that—he wanted to see her smile. It was astonishing that only a few short weeks ago he would not have cared if he ever saw her again, and that his opinion could have changed so. He had been beguiled by a beautiful, vibrant woman.

It was a shock to see Grace and John standing together when he entered the parlor. "Jeffrey!" John said congenially, coming forward. "How do you fare? You look well," he said, and extended his hand in greeting. "I should like to offer my felicitations on your nuptials and best wishes for a happy future. I was just telling Grace how fortunate you are."

*Grace.* He called her Grace. Jeffrey looked at her, and she smiled. "I'm so happy you're here," she said, and glided over to him, rising up on her toes to kiss his cheek.

His fist curled at his side and he tried to offer a smile for her. He looked at John, who was looking on with some conceit. "Where have you been?" he asked.

John laughed as if Jeffrey amused him. "I see we are to dispense with the customary greetings. I've come to congratulate you, Jeffrey. This is cause for celebration!" he said, gesturing to Grace.

Grace touched Jeffrey's hand; he felt that touch reverberate through him. "Thank you," he said stiffly. "I think there is much we need to discuss. Shall we talk in my study?"

Grace looked stricken by his rudeness. If Jeffrey could trust himself to speak amicably, he would have done so. But at present, all he could see was his brother on his wife, their bodies pressed together.

"Will you not even share a whiskey with me, Jeffrey? Will you not allow me to at least pay my respects to your new wife?" John asked, and stretched his arms out entreatingly.

Grace's gaze slid down, to where Jeffrey had clasped his hands at his back, then up again, to his face. Jeffrey said to her, "If you would be so good as to excuse Lord Amherst, there are a few matters we must discuss straightaway."

"Oh, dear, that sounds rather ominous, doesn't it?" John said amicably. "Very well, my Lord Merryton, if you insist on it, I shall keep my toasts to your conjugal happiness until supper. I am invited to dine, I should hope."

"Of course you are," Grace said. "I insist on it."

"Thank you," John said with a slight bow of his head. He walked to where Jeffrey stood and clapped his hand on his shoulder. "It *is* good to see you, Jeffrey. Did you say your study?" he asked, and strolled out.

"Jeffrey," Grace said.

Jeffrey took her hand and brought it to his lips. "I'll

see you at supper," he murmured, and dropped her hand.
He wanted desperately to touch her, to hold her in his
arms. It was churning in him, pressing against his insides. But he had more immediate matters, and left her
in the parlor, following his brother to the study.

## CHAPTER TWENTY

"WHY HAVE YOU taken all the paintings from the walls?" John asked when Jeffrey entered the study. "Another one of your peculiarities, I suppose."

How Jeffrey hated that word! His father had used it when referring to him—*my peculiar son.* The memory struck Jeffrey hard—he tapped against his leg, trying to push it down. "I should think that your concern would be the debt you have left on Sir Edmund, and not the decor of this study."

He could see that he had surprised John. "What do you know of it?" he demanded.

"Only that he has sent a solicitor to collect the debt from our family coffers. Once again, the Donovan family fortune is expected to pay your gambling debts."

"There is money enough," John said indifferently.

"And I suppose you believe there is money enough to support the by-blow you've sired."

For once, John looked stricken. "I don't—"

"Don't deny it," Jeffrey warned him.

John drew himself up. "I *won't* deny it, Jeffrey. Why would I? It is often the unexpected but natural consequence of taking a woman to your bed."

"A *tailor's* daughter?" Jeffrey said. He could imagine the poor girl, charmed by a handsome viscount, and now forever ruined.

But John laughed. "A woman is a woman."

"Not for you, John," Jeffrey said, his hand fisting against the rising tide of thoughts about this innocent young woman. "You are a viscount. Your name is a prestigious one. Even if we might somehow excuse the fact that your actions take money from the legitimate children of this family, we cannot excuse the fact that you have a duty to live an exemplary life. That is the price of the privilege you have enjoyed all your life."

"What hypocrisy," John spat. "You will lecture me about my behavior, when I know very well what likely you are doing to that poor woman. What you've done to others."

"What I'm doing?" Jeffrey repeated, not understanding him immediately. "I haven't the slightest idea what you mean."

"The hell you say," John said angrily, his face going red. "It is common knowledge around Ashton Down of the sorts of things you seek in a bedmate, Jeffrey. You will debase her with your lust and think nothing of it, and all while you are passing judgment on *me*."

The truth in that accusation stung Jeffrey quite deeply. He was well aware of his own hypocrisy, but that didn't absolve him of his responsibility to lead this family. He whirled about to his desk, crashing his fist down on it eight times in rapid succession. "You will *not* turn this conversation away from your reprehensible behavior, John! Say of me what you will, but I honor my word! What sort of man are you that you do *not* honor your bloody word?"

"A bad man," John readily agreed. "A poor excuse for a Donovan!" he shouted, casting his arms wide. "But at least I don't need to watch two women pleasuring each other with my cock in hand. At least I haven't married as a result of a tryst in a tea shop to a woman whose mother is mad."

"Mad," Jeffrey scoffed.

John's scowl suddenly lightened. "You don't know. How *rich,*" he sneered. "You think yourself so far above me, and *you* are the one who has brought madness into this family. I may have sired an illegitimate child, but I didn't bring the blood of the deranged into this family. That was all you, my lord."

Jeffrey's pulse had begun to pound. "You're lying—"

"Am I? Ask your lovely wife, brother."

Jeffrey's thoughts raced wildly as he tried to make sense of John's accusations. "That's enough," he said low. He rubbed his fingers against his forehead. His head felt as if it were splitting open with pain, and he needed to pace, to think. To *count.* "I have arranged a commission for you in the royal navy and we will meet with Admiral Hale on Friday at two o'clock." He looked John directly in the eye. "You will accept it. We will give this woman enough to go and raise her child comfortably on the condition she makes no more claims against you. You will go about setting your debt to Sir Edmund to rights. There is no argument in this, John. If you do not do as I ask, I will disown you. I will not allow you to taint the family name or drain the family coffers and the future of all our children for your own amusement."

"You're a heartless beast of a man," John said, his voice quavering with rage. "You've never said a kind word to me, do you know? I thought Father's death would change you, but you grow more and more like him every day."

John's insults were difficult to hear, but then again Jeffrey had heard them many times before. Every time he and John had one of these conversations—Jeffery demanding to know why John thought it all right to lose a substantial amount of money from coffers that supported the entire family, and John excusing his behavior by saying that he was distraught at the way Jeffrey had treated him—John would eventually come around to insulting him.

But today, John's words sank Jeffrey into a toxic mix of angry self-loathing and doubts about Grace.

"Our meeting is tomorrow at two o'clock," Jeffrey said, ignoring him. He wrote down the location and handed it to John. "You will be there."

"Of course," John said, snatching the paper from his hand. "It's a splendid idea. As far from you and Blackwood Hall as I can be is certainly *my* preference, as well." He brushed past Jeffrey, his shoulder knocking against him as he swept out of the study.

"You'll stay to dine," Jeffrey said tersely.

John paused at the door. Jeffrey could see his shoulders tense, could see the intake of breath. John looked back and smiled strangely. "I'd not miss the opportunity to dine with you and your lovely wife." He went out, slamming the door behind him.

"Four seasons," Jeffrey muttered. "Four windows, sixteen steps across the study…"

Counting wouldn't soothe him. Nothing would. He felt ravaged. His fear of what was said around Ashton Down about him was torment enough—a man could not seek the sort of diversions Jeffrey had sought and not expect for there to be talk. But to add to that the idea that Grace's mother was mad was more than he could bear. He didn't understand why she hadn't told him. He worried how the mix of blood from *two* mad people would ruin his children. What hope could there possibly be for them? But more than that, the weight of Grace's secret was pressing on him, making him a bit short of breath.

He opened the bottom drawer of his desk and withdrew a piece of vellum. He picked up a pen, dipped it in ink eight times and began to write figures, in rows and columns of eight. Sums. Sums divided and multiplied all by a factor of eight. It was a tedious, painstaking task that had, at times, taken an hour or more. But it was the tedium of it, the mind-numbing repetition that calmed him and allowed him to think.

He hadn't felt this anxious in days, if not weeks, he realized. He'd grown comfortable with the presence of a woman in his house, and the obsessions, the compulsions he'd felt about Grace, had eased. He was still plagued with images—but now the images were only of Grace. Only her. Even his unnatural fear of harming her had subsided. There was always that moment of uncertainty when he was with her, but even his tortured brain could reason that as he had yet to harm her, his fear of doing just that was nonsensical.

It was strange how it all came roaring back to him with one angry comment from John. The sad truth of his depravity was that even in times he felt quite normal, it was always lurking just below the surface, always in him. Even on those occasions Jeffrey believed he was improving.

And now, he began to imagine the number of secrets Grace was keeping from him. Too many, all of them salacious. The recording of sums helped ease him somewhat, and Jeffrey was eventually able to leave his study and go to his rooms to prepare for what he assumed would be an excruciating supper. The whiskey he drank only made his belly churn. There was a charge running through him, his thoughts alternating between lurid images of his brother with his wife, and the endless process of counting. *"Get hold of yourself,"* he hissed at his reflection. What sort of man was he that he could not control it?

*A peculiar one.* He tapped his fist against his leg and forced himself to go down for supper.

Grace and John were already in the parlor. John seemed relaxed, as if he'd somehow managed to suppress his rage with Jeffrey. Jeffrey wished he could do the same.

Grace looked lovely in a gray gown and pearls. "Good evening," she said, reaching her hand for Jeffrey's. "I was just saying to John how glad I am that he stayed for supper. I know you miss him."

Jeffrey leaned down and kissed her cheek. "Of course I miss him," he said. It was true. In spite of the adversarial relationship between them, Jeffrey missed the boy who once followed him around, chattering incessantly about swords and knights and battles on castle walls. There had been a period in Jeffrey's life when John had been the only bright spot.

Grace's grateful smile was brilliant, and Jeffrey could feel it slip through him like a whisper of silk. She was beautiful, surely the subject of any healthy man's thoughts. He couldn't be alone in that, and glanced at his brother. John was at the sideboard, pouring a glass of whiskey.

Cox appeared, carrying flutes of champagne. Grace took one. Jeffrey declined. She seemed nervous, he thought as she smiled at him and looked at his brother. "Your brother is incorrigible," she said.

"Pardon?"

She turned a sparkling smile to John. "He does a wonderful imitation of a mutual acquaintance, Lord Grimbley. Do you know him?"

Jeffrey shook his head.

"I am surprised you recall it, it's been so long ago," John said. "Let me think…he's a rather rotund fellow who has a tendency to sway side to side when he chats up the ladies," he said, mimicking the sway. He pinched his face, tossed his head back and peered down his nose with a squint. "You've twenty thousand a year, Miss Cabot? Why, you'd be the perfect match for me," John said in a gravelly voice, his hips swaying from one side to the next.

"It's uncanny," Grace proclaimed with delight. "You even *look* a bit like him. I think even Grimbley would be amused by your imitation of him."

"I wouldn't be sure of that," John said laughingly.

"He is at all the fashionable events," Grace said. "You must show him the next time you meet."

"It looks as if I won't be at any fashionable event," John said congenially. But Jeffrey could hear the thread of bitterness in his voice. "Perhaps my brother hasn't mentioned it, but he's been kind enough to seek an occupation for me. Very kind indeed," John said, and lifted his whiskey. "To my brother, a man who selfishly seeks occupations for his family, lest they be idle." John didn't wait for a response, but drained his whiskey.

Grace smiled uncertainly, as if she thought John was teasing her. "And what is your occupation to be?"

"Oh, I am to be an officer in the royal navy," John said grandly. "One must pay one's debts, you know. I never cared much for the sea. I had rather hoped for the clergy."

Jeffrey couldn't help the small laugh of surprise that escaped him. He was alone in it, however; Grace was looking curiously at John. Perhaps she was trying to imagine him in the robes of a vicar.

Cox announced supper was served. They made their way to the dining room, and John settled into a role Jeffrey had often seen him assume, that of entertainer. He launched into an amusing story about a race he'd seen in Hyde Park. Jeffrey had heard the tale before; John always told it affably, in that practiced way oft-told stories were related, almost acting it out for them. Jeffrey couldn't help but notice that Grace seemed to be on the edge of her seat, hanging on his every word leading up to the outcome of the race.

Jeffrey wished he had the ability to tell an amusing tale and have Grace look at him as she was looking at his brother. She was positively sparkling with pleasure. She glanced at Jeffrey from time to time, looking for a sign that he was enjoying his brother's story, and satisfied that he was at least listening, she would turn her sparkling smile to John again.

Jeffrey couldn't help but watch her and feel the weight of his depravity in a new way. Grace had not smiled at him quite like that, had she? Why would she? He wasn't engaging like his brother. When he attended evenings such as this, he remained quiet, for fear one of his unnatural thoughts would slip from his mouth. He began to wonder if there was more to this evening than he knew. His thoughts were so plaguing him, and he was ready for the interminable evening to end, to retreat to his rooms and his rituals, and yet the main course hadn't even been served.

There was no end to the tales John had to share, much to Grace's delight. By the time they had finished the last course, he had told so many that Jeffrey couldn't keep track.

At the end of the meal, as Jeffrey and John sipped port, John began to boast of his prowess at the card table and it was all Jeffrey could do to keep from exploding into a foul discourse, particularly given the untenable situation he'd put Jeffrey in with his latest debts.

Jeffrey suddenly stood. "I beg your pardon, but I have a headache. Grace?"

She glanced at John as she stood from her seat. "So glad you could come, my lord," she said.

"What, the evening is ended so soon?" John said jovially. "Come, Lady Merryton, won't you entertain me with your lovely singing voice?"

She laughed. "I haven't a lovely singing voice."

"Then will you play for me?" John asked. "It's early yet, and as I've been banned from the gaming hells, I am in desperate need of a diversion."

"It is late," Jeffrey said.

"Just one song," John insisted, his smile quite cool.

"Perhaps only one," Grace suggested to Jeffrey.

"Then it's settled," John said, and stood up, his port in hand.

Jeffrey silently offered his arm to Grace. He couldn't help the tapping against his leg as he led her to the parlor. His discomfort was growing, filling up his limbs and his chest. But Jeffrey wasn't certain from where the discomfort was emanating. It wasn't just in the obsessive thoughts, or the need to count.

No, he realized as he watched Grace take her place at the pianoforte, what agitated him was a feeling so raw, so unnatural to him, that he didn't know how to tamp it down, how to push it out of sight or bury it. He could not count his way from this.

What agitated him, what had turned him every which way, was that he *cared*.

He cared for Grace. Against all odds, he cared for her a great deal, and that made him feel more uncertain than he ever had in his life.

"Here's to Grace. Against all ...e...he cleared for
......th at ...tr... wavered. He hop... his glass
quickly, draining it quickly. ...

# CHAPTER TWENTY-ONE

GRACE WAS AGGRAVATED. Oh, she smiled, she laughed,
she declared Amherst a connoisseur of poor musical
talent. She was the perfect hostess, but she saw him for
what he was—a glib rakehell.

As she banged the keys—deliberately, for she would
not allow him to use music as an excuse to prolong this
wretched evening, and she could not very well box his
ears—Grace could feel her heart sinking with disappointment. She'd been so hopeful, even happy, these
past few days! She had truly believed that this marriage would flourish in spite of its less than commend-
able beginnings.

But then Amherst had arrived and tried to ruin it. Oh,
she knew what he was about. She'd been in far too many
salons and ballrooms not to recognize when a gentleman was playing a wretched game. What she didn't
know was *why*. He had denigrated his own brother to
her, telling her those awful things about him. Even if
they were true, there was no reason he would have to
tell her—other than to hurt her and make her afraid of
Jeffrey.

He'd been a wretched supper guest, telling long tales
that excluded Jeffrey. He talked of events and people

and London that only he and Grace would know, trying to draw Grace into a protracted discussion. Grace tried to bring the conversation around to be more inclusive, but Amherst was determined.

When it became clear that Jeffrey wanted to end the evening he sought to prolong it and, Grace suspected, had tried to arrange it where he would be alone with her. It was churlish behavior disguised as a guest, and Grace despised him for it. She knew it had something to do with the heated conversation they'd had. Oh, yes, she knew of that, too—their voices, raised in anger, had echoed up the flues.

To think she might have married that man!

Things were vastly different now. She felt things for Jeffrey she'd never believed she would feel—affection, esteem, perhaps something even deeper than that—but all the things she'd never really felt for a man. Whatever one called it, she thought too much of Jeffrey to stand for his brother's wretched behavior.

When they had said good-night to John, Grace expected Jeffrey to come upstairs with her. But he wished her good-night instead.

"You're not coming?" she asked him.

"No," he said. "I've some things to do." He walked into his study, his fist clenched at his side.

Grace went to her rooms and prepared for bed. She expected Jeffrey to come to her. She sat on the chaise beside the fire, her arms wrapped around her knees, waiting.

At one o'clock, he still hadn't come.

What had happened? What was she to do? Her instinct was to crawl under the covers and brood, but she heard Honor's voice in her head. *Are you afraid? If you need to speak to him, then by all means, go and speak to him! Don't be a milksop.*

Once again, Honor was right—which, by the by, was happening with alarming frequency. But Grace would never sleep with all the questions and doubts tumbling about in her head, so she pulled on her dressing gown, swept up the single candle from her bedside and went down the hall to Jeffrey's rooms before she lost her nerve.

She couldn't see any light from beneath his door. Was he asleep? She tried the handle; it turned easily enough. She rapped softly and slowly pushed the door open, peering inside. There was precious little light inside and Grace couldn't see. She leaned in, intending to have a look around the door—

She was suddenly grabbed at the waist and yanked inside, then pushed up against the wall. A hand went to her mouth, muffling her shriek of surprise. Grace would have dropped the candle had Jeffrey not caught her hand and righted it. "What the devil are you about?" he demanded, putting the candle aside. "You startled me half out of my wits."

"I knocked," she said defensively, and yanked her dressing gown closed from where it had come undone.

"You knock like a child—I scarcely heard it." He let go of her and stepped back, put his hands on his waist. He was still wearing his trousers and his shirt. He looked as if he'd been sitting in the dark, the only light from the dying embers in the hearth.

"Jeffrey—"

He reached for her wrist, then pulled her across the room, forcing her to sit in a chair before the hearth. He tossed a lap rug over her and squatted down to stoke the fire. When he had a flame again, he stood up and stared at her. "Why have you come sneaking into my rooms?"

"Because you didn't come to me," she said, and stood up, casting aside the lap rug. She put her hand on his chest, on the open collar of his shirt. She could feel his pulse racing beneath her fingers.

He put his hand on hers, curled his fingers around hers. "I've much on my mind, Grace."

"I know," she said soothingly. "I'm troubled by what's happened, too."

He gave her a suspicious look. "What has happened?"

"Amherst," she said. "My sister told me about his… indiscretion."

His surprise was evident. "I am saddened that you've heard it in that way." He pressed her hand against his heart. "But you needn't worry yourself with it. I've taken care of it."

Grace nodded. She supposed that Amherst would marry the girl, whoever she was. "When?"

"When?"

"When will they marry?"

Jeffrey snorted at that and dropped his hand from hers. "There will be no wedding."

"Then what did you mean, you'd taken care of it?"

"John will give the woman what she needs to move to a quiet hamlet and raise the child, and he will accept a commission in the royal navy. He should be gone from London. He does nothing but wreak trouble and scandal when he's here."

"You've sent him away?" Grace said, trying to understand his reasoning. "That seems…" She caught herself.

"Yes?" he asked, his voice cool, his eyes gone dark.

"Well, cruel, if you must know. It seems cruel."

"Cruel, is it?" he asked, stepping away from her, to the hearth. "I would say that dishonoring one's name is cruel to one's family. You don't carry the burden of a family's reputation as I must. John's actions affect us all."

Grace thought it the height of irony that he should say that, given what he'd only recently been through. "But must you cast him out as if he is unworthy of your esteem? He's your brother."

"Cast him—" Jeffrey made a sound of impatience and turned to stare at her. "Do you *condone* his behavior, Grace? Do you condone keeping unpleasant secrets from your family?"

"No—"

"Then do you think it acceptable to let your debts go unpaid and bear the child of any man who happens to put his cock inside you?"

Grace gasped.

"Pardon, does that shock you?" he asked, moving closer. "Perhaps you find it cruel. But that is precisely what he has done to the poor woman. He has put his cock in her and given her a child he does not intend to honor. He has given his word to Sir Edmund with no intention of paying his debts. He leaves that to me. He's made himself a pariah in our society. He has reduced his opportunity for a good match, and God knows I've not helped it."

That remark sliced painfully through her. She unthinkingly shoved against his chest. "How good of you to rely on principle and honor, Jeffrey. But for the rest of us impossible mortals, there are more important things than a name. We can withstand a bruise or two. But you? You place so much importance on it that it has isolated you from the people who love you."

He clenched one hand. "Don't speak of something you know nothing about. I'm the head of an important family. A *large* family that extends well beyond my brother and sister. I have cousins, two aunts still living, a niece and nephew. You've no idea the trials I've been made to suffer with John, deeds that affect me and affect them. But how could I expect you to understand? You and yours are rather careless with propriety."

Now Grace was truly affronted. *"Careless?"* she exclaimed heatedly. "My family may not be entirely free of scandal, I grant you, but we have lived and loved and laughed. Can you say the same? No, you can't. Not everything is perfect, Jeffrey! You can't control the world around you."

"I should think that a convenient view for the Cabots, as it is too bloody late to even try," he snapped.

Grace erupted into fury. She glared up at him, only inches from his face. "Say what you will of me, I don't care. Your good opinion matters far less than my own opinion. But he is your brother, and you should protect him instead of turning him out."

"That's right," Jeffrey said, stepping even closer to her, returning her glare with a rather hard one of his own. "He is my brother, and I am the only one left who can turn him into the man he deserves to be. If I coddle him, I do a disservice to the rest of my family. They deserve my protection just as much as John, do they not? Do they not deserve to be protected from the scandals he creates? Do they not deserve to be free of the taint to their lives and their children? Do you deserve to carry the shame of your sister's marriage in addition to your own?"

Grace reacted before she could think—she slapped him across the jaw. "You're an angry, *rigid* man with no feeling."

He brought his fingers to his jaw and gingerly touched the place she had struck him. "And you are a careless woman who is ruled by feeling. Tell me the truth—are you in love with John?"

The question stunned her. "*What?* No! Of course not!"

He shrugged. "It would seem a reasonable assumption, given the great lengths to which you conspired to trap him into making an offer for you."

"That is not true!" she insisted, flustered. "That is not *why.*"

"Then why?" he demanded, catching her arm. "Tell me the *truth,* Grace. Why would you ruin your reputation and risk the happiness of your sisters with such a deplorable scheme?"

"Do you want to know the truth?" she said, her voice quavering with anger. "Because you will not like it. You may very well toss me in the gutter alongside your brother."

"I want to know the *truth,*" he said tightly.

"I did it to protect my family. There, you see? We Cabots are capable of caring to protect one another."

His eyes narrowed. "You would have me believe you did it for money?"

Grace didn't respond. She merely lifted her chin.

He shifted closer, his gaze drilling through her. "I don't believe it," he said low. "I don't believe a woman of your standing would give herself up for money. You are Beckington's stepdaughter. You are beautiful, you come from a noble family. You might have had any number of suitors—you even boasted of it, as I recall. Why, then, would you risk so much for John's purse? I don't believe that you did."

"And I can't believe that a man who values propriety above all else and abhors risk would give in to temptation in the way that *you* did."

He took her elbow firmly in his hand. "On that, at least, we are agreed," he said. He untied the ribbon at the bottom of her braid and dragged his fingers through her hair, loosening it from the twists. "Perhaps we are two people with needs greater than either of us is willing to admit, do you suppose? Perhaps there are too many secrets that we simply can't divulge."

Her brows knit into a frown at that, and he hoped it was a frown of guilt. He leaned down to kiss her, but

Grace turned her head and brought her hand up between them. "I'm too...*angry*," she said curtly.

"Perhaps you would rather it was John standing here," he muttered as he filled his hand with her breast.

Grace's anger soared. "Perhaps you would rather it be two women standing here instead of one. I have heard your secrets, too."

His nostrils flared at the mention. "I won't deny that I've had more than one woman in my bed," he said. "But don't make the mistake of equating that with affection or love. Two women is a fuck. One woman—*you*—is more than that." He pulled her hair like a rope, drawing her attention back to him. "You are enough for me, can't you see it? You are the only one I want to fill."

A shudder shot through Grace. She didn't resist when he kissed her now, or when he slid his hands over her body. He was right—she had wanted him to come to her, to transport her with his mouth and his hands.

He pulled at her dressing gown, tearing it away, and then lifting her nightgown over her head and tossing it aside. He turned her around, pushed her up against a window so that Grace had to brace herself against the frame. He slid his hands up her belly, to her breasts, and began to slide his cock in between her legs, rubbing against her, making her slick with desire.

And then he turned her around and picked her up, wrapping her legs around his waist. He pressed her back against the wall and entered her, thrusting into her with a passion that Grace felt it scorching through her. She grabbed at his shoulders and dug her fingers into his flesh. "I gave you my word, no more secrets," he said breathlessly. "Now it's your turn. Can you be completely honest, Grace? Can you tell me what you desire? Can you say where you want me to put my hands and my cock?" he asked as he pumped into her.

She wrapped her arms around his neck and closed her eyes.

"*Tell* me," he said again.

"I want...I want you to ravage me," she murmured. "I want to feel your hands and mouth on every part of me, to feel you inside me—"

"*Where.*"

"On my breasts. Between my legs. My neck, my arms, my toes. I want your seed, I want a part of you to grow in *me*—"

He growled against her neck, his body pumping harder, his rhythm matching the pounding of her pulse. He lifted his head, roughly pushed her hair from her face and locked his gaze on hers. In the low light of the fire, Grace could see the ravenous desire in his eyes, and it pulled at her heartstrings. She hadn't imagined the closeness she felt to him was possible. She could plainly see his regard for her, his expression when she suddenly cried out in ecstasy, and the way he looked at her when he followed her into that ecstasy.

Their anger, their desire, was spent, but Jeffrey kept holding her. He turned around, carried her to his bed. They tumbled into it, and he gathered her close to him, draping his leg possessively over hers.

Grace sighed with deep satisfaction, touched his cheek and kissed his lips, then brushed a curl of hair from his eye. She felt safe in his arms, she felt desired, and entirely fulfilled.

He kissed her shoulder, and Grace felt herself drifting. *"Tell me the truth,"* he whispered.

Or had she whispered it?

Her eyes flew open.

Jeffrey kissed her shoulder again, but a shudder of fear snaked down her spine. She slowly pushed herself up, pulled the bed linen up to cover her and pushed her hair back over her shoulder. She took a deep breath. "My mother is mad," she said simply.

She expected him to cry out in disbelief, or for his eyes to shutter. But he merely rolled onto his back with a sigh and looked at the fire.

"Two years ago, she was in a carriage accident at Longmeadow, and she hit her head quite badly. Soon afterward, she began to forget little things. But it has gotten much worse. She lives in the past and she…" Grace caught an unexpected sob in her throat. "She doesn't know who I am any longer." A single tear slipped out of her eye, and she turned her head to wipe it away.

"That's why I tried to trap Amherst. Honor and I, we had no offers of marriage, and when Beckington began to worsen, and our mother was increasingly mad, we knew that if we didn't take matters into our hands, no one would offer for us. No one would invite four sisters and a mad mother into their coffers."

"Why John?" he asked, his voice sounding almost disembodied. "Did you have an understanding with him?"

"No," Grace said quickly. "He just seemed affable,

and I thought—foolishly—that he would be angry at first, but then his anger would subside and it would be something of a lark." She closed her eyes. "I'm so ashamed to even say that aloud. I was so naive and foolish—"

"Why haven't you told me before now?" he asked her. "When I told you the truth of my...ailment, why didn't you tell me the truth then?"

"A very good question," she admitted, and drew her knees up. "One I have asked myself many times. The truth is that I don't know exactly," she admitted. "I feared that you wouldn't be accepting because you demand perfection. And I didn't want to ruin the fragile peace we'd found because I had feelings for you. But I think mostly because I am a coward," she said, her voice much softer.

Jeffrey turned his head to her. Firelight glimmered in his eyes.

"But I can't be perfect, Jeffrey, not even for you. It's quite impossible, actually, and you must trust me when I tell you that I've fallen short of the mark all my life. We all have our secrets and our desires and our regrets, don't we? We all have families that are flawed. I have mine, and there is nothing I could ever do to change them. More important, there is nothing I would ever *want* to change. I love them as they are."

She could see the light flickering in his eyes again, but she wasn't certain it was the fire. He put his hand on her knee and squeezed it. "You think I am too unyielding, that I want perfection. But I am an earl. I have many more to think about than just myself."

"I know," Grace said. "But you can't control them any more than I can control my sisters. You can't make me the perfect wife for you. You can't make yourself stop counting. I don't know what your father told you or made you believe, but you can't be perfect and no one expects you to be."

He looked away.

"No matter what you may have decided about me, you should know that I love you as you are."

She saw a tremor course through his body.

"I do, Jeffrey." She laid her hand on his chest. "I don't care that you don't like paintings on the walls, or you can't abide more than one color in the vase, or that you don't particularly like dogs. I love you as you are."

He didn't speak, but he covered her hand with his.

Grace slowly eased herself down next to him again, pressing into his side. She was exhausted, emotionally drained. For the time being, she was content to remain in the moment, feeling the warmth of his body seep into hers, and not think of what might come tomorrow.

She closed her eyes, letting sleep wash over her. She felt his fingers curl tightly around hers.

Sometime later, she was awakened by a sound. Grace pushed her hair from her face and sat up, gathering the bed linens to her. The sun was just coming up, and Jeffrey was not in bed. Her heart sank on a wave of bitter disappointment.

But then he walked into the room from the adjoining dressing room. He was dressed, at least partially, in trousers and boots, a shirt and waistcoat. He smiled at her, touched his hand to her face. "You best rise, Lady

Merryton. Miss Barnill is pacing the hallway, ready to begin her day. And besides, you must call on your stepbrother."

"I must?" she asked uncertainly.

He splashed his face again, toweled it dry, then splashed again. "You must," he said as he toweled it dry a second time. "I should like to make your family's acquaintance this evening. I will see for myself who is madder—your mother or me."

Grace blinked.

Jeffrey looked over his shoulder at her. He was smiling. "It was a jest."

"But you don't jest."

He chuckled at that. "I suppose I don't," he said, and turned back to the basin.

Grace wrapped herself in a sheet and came up on her knees. "Are you certain?"

"I am certain. You want me to meet them, don't you?"

More than anything. More than air, more than food, more than even Jeffrey, she wanted him to meet her family. "Yes, I do. Very much."

He resumed his toilette, washing his face and toweling it dry. Grace fixed her gaze on the sheets, her mind whirling around the very idea of it.

"Grace...darling," he said. The word sounded strange coming from him, as if he had never used the endearment, and was testing the weight of it on his tongue. He had turned from the basin to her again. "No more secrets between us. Will you promise me this?"

"I promise," she said. "No more secrets."

He turned back to the basin.

Grace climbed out of his bed, gathered her clothes and donned them. She was tying the dressing gown around her when Jeffrey suddenly reached for her. He pulled her into his embrace and kissed the top of her head, shocking her with the sudden rush of affection for her. "I am trying," he said, and bent to kiss the corner of her mouth.

"Thank you," she said.

He smiled. "Go now."

Grace pulled away from him and walked to the door. But she paused there and looked back.

Jeffrey was splashing water on his face again.

# CHAPTER TWENTY-TWO

IT WAS AN embarrassment of staggering proportions that John did not appear at the appointed time to meet with Admiral Hale, particularly considering that the admiral had only agreed to meet as a favor to Jeffrey, for the sake of his father's memory, with whom the admiral had been closely acquainted.

At first, Jeffrey had believed that perhaps John had been detained somehow. After yesterday's bruising argument, he didn't believe for a moment that John would defy him in this. But as the minutes dragged by, and the admiral checked his pocket watch for what seemed the tenth time, Jeffrey had to accept that John had purposely missed the meeting. He had no intention of accepting the commission Jeffrey had paid dearly to give him.

The interminable wait left Jeffrey feeling as if his insides had twisted around on him. He wanted desperately to count, but had to make do with tapping his finger against his knee.

"I beg your pardon," Jeffrey said when the admiral stood to leave. "I can offer no excuse for my brother's absence."

"Yes, well, a life at sea is not for every man," the admiral said. He fit his hat on his head. "I understand

congratulations are in order on your recent nuptials."
He did not smile when he offered the congratulations,
but eyed Jeffrey curiously, as if he expected him to con-
firm whatever rumor the admiral had heard.

Jeffrey could only imagine the things that had been
said, the gossip having had time to percolate and morph
into whatever it was that society found amusing in another's folly. He could feel the pressure of his compul-
sion to count building up in him like a head of steam.
He smiled thinly and said, "Thank you."

The admiral eyed him closely for a few moments.
"Well," he said, apparently convinced that Jeffrey would
not divulge more than a thank-you, "happiest of tidings
to you and your bride."

Jeffrey accompanied the admiral out into the rain.
He stood there after the admiral's carriage had left, the
rain pouring down on him as his chest rose and fell with
each furious breath.

*Nothing had happened.*

Jeffrey had to see it, to accept it. The admiral had
clearly heard the rumors of his unconventional marriage. He had congratulated him. He had waited for
him to say more, which Jeffrey had politely refused to
do. *And nothing had happened.* He'd not been made to
stand on a black square in the foyer for hours. He'd not
been put in a cupboard, left to cry out for a mother who
would not come. He'd accepted the congratulations and
the admiral had wished him a happy life and a good day.
He had not made a single disparaging remark.

"Milord!" A footman from the club where Jeffrey
had met the admiral suddenly appeared at his side,

holding an umbrella high overhead. "Milord, will you come in?"

"No, thank you," Jeffrey said, and actually smiled at the footman. "I am leaving."

His search for John was fruitless. His brother had not been seen at White's Gentlemen's Club. Nor had he been in the infamous Southwark gaming hell that all the young Corinthians found so diverting, and where, so the story went, Honor Cabot had made an infamous proposal for the hand of George Easton. No one had seen John, no one knew where he might be. It was as if his brother had vanished into London's thick air. Again.

He rode back to Brook Street feeling helpless. He and John had gone around this before—John's refusal to take his title seriously, Jeffrey's insistence that he uphold the family tradition of honor and propriety— and it always had the same result. A standoff between brothers. Jeffrey was reminded of what Grace had said, that she couldn't change her family and didn't want to. Maybe, he thought, he had tried too hard to change John. Maybe, the sins of his father were being repeated in Jeffrey's insistence that John be what he thought his father would want him to be. Instead of allowing him to be his own man, with all his flaws. But if Jeffrey didn't look after him, what would John do? How would he survive? Was it possible that John was entirely satisfied with the life that he lived? Jeffrey feared he would end up in a gutter.

But another thought occurred to him as he rode along—how much fear inhabited him. Fear of discovery, fear of disappointing his family, fear of scandal—

all of them worked to fill in every crevice of his soul. Jeffrey scrubbed one eye with his fingers. It tingled with his exhaustion of being the man he was, of living with nebulous, dark and unformed fears that inhabited his body, rooting into his fiber like a cancer.

God, how he wished to be free of it. How grateful he was that John didn't seem to have those fears. And if he didn't have those fears, who was Jeffrey to instill them?

Jeffrey was halfway to Brook Street when he turned, and moved toward another part of town. He had an idea of how to find his brother.

Jeffrey arrived home much later than he'd anticipated. Grace was pacing the foyer and looked relieved when he walked in. She was dressed for the evening, a gown of silver and green that made her look like an angel come down from heaven. *His* angel.

"There you are!" she exclaimed, her voice full of relief. "I thought you'd changed your mind."

"I won't change my mind," he said confidently, and kissed her. He'd made up his mind about a number of things today, and the idea that he would be married to this woman, and give her children, and meet her family, was first and foremost in his mind.

"We'll be late," she said, glancing at a clock. "Augustine has sent a coach for us. He's quite pleased that you will grace his home."

Jeffrey had very little time, what with his rituals, but he was confident he'd be all right. "Wait in the parlor. I'll be down soon."

He remained confident when he appeared a scant half hour later, dressed in formal attire and clean-shaven. He was so confident that he smiled at Grace as he helped her into the coach, and listened to her list all the things he should know of her family. Mercy, the youngest, was vibrant and curious, prone to ask too many questions in her desire to know more of the world. Prudence, the next sister, would pretend it was the most tedious evening she'd ever spent, when in fact, she would hang on every word Jeffrey uttered. Honor and her husband, Easton, would offer free advice, as Honor fancied herself an expert on most things. Augustine would be gracious; his fiancée, Monica, would be watching closely for anything she might relate to her odious mother, and then, of course, Grace's mother would not know them and might say things that were inappropriate.

When the coach rolled up to Beckington House, Grace looked worried. "Are you quite all right?" she asked, reaching across the interior to put her hand on his knee.

"Grace—I am quite all right," he said. And he meant it. He meant it all the way to the door.

But then he was plunged into the chaos of the Beckington family, and his confidence began to seep out of him, beginning with the great hue and cry as three young women rushed at Grace, a fourth following behind them. Jeffrey handed their cloaks to a footman as the feminine voices, jubilant and loud, pounded like tin drums in his head. Five women, all dressed in sumptuous gowns, all chattering at once. It made no sense to Jeffrey—how could they speak in that manner? How could they hear what any of the others said?

"My lord! My lord, you are *most* welcome!"

Jeffrey recognized Beckington, having met him a time or two. He was hurrying forward across the expansive foyer to him so quickly that, for a moment, Jeffrey feared he might plow into him. But he managed to draw himself up at the last moment and bow low.

"Thank you," Jeffrey said. "Thank you for inviting us—"

"I am happy to have you!" he said with great eagerness. "Grace is like a sister to me, after all. Oh, allow me, do you know Mr. Easton? He has married Honor, who is also like a sister to me." He laughed. "I suppose they are all sisters to me, are they not?"

"Mr. Easton," Jeffrey said, and extended his hand.

"My lord," Easton said politely. He was an inch or two taller than Jeffrey and resembled the late Duke of Gloucester. And like Gloucester, or at least what Jeffrey could remember of him, Easton had a bit of a twinkle in his blue eyes.

"Whiskey or wine?" Beckington said excitedly. "We've both."

"Ah…thank you," Jeffrey said. Did he mean to serve it in the foyer? He looked to Grace, who seemed to be showing her shoe to the gathered women.

"Goodness, you won't want to wait for them," Beckington said. "They'll be nattering about shoes and whatnot for another ten minutes."

"Augustine!" one of the women cried. "Don't you dare steal him away!"

A woman with dark hair and blue eyes appeared on George's left. She was obviously Grace's sister, in spite of the difference in color—she had the same expressive eyes as Grace. "How do you do," she said, sliding down into a perfect curtsy. "I am Honor Cabot Easton, Grace's sister. You've no doubt heard quite a lot about me," she said, and gave him a slight wink.

"I, ah…" Good Lord, he had no idea what to say.

"Pay her no mind," Easton said low.

"I am pleased to make your—"

"What of me?" said another one, jostling in beside Honor.

"For heaven's sake, would you all at least *pretend* to allow me to introduce you?" Grace said, waving them all back. She introduced Jeffrey to Mrs. Easton, who was still smiling at him as if they shared a secret, then Prudence Cabot, and last but not least, in round spectacles, Mercy Cabot.

"And, of course, a woman who will soon become our sister, Miss Monica Hargrove."

"Well…perhaps not *sisters,*" Miss Hargrove said, and curtsied.

"Very well, very well, please don't crowd our guest!" Beckington said, shooing them all back, and ushered Jeffrey into a very grand salon. Jeffrey was certain the salon had the finest quality of furnishings, but all he could see, and feel, was the portrait above the hearth that hung a little lopsidedly.

He turned his back to it and caught Grace's eye. She smiled a little anxiously, as if she sensed something was off balance and expected him to collapse.

"We've been very eager to make your acquaintance, my lord!" Beckington said cheerfully. "That is, dearest Miss Hargrove has been eager, for I've met you from time to time. *My* eagerness has been more of a desire to greet you fondly as a member of the family. Miss Hargrove and I will join you in wedded bliss by month's end."

"What I think you mean to say is that we will be enjoying our own wedded bliss by month's end, dearest," Miss Hargrove said.

"Yes, of course, that's it," Beckington said.

"Are you in London long?" asked Easton.

"No," Jeffrey said.

Easton looked at him as if he expected more.

"We miss Blackwood Hall so," Grace said suddenly, earning a look of surprise from her sisters. "What?" she said to their unspoken questions. "Well, I do. It's lovely there. And I have dogs—"

"Dogs!" cried Mercy. "Hunting dogs?"

"Not exactly," Grace said. "Dogs that have been formally rejected from Blackwood's kennels as being too imperfect to hunt."

The young girl gasped. "That's outrageous!"

"Now, Mercy, let Merryton manage his kennels as he sees fit," said Beckington. "We are keen hunters at Longmeadow, my lord. I am particularly fond of the grouse season. I can see them a bit better, you see," he said, pointing at his eyes. "The hares, well, they're much too fast, and the deer, I've not much luck with. You?"

"I find them all challenging."

"I shall go and fetch Mamma, shall I?" Prudence asked Grace. "I might perish with hunger if we don't bring her soon."

At the mention of Lady Beckington, the room went

still. It seemed to Jeffrey that all of them were waiting on tenterhooks to see what he would say or do.

But Grace smiled and said, "Yes, please, Prudence."

The rest of them chatted amicably while they waited. Jeffrey stood with the gentlemen, nodding at things he thought to acknowledge, but holding one hand at his back, clasped against the rising tide of chaotic thoughts. He was counting, trying to calm his racing thoughts. The only saving grace that his thoughts were not particularly salacious, which, he supposed, given the number of lovely young ladies about him, was something of a personal victory.

He heard Lady Beckington before he saw her. There was quite a commotion—it sounded as if there was a disagreement. But then she appeared in the salon with Prudence, her eyes wild as she looked about. Lady Beckington looked tired, Jeffrey thought, and a bit haggard. But he could see the beauty in her still, could see where her four daughters had come by their fine looks.

"My lady, how lovely you look this evening," Beckington said jovially, and stretched out his arms to embrace her. But Lady Beckington pushed him aside and looked at her sleeve.

Beckington smiled without conceit. "She rarely allows me a proper greeting."

"Mamma, look who has come," Honor said. "It's Grace."

"Who took my cloak?" Lady Beckington demanded of Honor.

"No one took it," Mercy said. "It's hanging in the foyer with the others."

"Mamma?" Grace said. "I should like you to meet my husband, Lord Merryton."

He stepped forward, and Lady Beckington turned her head. She smiled at Jeffrey, but her smile was vacant. Her sleeve, he noticed, was unraveling. It reminded him a little of the way he often felt—unraveling into depravity.

Grace took her mother's hand and dipped down beside her. "I am married, Mamma. To an earl."

"You must be the girl William brought in for cleaning," Lady Beckington said curiously.

"Oh, dear," Prudence whispered, and smiled apologetically at Jeffrey. "William was our father."

Lady Beckington stood up. She looked at Jeffrey, her eyes quite clear. She stared at him, as if she thought she might know him. And then she said, "I know who you are. I know all about you, sir." But she said it with such sobriety that Jeffrey was momentarily confused— it almost seemed as if she was telling him she knew about *him*.

And then just as suddenly, her eyes clouded with confusion and she asked him, "Where did the maid get off to? We should have it all cleaned."

"Let's dine instead," Honor said, linking her arm through her mother's. "Shall I lead us in?" she asked Beckington.

"Yes, of course, whatever she likes," he said congenially.

Jeffrey watched Lady Beckington. She didn't want to go, but her daughter coaxed her along with some soothing words.

They gathered in the dining room, and Lady Beckington at first refused to sit, and then sat and began to pick at her sleeve. "Are you in London often?" Beckington asked Merryton, as if there was no chaos in this room. "I've not seen you in the club."

"I am not often in London, no," Jeffrey said, and politely continued the conversation, his foot tapping against the floor as quietly as he could manage. Grace put her hand on his knee under the table.

The evening was quite harsh for Jeffrey, but that was nothing new for him. He often felt the discord rattling in him in large groups. But with two glasses of wine, and an excellent bit of duck, Jeffrey began to see something different in this group. There was a lot of laughter. This family genuinely seemed to enjoy one another. The second thing he noticed was that none of them, not one, seemed to resent or otherwise dismiss Lady Beckington. Even in her madness, she was one of them.

It was something so foreign to him that it took him an entire meal to accept that was what was happening. Even Miss Hargrove, who said little, was solicitous of Lady Beckington, and helped her to consume her meal without any sign of rancor.

Grace had told him that no one was perfect. But at the end of that meal, when he and Grace finally took their leave with promises to return, he would privately disagree. That meal, that family meal, where everyone was accepted for who they were, was perfect.

## CHAPTER TWENTY-THREE

AFTER JEFFREY'S UNEXPECTED call to Mr. Ainsley the day before, a messenger arrived the next morning with a note for Jeffrey. True to his word, Mr. Ainsley had discovered the information Jeffrey needed. He went out before Grace had come down leaving word that he would see her at supper this evening.

He rode across town into a maze of streets with no rhyme or reason. It was very disconcerting, but the steady tap of his leg kept him moving forward.

At Tomlinson Street, the boy who took Jeffrey's horse said he didn't know Miss Louisa Peters. But he was aware of a Mrs. Peters and pointed to a small townhome.

Jeffrey had an uncomfortable feeling about Mrs. Peters and sincerely hoped his intuition was wrong. He walked up to the red painted door and rapped loudly, four times. Through an open window he could hear the sound of a baby crying and tensed.

A young woman opened the door with a baby on her hip. The baby looked to be several months old, had round, flushed cheeks and looked so much like John that Jeffrey was momentarily taken aback.

"Yes?" she asked, looking up at him, her gaze taking in his clothing.

"I beg your pardon, I am looking for Miss Louisa Peters."

The blood drained from the young woman's face. She put a protective arm around her child. She suddenly tried to close the door, but Jeffrey quickly stopped her with a boot in the door. "Who are you? What do you want?" she demanded.

What Jeffrey wanted was for his life to be different. He wanted to raise children to a better life than what his father had shown him. He wanted to be free of the peculiarities that gripped him. He did not want to be a man that women like this feared.

He forced himself to smile. "You know who I am, Miss Peters. And what I want is to hold my nephew."

She blinked. She held her baby closer, her fear obvious. *"No—"*

"Louisa…let him hold the baby."

John appeared behind her. He was in his shirtsleeves, his neck cloth missing, as if he'd been inside the small town house for a while. He looked as anxious as Miss Peters, and put his hand on her shoulder. "I won't allow any harm to come to him. Neither will my brother."

The young woman reluctantly handed Jeffrey the child.

Jeffrey took the baby in his arms and felt something warm rush through him. The little fellow reached for his neck cloth and made a sound of delight, and Jeffrey smiled.

"What is his name?"

"Thomas," John said. "Thomas Donovan. Come in, Jeffrey. We've drawn enough attention."

The house was small, and lacking in furniture. But what few pieces they had were of quality craftsmanship. In the parlor was a pair of wooden balls and a wooden toy soldier.

Jeffrey smiled down at the boy and ran his hand over his head. The baby reached for Jeffrey's nose. Jeffrey stood still and let him put his hands on his nose, his fingers in his mouth, all while Thomas's mother hovered nervously about.

Jeffrey at last handed the child to her and said, "Your son is beautiful."

"Thank you, milord," she said, and pressed the baby's head to her cheek. She picked up a rag, twisted tightly and bound on either end, and handed it to Thomas. He began to gnaw on the rag.

"You've been keeping a very big secret," Jeffrey said to his brother. "I assumed the child had only recently been born."

John didn't speak. He shifted to stand between Jeffrey and his mistress and her child. "Why have you come?" John asked. "What do you want?"

"An excellent question." Jeffrey sighed, and swept his hat off his head. "I came in search of you. When you didn't come yesterday, I was quite angry. I meant to have a word."

"You've said all that you need to say," John said tightly. "I suspect I know what you will do. But you can't threaten me, Jeffrey. There is nothing you can do that will change my mind or my heart. I have a son and I will not abandon him. I have a wife and neither will I abandon her. God knows I've not been husband enough to her as it is."

Jeffrey was stunned. He looked at the young woman. She was fair, with pale blond hair and big brown eyes. An image of her with her head tossed back in the throes of ecstasy, her slender neck exposed, flit through his mind, but he looked at the child and forced it down. "Married," he muttered. It was not what he'd hoped for John. But then again, Grace was not what he'd hoped for himself.

John shrugged. "I'm a scoundrel, it's true. But I could not bring my son into the world outside the bounds of marriage. And...and I love Louisa. It's as simple as that."

It really was very simple when one boiled it down wasn't it? A remarkable revelation to someone who'd spent his entire life avoiding the slightest hint of impropriety.

"I beg your pardon, Louisa, I have been remiss. This is my brother, the Earl of Merryton."

Her eyes were wide as saucers as she managed a curtsy.

Jeffrey nodded. He put his hand behind his back and held it tightly against the need for some order, a pre-scribed path. He thought of their father. He could still see him as clear as if he were standing before him, the disapproval in his eyes, the absolute censure of what John had done. Jeffrey wished John had had a care with himself, and with Louisa especially—he would recover from this sort of scandal, but she never would. John knew that, and he'd done what he ought to have done. He'd stood up, taken responsibility, and for that Jeffrey was proud of him. For once in his bloody life, when it mattered most, his brother had taken some responsibility.

Jeffrey sighed, seated his hat on his head. "I should like a pint," he said wearily. "Perhaps two."

John eyed him warily. "There is a tavern at the end of the street."

"Will you come?" Jeffrey asked.

John exchanged a look with his wife that Jeffrey wished he could wave away. They had nothing to fear from him.

THE TAVERN WAS crowded, but the proprietor recognized someone of Quality, and showed the brothers to a private room. Neither of them spoke at first, preferring to nurse their ales and their own private thoughts.

At last Jeffrey pushed his tankard aside, planted his elbows on the table, and gave John a stern look. "Why did you not tell me?"

John snorted. "*Tell* you? To hear your disgust? To be lectured at how I have ruined the family name? Is it not obvious why, Jeffrey? I hardly care what you say of me, but I will not hear such slander said against my son."

Jeffrey deserved that, he supposed.

"I know this is a match you will never approve of," he said, and then laughed bitterly. "Who would? She has no dowry, her father is a tailor…" He shook his head. "But she has made me happy. And my need to be a father to that boy—a *good* father—far outweighed my concern over losing my fortune." He rubbed his face. "It *is* a concern, but I have a bit of property I might sell."

"Surely you didn't think you could keep this secret from me. From Sylvia."

"I don't know—we've become quite good at keeping secrets from one another, haven't we?" He drank more ale then fixed his gaze on Jeffrey. "I know your concern is the Merryton estate and the scandal that will follow. But I've thought of that. My intent is to live quietly, out of the society's eye. Perhaps in a small hamlet, as you yourself suggested—"

"No," Jeffrey said, shaking his head. He wasn't entirely certain what was to be done, but he knew that the child he'd seen should not be tucked away to live in shame. "You should live as a Donovan, proud of your son and your wife. She's lovely."

"As a Donovan. What the bloody hell does that mean? Living with constant censure? With your constant fear of it?"

Was that what John thought of Jeffrey? That he feared censure? "What I mean is that, in this, you should live exactly the opposite of the way we were brought up. Openly. Proudly."

John blinked. A wry smile appeared on his lips. "Kind words. But I don't trust you, Jeffrey. You are a man who has insisted that honor and propriety and the family name are far more important to him than even a wife."

"I have, haven't I?" Jeffrey said absently. He felt the discord rising in him and tapped his knee. Protecting the family name had been ingrained into him since the time he could walk and talk. It was the thing that perhaps had driven him to madness, the constant need for perfection, the inability to absorb imperfections. That had all shifted a bit when he laid eyes on Thomas. "But you have a son, John."

"And you have gained a wife with a mad mother."

"Yes," Jeffrey said tightly.

John looked at his ale. "I beg your pardon. That was uncalled for. I'm sorry, Jeffrey. More than anything I regret what has happened to you and to Grace. It was my fault—"

"Don't," Jeffrey said. "I might have put off marriage all my life had I not been forced into it." He drank, washing down the bitter truth in that. "She suits me," he said simply, but it was more than that. It was far more than that. Jeffrey was finally beginning to understand just how deep and broad it truly was.

"She never cared for me," John said. "I hope you know that."

The image of John and Grace popped up, uninvited.

"There was a time, before Louisa, that I thought Grace Cabot was one of the most comely women in London. God knows I tried to ingratiate myself to her, but she wanted nothing to do with me," John said with a shrug. "But when she came to Bath, she'd had an abrupt change of heart and was far too determined to lure me to her. She'd never wanted for suitors. When I learned of her mother's illness, I understood that she realized she had to marry before it was too late, before the world knew that her mother had gone mad and she'd lost her best prospects."

Jeffrey studied the scarred table, thinking of the irony. On the surface, what Grace did was reprehensible. But he also understood that she was concerned for her family. Right or wrong, she'd done what she thought she should do for them.

"Yes, well, it's said and done."

"I'm happy that she suits you," John said.

She more than suited him. He had come to rely on her in a very short time. He had thought that he would manage his forced marriage from a distance, but Grace had had another plan.

Jeffrey drained his ale. "Speaking of Grace, I should return to her now." He stood up, put some coins on the table. "We've both turned a corner in our lives, have we not? For better or worse, as it were. We should not be enemies."

"No," John said. He came to his feet, offered his hand. Jeffrey took it. There was much more to say and to think through, but for now, he felt relieved. "Take care of my nephew."

John smiled. "Thank you for…for understanding, Jeffrey. I hadn't thought…"

"You hadn't thought me capable." Jeffrey said. "Nor did I." He smiled and went out.

There was quite a lot before him to weather—once news spread about John's child and marriage, there would be no end to the speculation. There would be those who would shun them, but for once in his bloody life, Jeffrey didn't feel the uncertainty rising up in him. He scarcely counted to his horse's trot.

He thought of Grace, and of how much she had

shown him in the short time they'd been together. He thought of her mother, and how her madness had been embraced by her family. He thought of the ridiculous, reckless thing she'd done in Bath—but at least it made some sense to him. Grace had been trying to protect someone dear to her from society and scandal, just as Jeffrey had tried to protect his brother from society and scandal. He had to admire at least her strength and willingness to sacrifice for the sake of her family. And he certainly had to admire that in less-than-ideal circumstances, in spite of his own madness, Grace had tried to be a good wife to him.

Things had changed in the complicated mess of feelings and compulsions in him. Truly changed—he could feel it in his marrow, in the lessening of the grip of his depravity. For the first time in his life, what he was feeling was love. Soft, asymmetrical, messy, imperfect love.

It was Mercy who heard the kittens, but Grace who gathered them up and put them in a box, bringing them into the parlor of the Merryton townhome.

Cox looked as if he might faint away, but Grace and her sisters put the box on the floor and gathered around the abandoned kittens.

"What will Merryton say?" Honor asked as she allowed a black kitten with one white paw to nuzzle her neck.

"He won't say much of anything," Grace said. "But he will not like it." She winked at Honor.

"He's very quiet, isn't he?" Mercy asked, holding a gray-striped kitten. "Is Blackwood Hall very big?"

"Enormous," Grace assured her. "And quite old."

Mercy blinked. "Have you heard any strange noises? Footsteps or the sound of someone crying?"

Grace laughed. "I've heard nothing but the wind whistling in the eaves."

"I'd wager it's haunted," Mercy said gravely. "Most old houses are."

"Mercy, for heaven's sake," Prudence complained. She had picked up the gold tabby, who had made a little nest in her lap and was watching the other kittens. "What *I* want to know is what happened that night in Bath." She leaned forward and peered closely at Grace. "You didn't do anything *very* terrible, did you?"

Honor laughed. "You sound positively enthralled, Prudence. I think you rather hope she did."

"Well, of course I do," Prudence said. "There's no diversion in proper etiquette, is there?"

"There is not," Grace agreed. "All right, I'll tell you." She stroked the gray cat with the green eyes and told her sisters everything that had happened that night in Bath...leaving out the more salacious details, naturally, as Mercy and Prudence were still too young to hear them.

She was in the midst of telling them about Molly Madigan and her very big cat when her husband returned. He walked into the parlor and seemed to take a step back, his gave riveting on the kittens bouncing around the four young women on the floor.

"Oh," Grace said, and quickly came to her feet. "We weren't expecting you so soon."

"Yes," he said, his eyes still on the kittens.

"You're right, Grace. He didn't say a word about them," Mercy said, peering up at him.

"Mercy, don't speak," Honor muttered. She stood, too.

"We beg your pardon," Grace said. "But the kittens were abandoned and we couldn't bear to leave them."

"*You* couldn't bear to leave them," Honor said.

Grace gave her sister a withering look. "All right, *I* couldn't bear to leave them. But Honor has agreed to take two. Mercy and Prudence each one, and so I'll have only one—"

"I don't care about the kittens," Jeffrey said, surprising her, and clasped his hands behind his back. He bowed his head to her sisters. "Have as many as you like." He looked at Grace. "Might I have a word?"

"Yes, of course," she said, and handed her kitten to Mercy. "Don't pet them too hard. They're still quite young."

She put her hand against her abdomen to quell her nerves and followed Jeffrey out.

He led her into his study and quietly closed the door. "Did you...did you find him?" she asked, vexed by how wobbly she sounded.

"I did."

Grace sighed and closed her eyes, assuming the worst. He had sent the woman away, had made John accept the commission. As disappointed as she was with John, she ached for that child. "Have you no feeling?" she asked softly. "People make mistakes."

He clenched his jaw and studied the floor a moment. Grace was certain he was counting behind his back, tapping away, his thoughts centered on the need to keep the Merryton name pristine, unsullied, pure. Which meant the truth would end in heartache and secrets, everyone living in the shadows along with him.

"You must understand—"

"You needn't say it," she said, cutting him off. "I understand. Part of me understands all too well. It's why I was in the tea shop that night, trying to maintain appearances and connections. But to what end?" she asked, more of herself than him.

"If you will allow me to finish," he said. "You must understand, more than anyone, how difficult it is for me to accept what John has done. Because I am mad, because I am lost without order and symmetry. Without them, the world descends into chaos and debauchery. You understand this."

"I'm trying to," she said helplessly.

"Then you must know how…" His voice broke, and his hand curled at his side. "You must know what it means when I tell you that you have changed me. Your love, your acceptance, has *changed* me. When I look at you, the fears I carry inside me begin to subside. I can see the possibilities—I can't grasp them all, not yet, but I can see them—and I *need* you, Grace. I need you desperately."

He had stunned her. Grace could only stare at him as those words wrapped around her heart.

Jeffrey clenched his jaw, tapped his hand against his leg eight times. "I have seen my nephew. I saw John in him. I saw all the possibilities stretching before him, and I want him to grasp them all. I want him to know he is loved. I won't press John into the naval commission. I won't press him other than to bring Thomas around."

Grace gasped. "You didn't send them away?"

He shook his head. "I left him to do what he must do."

It might seem like very little to anyone else, but Grace understood how hard that must have been for Jeffrey to do, fighting against himself every step of the way.

"Oh, my," she said, and couldn't help but touch his face. Jeffrey closed his eyes, turned his face into her palm and kissed it. "How hard that must have been. I'm so…relieved. And so proud of you, Jeffrey."

"Yes, well, I don't know that I will manage to keep from obsessing about it, questioning it all again, but I…I feel a bit proud of myself."

She smiled at him.

"I love you," he said, his arms going around her. "I will never be easy, I will never be free of my illness. But I love you, Grace, and I promise to love you as you are."

She couldn't have asked for anything more meaningful than that. With a cry of relief, she threw her arms around his neck. "I've never been so charmed in all my life, my lord." She kissed him. His hands began to move on her, but the voices of her sisters in the foyer brought their heads up.

"Mercy, I told you to keep a close eye!" they could hear Prudence say. "We'll never find it."

"Oh, no," Grace said. "I should go and head off whatever disaster is brewing." She kissed him once more.

It was strange, she thought, how the light in his eyes had changed. It was if the shutters had finally opened.

It was curious, Grace thought as she left him to go and find the lost kitten, how fate could take something so wretched—the night in Bath, in particular—and make it so right for so many.

She heard the kitten's meow and spotted it in the corner, near the umbrella stand. She scooped it up and held it to her chest, felt the reverberation of the kitten's purr against her, felt the strength of her feelings for a lonely earl sink deep into her roots.

# EPILOGUE

*1816*

IT WAS SUMMER at Blackwood Hall, and the long, dark hallways had been transformed by the children who now gathered here. Jeffrey no longer used the main corridor to count his way to sanity—how could he? It was littered with toys and forgotten blankets and bits and pieces of a house that seemed to him to being slowly dismantled by tiny hands.

Jeffrey loved the children, all of them. They had lightened his heart in a way he never would have believed was possible. He would have dozens of them if he could, and sometimes, he wondered if he might—he could not seem to keep his hands from his wife. His salacious and perverted thoughts were still very much part of him, but they were all reserved for Grace.

How fortunate he was that his wife had a rather amazing appetite of her own. She'd never been anything but an eager partner, no matter how far they slid down into the depths of his imagination.

Grace wanted more children, too—but their collective mayhem made his affliction rather difficult to manage. His fear of hurting Grace had been channeled into a very real fear of hurting the children. They were so small, their bones so fragile. And so *many* of them.

At present, there were eight of them in his house, which helped in that strange way eight had of soothing him. Two born of his brother, John, two from his sister, Sylvia. Three of the children belonged to Honor and George Easton. Easton had rebuilt the fortune he'd lost with a ship at sea several years ago, and now apparently believed that childbearing was something that should be done per annum, when the ships' receipts were counted.

The last child was his own fine young son, James Donovan, Viscount Ashton. Grace was due to bear their second child in the autumn of that year.

The large and extended family dined in the newly renovated dining room every night, where Jeffrey made it a point not to look at the paintings along the eastern wall. Two of them had been hung incorrectly, but there was no way in which he might convince Grace of it. She had insisted they'd been measured four times. She tried her best to see things his way, but she drew the line at measuring eight times.

Nevertheless, Jeffrey had managed to overcome the discomfort of the paintings and could concede that Grace was right—the rooms were far less somber than they'd been when he'd lived alone.

After the family dined, they repaired to the grand salon, where Grace was refused a turn at the pianoforte, given that her skill had not the least improved. Mercy, now seventeen, played as badly as Grace and was perfectly content to do so. "If one does not play the pianoforte well, one is not invited to play," she'd explained to Jeffrey, staring up at him with big blue eyes behind round spectacles. But as Mercy was not yet out, her sisters insisted that she play each night, presumably with the hope that she would improve. Jeffrey had tried to point out the flaw in her logic to Mercy—she was being asked to play more because of her lack of skill—but Mercy could be quite obstinate when she was of a mind. He understood perfectly why there was some discussion about sending Mercy to a young ladies' academy on the Continent. Privately, he feared for the academy.

Her playing was so awful that the dogs—there were four of them now, all with various flaws—took to howling. That annoyed the cats. Jeffrey wasn't entirely certain how many of them there were, as some remained outside, but he had seen at least three lurking about the house.

After Mercy's wretched song, generally Prudence would play, much to everyone's delight. Prudence was clearly the most talented of the Cabot sisters, and Jeffrey would say abundantly so. But Jeffrey had noticed that in the past fortnight, Prudence's play had seemed a bit disheartened. He had suggested to Grace that the burden of their mother's care, which had fallen to Prudence these past few years, weighed on her. Grace and Honor had children to care for, and Mercy was…well, she was Mercy.

"But Mamma is living with us now," Grace had pointed out. "Pru is free of the responsibility. I should think her disposition would be improved."

Unfortunately, Lady Beckington's situation had

worsened dramatically. She rarely spoke now, and was peculiarly attached to a ball of twine.

Together, all of her children and their spouses had decided that she should come and live at Blackwood Hall. There was no hope for her in London, as even the doctors had given up on her. Here, two women from Ashton Down had been employed to give her around-the-clock care in addition to Hannah. The burden was no longer to be on Prudence's shoulders.

But something was bothering Prudence. Perhaps it was that she was in her twenty-first year and had yet to be made an offer. Prudence was a stunning beauty, but Sylvia, who had been in London the past two Seasons now that her children were a bit older, had confided in Jeffrey that in spite of Prudence's fine looks and charming demeanor, there were no offers for her hand. "Too many scandals," Sylvia had said.

Jeffrey felt particularly uncomfortable about that. He was fond of Prudence.

One evening, after supper, after Mercy had pounded the ivory keys into submission, and Prudence had played a melancholy song that caused George to double the whiskey he poured into his glass, a mention was made that Miss Amelia Hawthorne, an acquaintance of the Cabot sisters, would be joining her brother in India.

"She's traveling to India alone?" Mercy had asked, clearly excited by the prospect.

"Not *alone,* silly girl," Honor said. "In the company of a chaperone."

Jeffrey swallowed down an image that was beginning to form in his mind—a young woman and her governess. He generally didn't think of other women now, but every once in a while—

Grace touched her hand to his arm, and he realized he was tapping. It was her habit now, to touch him and reassure him when he began to fidget with his counting. He found it soothing.

"Oh, dear," said Sylvia. "I should not like to travel all the way *there*. It seems far too treacherous. It's a long voyage and any number of things might happen. Why, George lost a ship on that voyage."

"True," George said. "But hundreds of ships sail it uneventfully."

"That is something I should very much like to do," Prudence said, and touched her fingers to a key of the pianoforte. "See a bit of the world."

*"India?"* Honor exclaimed, and laughed.

"Why not India? It's at least as interesting as Bath."

"Pru, don't tease in that way," Honor said as she peeled a figurine from her young daughter's hand. "Think of the peril. Sylvia is right—the chance for mishap is too great."

"Yes, of course, Honor," Prudence said curtly, and stood up. "God forbid I should put myself in the path of *peril*." With a dramatic roll of her eyes, she had gone out, leaving several to exchange curious looks behind her.

"What in heaven did I say?" Honor asked, exasperated.

"You said *peril*," Mercy answered matter-of-factly.

"Why should *that* displease her?" Grace demanded.

Mercy shrugged and adjusted her spectacles. "Perhaps she *wants* peril. It's so dreadfully boring here."

Honor and Grace looked at each other and laughed. "Mercy, you say the most preposterous things," Grace said.

Jeffrey noticed that Mercy didn't laugh along with her sisters. He supposed Mercy knew something about Prudence's ill humor and was unwilling to share.

*Good God.* He thought of his son in his nursery, only two years old. He thought of the weeks and months and years to come. How would he ever let James into the world? How would he ever bear it? How could he ever let go of the fear of harm coming to him? God help him, what if the next child was a *girl?*

He glanced up, caught Grace's eye. She smiled and rubbed her hand over her belly, their second child. He couldn't possibly bear it, not possibly.

Grace laughed at something Mercy said, which did not please Mercy in the least, and now they were arguing. Such chaos was this family!

But in all the chaos grew a love unlike any he had ever known, and for that he was profoundly grateful.

It was perfect.

\* \* \* \* \*

*Be sure to watch for Prudence's romance,*
*coming only to Harlequin HQN in 2015.*

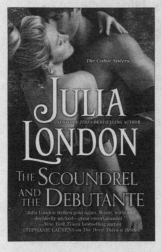

# JULIE PLEC

**From the creator of *The Originals*, the hit
spin-off television show of *The Vampire Diaries*,
come three never-before-released prequel
stories featuring the Original vampire family,
set in 18th century New Orleans.**

Available now!     Coming March 31!     Coming May 26!

*Family is power. The Original vampire family swore
it to each other a thousand years ago. They pledged to
remain together always and forever. But even when
you're immortal, promises are hard to keep.*

**Pick up your copies and visit
www.TheOriginalsBooks.com**
to discover more!

**HQN™**

www.HQNBooks.com

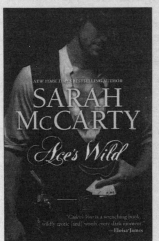

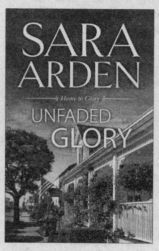

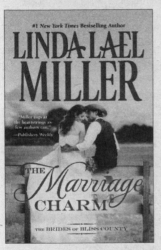

# REQUEST YOUR FREE BOOKS!

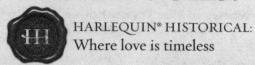

HARLEQUIN® HISTORICAL:
Where love is timeless

## 2 FREE NOVELS PLUS 2 **FREE GIFTS!**

**YES!** Please send me 2 FREE Harlequin® Historical novels and my 2 FREE gifts (gifts are worth about $10). After receiving them, if I don't wish to receive any more books, I can return the shipping statement marked "cancel." If I don't cancel, I will receive 6 brand-new novels every month and be billed just $5.44 per book in the U.S. or $5.74 per book in Canada. That's a savings of at least 16% off the cover price! It's quite a bargain! Shipping and handling is just 50¢ per book in the U.S. and 75¢ per book in Canada.* I understand that accepting the 2 free books and gifts places me under no obligation to buy anything. I can always return a shipment and cancel at any time. Even if I never buy another book, the two free books and gifts are mine to keep forever.

246/349 HDN F4ZY

| Name | (PLEASE PRINT) | |
|------|----------------|--|
| Address | | Apt. # |
| City | State/Prov. | Zip/Postal Code |

Signature (if under 18, a parent or guardian must sign)

Mail to the **Harlequin® Reader Service:**
**IN U.S.A.:** P.O. Box 1867, Buffalo, NY 14240-1867
**IN CANADA:** P.O. Box 609, Fort Erie, Ontario L2A 5X3

**Want to try two free books from another line?**
**Call 1-800-873-8635 or visit www.ReaderService.com.**

HHI3R